COMPELLING CONSEQUENCES

*A Tale Fashioned from
Pride and Prejudice*

RILEY ST. ANDISH

A LAUREN LITERATURE PUBLICATION

ISBN-10: 1481005847
ISBN-13: 9781481005845

Chapter One

"A MIND AT EASE WITH ITSELF"
–JANE AUSTEN

※

Charles Bingley was ill at ease with himself and everyone around him. How did a morning filled with promise turn as grey as a sudden storm in Hertfordshire? He had leased Netherfield with the prospect of purchasing. He would be a landowner, fulfilling his parents' last wishes. As heir to his father's coffee fortune, all he needed was ownership of a fine estate to elevate him to the coveted status—he would be a true English gentleman. He scowled in contempt at his good friend, Fitzwilliam Darcy who was reading a new book and so conveniently lost to its pages. A handsome man, Darcy was celebrated as a very well-respected gentleman, perhaps because the Crown had certified Fitzwilliam as the wealthiest man under thirty years of age. Darcy owned a fabulous estate called Pemberly, which boasted a mansion about four times larger than St. James's Palace, as well as nearly half of Derbyshire, a large estate in Scotland, one in Ireland, and of course, Darcy House, his London mansion. His vast wealth made Fitzwilliam one of the most sought-after unattached men in the British Empire.

Darcy had befriended Charles because he liked him. Bingley possessed something that could not be bought or sold: a sterling personality. Quite pleasant as a rule, Bingley was an outgoing charismatic, and cheerful optimist. Compared to the often dour and brooding Mr. Darcy, Bingley was his diametric opposite. Between them was a very solid friendship, in spite of the great differences of their natures. Charles knew his older, unmarried sister Caroline had nearly ruined their friendship with her shameless attempts to capture Mr. Darcy. Somehow, the eight-and-twenty-year-old woman did not understand that Fitzwilliam simply had no romantic interest in her. Failing to heed the prohibitions her brother—and the gentleman himself—had placed on her, Caroline persisted in her repugnant pursuit of Darcy. The old maid's hopes were as boundless as the sea, and her designs upon the man, were as intricate as a spider's web.

Longing to be outdoors, Bingley gazed out the window and allowed his eyes to follow the brick driveway out onto the road. Riding had been scheduled for the day, but Darcy predicted bad weather and refused to risk going out on horseback. Bingley's rare foul mood matched Darcy's weather prognostication.

"I say, Darcy!" Bingley called over his shoulder. "Do you have evidence of rain? If it does not rain, we will have wasted a full day, will we not?"

Startled, Darcy looked up from his book. Slightly annoyed with his friend, he sent a snappy retort, intended to quiet the man. "Of course! It is summer, we are in England, *rain* is expected! Trust me, Bingley and you will see I am right."

"I am quite out of sorts, you know," Charles responded, in a perturbed state of mind. "Yesterday the neighbors came to call. I had hoped to ride the property with you yesterday, but nay, we were thick with callers. Rising this morning, my dearest wish once again, was to ride the estate with you. Indeed, you shall need to ride and *see* the land before you can advise me to purchase it. I am, as you well know, quite ready for that occurrence. Good God! Here we are, with you reading, and I standing here, gazing at this prime land from the window!"

Fitzwilliam looked up at his friend, wishing to have sport with him. "Bingley, do you not know that a wealthy, unmarried man must be in need of a wife? Especially a fine figure of a man, such as yourself. Those neighbors were fathers of young girls, and old maids in search of an advantageous marriage. No doubt those papas saw a better use of your time yesterday. I am certain that each one felt he was doing you a great kindness. After all, you know the fault is your own. You, my friend, have elegant manners, handsome looks, intelligence, and graceful dancing skills. You are reputed to be good-humoured, and you have the good sense to possess more money than you shall ever be able to spend in one lifetime! Certainly any young man should be just like you, if he possibly can." Bingley forgot his poor mood and laughed at this. He smiled and added, "yes, and you quite forgot; I am also punctual, clean shaven and I almost never spit!" Darcy snickered and agreed. "All of this, makes *you* the better-half of a perfect match. Still, 'tis a pity there is only one Charles Bingley to purchase a fine estate in Hertfordshire and select a wife from amongst the local ladies. *You*, are a prize catch, my friend!" Darcy chuckled as he put his focus back on his book.

A loud crack of thunder blasted above their heads, as if God were announcing an impending disaster. In mere seconds heavy rain pelted the earth as fiercely as bullets being fired into the ground. Treacherous rainfall of such a hazardous nature was rare in Hertfordshire.

Bingley turned to the window and peered out into the grey and silver skies, watching the violent blows of the pounding rain. It was so forceful he feared it would rip patches of the earth wide open. Suddenly he yelled, "What in bloody hell is this? Dreadful! Darcy, come and help me!"

Tossing his book to the floor, Darcy reached his friend in a few strides and jerked the door wide open in one abrupt motion. He ran out to the circular driveway. Two small riders approached the house, boldly controlling their dangerously frightened horses. Incredibly, neither had been unseated. Obviously caught without warning in the sudden storm, they appeared drenched to the bone. Their horses had become nearly wild at the claps of thunder and stabs of lightning.

Two hands from the barn saw the drama as well and ran out to assist. Darcy's long legs gave him the advantage and he reached the riders first. He grabbed the reins of the black Warmblood and gained a steadiness to the animal. Thinking to offer his hand to the horseman, he was now close enough to see. It was not a small man, nor boy, but a woman atop the skittish animal. Accordingly, Darcy reached up with both hands and boldly took hold of her waist, lifting her down. As he did so, he liked the feel of her. She was slim with a small waist, yet her rather low-cut muslin gown revealed a very nice swelling of her bosom. A seductive scent of roses, spiked with sweet almond oil emanated from her wet hair. Obviously, it had just been washed and the fresh floral aroma had been revived by the rain water.

Looking into his beautiful blue eyes, she gave him a steady smile, almost a laugh. Good-naturedly, she thanked him. Her entire face lit up with her smile, and her exotic lavender-coloured eyes seemed to glow from within. Had it not been for the fierce storm, Darcy would have wanted to hold her longer, but quick action was needed. He placed her feet upon the driveway. Stepping onto the pavement she took the arm he offered and the two made a dash for the house. A quick-acting groomsman led her horse into the barn.

"My, what a lovely day!" she laughed as they crossed the threshold. Darcy could just catch the words. Turning to look at him, she continued her thought. "One moment, a beautiful sunny morning then suddenly—a downpour. A metaphor for life, is it not?" She smiled and locked her eyes upon his, as they stood for a moment just inside the door.

Darcy liked what he saw and heard of her. Immediately the man began to take a full inventory. She had the most sensuously beautiful eyes he had ever beheld, and her hair displayed a certain luster, though soaking wet. Even the grey of the morning could not cast a gloom over her naturally creamy complexion, or dim the healthy glow of her rose-coloured cheeks. She had a melodic voice that he found quite mesmerizing, and her laughter was soft and lilting.

As she walked deeper into the foyer, her drenched gown was clinging attractively to her shapely body. The wet garment was an inconvenience to her, of course, yet an excellent visual aid for one who possessed a natural talent for imagining how she would look without clothing. The thin fabric obligingly afforded him the freedom to determine her lack of stays and tempted him to stare at her bosom. She appeared to him as something of a rare vision; beautiful and refined, yet somehow refreshingly independent. He was intrigued, impressed, and very much inclined to think that she would appear quite lovely unclad. Indeed, he suspected that she might be nearly perfect when unencumbered by garments.

Stopping at the end of the entrance hall, she introduced herself, forcing him from his preoccupation. "I suppose I should identify myself, since it is unlikely I shall be announced. I am Elizabeth Bennet, and that nearly drowned princess is my dear sister Jane. We live at Longbourn, an estate just about three miles hence."

For the first time, Fitzwilliam Darcy was slow of speech. His manners had never completely failed him, and just in time to prevent a dire *faux pas*, he bowed and offered, "Fitzwilliam Darcy, a pleasure, Miss Bennet." When one is vastly wealthy, certain other economies are set in place. Rule number one: Do not encourage women. Limit the number of words spoken to them, and speak not at all to women who are unknown. Fitzwilliam Darcy was not looking for a wife, thank you. Yes, he found her to be extremely attractive, even beautiful to be sure, yet he would be over-careful around her.

She was an obscure woman, who lived an isolated life, in an out-of-the-way shire. Darcy always made it a point to avoid such ladies who were born to unknown fathers. His experience had shown them to be as dull and uninteresting as their unheard of families. Darcy was convinced that Miss Elizabeth Bennet would have little more than her obvious physical charms to recommend her.

"Very sporting of you, Mr. Darcy, to come out into the rain to assist us. Had I been alone I might have tried to make it home, but dear Jane should not be caught in rainstorms. Thank you for your kindness, sir."

At that, the door opened again and Charles came inside with Jane. He had taken his jacket off and was holding it over her head in an effort to provide a little shelter. Flinging the wet coat behind them, he took Jane's hand, bowed, and kissed it. One look at his friend told Darcy that Charles was already smitten with Miss Jane.

"Once again, I thank you, Mr. Bingley, you are all kindness," Jane was saying, "never have I heard of a gentleman sacrificing his coat as a protection from offensive water. You are too obliging, sir." She offered the compliment along with a beautiful smile. The two laughed as though they had known each other for years. With his easy manners, Charles Bingley had that effect on people of both genders. He laughed easily and often.

Introductions were completed in front of the large fireplace in the library. Towels and hot chocolate were quickly brought by a servant. Jane blotted her blond hair with a towel, and Elizabeth pulled her auburn hair back behind her head and wrapped it up in the towel to which she gave a twist. To Darcy, this was most efficient and sensible. Releasing the towel, she leaned her head sideways to expose more hair to the radiant heat from the fire. As she did so, the heavenly fragrance of roses spiked with sweet almond oil infiltrated the entire room. Again, as with his first whiff, the fragrance filled Darcy's senses. He thought it most unusual and pleasurable. At Charles's urging, the ladies removed their half boots, turning them to face the fire. Bingley averted his eyes as Jane drew her dainty feet under her skirts but Darcy took note of the graceful lines of Miss Elizabeth's shapely ankles and exquisite feet. She took the time to carefully dry them before drawing them under her skirts. The sisters' rather thin gowns appeared to dry very quickly. Apart from their hair displaying an out-of-doors messy aspect, (which both gentlemen found quite appealing) the Bennet sisters began to appear nearly as they had when they started their ride. It was a remarkable recovery which rather amazed both young men.

Darcy stared at Elizabeth's perfect profile and listened to the happy conversation. "You know, we too had planned to ride this morning ourselves" Bingley said. "Jolly good we did not, elsewise we might just now be sitting in front of a roaring fire at Longbourn, with the two of you here, might we not?" The girls laughed, but not too loudly, a fact which Darcy noted with pleasure. It seemed, that nearly everything about Miss Elizabeth Bennet had pleased Darcy, although he would never let that intelligence be known. He would not risk having his affections entangled.

The gentlemen excused themselves to change out of their wet clothing. It seemed neither one wanted to leave their visitors. Each man showed a remarkable interest in the newcomers to Netherfield. Passing Charles on the stairs, Darcy quietly cautioned, "Slow down, Bingley. Use prudence, my friend." Although it was obvious that Darcy himself showed no signs of going slowly.

In truth, both hurried to return to their recent arrivals. Each man was eager to be reinstated in the library. Dressed impeccably, they wondered how best to resume conversing. But when they discovered the ladies engaged in a lively topic, both gentlemen gladly joined them. It was apparent that the Bennet ladies were well versed in current events, and Elizabeth especially possessed natural talent as a conversationalist. Two hours passed in congenial exchanges, with each one making a favorable impression upon the others. Showing his good disposition and affable manners, Charles stood and announced that he would ask Cook to prepare a nice hot meal for the four of them. Darcy could not help but note how Bingley's mood had lightened. In truth, he had never seen his friend so happy and well occupied with a beautiful girl. Soon they were seated at the dining-room table, enjoying hot, nourishing food. It was a pleasant event to everyone's liking—even Darcy could find no fault in good food, gratifying company, and intelligent conversation. To his surprise, Miss Elizabeth was very well read, and in fact, she had just completed the new book he had begun only that morning. He found her to be witty and sharp minded, well spoken, strongly opinionated, and quite prepared to capably debate her points of view on varied topics. She displayed a sort of sparring attitude towards him which he supposed was a good-tempered type of exchange. He loved the way her eyes sparkled when he disagreed with her; this told him she enjoyed the volley as much as he.

At the close of the meal, Caroline Bingley made her way into the room. She wasted no time in letting her brother know it was improper to order a hot meal at that time of day and harangued him for not ordering a simple tea. Speaking to him in such a manner demeaned not only Charles, but revealed her disdain for the Bennet ladies. Soon the sisters would become accustomed to Caroline's pejorative remarks. "Tis a pity they shall cancel the Meryton Assembly due to rain," Caroline said, standing possessively by the chair next to Darcy. He answered not, but rose and assisted her into the seat. Then smiling at Charles, he said, "Shall we escort the ladies into the library, my friend? Perhaps we can best check the storm clouds from that east window?"

The cheerful party rose to their feet, the ladies tipping their heads to Caroline and telling her how good it was to make her acquaintance. Jane was very sincere—she saw only the best in everybody at all times. Not so her sister; the briefest glance told her all. She had already sketched the character of Miss Caroline Bingley and understood her devious manners. Elizabeth gave a nod to propriety in doing what was expected.

Charles suggested they send his man Crawford to Longbourn with a missive to inform Mr. Bennet of his two eldest daughters' whereabouts and alert him to the fact that it might not be possible for them to brave the storm to return home. Agreed and quickly executed, Crawford was on his way and Charles mentally planned that the beautiful angel Jane should be situated in his very best guest room. Darcy fondly hoped the two Bennet sisters would soon take their leave, as Miss Elizabeth was beginning to tempt him in dangerous ways that he must not allow himself to contemplate.

The conversation turned to parlor games children play during the rainy season. Charles reminisced about an active child's game called "Ragamuffin Tin Cup," and Jane recalled "Riddle m' Riddle m' Riddle Marie"—then, spoken at the exact same moment and using the exact same words, Darcy and Elizabeth exclaimed, "Bethink the next line of poetry!" Everyone laughed. Charles loudly protested, claiming that he did not have the patience to memorize poetry, having left that necessity at Oxford.

Darcy and Elizabeth smiled at each other. He fixed his steady gaze upon her lovely lavender eyes. Impulsively, he suggested a game of chess. She held his gaze and remarked that she would enjoy a game, but warned him that she was a slow thinker and sometimes, to her father's vexation, a slow mover.

"I shall time you if it comes to that!" he laughed.

Charles looked up at him, startled at the sound of Darcy's solo laughter. Elizabeth noticed his beautiful white, straight and evenly matched teeth. She nearly remarked upon his dazzling smile, before she caught herself.

The two moved to the small table by the window. Darcy set up the board, then put one king into each hand. Smiling at Elizabeth, he put both hands under the table and without looking, he passed the kings from hand to hand, mixing them up. Lifting his hands up slowly, he held both before Elizabeth, allowing her to make a selection. Maintaining a level eye contact, she touched his right hand gently with her fingertips. To Darcy, it was a very sensuous touch that lingered longer than required. Elizabeth had certain enticing qualities about her that lent a bewitching enchantment to everything she did and said. He felt the best aspect of this allure was her total unawareness of her own earthy sensuality and exquisite beauty.

Remarkably, they each felt a shudder course through their arms at their skin-on-skin contact. Slowly, and with more meaning than chess, he opened his hand and offered her the white king she selected. His sensual smile caused a sudden shiver down her back. Reaching out, she held his stare and slowly took the piece from his hand, brushing her fingertips lightly over his palm. Elizabeth lowered her eyes as an excited tremor coursed downward into her epicenter. Her breathing quickened, her heart pounded. Even a casual observer might have seen these exchanges as those of lovers, remembering with fondness the intimate details of their last interlude and now flirting covertly whilst in the company of friends. Yet their companions failed to notice. Bingley and Jane looked only at each other. Placing her thoughts upon the chess board, Elizabeth began the game. Her eyes were upon the board, Darcy's were upon Elizabeth. Their first few moves were not slow.

Caroline Bingley entered the room, as if her company had been requested. She chatted briefly with Jane and Charles, then moved closer to the chess game and began speaking with the players. Her first attempt was to engage Darcy, but he ignored her efforts. Next she turned to Elizabeth, condescendingly calling her "Eliza," whereupon, Darcy sharply raised his head and corrected her smugly, "Miss Bennet's name is Elizabeth, Caroline. Perhaps you remember that name because we once had a queen called the same. I daresay no one in the realm would shorten such a lovely name to Eliza during her reign!" Then, looking up at his opponent, he asked cordially, "Miss Elizabeth, have you a nickname, used by family or others?"

She smiled, but did not look at him. Studying the board she answered as she moved her rook, "Lizzy is my family nickname."

"Oh, Barnacle! That is what I get for listening to conversation. I did not see that move on the board," Darcy protested.

Outside, the sky darkened; inside, Caroline's sky was crashing down around her as she could clearly see that this Bennet creature represented a threat. She sat down upon a sofa to think about ways to remove the Bennet sisters from Netherfield.

Time progressed much to Bingley's satisfaction. He was getting to know an angel. Even Darcy was having a wonderful day. He could not remember ever being so at ease in the company of a beautiful woman. Elizabeth was not only beautiful, but Darcy was convinced that she was the most intelligent young woman he had ever encountered. It was his delight to discover that she could be filled with humour and playfulness, as well as converse seriously upon any number of topics. He felt one of the most pleasing aspects of her character was that she did not fawn over him, nor attempt to curry favor with him. In truth, Elizabeth was strong of opinion and seemed to relish taking an opposing point of view. She showed no signs of being impressed by his great wealth and displayed no special interest in his holdings. He greatly enjoyed being with Elizabeth, even though he knew he was treading a path he would regret. Charles gave the order to ready two guest rooms, and the ladies went to freshen up as best they could with no toiletries, not even a hairbrush between them. Nonesuch was offered to them. Little matter, for their natural good looks had only been enhanced by the wild rainstorm.

Dinner was wonderful. Everyone— except Caroline— felt the meal had been a delight. The happy dinner conversation was lively and most amusing. Afterwards, the gentlemen did not wish to leave the ladies, and Caroline sat down to open the instrument. She played the pianoforte for about an hour and then thinking she would embarrass Elizabeth, requested that she play and sing. Rising to the occasion, Elizabeth accompanied herself and sang a beautiful Scottish folk song. Her impromptu performance was equal to any seen upon the stage. Caroline grew more angry and impolite. She began a sniping campaign against Elizabeth, who barely took note of her existence, much less her unsavory comments.

The Bennet sisters were thrilled when Crawford entered the salon, bringing them a missive from their mother, some fresh clothing, hairbrushes and other sundry items they required and were dearly grateful to receive. They considered these things necessities. Neither girl had ever been without the basic essentials of life. Their necessary items were among the very finest quality of grooming products and fine cosmetics of the day. Members of the Bennet household were provided with a constant supply of the most luxurious toilet items. Each of Mr. Bennet's daughters possessed a wardrobe that was refreshed with each new season of the year. The girls had never known lack.

Too soon the evening was over and the two ladies went to their rooms. The gentlemen went elsewhere, but did not retire. Not more than an hour later a servant knocked lightly upon Elizabeth's door and urgently requested that she meet Mr. Bingley in his study. Thinking it odd, she complied, although the servant eluded her and she was left alone to navigate the house in semi-darkness. Seeing an open door emitting light from within and hearing voices, she surmised the study was in view and stepped inside as requested.

Darcy was standing with his back to the door and was speaking to Bingley, "I know, old chap, I quite agree she is perfect. In fact, they both are perfect and completely wonderful, but we must consider their low birth and the inferiority of their connections. I have never heard of the family, and I daresay, no one I know has heard of them. They are completely unknown, Bingley, and without influence. Pity that these two very remarkable and beautiful young ladies will not marry well, and certainly not to anyone of our class!"

Elizabeth was just inside the doorway of the study. Naturally, she heard Darcy's cutting remarks. Not being one to shrink away, she straightened her back and cleared her throat loudly. " Pardon me, please, gentlemen. Mr. Bingley, your servant advised me to present myself to you, posthaste. I am here, sir, pray how may I help you?" Upon hearing Elizabeth's voice, Darcy turned to face her. His eyes smarted, his face crimsoned, and his mouth went completely dry. He spoke not one word, but neither did he lower his intense gaze. He kept his eyes riveted upon Elizabeth.

Recovering his shock at seeing her, Charles tried to make amends. "Miss Elizabeth, I do so humbly beg your pardon. It seems there has been a very great mistake, as I certainly did not send for you. I do, however, have an inkling of an idea as to who might have done so, and madam, I offer my most sincere apologies to you. I wish you to know that your presence is most genuinely appreciated, as is your friendship, and of course, that of your sister. Both of you are exceptionally worthy and respected. It is an honour to have you sheltered from the storm here, under my roof, as my esteemed guests. I afford you both my deepest regard and hospitality. May I also tell you that I look forward to visiting your father at his estate, to pay my respects and to compliment him upon his excellent daughters."

Elizabeth smiled charmingly, and looking straight at Mr. Darcy she said, calmly and clearly, "Mr. Bingley, you are, sir, everything a young man ought to be, and I and my sister are honoured to be named among your friends. Surely you are a man of integrity, and you value each person according to their giftings and talents, notwithstanding their station of birth, or their rank. You are certainly most Christian in your deeds as well as your unaffected words. I most humbly thank you, sir. Our father shall very much enjoy your visit. Enduring life with five vexing daughters, he shall delight in a gentleman calling upon him. I appreciate your thoughtfulness, sir. I bid you both a very good evening, Mr. Darcy, Mr. Bingley." Elizabeth was certainly not framed for ill temper; and although all prospects of her own had now been destroyed, she would not allow her spirit to be crushed. Likewise, she would never allow the sentiments expressed by Mr. Darcy, to reach the hearing of dearest Jane. Maintaining her smile, without showing any sign of feeling displeasure, she held her eyes level. Without malice, she curtseyed nicely and quit the room, leaving the men to gaze upon the spot she had occupied.

"Damn that Caroline! Darcy, she must have been listening to the trend of your remarks to me and wanted Elizabeth to hear them from your own lips to discourage her—and I hate to admit it, but to wound her, if possible." Bingley pounded his fist upon the mantel as he spoke to his friend. He was at his wits' end with Caroline.

"Have no concerns, my friend," Darcy answered him, placing his hand over his heart. "Your speech confirmed your reputation. Miss Elizabeth was impressed, and she shall certainly tell her sister of your gallant remarks, which verify your good name. Your *angel*, as you refer to her, will think very highly of you. I am the only one whose good image was destroyed, and I daresay, it is probably for the best. Although quite cruel, it is possible that Caroline did her a favor. I do not wish to lead any woman on when it comes to a friendship with me. When I marry, I must consider fortune, position, rank, and even the power of the family connections. As should you, my friend." Darcy was blushing. The sight of the beautiful Elizabeth Bennet in the doorway had scorched his soul. He repented his harshly honest words and deeply regretted that a wonderful woman like Elizabeth had not only heard them, but most certainly been injured by them. He hurt her deeply, and he knew it, but once spoken, he would not retract his sentiments.

Charles clearly saw his friend's pain and embarrassment. His anger was kindled against his sister, who would stop at nothing in her attempts to ensnare Fitzwilliam Darcy. "Darcy, I say, I quite pity you, my good friend. I could not deny love. Nay, I could not and would not. I must tell you plainly, this afternoon was the first and only time I have seen you laugh out of pure joy whilst talking with a beautiful young woman. My God, man, you have the most attractive teeth I have ever seen, a fantastic smile. I daresay, Darcy, I had no earthly idea that your face could look so very pleasant! It was obvious to me, and probably to the Bennet sisters, that you were enjoying yourself quite well. 'Tis a pity, my friend. I shall pray for you that the great and mighty considerations needed to qualify a woman as your future wife, may be packaged as agreeably as Miss Elizabeth Bennet."

Bingley smiled and continued. "My friend, advise me on the estate, my finances, my selection of servants, direct me to the best business associates and opportunities and even critique my wardrobe and select my fashions. Yet, when it comes to affairs of the heart, I shall let my guiding spirit be the one that shows me the most agreeable nature, a beautiful face and beguiling figure. Yes, give me a gentlewoman, such as Miss Jane Bennet, who can lighten my day, lift my spirits, and ignite my passions! That is love, and in marriage, love is all I am looking to obtain. I want my wife to be my lover. I want to wrap my arms around her and enjoy her charms, sleep with her, and awaken each and every morning with her. My friend, I believe that fate has brought my future wife to my very own doorstep. Ay, by God, indeed I do!"

Ending his lecture on love, Bingley clasped Darcy upon the shoulder and inquired, "Now, how about billiards my friend? We shall take this bottle of port with us."

Elizabeth supposed herself to be awake before anyone in the household. Quietly descending the staircase, she looked out the window towards the east and decided it seemed clear at the moment; however, the dark clouds threatened more rain. The question of how high the standing waters might be and whether the horses could make the trip to Longbourn remained, even if the sky held clear. She would wait for Jane to rise.

She stepped silently into the library and selected a volume of Shakespeare's Sonnets. She had not noticed that Mr. Darcy was already in the library, seated upon a chair towards the back wall. He had paper and pen, and upon his knees he carefully balanced an atlas, which he had conscripted as a desk. He had been writing a letter, but stopped to watch Elizabeth take a chair. He observed her. She opened the book reverently. She smiled pleasantly as she read. Even in the dimly lit room her face was radiant.

Soon Darcy was fascinated by a ritual. She would read the sonnet, then placing the top of the book to her bosom, she lifted her chin and soundlessly mouthed the words, as if checking her recollection of the work. Closing her eyes to recite from memory, her lush, black eyelashes took a brief rest upon her rosy cheeks. Darcy had never seen such lashes, so luxuriant and dense. Slowly lifting her eyelids, the black fringe seemed to deepen the lavender glow of her eyes. Those lovely orbs appeared to dance with delight, showing her enjoyment of the sentiments she had committed to her memory. He thought her fine eyes to be far more beautiful than any he had ever encountered.

It was a charming scene. She appeared to practice her memory work, perhaps for a formal performance, or to delight and entertain at a friendly gathering. He thought it more likely that she prided herself upon her good memory and dared not let one sonnet slip. Slowly turning her head towards the fireplace she held it there, displaying her perfect profile. He admired her faultless facial features and her graceful neck. She was a splendid paragon of loveliness.

Quietly turning to a fresh page of paper, Darcy began to sketch her classic beauty. He had not sketched anyone since Cambridge, and it was a joy to record her good looks, even if her wonderfully spirited personality defied the best efforts of his fist. During that half-hour he accomplished three sketches before she suddenly quit the room. Listening carefully, he heard her whispering to Jane, just outside the door. Elizabeth seemed to be trying to persuade her sister to leave for home at the earliest opportunity. She said nothing of his cruel remarks of the previous evening. In truth, answering Jane's comments on the positive aspects of both men's characters and natures, Elizabeth readily agreed and added her own careful commentary of noteworthy attributes.

At once it occurred to him— Elizabeth held the role of protector for Jane. Even though Jane was the elder, Elizabeth was the stronger of the two. He remembered the first remarks she had made about her sister were for her welfare during the rain. Nay, she would never reveal the cutting, cruel, and even baseless comments he himself had so thoughtlessly made the night before; as it was not in her nature to cause even the slightest discomfort to her beloved sister. He would wish for such a sibling for his own Georgiana. His little two-and-ten-year-old sister had lately been begging him to marry so she might gain the warmth and fellowship of such a one as Elizabeth. Darcy who was also guardian of the little girl, reflected on what this type of care could mean. The thought stung him with a sharp pain. Perhaps there were other reasons to marry such a woman, in addition to those Bingley listed. Ay, this and those thoughts of love that his friend kindly reminded him of were simply added to the ever growing list of Miss Elizabeth's attributes. He turned the page and actually began listing them, including even this early morning's memorization work, which he identified as "constantly seeking to improve her mind."

Darcy began to think more seriously about Elizabeth Bennet.

The bleakness of the weather continued, creek beds were swollen, and no trails were passable. The Bennet sisters continued at Netherfield. Darcy felt the weather, and even the poor condition of the roads and trails, correctly reflected his current relationship with Miss Elizabeth Bennet. He was reminded of his unfortunate oration each time he saw

Elizabeth. He sought her company, and was painfully put in remembrance of the rift he, himself had created. His lofty and high-minded ideals had formed an awkward split between them. It seemed Elizabeth also had very high standards. She held herself aloof, perhaps, in an effort to assist him in keeping away from unsuitable young women. He fancied he could not blame her. What intelligent lady would willingly seek the company of one who had made his tastes and preferences known in such emphatic terms? Alas, none but Caroline Bingley would force herself upon a man who had expressed his exclusive wishes in such a definitive manner. Oh that Caroline would avoid him, and Elizabeth pursue him. Yet, he knew Elizabeth had not the nature to pursue men, nor the necessity. Gentlemen would no doubt, be drawn to Elizabeth Bennet as moths to a flame. He studied his situation with a new intensity.

His friend was experiencing the opposite situation with Miss Jane. Charles Bingley had never been happier. He enjoyed each day and evening spent in the company of his angel. Their voices could be heard joyfully sharing conversation and laughter, all over the house. Elizabeth spent much of her time reading in the library, quite often joined by Darcy, as he was content to sit and read in silence. Elizabeth oftentimes fancied she could feel his steady gaze upon her. Yet she remained composed, and was able to maintain her concentration upon her book. Caroline found occasions to venture into the library, to watch Fitzwilliam as he read. Curiously she would hold a book up, but keep her sharp eyes fixed upon Darcy's face. She was always more interested in his progress through his pages, than she was in looking at the lines of print, within her own. Easily bored in the library, Caroline rarely stayed longer than ten minutes at a time. Her mournful sighs, yawns and moans were never missed. The woman was most audible in her *silence*, and equally annoying with her frequent stretches, and shifting of her body. In truth, Caroline had no shortage of physical tactics to employ, in her efforts to obtain Mr. Darcy's attention. Quite frequently, her book would slide to the floor, just within reach of his hand. He would patiently retrieve the volume and return it to her. Often Caroline would enter the library, clear her throat loudly, and then consult with Fitzwilliam as to the day's menu, questioning him upon his favourites of the finest cosmopolitan foods. Upon another excuse, she sought his sophisticated advise as to which colours were most flattering to her own complexion. His worldly-wise knowledge of beauty was needed to advise her as to how she should style her hair, so that it would be most appealing. Her most successful ploy was found to be the times Caroline brought her one and only letter from Georgiana to read to Darcy. She would express her complete delight in the girl, and then with the utmost dramatic flair Caroline would open the missive and begin reading it, along with a full commentary. Elizabeth found these attempts to gain Darcy's attention (and affection) nonsensical, preposterous and shamefully transparent.

Fitzwilliam and Elizabeth both felt great relief, each time Caroline made her retreat. In truth, Caroline's own voice often seemed to reveal a level of relaxation each time she made an exit from the library.

Upon the fifth day, Elizabeth and Fitzwilliam were once again alone in the library. Both had been reading poetry and they each lowered their book at the same time. At once, they realised they had been reading two volumes of the same book of poems. Then, their eyes met and they smiled at each other. No words passed between them. It was a wonderful silence, each one admiring the other. Elizabeth broke the stare. She cast her eyes upon the bottom row of the bookshelf, suddenly remembering the boxes of children's games stored there. She had visited the home many times in her youth. Seeing the faded red box she had loved as a little girl, she rose to retrieve it. Smiling a delightful smile, she quietly carried it to the large conference table, pulled out a chair and seated herself. With a joyful reminiscence, her hands gracefully and respectfully removed each alphabet letter, one at a time and placed them upon the table top. Darcy was spellbound. He watched her in silence as she wordlessly moved the letters over the surface of the table. Gliding them along, she arranged them in order, then looked at them, with a glorious smile upon her face. Darcy desired to join her, yet he feared she might not wish to have him in her close company. They'd not had a private conversation since she overheard his harsh words in Bingley's study. Gathering his courage, he silently walked to the table, and seated himself in the chair opposite her. Once all the letters were out of the box, she lifted her head, and seeing him there, she showed her pleasure in a slight smile and subtle nod of welcome. "There are but six and twenty letters in our alphabet— yet many more are on the table." He mused, somewhat to himself, yet she took his comment as a question and answered him. "Ay— to be sure— but children must learn to spell, and many letters are required for those blessed lessons. I quite remember my much smaller hands spelling words with these very letters. I used these letters each time I visited my friend Nancy. I do believe this room was our very favourite. A most pleasant: M-E-M-O-R-Y, she spelled with the letters. Darcy's face lit up in a wide smile. He was quite enchanted with her childhood recollections. Silently he lifted one brow, and tilted his head, then he motioned to the letters, seeking her permission to spell his own word. She nodded and smiled. Her eyes locked upon his handsome face. He reached for the first letter, and turning it to face her, he began to spell one word only. Completing his word, he boldly leaned over the table, took her hand, and held it briefly. He smiled again, inhaling the scent of roses and sweet almond oil in her hair as he bowed and quit the room. She watched him away, smiling to herself, then she lowered her gaze to read what he had just spelled. His letters were arranged just in front of the word she had displayed. Her eyes fell upon the word: L-O-V-E-L-Y. "Lovely memory," she said aloud to herself and smiled. Casting her thoughts upon Mr. Darcy, she could still feel the touch of his hand upon hers.

The evening of the sixth day, Elizabeth was taking a stroll around the first floor of the house. Seeing the pianoforte unoccupied in the grand salon, she thought to play for a while. Sitting down at the instrument, she began to play Mozart's Sonata No.16 in C Major, for pianoforte, "Sonata facile": I Allegro. It was so lively and cheerful that soon Jane and Charles entered the room and sat upon the sofa to enjoy listening. The pair were speaking many compliments to Elizabeth on her execution of the piece. Only a few minutes into the sonata, Caroline entered and ever so sweetly approached Elizabeth. "Do forgive me, please Miss Elizabeth. I have not as yet practiced the instrument today, and I feel I absolutely must. Would you mind awfully?" Elizabeth took a deep breath and replied, "Indeed Miss Bingley, I would be honoured to know you were engaged so agreeably in your practice." At that, Elizabeth rose from the pianoforte, gave a pretty little curtsey, and allowed for Caroline to commence. Charles and Jane were agreeably situated and took no notice of Elizabeth's departure. It was a scheme, of course, Caroline was desirous of Mr. Darcy coming to hear her play. This was the usual time of day when Mr. Darcy sat with Bingley and oftentimes, Caroline would open the instrument. With her back to the door, she could only imagine that the gentleman had entered to listen to her. She played on and on, to the great appreciation of Charles and Jane.

Feeling the need to move, Elizabeth quit the grand salon and began to walk from common-room to common-room. Thinking it unoccupied, she entered the billiard-room just as Mr. Darcy was preparing to practice. He had removed his jacket, waistcoat, and cravat. His linen shirt was one-half open down the front, revealing his neck and chest. Clearly he had made himself comfortable for his sport. He had just taken a cue rod from the rack at the back of the room and was turning around when Elizabeth entered. He moved quickly toward her. Never had Elizabeth seen a man's neck and chest, and as he turned to face her, she did not quit the room for the sight of him. His dark chest hair was revealed through the partially opened shirt, and she thought the sight of his bare neck also very appealing. Darcy's well-developed muscles were quite easily appreciated through the thin linen fabric. Elizabeth wondered as to their density and strength. She had never before seen so much of a man's body. She thought Mr. Darcy's body quite fetching. There was little about Mr. Darcy she did not fancy, excepting of course, that proud, arrogant, imperious, and demeaning attitude he had articulated in Charles's study. Seeing her, he stood straight and engaged her fine eyes. There they were, just the two of them. Wordlessly, they communicated, each one telling the other of their profound appeal. She broke the stare by allowing her eyes to slowly travel the length of his body, and then back to his eyes again, and he taking the same liberty when he thought she would not see.

At last, it was Elizabeth who smiled at him, causing him to wonder if she was holding him in contempt— or making sport of him. Not knowing her character, he was unsure of her feelings. Sensing his discomfort, she spoke. "I do beg your pardon, Mr. Darcy. I can see you are engaged in your practice. Please do forgive my intrusion upon your privacy. I shall leave you."

"Nay!" He protested, a bit louder than he had intended. "It is a pleasure, Miss Elizabeth. I was just amusing myself—not really a practice." He watched her closely, trying to judge her response to him. Wishing to engage her in conversation, and to find a way to say something respectful about her family, he asked," Does your father play?"

Smiling and lifting a single brow in surprise at his question, she answered, "Perhaps he did at one time, in his younger years, now I fancy he finds his pleasure within the pages of his books. I thank you for asking after his interests."

Wishing to find his way back into her favour, he inquired: "Have you learned to play? In town, many ladies are taking the game with vigour." Elizabeth ran one finger sensuously along the side of the cherry wood billiard table as she walked its length. Darcy was most taken with her physical movements. He felt her every motion was endowed with a bewitching quality. To Darcy, her fingertip seemed epicurean— hot— as she drew it over the smooth wood. It made him wish to touch it, and feel the heat. Hearing his question, she looked into his eyes and slowly offered a thoughtful response to his inquiry. "Indeed, I have not—although I must say the game does have appeal. You are using geometry, are you not? It seems to be a game requiring much skill and thought." Her answer expressed her genuine interest in the game.

Suddenly realising she had answered him with a thoughtful response, he recovered himself from his musing and met her gaze. "Precisely," he said, "I rather think you would be quite good at it. If you wish, I could show you how to shoot," he offered, without applying the caution of forethought.

"Ay, if it would not be too much trouble on your part," she smiled. "Thank you." Stepping next to her, he placed the cue in her hands and showed her how to hold it. He did not notice that in this process, he had actually placed his arms around her, and she being focused upon the mechanics of the game, remarkably took no notice. Turning around to thank him, and ask permission to begin playing, their faces nearly touched. Their bodies did touch, and Darcy's arms wound snuggly around her. Too shocked to speak, there they stood—she feeling as though her heart would break free of her chest, and he feeling another part of his anatomy bursting forth.

Once again, their bodies communicated without words. After several magical moments, with each one enjoying the embrace, she found her voice, and in a volume she had rarely used before, she nearly whispered, "Have I the correct form? May I shoot now?" Taking her shot, she was thrilled with the result. She took a few more shots, enjoying the game and her time in his company. And then, with a shallow curtsy, she thanked him for teaching her. Wishing him a very good evening— she abruptly quit the room. Quickly and quietly she set out, making haste for her quarters. Once inside, she sat enveloped in the darkness, pondering Mr. Darcy. Never had she entertained such thoughts. Thoughts she could not control, indeed, such folly! She was forcibly struck. Time spent alone in her room did nothing to compose her.

≻≁≺

Life at Longbourn continued at a hectic pace. Steadily falling rain did nothing to dampen Mrs. Bennet's spirits; she was thrilled that her two eldest daughters were occasioned to spend so much time in the company of two reportedly wealthy bachelors. She was in no hurry for them to return home. Upon the whole, she was most eager for them to be wed and gone. She especially wished to see Lizzy out of her household as soon as possible. She thought it all the better if the two eldest could be wed to men of means. The less they would take from Mr. Bennet's fortune, the better, she reasoned. She would be quite pleased, if they could be gone before the change of season required new wardrobes. She would not miss the girls, her little Lydia would be quite wonderful company for her. As far as Mrs. Bennet was concerned, Lizzy had thoroughly disgraced herself in her disrespect for her mama. Mr. Bennet sat in his bookroom, missing his two eldest daughters, especially Lizzy. He longed for the girl's society. His favourite daughter was a sweet distraction from his constant worries. He noted that the nagging pain in his stomach was indeed becoming more frequent.

All was quiet at Netherfield. An atmosphere of peace filled the house, and its occupants slept blissfully. All except Fitzwilliam. Slumber was eluding Darcy. Even though he was naked atop the sheets, he began to sweat from the humid heat in the second story guest room. Rising up to open the windows, he became startled as the door to his room was slowly opening. Blinking to adjust his vision in the limited light, he began to squint. To his delighted amazement, the intoxicating aroma of roses spiked with sweet almond oil began to fill his room and tantalize his senses. The seductive form approaching him, teased his desires, and baited him with insistent urges he could not deny. At last his eyes adjusted to the moonlight streaming through his window and he saw well enough to identify the lovely face and exquisite form of Miss Elizabeth.

She walked towards him. Even in the darkened room she appeared perfect, and so beautiful. Clad in a thin nightgown, her body looked impeccable. She displayed a ripe suppleness, in her graceful and fluid movements. His breath quickened— and his heart raced as he approached her. Her nightgown was nearly transparent, revealing her tantalizingly curvaceous body. Darcy held his breath in anticipation. When they touched, they embraced so tightly that their bodies molded into one shape. This contact was magical— unbelievable. His appetite for her body went far beyond a hungry lust. Holding her so tightly became a stimulus which evoked an intense excitement he had never before experienced. It revealed his emptiness and awakened a deep desire, making him marvel at his own deficiencies. He startled at the sudden notion of two people. The embrace was made, not of him, nor her, but them! The sensation of their two bodies as one, compelled him to refocus his life's vision and acknowledge his own great need. For all his wealth, Fitzwilliam Darcy was a solitary man, a lone man— a lonely man.

Darcy knew this woman was ideal for him. His hands followed the curves of her back and smoothed over her derriere, where he repeatedly squeezed her firmly and seductively. He buried his face into her beautiful hair and breathed in that delicious bouquet which seemed to be her signature scent.

Silently holding her, he pressed his hardness onto her with great longing. Her body was very responsive as she exhibited her own hunger, pressing herself onto him. "I had to come to you," she whispered, her hot breath nearly scorching his ear. "I know it is the right thing to do. I understand why you and I may never wed, but how can we continue to deny that we are perfect for each other? In a few short days, Jane and I shall away, and we shall have so little time to love each other. I knew you would not be able to come to me, but I have not had the breeding and education you have enjoyed, therefore, it had to be me, coming to you. What prevents you— pride or prejudice?"

He followed her to the bed, and she stacked the pillows for his head. "I have wanted to do this since the first day we met," she confessed. Then, gently pushing him down upon the bed, she stretched out on her side next to him, rubbing her hand over his back. Darcy spoke not one word, but moaned with desire. He closed his eyes, and tried to be very quiet, to prevent their discovery. He would not want others to think poorly of her.

He ran his fingers through her beautiful hair and told her she was all he could ever want in a lover and even a friend. He began to recite his list of her many attributes. To his enjoyment, she began kissing him softly, slowly and passionately. Darcy accepted her kisses as she bestowed them, for his emotions were equal to hers. He relaxed, and they enjoyed mutually enchanting kisses, which demonstrated their total affection. Peace enveloped him.

"Oh Elizabeth, you are so perfect for me. I think— I may be falling in love with you."

Pushing him firmly away from her, she said, "Do not waste your time on what shall never be, my love."

"Nay!" he cried, and tears began to fill his eyes. "Do not say never be…" As he lamented this, his tears awakened him. He sat straight up and could not seem to stop the flow streaming from his eyes. It was only a dream, but it all seemed so real. He could actually feel everything that he dreamt about, and the smell of roses had seemed so strong as to convince him it might have been real. "Ay," he said softly to himself, "I forgot, there are roses growing outside my room." But, looking up, he saw the windows were tightly shut.

Chapter Two

"IN VAIN I HAVE STRUGGLED...MY FEELINGS WILL NOT BE
REPRESSED."

–JANE AUSTEN

Breakfast at Netherfield was lively. Bingley was in a capital mood, and Jane enjoyed his jocularity. Elizabeth also laughed with much amusement at the clever young man's discourse. Upon this scene Darcy entered, followed closely by Caroline Bingley. "Charles, you are the cleverest gentleman I have ever occasioned to meet," Jane stated adoringly. "Did you learn your quick repartee at Oxford, or pray, tell us, were you born so and simply grew up an enchanting boy?"

"Miss Bennet, I beg you," Darcy interjected, "kindly stop! You will create a monster from which we shall never cease to be amazed. His head shall swell three hat sizes and there shall be no living with the man after today. Do not praise Bingley, I must insist!" The group laughed at Darcy's merriment. He was obviously feeling himself in a lighthearted mood, as well. His eyes sparkled as he spoke, but it was quite clear that the focus of his eyes was none other than the beautiful Miss Elizabeth Bennet.

Bingley saw a chance to tease his friend. "Darcy, jealous as always, I see!" Bingley retorted. "Ask Caroline. I have always been a friendly sort of fellow, and conversation simply rolls off my tongue. I cannot help it!" With that, the trend of thought died out, for no one really desired to inquire of Caroline.

Elizabeth looked up at Darcy and smiled, offering a cheerful wish for a good morning. He returned the smile and the sentiments and held her gaze a bit, trying to judge her mood. It nagged him that she quit the billiard-room so suddenly, and the dream of last night seemed so very real, to him it was as if they had a very deep relationship already. The friendly exchange of smiles between Darcy and Elizabeth did not escape the notice of Caroline. Such expressions of mutual admiration were fathomable to her, although she very much desired them not to be. A servant had just filled Darcy's coffee cup, he nodded his thanks, then lifted his hand— directing the man to refill Elizabeth's cup. It was but a very small gesture, yet it was observed by everyone in the room. Attending to his coffee, Darcy gave no more thought to his token of consideration towards Elizabeth. He was quite accustomed to ordering servants at mealtimes, and his preference for Elizabeth seemed so natural to him, he nearly did it by rote. All things considered, Darcy was very well pleased with the nearness of Elizabeth. He quite enjoyed having her close enough to be watched and appreciated— even if he did not converse with her.

Feeling his eyes constantly upon her, Elizabeth became somewhat restless. She looked at the window and saw that it had begun to rain again. Jolted by a harsh sound, Elizabeth startled. The abrupt and unkind voice of Caroline Bingley trumpeted at her, nearly jarring her out of her chair. "I say again, Miss Elizabeth. Have you a modiste in Meryton or do you and your sisters go into town?"

Caring little for the question and even less for the one who posed it, she looked straight into the eyes of Caroline and said proudly, "Miss Bingley, there is an excellent modiste in Mertyon. It is our family's delight to patronize the local businesses of our village and give them our full support." Elizabeth continued to hold Caroline's gaze. "Does that satisfy your curiosity, or did you simply wish to draw our attention to the fact that country costumes are inferior to those of town?" At that, she caught herself and softened her tone and her voice. "Pardon me," Elizabeth asked, sorry for her retort. "I am too direct in my speech, I suppose 'tis the close confinement. I do thank you for your kindness to us, and your most generous support and encouragement. 'Tis much appreciated." Elizabeth sighed, looked at her hands for a second, then back to Caroline. "If you were indeed seriously inquiring," she continued, "Miss Mimi would be honoured to serve your needs whilst you and your brother are in the country." With that, Elizabeth stood up and excused herself from their kind company.

Quitting the room, she turned the corner and was out of their sight. Knowing the house from her childhood, she entered the butler's pantry and pushed a secret panel. It opened to her, and looking around, she stepped inside. It was dark and somewhat damp, just as she had remembered. It did offer a quick escape, and that was what she was seeking. Carefully stepping toward the secret butler's passage leading to the library, she slowly began to follow the course, in almost total darkness. Stopping, she leaned against the wall and tried to clear her head of Caroline Bingley. She made a mental note never to allow that woman to get under her skin in the future.

Hearing the butler's door creak open, she startled, for she thought it was not in use. The house was at a low census and there seemed little need of the butler's passageway. Quietly stepping up on the small curbing she leaned against the wall to listen. There were footsteps slowly advancing toward her. Almost hearing her own heartbeat, she could feel it begin to pound within her chest. It was all quite similar to the fleeting moments of fear she had sometimes experienced in this very passage. Although as a child, the unexplained and scary noises were always servants quite bothered by children underfoot. She was now an adult, and she would confront her fears and the intruder. Most likely it would only be the housekeeper looking to save some steps. Bravely she whispered, "Who is coming, please?"

A deep, sensuous male voice answered her in a whisper, "It is I, Miss Elizabeth, Fitzwilliam Darcy."

"Mr. Darcy, how did you come to find this passageway, sir?"

"From the library," he said softly," I often use it in avoidance of Caroline."

"I certainly cannot fault you for that, such is my intended use at this very moment. I blame myself for letting that disagreeable woman get under my skin with such regularity." She whispered her response in a matter-of-fact manner, and then she fell silent.

"Indeed." he whispered his agreement, then he continued. "I am here with the object of seeking a few moments of your time. May I speak with you, Miss Elizabeth?"

"As well as you may whisper, I warrant. Whatever is on your mind, Mr. Darcy?"

He began haltingly, "I wish to tell you how deeply I regret the distorted values I was expressing to Bingley in his study when you entered. I have completely changed my mind upon those sentiments and wish to ask you to forgive them, and me for having espoused them."

"Is that correct, Mr. Darcy? What has changed your mind in that regard, if I may inquire?" she whispered.

"I must admit, I have been observing you and your gentle sister. You have shown me many fine and wonderful qualities that I deeply admire. I feel I have been accustomed to having so much female attention that I have built a rather strong and somewhat ridiculous shield around myself. I know that makes me pompous, and once again, I simply ask you to forgive me." Here he paused and waited, hoping she would answer.

She answered not.

He continued, "Miss Elizabeth, I have so closely observed and admired you that I wonder if I may ask your permission to court you? It would be an honourable courtship and I shall certainly seek your father's approval as soon as it is possible."

She remained silent.

Perceiving her to be still doubtful and reluctant, he whispered, "I do indeed desire to know you much better, just as I hope you will know me better and find me to be so much more pleasant than your present assessment ranks me."

"I must say," she replied after some moments of consideration, "I am all astonishment, Mr. Darcy. I do wish to tell you, these expressions now lend me a much more favourable opinion of you and your values." She felt him step closer to her. He was standing in front of her, she being almost the same height as he, for she had accessed the step used by the servants when they needed to pass one another.

"And, are you now so inclined as to consent and allow me the privilege of knowing you better, Miss Elizabeth?" He asked, fondly hoping she could feel his good wishes. He desired her to know that he was attempting to admit his egregious mistakes and confess his most offensive vanity. That he should fancy himself in love with her was a matter of Darcy's own astonishment. He had given this little talk with her the utmost consideration, but he was yet unwilling to beg, and plead his cause. He resolved to remain quiet and allow her to perceive his affections. He fell silent in order to avoid speaking with too much haste. He did not want to reveal too much, too soon.

"Mr. Darcy, it would seem that you are a logical thinker, as am I. Why would I refuse when considering the argument you have presented for yourself? In this new light, I feel I would be so inclined as to consent, upon one provision," she answered.

"I am most eager to hear it, Miss Bennet."

"I am the daughter of a gentleman, you are the son of a gentleman. Are you able to meet me upon that common ground? A ground, which, by the way, elevates us both within our current society to the very same level." She waited for him to respond.

Taking him by much surprise, Darcy was forced to take his time, and consider a point of view he had never once contemplated. A warm smile spread across his handsome face, although she could not see it. Stepping even closer to her, he gently placed his hands upon her shoulders and murmured, "Miss Bennet, your point is profound. Indeed, your father owns an estate with tenants— as did my father. Ay, we are both children of gentlemen land owners. A wonder it did not occur to me earlier. I am bested and must therefore say that our relationship has begun with you already showing yourself to be the better person. You had the correct understanding of our equality. As to our differing connections, dare I ask where your father received his education?"

Elizabeth did not follow his trend of thinking, and this vexed her exceedingly. Nevertheless, she answered him without hesitation. "Oxford."

Darcy made his reply, whispering in her ear with much affection. "There, that answers forever the question as to why our spheres of influence differ so greatly. My father attended Cambridge, as did I. Little wonder my father had never known Mr. Bennet. We may fancy, that had they both attended the same institution, the two of us might have known each other all our lives." He smiled widely at this, knowing that he had now, with her help, mended the hurt he'd caused the night he verbally assaulted the Bennet sisters.

"That said, just for my own benefit, would I be able to hear you simply say, that I, Fitzwilliam Darcy, may officially court Miss Elizabeth Bennet?" He asked so sweetly that Elizabeth was nearly stunned at his affection for her. It took her by much surprise. Her heart was swelling with emotion, therefore some few moments passed before she found her voice to answer him. She felt her body trembling, yet she steadied her voice. "Indeed, yes—Miss Elizabeth Bennet agrees to enter into an honourable courtship with Mr. Fitzwilliam Darcy," she said, smiling at him although he could not see her.

"And thanking you for that, I must offer my first heartfelt apology to you, Elizabeth, for that which I am about to do. I must tell you that I am completely unable to restrain myself any longer." He gave her little time to wonder at this strange statement and apology. He knew his words would create some confusion. He hoped she would feel joyful anticipation. In truth, he wondered if she could guess his next actions.

Reaching his fingertips up to her face, he began to slowly trace her cheekbones over to her jawline, which he gently and ever so slowly stroked, up and down. She gasped, not expecting his touch, for she could not see his hands in front of her face, it was so dark in that part of the passageway. She wondered if he could see.

Patiently waiting to determine her disposition, he licked his lips, offered a prayer that she would accept his attentions and, leaning forward, pressed his body firmly against hers. His lips lightly brushed hers. She moaned softly, and he parted his lips to lightly caress hers, tenderly drawing her lower lip into his lips and slightly sucking upon it whilst his fingertips ever so softly brushed over her hair, from the crown of her lovely head to her shoulder. It was all so gentle and with just a whisper of touching, so lightly executed, she was not certain it was happening at all. Then she felt his softly smooth tongue lightly licking her lips. Her mind began to reel. She tried to think if this behaviour was proper for a courting couple, but her thoughts were not organized. Her brain did not want to think, her body simply wanted, nay, needed to enjoy these very new sensations. Her lips were burning. Somewhere deep inside her core, there was a profound and very urgent longing. She was not sure what was being longed for, nor how it could be obtained.

More disturbing than all of this, was a certain spot, just beneath her mound that was sending powerful explosions of pure pleasure throughout her entire body. That certain spot was perturbing, as its sensitivity was becoming intrusive, due to its direct contact with a hard and somewhat large part of his anatomy. The unsettling power of this small spot on her person, troubled her greatly as she absolutely could not resist its urgent need to press firmly into his large part. Press into him she did, and to her delight, he pressed back. This new feeling, made her arch her back, pressing her breasts suggestively into his chest. She sighed sweetly. It was overwhelming. It was wonderful. It was new and exciting, for both of them. All the while, the delicious kisses continued. She reached up and touched his face and then ran her fingers through his hair. At this, he moaned, emboldening her to tenderly touch the tip of his tongue with her timid tip. This was the most intimate act she had ever experienced. Without realising it, she began a series of soft sighs. At once their lips ceased and their tongues began lightly touching one another. She tipped her head back slightly, in order to place more of her tongue onto his. It was a spontaneous, rhythmically perfect succession of movements. Their gestures of devotion, and mutual passions, became a celebration of merged sensual commitments. Their tongues were at a gentle play, and their bodies were certainly confirming a shared desire. It was a yearning that could not be satisfied now, nor in the near future. Slowly, reluctantly, he pulled his body away from hers, and turned his kisses back to her lips. At last, he drew his head slightly away from hers and turning her head, he gently pulled it onto his shoulder.

"Oh my!" her shaky voice confirmed her excited joy. "Where did you learn to kiss like that, with such powerful feelings?" Her breathing was ragged and heavy, reflecting her highly aroused state. It made her feel breathless.

"France," was the one-word answer he hoped would stop that line of thinking. "Elizabeth, I must remind you that I offered an apology before my actions. After you accepted my courtship, I knew I could not go one moment longer without enjoying our kisses. Can you forgive me, please?"

"Absolutely not!" she teased. "Or, perhaps I shall, if you promise to let it happen again." They smiled at each other in the darkness.

"I have some questions, if you please." she said quite simply. "I suppose I must start with a confession of sorts. When we first met, I began experiencing certain specific feelings towards you. An attraction to you, I would say."

"Elizabeth, those feelings are God given. Could you give me an example, please?" He felt slightly improper asking such an obviously honest woman to tell him of his particular appeal, yet he could not resist the temptation. He heard her take a deep breath.

"When you helped me off my horse in the rain, I felt a certain— unidentified something for you. Then, as I touched your hand to select my king there was a surge of strange feelings running through my arm, into my body, and then down to..." Here her whispery confession stalled, as she was suddenly quite shy. "And, most illogical," she continued, sighing, "yet very powerful, when I saw you in the billiard-room, in your casual attire, I had very strong feelings. What made these so overwhelming was the sight of your neck, and the hair on your chest. I finally had to rush from the room, in order to protect you, and me, from some illicit behaviour I desired to perform." She closed her eyes and waited for him to respond to her confession. Silently, she hoped he would understand.

"Oh, I see. And before I answer, pray just what was that illicit behaviour?" he asked. He could hear her swallow hard in the darkness. The delicacy of her response required her full concentration. It was difficult to describe feelings and emotions she had never before experienced. For the first time in her entire life, Elizabeth found herself to be inarticulate. She took a deep breath and whispered, "The urge to touch you was overwhelming. Just the sight of your neck made me, ah . . ." She paused a moment, then went on timidly, "And, your chest, dear Lord —" Here her confession broke off for a bit. "I felt an urgent need to reach inside your shirt and run my hands up and down your chest, and kiss your neck. 'Tis so very improper, is it not? Yet, it was all so overpowering, I was overwhelmed. And my guilt—" she whispered," was all the more extreme due to your complete innocence. You were, after all, alone in the room. I entered upon your privacy without your expectation, or even your consent. Finally, I could stand it no longer and had to flee for never had I observed a gentleman in so casual attire. I was astonished at these thoughts and I could no longer trust myself being alone with you." She blushed wildly at this, although he could not observe it, owing to the darkness.

"Oh, I see," he said softly, his lips touching her ear as he responded. At last he understood why she had left him so abruptly. He found her honesty quite endearing.

"You do see my point, do you not?" she pleaded somewhat nervously. "Never had I these feelings before, not at any time nor with anyone else. And just now— heaven help me; that wonderful and astonishing kissing unleashed new feelings that could easily overpower me."

"How so, please explain them to me." He requested the additional information. Now he was feeling very guilty. It was as if he were reading her private journal.

"I am not sure where to begin," she uttered breathlessly. "I felt my thighs were in urgent need of feeling yours pressing firmly against them. And certain other parts of my person were strongly demanding to be pushed tightly against your, ah— corresponding parts. All due to the throbbing demands that are unique and unknown to me. " In addition, my breathing was shallow and uneven. My heart felt it would leap out of my body, and I began to shiver— even though I felt quite hot. All of these sensations were quite out of my control."

"Oh my dearest heart, Elizabeth. We both enjoyed our embrace and kissing— did we not? You are describing very nearly the same feelings I experienced. You and I have a very powerful attraction for each other. When we met outside in the rain, the smell of roses in your hair— drove me mad. The sight of all your natural beauty, enhanced by the storm, created a strong allure. And our hands touching so innocently with the chess pieces sent a sudden momentary jolt through my hand and arm. Your eyes captivate mine, and I could listen to the sound of your voice all day long. These are all very spectacular feelings. As I said— they are God given and meant for us to enjoy greatly the physical acts of loving each other. Our relationship is not ready for them, but they shall continue to drive us both wild with excitement and desire. We may have these feelings, just thinking about each other— even when we are apart."

"You liked me, even when I looked like a drowned rabbit out in the pouring rain?" She asked, astonished at his revelation.

"Please tell me you heard my sincere words of admiration, Elizabeth?"

"Yes. I heard you." She responded with a very simple answer. "Thank you." At this, she slowly slid her fingertips around his neck, stroking it lightly as she reached up to link her fingers into a holding position. Licking her lips, she softly brushed his, gently pulling his lower lip inside both her own, and sucking it ever so lightly. He moaned deeply and pressed himself even more decidedly against her. She parted his lips very gently with the tip of her tongue. Moving her fingers upward, she gently outlined his ears. Then, taking her time, she slowly traced the margins of his mouth with her tongue— quietly moaning her own enjoyment.

Her tender attentions continued as she softly moved her lips to his neck and began to kiss him there. Boldly her hands began to rub eagerly up and down his chest. Each stroke demonstrated more and more desire as she sighed deeply with each breath. Her moans had an aphrodisiac affect. Darcy thought he would spill his seed when she began to push her mound firmly into his erection and rhythmically move her hips against him. He wondered if his resolve was strong enough to endure what this innocent virgin might do.

Finally, she lifted her head and rested it once again upon his chest. Sighing, she said simply, "very nice. Curiously not enough to satisfy me, but very wonderful all the same, was it not?"

Darcy swallowed hard, "Elizabeth—" he whispered, "where did you learn to do all that?" "Netherfield, in the butler's passageway. Your body taught me, Fitzwilliam." They smiled in the darkness. Although they could not see, they knew of their smiles.

Chapter Three

"...SO GROSS A VIOLATION OF EVERYTHING RIGHT COULD
HARDLY BE CONCEALED FROM THE WORLD..."
–JANE AUSTEN

The day arrived when the Bennet sisters entered the Bingley carriage, their horses in tow. With two attentive gentlemen riding next to them, they headed to Longbourn. Mrs. Bennet was in her glory as two very wealthy young men entered her home with her two eldest daughters. The girls were not welcomed home very cordially by their mother, to be sure. Yet their father, though very laconic in his expressions of pleasure, was most happy to see them both; he allowed them to see their importance within the family circle. Especially so with Lizzy— a very important person in the Bennet household. She was quite dear to her father's heart.

Mrs. Bennet ordered a dinner and invited the guests. Mr. Bennet was pleased to meet with both gentlemen in his bookroom. He offered them each a glass of port, but he declined to imbibe himself, declaring a somewhat sour stomach of late.

Before they quit the room, Mr. Bennet had given approval for each of them to court his two favorite daughters. Mr. Bennet rose from his chair, smiled and requested Mr. Darcy to remain one moment longer with him, allowing for Mr. Bingley to leave them. He put his hand upon the younger man and offered, "—Mr. Darcy— might there be another item you wish to express to me— before we join the others?" His eyes sparkled and he stood eye-to-eye with Darcy. Fitzwilliam was silent for a moment. He wished to speak to the man and confess his ardent love for Elizabeth, yet something was stopping him. In his silence, Mr. Bennet spoke to him. "Mr. Darcy, Lizzy is a very special woman. I sense that you know this about her by the way you say her name, and the respect you show when you speak of her. I would like it to be known that she is the best of the five, sir. Now, if you are certain that you have omitted nothing, and have no additional sentiments you wish to declare at this time, we shall away, sir." Darcy nearly lost his senses at this bold conversation. Mr. Bennet left no doubt that Elizabeth was very special to him. He knew that Mr. Bennet understood he wished to ask for her hand in marriage. His reluctance at so asking— kept him in awe of himself. He could not understand himself in the matter. Even her father knew and understood; why could he not tell Elizabeth of his feelings?

Mrs. Bennet was mentally planning the weddings and calculating the wealth of her prospective sons-in-law. In truth, she longed to be rid of her four elder daughters. In all respects, her love and affection had been lavished only upon her dear little Lydia. In the secret corners of her heart, Mrs. Bennet had felt love only for her baby. She could scarcely wait for the older girls to leave home. If it were possible for them to depart without taking one shilling with them, it would suit her right down to the ground. She dearly wished to have all four removed from her—and from Mr. Bennet's fortune, as well.

Halfway through the three-course meal, the occupants of the dining-room ceased all conversation. The sound of pounding hooves alerted them to a single rider rapidly approaching the house. Express messengers seldom brought good tidings. Each one looked to Mr. Bennet, and Mr. Bennet looked to his man, Mr. Hill. All inside the house jolted at the insistent knocking upon the front door. Mr. Hill answered and showed the rider into the vestibule. Approaching Mr. Bennet, he whispered that a courier from Pemberly awaited Mr. Darcy with an urgent missive. Bennet summoned Darcy and directed him to the man who delivered the letter. Darcy immediately sent the rider back to Pemberly. Fitzwilliam was gone but a few minutes, an eternity to Elizabeth as her imagination held her in its dark grip. The mystery of the urgent messenger threw Elizabeth into a flutter. Fear gripped her heart and held her hostage to the powers of the unknown. For all his wealth— Elizabeth knew that fortune did not prohibit problems.

Upon his return, Darcy asked Elizabeth to accompany him to the front parlor so he might speak privately with her. She arose reluctantly, knowing ill news awaited. The great concern taking root in her heart was now spreading across her beautiful face. Entering the parlor hand in hand, Elizabeth could scarcely breathe as Darcy read the entire letter to her. It was from a Mr. White, the Darcys' personal surgeon. It detailed the very serious condition in which Georgiana had been found. Whilst she sat in the garden, a poisonous spider bit her ankle. Although this variety of spider was thought to be deadly, the bite administered to such an extremity was to be an advantage—the poison was not introduced close to her heart, therefore proper treatment and time would be the biggest factors influencing her recovery.

Before he could say he was to away, Elizabeth placed her hands upon his and said, "Fitzwilliam, this is most urgent. Your sister is in complete need of your love and support at this time. Please go to her as quickly as it is safe for you to travel. How I wish I could help, but do tell her that my fervent prayers shall be ascending into Heaven on her behalf, and I shall beseech the Almighty for her healing. And for you— my dearest heart, I shall pray for a safe journey and that you shall find her to be whole and safe when you arrive home." In the privacy of that room, he wrapped her in his arms and kissed her with such feeling that they both cried.

Knowing that he wanted to stay with her, she was required to send him away to his precious charge. "Dearest heart," Elizabeth pled, "would you please wait five minutes for me to prepare something for you to take to your sister?"

"Indeed. I thank you," he said, and with great sadness he watched her quit the parlor. Once again, Darcy was faced with the temptation to make an acknowledgment. He dearly wished to tell her that he loved her— most ardently. He thought about what might happen if he expressed his feelings. There was no denying what he felt in his heart, yet he was, at the same time grieved. Surely this would be the appropriate time to confess his emotions. He told himself that she guessed his warmth of feelings and he need not speak with words at this time. They would see each other soon enough, perhaps then he would feel more comfortable, more at liberty to say what he felt. Elizabeth rushed to her room and selected two of her own blended oils. She chose a pretty little jar and one larger plain bottle. Sitting down she wrote two short notes, one to go with each preparation. Pausing before she left her room, she thought about her profound affection for Fitzwilliam. Truth be told, she loved him, longed for him, desired him physically, and was uncertain as to whether or not she should ever confess it to him. She wished above all things, that she could be alone with him, back at Netherfield. Yet, even if they'd been given one more night at Netherfield; Elizabeth would have been unable to arrange being alone with Darcy. She was completely inexperienced in such matters.

Rejoining Fitzwilliam in the front parlor, she handed him a plain brown sack containing the large plain bottle. She pulled the bottle out and told him it was a combination of chamomile, sandalwood, hops, and lemon oils. She instructed him to put it in his bathwater when he needed to relax. Explaining that the smaller jar in the floral bag was for Georgiana, she quickly slid a letter into the pretty sack. The short missive wished the little girl well and told of the preparation.

"You make these oils yourself?" he asked, smiling and stroking her hair with a look of pride and approval lighting his eyes. "So— that is why your hair smells so absolutely wonderful." She reached up and took his hand from her hair, brought it to her lips and kissed it. She gave him a sad little smile and responded, "I do, and thank you for the compliment."

He lifted her chin up causing her to look into his eyes and asked, "Elizabeth, I quite fancy such things. Where did you learn to do this, dearest?"

"From books, of course," she answered placing her gaze upon the floor as if to prevent her eyes from filling with tears. She found it painful to be in his presence, knowing that he must away. Looking at her feet, she said, "—I fear— I am a strange creature. I wish above all things that I could remain with you forever, but knowing that you must away without me— suddenly I desire you to start on your journey. Standing here with you, knowing that it cannot last, but a few fleeting moments, makes me wish to see you go, and end my despair; yet— I know full-well that my despair will truly begin as you go away. Oh, if I could have *carte-blanche* and be given all things in this life as I desire them…"

"I wish you were coming with me. I need you and Georgie would benefit from your help." At these words, she took his hand in hers and kissed it. Her tears now knew no delays and she could not interrupt their flow. Seeing her weep, Darcy wept. He wanted to rush back to Mr. Bennet and demand to take his second daughter to Pemberly. He thought most seriously about asking the man to return to his bookroom with him. Once there Darcy would ask for Elizabeth's hand in marriage. He loved her— he knew he loved her. Would it not be more sensible to leave as her fiancé? He knew for a fact the man would understand. After all, he realised in his heart and mind that was exactly what Mr. Bennet was trying to help him accomplish earlier in the evening. For some strange reason— he was holding back. He had been given an opportunity with her father. Mr. Bennet was making it so easy for him. What more could her own father have done to assist him? What prevented him? He could so easily have declared himself— asked for her hand and she would right now be packing her bags to go with him. His lack of being more serious with Elizabeth was driving him to melancholy. Why was he unable to declare himself?

She leaned against him and he bent down and kissed the top of her head. "I scarcely know how I shall face each day whilst we are parted," she murmured, continuing to look at her shoes. "Yet we both know that I cannot come with you. Please do go now. Although 'tis painful to see you leave— I should not wish to delay your sister's comfort one minute. Please write to me—" she pleaded. He nodded and then went to collect Bingley for their return to Netherfield. Within five minutes both gentlemen prepared to away. Bingley pledging that he would journey with Darcy and see what support and help he might offer his friend. Jane was proud of his loyalty, although she wished he would stay home. Promising they would all meet again soon, the Bennets' front door opened once more. Darcy and Charles quitted the house and the Bingley carriage took them swiftly into the darkness. Jane and Elizabeth retired to Jane's room to comfort each other and to talk about their week at Netherfield. Both girls wished they were still there…

Just before sunrise, Elizabeth was dressed and set to depart for her early morning ramble. As she passed her father's bookroom she saw him seated at his desk, his head resting upon a book. Knowing it was too early for him to be out of his bed, she approached him with her heart in her mouth. Her voice shook with trepidation as she called softly, "Papa," and waited for a response.

He was quiet and made no move whatsoever. Frozen where she stood, she whispered a prayer to God for help. She walked to him and placed her hand upon his back to feel for movement as he breathed. She felt no movement. Picking up his arm, she placed her trembling hand upon his hand, it was cold. Her breath left her, tears filled her eyes although she did not spill them. Her thoughts refused to believe yet the evidence would not change. He was gone. Amazed that her legs still moved upon demand, she quit the room, and went very quietly upstairs to Jane. Shaking her sister gently she beckoned her to come downstairs. Once there, her eyes spilled their tears as she whispered to her dearest sister, the saddest of news. Their wonderful papa was gone. Events moved quickly. The eldest sisters called for Mr. Hill and quietly told him the news. He sent for the undertaker and the cleric. The apothecary was called for Mrs. Bennet, who was not awakened and informed until all of the other arrangements were in place. Both girls had enough experience with their mama to know that she would be nothing but a hysterical nuisance and hindrance.

Elizabeth especially feared her, ever since she herself had recently refused the proposal offered to her by the male heir to the Bennet estate. Her father's cousin, cleric to a Lady Catherine de Bourgh, had asked for Elizabeth's hand, and she had flatly refused. Her mother had warned her that the consequences of such an injustice on Elizabeth's part would be visited upon her. She told her daughter to fear the day Mrs. Bennet would be widowed. The warning had made Elizabeth shrink from her mother's anger. When William Collins married Elizabeth's best friend, Charlotte Lucas, Elizabeth received a letter from her mama. Mrs. Bennet had called her second daughter 'an enemy' and told Elizabeth of her disdain and disregard. This broke Elizabeth's heart and filled her with shame. She burned the letter and told no one. Here was the moment of truth: Mrs. Bennet had been widowed. Elizabeth tried to brace herself and await the fierce storm.

Now Collins would take up residency in the house, moving Mrs. Bennet into the tiny dowager cottage, forcing her to follow in the footsteps of her own late mother-in-law. This had been a misfortune Mrs. Bennet had dearly wished to escape. She loved her lavish home and could not face the idea of being forced to release the house and all its contents for others to enjoy. Her plan had been to secure her home by marrying Elizabeth to Collins. She had selected Elizabeth because she was jealous of her husband's love and devotion to Lizzy. She had long desired to send the girl away with Collins, at the earliest opportunity. However, when the day of the proposal arrived, Mr. Bennet had come swiftly to his little Lizzy's rescue. Mrs. Bennet had hardened her heart against the girl. She had begun to reason that all four daughters should find their own way. She fancied herself a good mother and if her daughters had not the good sense and training she had given them, life would become their teacher. As to Lizzy, the girl had sealed her own fate. She was merely reaping a harvest from a crop of cruel selfishness, sown when she refused a perfectly wonderful proposal, claiming she would wait for love.

Ridiculous. Mrs. Bennet herself had wed for security, and Lizzy's marriage to Collins could have secured all of them.

Elizabeth and Jane walked to Meryton together to alert their Uncle Phillips. An attorney by profession, Mr. Phillips would handle all the legal requirements of the transfer of the estate. He would also settle the amount of money Mr. Bennet had bequeathed upon each of his five daughters.

Uncle Phillips had an unusual expression upon his face as he spoke what seemed to be a prepared speech. "Lizzy, my dear— I fear I must be the bearer of some very sad news for you. Your mother has directed me to tell you, that because of your refusal of Collins, you will not be allowed to live in your home. I am to settle your amount at fifty pounds. It is unusual for females to inherit. When your papa told me of his failing health, I arranged with a Mrs. Margaret Dart in Devonshire to hire you to work as her companion. You will go to her in Exeter when the post departs. He sighed and shook his head.

"Elizabeth, I know you to be a wonderful girl. It grieves my heart to treat you so unfairly." He looked away from his niece, as he could not look directly into her eyes. He knew very well the cruelty he was perpetrating upon the girl. He had always taken such pride in the older Bennet nieces. In truth, all four of the elder sisters were wonderful young ladies. He was angry with himself for taking part in this administration of their father's will. Elizabeth was taking the news very poorly.

Just as the two sisters began to cling to each other, Lydia rushed into the room. She had been alerted to the news by the noise in the house, after her two elder sisters awayed. Seeing the older girls walking to Meryton, she quickly dressed and followed them. Lydia ran most of the way, and by the time she reached her uncle's house she was panting and covered in sweat. Neglecting to brush her hair, it was now matted together, and standing up over her shoulders, rather than falling over them. Lydia looked every bit the part of a wild girl. Her eyes flashed with her extreme anger. She did not look like their sweet little sister, nor their mother's little pet.

"Mama has told me we shall be forced to leave our home, and it 'tis all your fault, Lizzy!" She yelled at her sister as soon as she saw her. "I hate you, you selfish girl!" Lydia ran in front of Elizabeth and reached up, soundly slapping her big sister across the face. Elizabeth flinched and cried, "Lydia— control your temper!" Uncle Phillips took Lydia by the shoulders and called for his son Robert. Entering the room, Robert took his little cousin Lydia by the hand and led her, not gently back to her home. The child's loud protests could be heard as she quit the house with her older cousin.

Uncle Phillips made to cross the room to look at Elizabeth's cheek. Although it was quite red, she kindly smiled and waved him away. "Uncle, the child is grief stricken. I forgive her, and I quite understand her ill humour. I suppose without Papa's support I can certainly expect the wrath of Mama. Looking at Jane, Lizzy warned, "take care, Jane, to stay on the good side of both Mama, and her little Lydia."

Uncle Phillips raised his eyebrows at Jane as he heard this warning. He knew he needed to prepare her for her bad news. "Jane, I fear you are also to be sent away with the same meager sum. I do not as yet have a placement for you; however, because your mother is not angry with you, you may stay in the dowager house until you secure employment." At this sad news, both girls burst into tears and clung to each other, just as they had done when they were little. Their attempts to comfort one another failed miserably. Shock and fear ruled their senses. They were undone. Looking at the girls, their uncle decided to keep the bad news about Mary and Kitty to himself. He felt there was plenty of time for the younger girls to write about their expulsion. Lizzy might just as well read about their situation. She and Jane had heard enough from him for one morning.

When they had a little time to reflect upon this awful news, Jane spoke of the comfort she had, in knowing the mailing address for Lizzy. They would be able to write to each other. In addition, they would have the support of Uncle and Aunt Gardiner in London. Letters could be sent and news could be obtained through them, if necessary. It might not be swiftly done, but they would not lose track of one another's where-abouts. Although they had not the room, nor the means to offer a home to the Bennet sisters, the Gardiners would provide a sort of safety net— to ensure that no girl would ever be lost to her family. They had a permanent address and could offer temporary shelter in an emergency.

Jane and Lizzy walked back to Longbourn for the final time. Jane helped Lizzy pack as many belongings as she could take with her. Some few books, oils, and as many clothes and shoes as would fit into her two bags. She packed her winter clothes, but she was obliged to carry her best winter coat in her arms. Lizzy wrote a letter to Fitzwilliam telling him of her new situation and one to Georgiana wishing her well. At Lizzy's insistence, Jane wrote to Charles. Elizabeth also took the liberty to write to Charlotte. She told her friend of her mother's wrath. Then, she requested a favour, asking her lifelong friend to please secure and safeguard all her oils, dried flowers, equipment, tools, instruction books and glass bottles and jars. Somehow, Lizzy felt she would have them again, yet she freely confessed that she had not the slightest idea of how. She wished her friend the best in life, and then asked a servant to see her missive safely delivered to the new Mrs. Collins. Having accomplished a great deal in a small amount of time, the two girls walked back to Meryton, and to Uncle Phillips's house where they spent the remainder of the day together.

Devastated at being forced to leave before seeing her father's final resting place, she resigned herself to the will of her fiercely angry mother. By two o'clock on the following day, Lizzy summoned her courage and stepped up into the post wagon. Jane, Mary and Kitty waved a tearful good bye. A life always lived in the brightest of sunshine had encountered the sudden onset of a savage storm. The longest ramble of her life commencing, she would learn how vicious the world could be when suffered alone. She did not know what life would hold, but she knew that, whatever it would be, the experience would change her. Elizabeth Bennet would never be the same.

At Pemberly, Georgiana mended slowly. The bite was a threat, but even more so, was the infection created as the child scratched at the wound. Healing was slow in coming. The preparation of oils sent by Elizabeth was praised by Mr. White, the surgeon, and he instructed the little girl in their use.

Darcy was sitting in his study with Bingley when the day's post arrived. Looking through the day's letters, he spotted a pristine hand, and noted the return address was Hertfordshire. Knowing it was from Elizabeth he tore the missive open quickly. Just as he began reading, Bingley was handed his letter from Jane. Within moments, both men blanched; Darcy was especially upset hearing that Elizabeth had felt her mother's wrath. The two had not spent enough time together for Elizabeth to tell him the story of the insufferable Collins, but she revealed it all in the letter. He was doubly angry when he learned that this disgusting pig of a man was the cleric to his own Aunt, Lady Catherine de Bourgh. He was outraged to think such a man would leverage his legal position to force such a beautiful woman to become his wife.

Darcy rose from his desk and poured two glasses of wine. Handing one to Bingley, he shook his head. "Bingley, why does trouble come to us like this? I am stuck here with a very ill sister— when the woman I love is being sent off into the world, and all I have of her is this address. How I wish she had come directly here, to Pemberly, rather than take that post wagon to a stranger's house." The thought suddenly pierced his heart. He had not declared himself to Elizabeth. He had postponed telling her of his affections. Darcy knew her well enough to realise that she never would presume an invitation. If he had asked for her hand in marriage— she would have come to him. But, upon the strength of a courtship— what could she do? Without a plan for marriage, he knew she would be obliged to make a way for herself out in the world. What of her position? How was she to be treated by others? He roused himself and murmured, "What is to become of her, and of Jane?"

"Darcy, I am beside myself. To think that Elizabeth is punished because she wanted to wait for love, rather than marry advantageously, breaks my heart. And now that I hear Jane is being turned out, and I know not where, I am ready to go to Longbourn immediately."

Darcy nearly sprang from his chair. "Of course, old chap, you absolutely must go now! There is nothing stopping you, Bingley. I shall send my man Collot with you. He is a fighter and a no-nonsense bodyguard. Who knows what you may face? We do not have any idea where Jane is being sent. Bingley, I shall send for Spencer and Collot. My men have amazing skills and they are clear thinking. Let us bring them in to help us with this dire situation. Together we shall plan a strategy."

Within minutes, both big men entered Darcy's study. Darcy explained the plight, and the importance of the two Bennet women. In addition, he outlined his plan for Mary Bennet and Catherine, also known as Kitty. Were these two sisters being turned out as well, but no information about either of them was available? He told his men to return in one hour. He instructed Collot to be ready to depart for Hertfordshire with Bingley. Darcy sat down and sketched Elizabeth's three sisters from his memory. Bingley sat in awe of his talent. He had no idea that Darcy possessed this gift of artistic genius. Reaching into his desk drawer, Darcy removed a folder with over two dozen sketches of Elizabeth. Most of them were works of memory, but some were done when she had no idea he was sketching her likeness.

Bingley studied the sketches. "Darcy, I say I am overwhelmed at your talents, both in sketching and in memorizing each person's features. I must admit, I lack the command needed to recall descriptions both of locations and human features. I should make a poor witness to crime." Darcy did not respond, he simply continued his efforts and prepared for his footmen. One thought consumed him; he must find Elizabeth Bennet as soon as possible. Should any harm come to her, he would never forgive himself. All could have been prevented— had he only declared himself when he'd had the opportunity.

When his men returned, Darcy displayed the sketches of the Bennet sisters, their name and a description of each girl was listed on the back of their likeness. Putting the drawings into three envelopes, he gave one to each man. After taking Jane's likeness out and looking at it for several minutes, Bingley put the envelope into his breast pocket. "Darcy," he said, "is it not disturbing how life can turn in a minute? One fine day, all is perfect with your world, and then in a heartbeat, the bottom falls out."

Standing up, Darcy clasped his friend on the arm and tried to offer him some measure of hope. "Old chap, I know we both feel lonely and somewhat dismayed. We must never give up hope that we shall all be reunited very soon. Let us keep our eyes on the day's requirements and our hearts set firmly on the vision of finding Elizabeth and Jane."

Bingley nodded, turned his head away from Darcy and quitted the room with Collot following him. As he awayed, Fitzwilliam wished him safety and good fortune. Then he directed Spencer to go to London and speak with Mr. and Mrs. Gardiner at number five Gracechurch Street, near Cheapside. He was to take a letter from Darcy to Mr. Gardiner, and learn all he could about the locations for the other sisters and inquire of any changes with Elizabeth's whereabouts. Both footmen were instructed to give a letter to each sister if they were found. The letters from Darcy would describe his wish to bring them to Pemberly and offer them a paid position. Mary would be asked to assist Georgie with music and scriptures, and Kitty would be hired as a companion. His plan was to have the sisters at Pemberly so when he found Elizabeth he could marry her, and bring her home to her family.

Charles was on his way to Jane in Hertfordshire. Collot was with him and he had plans of his own. Collot would canvass the area and inquire after Miss Elizabeth as well. He had also been directed to look after Mr. Bingley and safeguard the man's very life. In addition, Darcy directed Collot to interview Mr. Phillips. He felt there was a story lurking there. This was a man who had taken quite a large role upon himself. He had placed Elizabeth's employment, sent her to Exeter, and disbursed her pitiful inheritance money. Darcy wondered if this had been by Mr. Bennet's directives. He had many questions about Mr. Phillips. Mrs. Bennet's close relationship to the man caused Darcy to feel a deep concern and perhaps a caution. He continued to worry about Elizabeth.

Darcy sat down at his desk and put his face in his hands. He could not remember ever feeling so completely helpless. What hardships would Elizabeth face before he could reach her? He knew quite well that the world is a very dangerous place, indeed. Taking his writing materials out of the drawer, he began a letter of great importance to his beloved. He declared his love for her, and asked her to marry him. His one regret had been, that he had not confessed his ardent love for her, when they were last together. In this missive of some length, he poured his heart out to Elizabeth.

More time would be needed before the surgeon would declare Georgie fully recovered. Georgiana understood the urgent situation with the Bennet girls. She knew that her brother would ask them to come to Pemberly, and she was excited to think they would become her new sisters. Georgie prayed that Fitzwilliam would find and marry Elizabeth as soon as possible; for he had talked of Elizabeth daily. The girl felt as though she already had an acquaintance with her brother's beloved. She had received the gift of essential oils from her, and Elizabeth had sent her two missives. Daily her brother talked of the woman he deeply desired to become her sister. Even though she was just a child, Georgiana could clearly see the happiness in her brother's eyes when he spoke of Elizabeth. Georgie prayed for Elizabeth and all the Bennet sisters daily. She knew they were praying for her, too.

Spencer called upon Mr. and Mrs. Gardiner in London. The couple had concerns about their four nieces. Mr. Gardiner had no additional information to share with Mr. Darcy, but he expressed his willingness to assist in any way possible.

Next, Spencer set out to Hertfordshire to conduct his own investigation. Mr. Darcy was a very careful man. He demanded an intensive search, characterized by attention to the smallest detail. Spencer was faithful to send messages to his employer, keeping him informed of his inquiry. Darcy likewise sent his own messengers to Spencer, telling him of his planned trip to Exeter. He had been writing daily to Elizabeth, to keep her informed of Georgie's progress. It was such a relief, and pleasure to write his last letter, revealing his soon planned arrival, and telling her of his own excitement. He was hopeful that their relationship was still viable because the last and only letter he had received from her, was the one written in Longbourn, before she left her home. Georgiana had tried to comfort him. She reminded her older brother that often the postal service lost or misdirected letters from shire to shire. This reminder, made him pleased with his own couriers. His messengers were the very best. In truth, he could not think why he had not remembered to use them. He could have sent his own men to Elizabeth's door. What a comfort it would have been to have heard from them of her appearance, and the expression on her face as she received his missives. But, that was an opportunity gone by, perhaps he did not think of it because he was so preoccupied with his sister's ill health.

One week before Mr. White declared Georgiana to be completely healed, Darcy became so restless, he made a very quick trip to London on horseback. He wanted to see the Gardiners for himself. In Mr. Bennet's absence, he looked to Mr. Gardiner as Elizabeth's head of household. He declared himself to Gardiner, and asked for Elizabeth's hand in marriage. A visit with his godfather, the archbishop of Canterbury, gave him the special license, which provided consent to their marriage, without the usual requirements of the church. A stop at Darcy House allowed him to check on the property, and send a missive to his solicitor, with instructions to draw the settlement papers on Elizabeth, and forward them to Edward Gardiner in Gracechurch Street. Darcy made some needed purchases in London, then walked the streets. He knew Elizabeth was in Exeter, but he searched the faces in town. Perhaps he would see Jane, Mary or Kitty...

On the day Mr. White pronounced Georgie healed, Darcy set off by himself for Exeter, to the home of one Mrs. Margaret Dart. Elizabeth had arrived several months earlier to serve as her companion. Finding the grand home would present no challenge, yet it would be an urgent journey. The weather was fine for the carriage ride and Darcy congratulated himself on the remarkable speed at which the new vehicle accomplished the trip. Finally arriving in Exeter, the driver made haste to Dart House. In moments, Darcy entered the unearthly quiet of the somewhat eerie home.

"Good afternoon, sir." The elderly butler, greeted him. The man wore a grim expression on his ancient face. He was a straight, tall, and very proper man with a genuine sadness about him.

"Mr. Fitzwilliam Darcy to see Miss Elizabeth Bennet, if you please." Darcy snapped.

"Sir— I am so sorry to inform you that there has been a recent death in the house. We do not have a wreath, as none has been directed. May I inquire as to your business?" He asked in a rather stilted voice.

Not realising the man was nearly deaf, Darcy announced himself a second time and then requested to see Miss Bennet.

The butler nodded, without a smile. "Ay," he said sadly.

"I say, Bennet, companion to Mrs. Margaret Dart, do you hear me, please?"

"Ay," he answered slowly. He heard not a word that Darcy spoke, but his experienced, professional eye scanned the young visitor. Obviously very wealthy, perfectly dressed and he possessed a very powerful presence. The butler sized up the young man almost instantly. He reasoned Darcy to be related to the very wealthy Mrs. Dart. How he loathed giving the sad news.

The old butler looked down at his own shoes, then back into the eyes of the young man. Normally, he would not make eye contact with a visitor of Mrs. Dart's, but he knew he must show compassion to the young man. Slowly he gave the grim details, "Ay, with deep regret, I tell you of your loss, sir. She was most recently deceased. She passed away right here in this house at three o'clock on Tuesday, last. Services have been conducted, but if you wish to visit the gravesite, please see the cleric at the Church of St. Peter, Mr. Thomas Cole."

Darcy reeled at the news of Elizabeth's untimely demise. He grabbed the old man's shoulders and shook him. "Please be certain—Miss Elizabeth Bennet is gone? Is there not perhaps a misunderstanding? Do you hear me, please? Miss Bennet? What of Miss Bennet?"

"Ay, that was the name, Miss Elizabeth Bennet, lately of Hertfordshire. *She* had been the companion, sir," he concluded, not realising the confusion he had just created with his response.

Darcy was stunned. His world turned upside down. He wished to inquire further yet he had suddenly become mute. Dazed by the crushing shock of his great loss, he returned to his waiting carriage and directed to make way to the Olde Roman Inn.

Checking in, he bought four bottles of port, took one glass, and went straight to his rooms. Sitting down at the table— Darcy pulled the cork on the first bottle and drank it without use of the glass. He stared at the wall. His breathing was shallow, his eyes held a hollow look, and his mouth was as dry as cotton. He consumed all four bottles in this manner, and then stretching out across the bed, he began to ululate. His wailing was so mournful that the clerk tapped upon the door and entered to ask if he could be of assistance. Upon waking the next day, Darcy went downstairs and purchased another four bottles. Once in his rooms he repeated the process. This became his daily ritual.

Spencer appeared four days later. He entered the inn, made his way straight to the master's rooms, and went inside without knocking. He had feared foul play, but he found foul living. Darcy had eaten no food, failed to bathe, and simply drank enough each day to remain in a drunken stupor. The man was insensible and numb with grief.

Ordering a bath immediately, Spencer took the part of a valet, and the bodyguard washed and fed the master of Pemberly. As soon as Darcy could speak coherently, Spencer demanded answers. Darcy explained Elizabeth's death and declared that he would not return home. He insisted he be left, in the town where she had last lived. Spencer knew he had to get Mr. Darcy moving in order to motivate him towards the land of the living.

He needed to speak to him of Pemberly and his sister, Georgiana. In an epiphany, Spencer suggested, "Mr. Darcy, have you been to the church gravesite to pay your respects to your beloved, sir?"

Shocked to know that he could be so coarse as to neglect his last respects to the woman he dearly loved, he asked for help to prepare for the visit. Sadly, Darcy thought (to himself) of his own responsibility for her death. If only he had declared himself to Bennet and had claimed her hand in marriage. She would be alive, and the two of them would be happy together at Pemberly. He told Spencer that she had been buried at the Church of St. Peter in Exeter. Breathing a slight sigh of relief, Spencer ordered a bowl of soup and then helped Darcy dress for the day.

Arriving at the church, Darcy requested a visit with the rector, Mr. Thomas Cole. Mr. Cole's assistant arrived and ushered them into his study. After a fifteen minute wait, a short and stodgy Mr. Cole approached the men. "Pray, how may I be of assistance to you gentlemen?" Darcy could hardly state his sad business through his tears. He mournfully asked to be directed to the recently interred remains of Miss Elizabeth Bennet. "Let me check the register." Mr. Cole offered, "I do not recall the name."

"She would have been new to your church," Darcy said," having been here nearly three months. She hailed from Hertfordshire. Elizabeth Bennet. Without thinking he reached into his pocket and withdrew her sketch. As soon as his fingers touched the paper, a fresh revelation of the awful news flashed through his mind. Once more he felt the crushing blow of the newly bereaved. It hit his body as though someone had thrown a boulder on his back and took all the wind from his lungs.

"I am sorry to tell you there is no record of her here. Would you have any other additional information for me, perhaps a married name?"

"Nay!" Darcy barked in anger at the man. Recovering his manners, he took a deep breath and began speaking very slowly. "— Excuse me— she was unmarried, sir. She had only been in Exeter a short while, employed as companion to Mrs. Margaret Dart."

The cleric's face broke into a broad smile. It lit as though a beam of light was turned on inside his head. "Gentlemen, I do have some very good news for you. I am afraid there has been a gross misunderstanding. It was Mrs. Margaret Dart who was recently deceased. Her companion was in excellent health when she left Exeter just four days ago."

Darcy turned white at the news. He was thrilled, naturally, but even news as wonderful as this registered as a shock to his system. The assistant was ordered to bring wine for Mr. Darcy. Sipping the wine, he asked for additional information about Elizabeth.

"Ay, Mr. Darcy, Miss Bennet left town with the daughter and son-in-law of Mrs. Dart. It seems the lovely elderly lady made provisions for Miss Bennet out of an unusual fondness for the girl. She engaged her as governess to her very own grandchildren. Miss Bennet is now at the home of Mr. and Mrs. James Brookfield in Salisbury. No doubt the party has had ample time to arrive home. I believe I have an address for you, if you care to wait. The Brookfields have recently moved from our parish to Salisbury." Once again the assistant entered the study, and this time presented Darcy with a slip of paper detailing the address for James and Mary Alice Brookfield in Salisbury.

Charles Bingley met with failure in his attempts to locate Jane. He did not find her in Hertfordshire. Uncle Phillips did not have any information to share with him, and the once friendly Mrs. Bennet was in no mood to help him find her eldest daughter. Not being far from London, Bingley decided to go to his home and check on any word from Darcy. Perhaps there would be a letter from Jane waiting for him. His only dread was of seeing Caroline. This sort of news would elate her. It grieved him that his sister had such a cruel streak in her character. She so wanted to marry Darcy that she would find great joy in knowing Elizabeth had been turned out of her home, and was possibly lost.

Entering his study at Bingley House, he called for Caroline to attend him. As he crossed the room, his heart quickened to see a message upon his desk. "What have we here?" he mused aloud, "a missive from Jane, perchance?" Charles smiled widely, took the paper in his hands and walked towards the window into better lighting. In seconds he yelled, "Stone the crows! What is this?"

Bingley House, London

30 September 1801

Dear Charles,

Upon hearing the sad news of your little friends, and imagining how distraught Fitzwilliam and dear little Georgiana would be, I have awayed to Pemberly. The joy and support that I bring to both Darcys will be well received. You may reach me by mail at Pemberly. I shall see you upon my return to town, brother.

Fondly, Caroline.

"What in bloody hell is this?" he shouted. Knowing his younger sister would be aware of Caroline's actions, he yelled for her at the top of his lungs.

"Louisa!" His voice nearly shook the hallways. Hearing her name, the girl began to walk reluctantly towards the demanding call. Louisa Hurst and her husband also lived with Charles. His fortune kept his sisters and brother-in-law close at hand. Bingley's generosity and kind heart provided a livelihood for all of them.

Louisa entered the room. Maintaining a safe distance from Charles, she inquired how she could be of assistance. In truth, she had been dreading the questions coming from her brother. Louisa was closer in character and nature to Charles, than was Caroline. She had a tender heart and had been pricked in conscience about her recent conduct.

"I must know how Caroline got involved in this search for the Bennet sisters," he raved.

"Oh, it is quite easy to explain…" Louisa began lying to him, as she boldly inserted herself into his wrath. "—She wrote a letter to dear Jane—and Mrs. Bennet answered. She seems to be quite angry with Eliza, did you know that, brother?" Charles turned his back upon his sister. Louisa took that opportunity to whirl around and swiftly quit the study.

Sitting down to write to Caroline and demand she return to London, he also wrote to Darcy. He felt certain that the man would not be at Pemberly but a letter of apology was necessary all the same.

When the missives were prepared, he called for his carriage. Stopping at Darcy House he found no one at home, as he suspected. Continuing on, he went to number five Gracechurch Street, near Cheapside. A short visit with the Gardiners told him that Jane had written to him about two weeks earlier. Charles was encouraged to know Jane had written, indeed, but he was discouraged in knowing that the letter was not available to him.

Mrs. Gardiner was happy to outline all she knew of her niece, Jane Bennet. "Ay, Mr. Bingley. She had mentioned going to serve as a companion for Mrs. Prudence Cooke. She did indicate that she had sent a long letter to you at your London address. That letter was sent to you a few weeks ago. She heard no reply and assumed that you no longer had an interest in her, as she is now a turned-out girl."

Bingley shifted in his chair, sorry to interrupt the woman, but he had to speak. "Mrs. Gardiner, I must assure you that is not the case. May I make you aware, please, that I would marry your niece right this moment— if I could only locate her. Mr. Darcy says the same about Miss Elizabeth. May I assure you that we are both most serious and have honourable intentions regarding your eldest nieces. In fact, we are both out daily searching for them."

Mrs. Gardiner smiled knowingly at the young man. "Mr. Bingley, I am very happy to hear you tell me that your affections match those of our Jane. Her letters are always filled with her regard for you, and her hopes for the future."

Bingley sat back in the chair. A look of relief flooded over him, and he smiled at the woman. Jane had told him that Uncle and Aunt Gardiner were favourites. After speaking with them, it was easy to determine her attachment. Charles was very much impressed with the Gardiners.

"Mr. Bingley, at my urging, Jane wrote a second letter to you at your London address and one also that she sent to Pemberly. I have absolutely no idea why you did not receive any of her missives. The most recent information we have for Jane is an address for a Mrs. Cooke, in Hinckley. I do not believe it is very far from here, actually." She gave him a sad smile, wanting to do more to help the couple reunite, but nothing could be done. Mrs. Gardiner voiced her concerns and expressed her wishes for success.

"Mr. Bingley— we are heartsick about our wonderful girls. Jane and Elizabeth are very precious to our family. Please do send us word immediately when you find Jane.

"We are quite at a loss as to why my sister-in-law would have turned her four older girls out of her home. We have seen the cottage, and even though smaller than the manor house, it is a suitable dwelling for the six of them. Have you any ideas, sir?" She asked.

Bingley looked at his feet and waited for thoughts of something to say to Mrs. Gardiner. "Madam, it seems to have something to do with Elizabeth's refusal to enter into an advantageous marriage. As to why Mrs. Bennet would wish to send her four older daughters out into the world, I am at a complete loss. Perhaps she felt her new cottage would be too small, or perhaps their fortune was depleted. In any case, it is heart-breaking, to be sure.

"Mr. and Mrs. Gardiner, I shall send word to you when I locate Jane. I wish to ask her to be my wife as soon I see her. The very night before his death, I asked Mr. Bennet for the honour to court Jane, and he heartily gave his consent. I too, am heartbroken at the loss, madam."

Charles awayed to Bingley House and questioned the staff about letters from Jane. His butler assured him that he had indeed received two letters from Miss Jane Bennet and both had been placed upon his desk to await his return. With the sad realisation that his privacy had been violated, and his personal letters were missing, he was furious with Caroline. It was so like his eldest sister to do such a thing. Louisa was just the person to confirm this evil, no doubt she was a witness.

In despair, he sent for Louisa. His face was set in a harsh stare as she entered his study. "Louisa— I have been told the truth. Caroline learned of Jane and Elizabeth's troubles because she opened my letters from Jane, did she not? If you lie to me this time you and your husband may remove yourselves from my home this evening."

"Brother, it is true. Caroline saw both letters, she opened each of them as they arrived and read them to me. We laughed at those rag-tag girls, out of a home and with no way of support except to bow and scrape to the will of others. Caroline burned each letter after reading them to me. Jane Bennet is so far beneath you. Charles, you are saved and so much better off!"

He looked at his baby sister in disbelief. Shaking his head, he stood and walked to the fireplace, gazing at the hearth where two letters from his angel had been consumed in flames. Louisa took advantage of his grief and tiptoed from the room. Benumbed, he sat at his desk and penned a second letter to Caroline. This missive told her not to come back to his home. He would send all her earthly possessions to Bristol and henceforth, she would be living with their aunt Mildred. A second letter went to his solicitor instructing him to settle Caroline's portion of their financial agreement. Funds were to be sent in the care of their aunt. Quitting the house, he entered his carriage and made for Hinckley and to his angel.

❧

Darcy's head was reeling. The man was scarcely able to contain his excitement. He sent Spencer back to London to check on any messages or needs from Pemberly. Without delay, he directed his driver to make great haste to Salisbury. Darcy's excitation grew during the trip, but it seemed to him that the carriage was moving very slowly. He felt his driver kept the horses at a slow pace. He was so eager to reach Elizabeth, he checked his watch every five minutes and he began to feel the relatively short journey would drag on endlessly. Darcy held steadfast in his opinion that he would find Elizabeth at Brookfield House and became more and more restless seated in the carriage. Never had the man been more unquiet, nor more eager to reach a destination.

Arriving at Salisbury in the late afternoon, the coachman took an inordinate amount of time looking for Brookfield House. The man tracked up one lane, then down another without results. Darcy was growing immoderately anxious. The ineffectiveness of his driver was not to be tolerated. He was desirous of seeing Elizabeth before the afternoon ended. Rapping his cane impatiently on the top of the carriage, he ordered his driver to pull to the side, and allow him to get out and walk. The carriage was taking too long to do what he felt he could accomplish faster afoot. He was convinced that he was in the correct neighborhood, and he was, of course, intensely desirous to see his Elizabeth. It was insupportable to be this close and not see her before dark. He would not allow another day to pass without seeing her. He absolutely must see her and speak with her. Had she received his letter of declaration, and his offer of marriage? He had obtained Uncle Gardiner's consent, was she pleased? He had obtained a special license from his godfather in London, and the settlement papers were being drawn. How soon would she wish to be wed? Where? In London— or Pemberly where Georgiana could attend their service in the chapel. He was very eager. He had waited months for this reunion. He must assure himself first hand, of her wellbeing. He must hear her wonderful voice, look into her beautiful lavender eyes and know that she still cares for him.

Even though the ground was exceedingly muddy, Fitzwilliam nearly sprinted in his desire to reach Brookfield House. His plan was to make arrangements that evening and call for her first thing in the morning when they would away to London, together at last.

Earlier that same day, Elizabeth was in the room she occupied, which connected to the nursery. She was happy with her adorable little charges and liked Mrs. Brookfield very well. Mr. Brookfield, a surgeon, was another story. He made Elizabeth feel quite uneasy. She had been alone in her room for the last two hours, filling the time by writing letters. Mrs. Brookfield had taken the children out of the house on her errands and Lizzy looked forward to some quiet time. It was only a minor worry that Mr. Brookfield was in his study downstairs. Other servants were in residence, so she was not alone with the man.

Thinking she heard him call her name, Elizabeth rose and walked out into the hallway. She listened and heard nothing. Returning to her desk— she heard him once again. She descended the stairs to see if she was needed and entered his medical study. He was not at his desk, but as she turned to quit the room he jumped out from behind the door and grabbed her. His right arm went around her, his right hand tearing at her left breast. His left arm went lower and he wound it around her lower belly with his hand grabbing at her crotch! She struggled with him, but he laughed and told her he had his eye on her and noticed how she flirted with him constantly. Knowing this was a gross falsehood, she realised he was mad. She tried to fight him but the greater the opposition she presented the more intense were his advances. It was clear he intended to rape her.

She ceased struggling a moment to think. Lizzy was quick thinking and quick acting. She grabbed a bronze bust which was upon his desk, and held it down below her waist. Brookfield, thinking she was going to surrender to him, relaxed his grip upon her, which allowed her time to whirl around, facing him. Using the momentum she gained, Lizzy swung the heavy object with all her might, and directed it up into his groin. The extreme pain rendered him helpless. He slumped to the floor, holding himself and moaning oaths and obscenities at her.

Elizabeth put the bust back on the desk and ran from the study. Entering her room upstairs, she opened her two bags and hastily jammed all her small worldly goods into them. Grabbing her coat, she fled as swiftly as possible. Mr. Brookfield was still writhing in pain upon the floor of his medical study, calling his servants for help.

As she ran from the house, the heavens opened and burst forth with a storm to nearly equal that of the Netherfield episode. Having nowhere to go and no connections in Salisbury, she made for the Cathedral View Inn and promptly checked in at the desk. She was taken to a small second floor room with just a bed and a stool.

Elizabeth was soaked to the bone. Her stockings and slippers were muddy and probably ruined. Another financial disaster for her, and she had very little cash left. Most likely enough to cover the cost of the tiny room and that of a post wagon passage to London. Within the hour, Elizabeth was feverish and suffering a great headache. She developed a violent cough and a very sore throat. Her chest was so tight, she could scarcely breathe. She could not remember ever feeling so ill and all alone.

༐

Darcy watched his carriage pass him. It was on the way back to the Cathedral View Inn they had just passed. At last he felt he was making good progress in reaching Brookfield House. Imagining he would see Elizabeth within minutes, he felt a lightness of mood he had not experienced in months. Nearly out of the town's limits, he found himself in an exclusive residential district. Seeing two youths, he hailed them to inquire of directions to Brookfield House. They took him around a corner, dense with foliage, as though they would point to the house. Then the two suddenly jumped him. The third, a tree of a man, came from out of nowhere and commenced to fiercely beating him. Finally, thinking they had killed him, they picked his pockets clean and fled.

To Darcy it was as though he had entered a maelstrom. His vision blurred, his head throbbed with unbelievable agony. Fearful thoughts of never seeing Elizabeth again tumbled through his mind. His breathing was so terribly painful and difficult he was convinced his very lungs had been crushed. Efforts to use his legs had been brutally ineffective owing to damage in his left knee. Any lifting of his head nauseated him beyond his control and his body ached from numerous kicks powered by evil boots. His present abilities were simply to lie upon the cold muddy ground and moan. He knew he was at the mercy of the next person to encounter his defenseless form. Unable to stand or call out for assistance, all he could do was suffer and wait, if he did not die.

༺⚬༻

Elizabeth curled herself into the fetal position upon her little bed and shook horribly with chills. She could not move or speak. Her throat felt afire, and her body was stiff and filled with pain. Within a few hours she developed a deep, body-wrenching cough which caused sharp pains in her back. These pains seemed to stop her lungs from working, and when she was able to take her next breath, it was short, shallow and very hurtful. The thin blanket and worn counterpane gave small warmth. Her coat was soaked and would take nearly a week to dry completely. She needed to use the water closet, but she could not rise. She had not received one letter from Fitzwilliam. Suffering in this current distress, she whispered a short prayer to God. "Lord, help me remember he only asked to court me. He did not propose marriage. Help me not to expect anything from him. He has not answered any of my letters. Please let me accept his rejection, and if I cannot improve my miserable life, let me die!" Soon her fever dreams took over and she was lost to a world of pain and hopelessness.

༺⚬༻

At eight thirty-five of the evening, a man and wife were riding in their carriage when their driver spotted Darcy. They stopped and took him directly to the Cathedral View Inn, where a grievously injured Fitzwilliam, without a farthing to his name, registered as a guest using only his pledge for payment. Painfully he penned an express missive to Spencer relating the events and ordering his help.

Darcy requested a surgeon. The clerk at the desk informed him that the only surgeon, a Mr. James Brookfield, suffered a fall down his stairs earlier in the afternoon and would be unable to attend any patients for approximately one month.

One hour later, the local apothecary, Mr. Wilson, left his patient after rendering several remarkable treatments for two cracked ribs, a dislocated knee and extreme headache. He then quit the Darcy room and knocked softly upon the next immediate door, entering when a soft female voice bid him to come inside. She was suffering a high fever and a violent cough due to sudden exposure to the rain.

Darcy could not eat or drink. His only competency was found in lying upon the bed and trying to sleep. It was in vain— for the loud and painful sounding coughs emanating from the room next to his kept him awake all night long. At times, he could hear a girl's very hoarse voice in that room crying. She seemed to be calling for Fitzwilliam. Holding his hands to his throbbing head, he doubted that he heard correctly. However, he wondered in his fog, just how many men bore his name.

At eight the next morning, Mary Alice Brookfield entered the small, dark room at the Cathedral View Inn. She brought soup and an envelope with one hundred pounds. Cook had told her everything that happened to Elizabeth. Mrs. Brookfield visited her tiny room upon six additional occasions. Each time she brought soup and stayed for one-half hour. She proved to be a godsend for Elizabeth.

Arriving upon the ninth day of Darcy's stay at the Cathedral View Inn, Spencer helped the master of Pemberly once again to find his land legs and get on with his life. At present, Fitzwilliam Darcy's entire life was his relentless search for Elizabeth Bennet.

Darcy and his man Spencer stood at the desk awaiting service. To Darcy, it seemed the clerk was very inefficient, and his slowness was most irritating. Fitzwilliam decided to pass the time pleasantly, rather than show his irritation. Taking out his sketch of Elizabeth, he showed it to Spencer and said, "They robbed me of everything I had which they thought of value. The only thing they did not take was my sketch of Elizabeth, and that, ironically, was the only thing I did value!"

Overhearing their conversation, the clerk looked up and saw the sketch. "I beg your pardon, Mr. Darcy. You have a sketch of Miss Elizabeth Bennet? Is she in trouble, sir?" he asked earnestly.

"Nay, but how is it that you know her name and recognise her face?" Darcy barked.

"Sir— Miss Bennet checked out of our inn only two days ago. She had been quite ill, suffering a terrible cough, and we worried for her survival. Mr. Wilson treated her every time he saw you. Her room was next to yours, sir. We were concerned that her awful cough would disturb you, Mr. Darcy. She left ten pounds to be applied against your bill here and also for Mr. Wilson's services. The remaining amount is to be rendered unto you. She said she wished to assist you because Mr. Wilson told her you had been robbed of all your money and valuables. She sternly admonished me not to tell you the source of your assistance. Of course Miss Bennet had no idea it was you, Mr. Darcy."

Darcy nearly sank to the floor upon hearing that Elizabeth had been in the room next to his for the past week, and he knew it not. She had been so close to him all those days and nights, and now she was gone, again. He shook his head slowly in utter disbelief. He was shocked and dismayed to realise it was her prayers and her voice crying out for him. Ay, it had been Elizabeth herself, calling his name, crying and praying for him.

Questions began to form in his mind. How came she here to the inn? Why? "Pray— tell me everything of her," he demanded, "anything you may remember— even a little word or two. She is lost to her family and we are desperate to locate her."

"So you are her family, then?" the clerk asked.

Darcy did not hesitate. "Ay, of course, what can you tell me, man, please."

"She left me with letters to post and just this morning Mrs. Brookfield brought over two letters addressed to her. It would be a great relief to my mind to release these to your care, Mr. Darcy. Would you kindly take them, sir?"

The clerk handed Darcy the outgoing letters, which Elizabeth had tied together with a thin blue ribbon. Just under the ribbon was a small square of paper upon which she had written, "Please post in your next outgoing service. Thank you, E. B."

The letters addressed to Elizabeth were placed inside a larger envelope by Mrs. Brookfield, with Elizabeth's name penned on the outside.

Taking the clerk by the lapels, Darcy demanded, "Where did she go? If not on the post wagon, how did she depart from the inn?" Fearful of Mr. Darcy's wrath, the clerk stepped back and said, "Please understand— it has been very busy and I have no assistant. I did overhear a husband and wife with one child offer her a ride in their carriage. The family stopped here for a meal, they were not overnight guests so I did not learn their names. I know not where they were headed, sir."

Darcy took the letters and hurried to his carriage to read them. His hands were shaking as he untied the blue ribbon. Taking it to his lips, he kissed it and then placed it in his pocket. Carefully he opened the letter she had just written to him. He had not yet recovered from the wave of nausea that flooded over him. She had been in the room next to his and so very ill for one week. He had heard her horrible-sounding cough and listened to her whispered prayers. It had indeed been his name that was called out in the middle of the night on several occasions along with heart-wrenching crying. At the time, it had tugged upon his heartstrings. But, now, knowing it was her grief, it was almost more than he could bear. Her generous gift of ten pounds to a stranger who had been robbed—and her request that her gift never be made known—touched his heart.

Holding the letter to the best advantage of the available light, he began to read:

Salisbury, England
Cathedral View Inn
30 September 1801

My dearest Fitzwilliam,

I boldly call you my dearest even though after all this time with no word from you I feel it is in vain that I dare to continue to hope. Daily I remind myself that your offer was only one of honourable courtship, in an effort to know me better. Such a slight consideration does not obligate you to write to me, and I know I am improper to send a missive to a gentleman. In a different time, I may have made a jest about such an arrangement, but these days I find I am far less impertinent.

My prayers for Georgiana continue. It is my hope that she has been returned to robust health and that she is enjoying the change of seasons at Pemberly.

Are you well, Fitzwilliam? It is my prayer that you are well and very happy. Are you shooting? If so, I hope you are enjoying your sport. I know not whether you are home at Pemberly, in London or even back at Netherfield. My— was it only just three months since the most magical moments of my life in the butler's passageway? I am still but a naive girl, I fear, yet you were correct in telling me that the feelings I had shall come to me, even when I think of you. I think of you so often, Fitzwilliam.

I lost my position with Mrs. Dart. The poor soul was ailing so, yet before her death she thought of me and arranged for me to become governess to her grandchildren.

I write this as I leave my most recent employment. It was a very unhappy and frightening event which sent me away from an otherwise wonderful position. The three children were adorable and I shall miss them so very much. Their mother is a saint, and I shall not trouble you with information of their father, the surgeon of Salisbury. May God protect his patients—and that last statement was not in jest.

I am nearly en route to an elderly Susan Boley of Swindon, somewhere near London, I do believe. Perhaps it shall be a pleasant installment. I do hope she is in good health. Should the Boley position fail, I shall feel rather like a fish out of water. Perhaps I shall make my way to London and seek advice from Uncle and Aunt Gardiner. How I wish Father were here to guide and direct me, and I am sure you can agree with that same sentiment upon your own behalf, many times, can you not? Do you ever stop missing your father? It is still a painful loss for me, and I confess I do weep for him, almost daily.

After seven days of acute illness, I am better and able to travel. I became unwell after being forced to run to the inn during quite a downpour, reminding me of Netherfield. My cough is all but gone. However, I do not complain, as Mr. Wilson, who attended me, informed me that the lad in the room next to mine suffered so much in his body because of a cruel beating administered by three strong men. He was robbed of all his earthly goods and left for dead. Mr. Wilson told me except for God's intervention he may well have expired. I have been praying for his total recovery and wishing him complete mending by this time. I had it in mind to seek to visit and encourage him in his suffering; however, it would have been most improper, so I prayed for him instead. Had he been a girl, I would have tried to provide some measure of comfort. One can always see others involved in even more trials and adversity than our own, can we not?

No doubt you wish to be done with my many words. I shall relieve you and be through except to tell you that I do miss you so very much. I visit you in my memory. My constant quest is for the sight of you and the sound of your beautiful voice. At times I close my eyes and picture you in the billiard-room. I try to remember your scent.

Stay well in Christ's strength, and 'tis my greatest hope that we are still friends, E. B.

Darcy read this letter three times before asking Spencer to join him. He wanted the man to check into the situation with Elizabeth. What caused her to flee the house in a vicious rainstorm? Knowing that Spencer would inquire of the household help, he asked him to "see to the surgeon, as needed."

Darcy watched Spencer take off for Brookfield House. He boldly opened Elizabeth's second outgoing letter. It was written to Jane.

Salisbury, England
Cathedral View Inn
30 September 1801

My darling sister Jane,

How I do miss you, dearest sister. I pray daily for your health and continued strength. I should like to be with you again, and keeping hope alive, I can see that day by faith. Are you off to Hinckley? Aunt Gardiner said that was her last word of you. I do hope that you are highly valued, as you certainly should be. I have no doubt that you are well appreciated and that you find favour with all you serve.

Jane, do guard your health. Be sure that you take your walks at every opportunity. I recently read that walking is most important to keep the constitution robust. Perhaps we may spend some part of Christmastide together. We shall want to be healthy and strong for that visit, shall we not?

Every time I face a challenge or a difficult moment, I ask myself, "What would dear Jane say about this or that?" and then I laugh with great mirth remembering what a wonderful soul you are and how you never see evil in anybody. I know that C. B. certainly sees the good in you. I hope you have heard from him by now, and if possible he has been able to visit with you. Before I left Meryton, you expressed your fears that he might not wish to be acquainted with a cast-out girl. Jane, please do not let that thought enter your beautiful head. You must keep your chin up and your thoughts always confirming a wonderfully bright future; for yourself, and all of your sisters, of course!

Jane, Aunt Gardiner told me how Mama cast you out because Lydia complained about you. I wish we could have gone together, to the same town, or perhaps at least the same shire. At night I look up at the moon and remember our talks at home and how we wished upon the moon. Jane, please continue to do that. We still share the same moon each evening, do we not? Confession, I wish upon the moon every night that I might see F. D. once more. I do so ardently love and adore him! Oh Jane, I have lost so much weight, I hardly look like myself, should he even know me if we meet again? Would you know me? At my new position, I shall pay more attention to my rations. I go to Susan Boley in Swindon. I do hope this shall be a good opportunity of lasting employment.

Do embrace yourself for me, I long to see you. Be forever strong and well, my darling. I love you so very much, my dear Jane.

Your loving sister, Lizzy.

Glad that Spencer had not yet returned, Fitzwilliam wept at reading the second letter. He had been correct, Elizabeth had assigned herself the role of protector and she tried so hard to offer her strength and hope to her sister. He thought of Georgie and thanked God that she should never even know the word *rations*. He tried to picture the perfect body of Elizabeth at a lower weight. She was so excellent. He asked himself how this happened in England? Darcy did not think it possible that a man like Mr. Bennet would make no provisions for his daughters. He had met the man after all, he certainly did not seem to be irresponsible and he had made it plain that he held Elizabeth in very high regard.

He reread the line that spoke of her confession. She 'wished upon the moon every night just to see him once more. And she does so ardently love and adore him.' Then he recollected standing in front of the fireplace at Netherfield and lashing out against her poor circumstances, stating that the two sisters could never hope to marry anyone of their upper class. Is she remembering those words now? Oh, how he hoped she had forgotten all he said. If he could only find her, he would take care of her. With a new resolve, he promised himself that he would find her. He would see to it that she had good food, safety, rest, and all the comforts of having the security and peace of living in her own home with her husband and sisters.

Darcy had written to Elizabeth many times and yet it was apparent she had not received even one letter. He had found refuge in his study, and a sort of comfort, writing letters to Elizabeth. He wondered how many weeks he had spent in such activities. The inefficiency of the postal service made him marvel. He had posted letters from Pemberly, and even from London on the occasion he had travelled there. Again, he berated himself for failing to use his own couriers, yet this was too late to be of help.

Just as he finished reading Elizabeth's letter to Jane, Spencer returned. "Mr. Darcy, the cook at Brookfield House told me that she was personally aware of an attempted attack upon Miss Elizabeth. It seems the doctor has done this before, so Cook was alerted to potential danger as she clearly heard the man call Miss Elizabeth two times. Cook then went towards the man's study just in time to see him jump out at Miss Elizabeth. From a crack in the door, Cook saw him grab Miss Bennet in a savage grip. Then he groped her. Cook said the doctor used one hand to open his trousers, allowing Miss Bennet to grab a bronze statue from the rapist's desk. She held the object low, and when Mr. Brookfield slacked his hold, she had opportunity to forcefully raise the statue upward, striking him in his groin with the heavy sharp-edged object."

"Damn that monster to hell!" Darcy interjected. "I am proud that she did well, yet I regret she had no weapon. Such a man should be shot!"

Spencer nodded and continued his account of the attack. "Cook said Brookfield writhed in pain upon the floor, calling for his servants to help him. They responded very slowly to the emergency. As we know, Miss Bennet made haste, running from the house with her two bags.

"Listening at the door, Cook heard Mrs. Brookfield confront her husband, telling him she knew he had 'done it again.' The man denied it all. Then he admitted that he had somewhat put his arms around her, but the 'little beast' assaulted him. Mrs. Brookfield informed him she was going to take the usual amount of money to Miss Bennet for her suffering and severance pay, and hopefully the girl would not go to the magistrate.

"Cook said Miss Elizabeth was not raped, due to quick thinking and bold actions of her self-defense. The sixty-year-old Cook was concerned about what she could have done to help her, but apparently Miss Bennet was capable of taking care of herself. Cook confirmed all of this to Mrs. Brookfield."

Darcy was filled with anger. Spencer had to remind him that he had men who would take care of this type of person. Nodding his head in agreement no more was said between them about Mr. Brookfield. Darcy knew Spencer would see to it, and set it right, if necessary. He would await the man at their agreed upon location, on the way back to London.

Darcy put the two letters sent to Elizabeth into his pocket. One was from her aunt Gardiner, and the second one from Kitty. He checked the return address for Kitty and happily saw she was in London. This would make getting her to Pemberly much easier. It was the first real breakthrough Darcy had experienced in months.

❧

Charles Bingley was sorely disappointed to learn that Jane was never installed in Hinckley. She reached the house just as her prospective employer was being taken to live with her son. Someone remembered Jane saying she would try to reach her relatives. He presumed the relatives to be the Gardiners. With a dejected spirit, Charles turned back to London. Hopefully he would have a letter from Jane waiting for him upon his return. Or perchance she would be with the Gardiners.

❧

Darcy went to Winchester. He had agreed to meet Spencer at King Arthur's Inn. He would hear the report about removing the menacing threat of the surgeon of Salisbury. The two had just finished a confidential conversation, which they had conducted behind the establishment. Spencer had it on very good authority that a particular surgeon had quite recently sustained a somewhat serious injury. He assured Mr. Darcy that the man would not expire— although it was a certainty that the fellow would have no additional children. His masculine anatomy had been dramatically altered as the result of an *accident*. He pronounced his own self-diagnosis: lesion of the prostatic plexus which caused impotence. The learned man had only recently sustained injuries caused by a severe blow to the groin, administered by a 'heavy, sharp-edged object.' Consequently his member was rendered useless, except for urination purposes, which might hereafter be best performed whilst sitting. Spencer assured Mr. Darcy that the man would continue to be a sound financial earner for his family, possibly a better influence upon his children, and most likely a much more respectable husband to his wife. Upon hearing this news, Darcy thought it fitting that the man had received the consequences of his evil actions. He began to think about telling Elizabeth. Perhaps she should know about the success of her self-defense against her attacker. He thought it fitting that the man was tamed in such a permanent manner. No doubt, Mrs. Brookfield would be thankful to Elizabeth forever.

Concluding his report, the men entered the common-room of the Inn. There they happened to spot Mary Bennet eating at a table against the wall. The girl looked thin as a rail and her poor eyes were dull. Just as Darcy approached her, she spotted him. A look of profound relief spread over her face as she recognised him. Quickly, she rose to her feet and walked very swiftly to meet him.

"Miss Bennet? Miss Mary? Do you remember me? I am Fitzwilliam Darcy. We met on only one occasion when Charles Bingley and I escorted your two charming sisters home from Netherfield. Do you remember me?" She nodded her head and leaned very close to him whispering, "Please do forgive me, Mr. Darcy, but do you see that man sitting by the door? He has been following me very closely for the past two days and actually had the barmaid pass me this message to me only moments before you entered the room."

Darcy took the note and led the girl back to her table. The men sat down with her. Observing her for a moment Darcy smiled and reassured her. "Please be at your ease, Miss Mary. Allow us to read this missive and we shall bring a remedy to whatever situation is at hand." His keen blue eyes quickly scanned the soiled piece of paper and he deciphered the poorly written document. Although the script was ill-contrived and the words were nearly all misspelt, the intended threat was very clear. The evil-doer promised he would kidnap her and take her to live with him in his cottage. His wagon and the necessary rope and gag awaited. He promised to use them both on her if she resisted his efforts to put her in his wagon.

The barmaid attended their table and the two well-dressed men calmly placed their orders. They acted as if they had not a care in the world. Smiling, Darcy handed the note to Spencer who also smiled, and began a lively conversation. Then he quietly rose from the table, and quit the room through a back door. Darcy assured Mary all would be well and continued to engage her in conversation about Elizabeth. Mary sat very quietly. She knew help had arrived and she tried to relax and remain calm. She did not look at the man sitting by the door. Had she turned her head, only slightly she would have seen Spencer enter the room through the nearby door, and take the man by complete surprise. Spencer briefly sat in the chair opposite the stranger. He spoke a few words and then the two walked calmly from the common-room. One of the men was never to be seen again. His horse and wagon would be held for a time in the stable of King Arthur's Inn. Eventually, the wagon and horse would be claimed by the inn as payment for the animal's keep. It would prove to be a better situation for the horse.

Mary had learned a servant's manners very quickly—and under the lash, for her trouble. She spoke with her eyes lowered, "Mr. Darcy, how kind of you to remember me. I do give thanks to God for sending you into this room. I greatly fear what would have become of me had you and your man not arrived to benefit me. How I thank you, and God for the remedy, sir. My sister Elizabeth holds you in very high regard, Mr. Darcy. Are you well? I should like to inform Lizzy of your wellbeing when I write to tell her of this rescue. I own to being completely without an address for her at the moment, however, I am in hopes that Uncle Gardiner may assist me in getting a letter into her hands."

Darcy looked at Mary. She was not much older than Georgiana, and the thought of that evil man taking her as a kidnap victim made him ill. He too, thanked God for the timing. "Indeed I am well, but be at complete ease, Miss Mary. That man will not trouble you anymore. There is now absolutely nothing to fear. I too, am thankful that we came upon you just in your hour of need.

"I was distressed to hear of your father's passing, Miss Mary. I have— if I might, an offer of employment for you. Georgiana, my sister is two and ten years of age. Perhaps you recall my telling your family about her, and you might remember the news I received of her spider bite. She has fully recovered, I am happy to tell you. However, I have been in need for quite some time now to find someone to live at Pemberly and assist her with the Holy Scriptures a half-hour each day, except Sunday, of course. Georgiana also plays pianoforte, and I wish to have someone to turn her pages and perhaps play duets with her on occasion. Does this type of employment sound as though it might fit your needs, Miss Mary?"

Mary melted before his eyes. At last she met his gaze and nearly swooned as she answered, "Oh, Mr. Darcy. Elizabeth has told me so much about your sister. I have been praying for her since the evening I first learned of the dangerous spider bite. It is wonderful to hear that she has made a complete recovery."

"Indeed, I thank you Miss Mary for your faithfulness to pray for her health. I am happy to agree with you, it is wonderful that she is fully recovered," he answered.

Mary smiled at him. She felt it had been years since she had smiled at anyone. She said, "It should be such an honour for me to read the Holy Scriptures with her thirty minutes, six days per week, and I should be ever so joyful to turn her pages and listen to her play the instrument. I also play. If she should wish it, I would gladly play duets with her. Oh, thank you so much Mr. Darcy. I thank you, sir. You have rescued me twice in one day, sir. My thanks to both of you for removing the threat of that horrible man. I shall be so pleased to go to Pemberly and Miss Georgiana at once, sir. I have been without employment for several weeks. I do not mind telling you freely that my financial need has been grave, sir. I thank you for the employment, Mr. Darcy. I am so happy to serve Miss Georgiana."

"Miss Mary, this is Spencer. He will arrange your transportation to Pemberly. Have no fear about your travel, Spencer will accompany you. Will the next available wagon for hire be acceptable to you? Spencer will ride horseback and watch over you. I suggest a hired wagon as it will most likely be the quickest available means of travel. I shall write to Georgie this very moment and tell her you are coming to join her. Mrs. Reynolds, our housekeeper, will take you in hand, and help you settle in, and find a room to your liking." She stood smiling up at him. He returned her smile and continued. "Miss Mary, have you heard from Elizabeth?" The girl started to cry at the question. She dabbed at her eyes and looked down at the floor. He was sorry to have caused her pain. Apparently, one of the countless difficulties in being homeless was that communication by mail seemed nearly impossible. Reaching into her Bible, the girl withdrew a much folded and tearstained paper. She handed it to him and nodded, silently. He opened it and read.

Exeter
Devonshire, England
4 September 1801

My dear little Mary,

I write from the lovely home of Mrs. Dart. She is a lady of refinement and I have every hope her delicate manners and gracious treatment of others shall begin to help me change. I should like to be just like her, and I should like to be more like you, Mary. You will be glad to know that I read my Bible every day and I say my prayers as well. See what a good influence you are upon your too lively older sister?

Mary, I must be brief. May I ask you to pray for me, please? Pray for me, as I pray for you, dear sister, and continue to pray for Georgiana and Mr. Darcy. Do practice your pianoforte, if you are able. I have not had opportunity to play nor even sing, as my life is so altered at the moment. I do sing in my heart and sometimes I play a duet with you, just in my memory. Do you ever play using your memory? I encourage you to try. It is quite diverting. Oh Mary, do try it sometime. We could perform that Bach piece we last played together at Longbourn. If you use your imagination, you can actually feel me beside you at an instrument.

I write thinking you are still in Meryton with Uncle Phillips. See, I have addressed this to his attention in hopes that if you have awayed, he will by some method or other help it to reach you. Remember, you are never out of my thoughts, therefore, you are never really far from me, are you? Keep looking up and smiling at all you meet. I adore you, Sweet Mary. Your Loving Sister, Lizzy.

Darcy held his feelings in check. He could hear Elizabeth's voice in her letters. He was beginning to realise she was a powerful woman in the Bennet family. Folding the letter carefully, he respectfully handed it back to its owner. "That is a lovely letter, Miss Mary. Thank you so very much for sharing it with me. It was just like having a visit with Elizabeth, was it not? By faith, we must believe that we shall see her soon.

Miss Mary there is something more I should like to say to you. I am searching daily for Elizabeth. When I find her, I shall ask her to be my wife. If she accepts me, the two of us shall join you at Pemberly as soon as possible. My sister knows of my plan. Feel at your ease to converse with her if you wish. If Elizabeth consents to marry me, you and I shall be brother and sister, Miss Mary."

The girl's eyes became brilliant at this intelligence. "Oh, Mr. Darcy, what wonderful news. I shall pray that you will be blest to find my sister very soon. Your proposal will make her so very happy. Lizzy has confided in me that she loves you with all her heart. I have no doubt that she will marry you. You are going to make her very happy."

Darcy smiled at her and added, "Miss Mary, Georgiana and I are very happy to have you in our household now, and we shall be even more blest to welcome you into our family. Be certain that I shall keep you and Georgie informed. You will receive word the moment I find Elizabeth. I shall be sure to give her your love, and your good wishes for our wedding." Smiling at her response to his news, he thought to give her more information. "I have more good news for you, Miss Mary. I have recently obtained Kitty's address. If it is indeed a valid location for her, I shall see her very soon. Should it be possible, I shall send her to Pemberly. If God is with us, she shall join you and Georgie." At this, he bowed to her, turned and left her in the care of Spencer.

"Mr. Darcy, I thank you." Mary called after him, "Lizzy would want me to give you her kindest regards. She made a great point of telling me when she left, that if our paths should someday cross, I was to tell you that she highly regards you and holds your friendship as very dear. She would also want me to say thank you for your kindness to me and to Kitty. I shall pray for your success in finding Lizzy and Kitty." With that, she curtseyed, and turned towards Spencer.

Darcy headed out to his carriage. Swindon would be next on the list. He told himself that if he failed to locate Elizabeth in Swindon he would return to London and team up with Bingley. The two could take care of Kitty, speak with the Gardiners and possibly unite the search for both sisters at once. He would talk to Collot and see if he had any better plans.

Chapter Four

"THEIR JOURNEY WAS PERFORMED WITHOUT MUCH
CONVERSATION . . ."

-JANE AUSTEN

❧

Allister Mason headed for his study. He had many papers to review and the lack of his assistant was beginning to wear him down. He could not fault the man for taking some time off the position. Monty's wife Hannah was about to deliver their first child, and he was quite filled with nerves. Allister was very fond of Monty and often found himself filled with envy. Hannah was completely devoted to Monty Knox. Watching the young couple, he felt the need of having a Mrs. Mason in his own home. Someone to love him and share his life. He had known many beautiful young women, of course, but he had been serious about none of them. His years at Cambridge, and the two years of his grand tour had brought many willing young ladies. They thought him to be a good catch. He was handsome, a desirable lover, and a very wealthy man. Many had matrimony on their mind, but none were right for him. He preferred the single, academic life. He had become a full professor, published two books, acquired three patents on his inventions, and amassed even more money. Perhaps now it was time to concentrate his efforts in finding someone as beautiful and loving as Monty's wife. Marriage and family were beginning to seem more important to him with each passing day.

Allister was brother to the famous builder of the world's first practical steamboat. The Mason brothers were known for their genius and timing. March third, 1801, had been the maiden voyage of the *Virginia Proper*, launched in Glasgow to the pride of all Scotland. Now, Allister himself was working on a high-powered steam engine designed for use as a rail locomotive. The secret nature of this undertaking made him a nervous wreck. He had little doubt that Monty suffered nerves owing to the strain of being his assistant engineer on the project. Working covertly was difficult. Work of this nature could not be done at the university, and use of his home as an inventor's workshop held certain risks. He feared too much exposure with servants coming and going. In addition, his younger brother Alden did not use discretion where friendships were concerned. Even when speaking with strangers, the lad did not use good judgment. So far, at least, all was well. He was waiting now to speak with a small group of men he would approach as potential investors. First on the list was his childhood friend and Cambridge brother, Fitzwilliam Darcy.

He picked up the letters that most urgently needed a response. Professor Mason needed Montgomery Knox. The man was brilliant; only his youth and inexperience kept him from having a full professorship. For now, Allister was glad to have him as his assistant. Mornings like this one confirmed that Monty was worth his wage. Gathering up some light work, he headed out the door and walked the six blocks to the staff housing. The Knox flat was on the second floor. He knocked lightly on the door. He did not want to disturb Hannah. Her baby was due to arrive soon, and he did not want to intrude.

"Welcome, Professor. Please do come in," Hannah smiled as she invited her husband's supervisor into their humble home. Not wishing her to worry, Monty kept her in the dark about their covert work. He adored his wife and wanted to protect her from any undue anxiety.

Looking around the humble dwelling, Allister wondered how the young couple made do with his meager wage. Monty's intellect would someday put him on the faculty at Cambridge, but at present his alma mater required fifty years of experience from twenty-year-old men. Impossible math, even for a genius like Montgomery Knox. "Professor Mason," Monty greeted him. "I see you have brought me some things to help me pass the day."

"Ay, and I feel somewhat guilty asking for your assistance. Are you both well? Are you able to have any additional help with the new arrival?"

"Indeed," Monty answered. "I thank you— we are both well. This morning's post brought word that our cousin Elizabeth shall soon arrive. She is unmarried so I am not sure how much she will help during the birth, but she is a very industrious lady and will no doubt lend a hand with all other matters. She is kind to come, and says it is a labour of love on her part."

Allister smiled at the younger man. He worried for him. "It sounds as though Hannah shall enjoy the support of her cousin. I am happy for you."

"Oh, I thank you," Monty replied. "She is from Hertfordshire, so I hope she fares well in our cooler climate." He smiled at the slightly older man. "I am certain you shall make her acquaintance whilst she is in Edinburgh. She is a most agreeable girl."

Bidding his assistant a good day, Allister quit the home and returned to his study. He wanted to do anything he could to help the young couple. He feared losing such a valuable assistant. He knew the rail locomotive project would stall without Monty. Indeed, he knew he would be completely lost without the man.

Heading for London, Darcy began to feel fear. All manner of crime scenes invaded his thoughts, but he knew he could not allow his imagination to run wild. He must stay rational and hopeful. He was thankful to have Kitty's London address. The morrow would be spent trying to contact her. Without the opportunity of seeing Kitty, he would have done what he did in Swindon: pound the streets of town, carefully searching for faces that resembled his love. He thanked God for the letter in his coat pocket, giving him one more reason to hope. He would see Kitty—provided that she was at the address he possessed. She might have news from Elizabeth, or possibly even from Jane. If Kitty is not at the address, he would see the Gardiners in Gracechurch Street.

Darcy tried to keep his thoughts bright, as the skies grew darker. The landscape began to disappear, with evening giving way to night. It was dark outside with no moon to light the heavens. Darcy missed the moonlight. He wondered if Elizabeth missed the moon. A sky without a moon gave her no opportunity to wish to see him again. He hoped she was wishing for him anyway, even without the moon. He tried not to think about Swindon. It was a mystery he could not solve, yet he continued to rethink all the information he possessed. Did she reach Swindon, indeed? To Darcy, she seemed to have vanished. He looked out at the black surrounding his carriage, and prayed that Elizabeth was well.

Arriving at his mansion, he summoned the energy to bound up the steps of his London home. He entered the comfort of his study and poured a glass of port, before removing his jacket and making himself comfortable. His butler entered the room and attempted to announce Bingley, but the man eagerly brushed past him.

"What news, Darcy?" he demanded, wearing an anxious expression.

Darcy turned and smiled at his friend. Taking off his jacket he replied, "ah yes, and a very good evening to you, Bingley." Charles gave him a quick smile and made an apology for his rush. He confessed that he had been checking in at Darcy House each hour on the hour, nearly all day long. He was eager to hear anything Fitzwilliam would report.

I do have news, yet not the sort you are hoping for, I fear. Spencer and I located Mary. Old chap, we happened upon her just as an evil man was stalking her. He had planned to kidnap her and take her to his home. God only knows what other vile intentions he had for the girl. He confessed his evil plans in a note which had been delivered to her, moments before we encountered her. It seems she had lived in fear of him for two full days before our rescue. Thankfully she is now safely en route to Pemberly with Spencer as her escort. She had in her possession a letter from Elizabeth which had been sent nearly three months ago, but she has had no current news of either Elizabeth or Jane. Have you learned anything, old chap?"

Bingley looked at Darcy and rolled his eyes. "Darcy— I have and upon my word, I am afraid you are not going to like it one bit. Caroline opened two letters from Jane, that arrived here in London, whilst I was away. Louisa admitted that Caroline read them, made sport of the two eldest Bennet sisters' plight, and then burned both letters in the fireplace of my own study. Darcy those letters had her return address, and their contents possibly told even more of her whereabouts. When I think of all the hours I sat at that desk, praying for a letter from Jane, and my angel hearing no response from me…"

Darcy looked up at his friend, shook his head, and spat his words. "Bingley, that sister of yours should be horsewhipped! I am mortified to hear of such offenses. I am so very sorry, old chap."

Nodding his head and frowning deeply, Bingley declared, "Darcy, it gets worse. She has taken it upon herself to go to Pemberly." Fitzwilliam shook his head in disgust. Bingley threw his hands in the air and continued, " Ay, that is terrible I know, yet even worse, my friend, she has installed herself as care provider and temporary guardian of Georgiana!"

"Bloody hell, Bingley! I cannot have that woman there. As I have just told you, Mary is at this moment on her way to Pemberly and Georgiana. Caroline will eat that humble little Mary for breakfast. By Jove, it astounds me that you, and she, could be siblings. Your sister does not equal you in character— she is decidedly inferior old chap!" Darcy was unable to hide his agitation as he sat down at his desk. He wrote an urgent missive to Mrs. Reynolds, and one to his steward. He directed that Miss Caroline Bingley be removed from the property immediately. He informed his friend of the contents, rang for his butler, and ordered the missives to be taken posthaste by his fastest messenger. "That should do it, Bingley." Heaving a deep sigh, Darcy slumped into his chair.

Bingley pointed to the glass of port and asked, "Darcy, I say, I could use one of those myself, if you do not mind."

"Forgive me, Bingley." Darcy crossed the room and poured a glass of port. He tried to offer a slight smile as he handed it to his friend. Their discouragement was profound. "What should be our next move?" Bingley asked, scarcely lifting his eyes up to look at his friend. Pleased to have a bit more hopeful news to report, he smiled and leaned forward in his chair as he answered his good friend. "I have in my possession." he said, "two letters addressed to Elizabeth. One is from Kitty. She has a London return address, and tomorrow morning I shall go and offer her employment at Pemberly as a companion for Georgie. This way we shall have the two younger sisters safe and secure, and perhaps Kitty has news of Jane and Elizabeth."

Bingley smiled and relaxed. "At least we have one small ray of hope, have we not? The girl may have heard from Jane and Elizabeth both—she may have important information for us, Darcy! I would certainly like to go along with you. Even if she knows nothing, it would feel like progress, just to be speaking with one of the Bennet sisters."

"Precisely, my friend we shall take this challenge one day at a time, shall we not? Now, Bingley," Darcy began, "allow me to tell you of my ill-adventures." Refilling both glasses of port, Darcy sat down and began to chronicle events as they had occurred. He began with Exeter, and his supposing Elizabeth to be dead. Then he told of Salisbury, recounting the story of Elizabeth's near rape— which sent her running through the rain. He told of his own savage beating, and how heart-wrenching it had been listening to a young, desperately ill girl in the next room cry and pray and cough for the entire week. At some few times she had cried out his own name! But, with his blurry head and crushed body, he could not think clearly and only vaguely wondered how many men were called Fitzwilliam. He told of his unbelievable heartache when he learned that he had unknowingly spent seven days in the room next to her— only to learn the truth two days after she awayed. Bingley was moved as he listened to his friend's sufferings. "Darcy, it is so frightening to realise how quickly one can become lost, right here in England. With all our resources the simple task of finding someone should be without worry or effort, should it not? Your experiences are horrifying, my friend." Darcy nodded his head and ended his account with the telling of his recent disappointment in Swindon. He admitted that now, Elizabeth and Jane were both missing, leaving no clues as to their whereabouts. Bingley's eyes filled with tears. He rose from his chair and stood at the mantel, to avoid Darcy's eyes. He could so easily imagine himself in his friend's place; it could have happened to him in his search for his angel. Taking a deep breath, he turned around. "Darcy, this is a terrible saga. When— oh when— will this agony end? Do you think Mr. Bennet had any idea that his lack of financial planning for his daughters would result in such dire circumstances for them? Elizabeth could have been raped—or killed. God knows what that evildoer had planned for Mary. What was Mr. Bennet thinking, Darcy? It seems he simply neglected his daughters' future wellbeing."

Darcy stood to his feet and said, "Bingley, I have been giving this much thought. Do you suppose it could be possible that Mrs. Bennet simply directed her brother to settle only fifty pounds upon her four daughters? Bingley, suppose Mr. Bennet's last will and testament bequeathed them more? The girls would have no way to dispute the amount settled upon them and no opportunity to inquire and learn the truth. I did not know the man, but upon my interview with him, he made it abundantly clear that he held Elizabeth in very high esteem. I find it difficult to believe he would treat her ill. He certainly communicated his love and devotion for her when he spoke with me. Even in that short amount of time, I well understood his high regard for Elizabeth."

"Darcy, that is possible, of course. I shall send my solicitor a missive and ask him to look into the matter. No doubt, such wills are registered with the courts."

"It does make me thankful that Georgie has been taken care of," Darcy declared. "And of course, I shall provide for any children I might have in the future."

"I agree with you." Bingley nodded. "This changes the way I look at everything in life, my friend. One must not live in the present without consideration for the future."

The two men planned to go together as early in the morning as possible to secure Kitty to Pemberly. Then they would visit the Gardiner home once more. Darcy and Bingley had no earthly idea of where to look next for

Elizabeth and Jane. Although neither of them would own to it, each one felt better uniting the search.

"Darcy, the moment I find my angel, I am going to take her across the border to Scotland and marry her immediately. Caroline is being sent to live with her aunt. That girl is a menace, to me and to others. I only hope she is being good to Georgiana."

"Ay, Bingley. We can hope, but after all, Caroline is Caroline, is she not, old chap?"

The morrow brought a very sober looking morning, the sun making only a few good attempts to shine. It was early for a visit but the two could ill-afford to wait any longer. The men, eager to see Kitty, arrived early at number seven Brightly Street, London. The butler opened the door. He knew the Darcy name and called for Kitty to join her visitors in the large salon. Fitzwilliam thought the man seemed somewhat nervous and he wondered why such a visit to Kitty would make the man uneasy. The jittery servant led the two wealthy gentlemen into the best receiving area of the home. As far as he knew, the very powerful and influential Mr. Darcy was not acquainted with his master. Nevertheless, Mr. Darcy and Mr. Bingley could be installed nowhere else, even though they had requested to visit a servant girl.

The edgy man led Kitty down the hallway towards the grand salon. He had simply told her she was wanted in that part of the house. Then, the anxious man took a position just outside the door as the girl entered the large room. There he listened with his ear upon the great door.

Kitty came into the large room very quietly. She scarcely resembled the giggly girl they had family dinner with at Longbourn. She remembered the gentlemen and was quite confused about why they were visiting her. Suddenly it occurred to her. "—Mr. Darcy, are you perhaps here to ask me about Lizzy? We had a wonderful visit a few days ago. She is on her way to help our cousins Hannah and Monty. They are to have a baby and Lizzy will be there to make things easier for Hannah. Lizzy sent a letter asking to be released from her employment with Mrs. Boley in Swindon, as it would not begin until next month. Hannah wrote to Lizzy— telling her she would be without help as Monty could not afford to hire anyone to assist her. But, do not tell Lizzy that I told you. She asked me not to tell anyone, as she did not want it to reflect poorly upon Monty."

Darcy nearly jumped out of his chair. Elizabeth had been in that very house just days prior. He wondered if she had gone to Darcy House. "That is wonderful, Kitty. Did she visit Uncle and Aunt Gardiner as well?" he asked, trying to remain calm and sensible.

"She tried but they are out of town for two weeks. She went to Darcy House twice, but no one answered the door. She told me someone saw her both times, but the door was never opened, and she was given no opportunity to ask after you and Miss Georgiana. She left a note for you, but she was uncertain that it was secured. She worried that it might not be found, or that someone within Darcy House would find it, and discard it. She told me that she greatly feared that you might never receive her missive. She said she would write to you from Scotland."

Darcy felt a wave of nausea as he imagined Elizabeth standing at his own front door and not one of his servants answering to speak with her. It was insupportable that one of his servants saw her and failed to welcome her into his home. The fact that she was aware of this rejection from his servant, caused him to worry that she might think he had so ordered his staff. Darcy would look for her message at his front door, and he would ask his servants for any additional information. He would know more of this when he returned home. He collected his thoughts back to Kitty and organized the questions he needed to ask. "Do you know where Monty and Hannah live, Kitty? And can you tell me their surname, please?" He questioned her trying to stay calm. He certainly did not want to pressure the girl. It was clear that she was under great stress in her daily life.

Kitty smiled at these questions. She was happy to help Mr. Darcy as much as possible. "They are Mr. and Mrs. Montgomery Knox." She said proudly. " They live somewhere in Scotland. Monty is an assistant. Nay, I am sorry—that is not correct. He is called an associate. Ay— that is what he is called. He is an associate professor at the university in Scotland but I cannot remember the name. Lizzy mentioned he is also someone's assistant." Kitty remembered as much as possible. "Oh, please do forgive me, Mr. Darcy. I cannot recall the name of the university, or the name of the man Monty assists."

"Kitty, do you know if the university is in Glasgow or Edinburgh?" Darcy tried to ask kindly. He did not wish to bring undue tension upon the child. His thoughts were not far from his own dear Georgiana. He was thankful that she was not in such a cruel circumstance.

"Oh, I am so very sorry, I know it is important. Lately, thinking is difficult for me. Lizzy knows how to find people through the university. I am sure she knows which city. She told me she would send her address once she is settled. Monty and Hannah have recently relocated their residence."

"Ay, Lizzy is very capable, is she not?" he reassured her.

"She is wonderful." Kitty looked out the window, as if she could see Lizzy. "She said once she is settled and is able to support me, she will send for me to live with her. She gave me twenty pounds when she was here. She says she has the same amount for Jane and Mary as soon as she can find them. She told me to tell Uncle Gardiner about the money and he would advise me what to do about keeping it safely in a bank. Lizzy told me I should be saving as much of my earnings as possible. I did not want to tell her that I have not as yet been paid any money for my service. I felt she might become upset."

Darcy frowned at this news and made a mental note to inquire after her wages with the butler. By Darcy's calculations, the girl should have received three separate payments. "Kitty," Darcy began, "I shall inquire about your fair wages. It pleases me to tell you that your sister Mary is now living at my home. Do you remember when I told your family about Pemberly in Derbyshire? She is helping my little sister, Georgiana. I told you about my sister as well, do you recall?

"Ay, Lizzy spoke of Miss Georgiana, reminding me to pray for her to recover from her spider bite. Is she well? I am happy that Mary is living at Pemberly." Kitty smiled, "Mary deserves a good home and good employment, Mr. Darcy. Thank you for helping her. I know she is well pleased. Miss Georgiana will love Mary very much."

"Ay, Georgiana is well now, and I thank you, Kitty," Darcy answered, smiling. "I am also very happy to have Mary living at Pemberly." Darcy thought well of Kitty. He could see her genuine pleasure at hearing of Mary's good fortune. Kindly greet Mary and Miss Georgiana for me. When I am able to write to Lizzy, I shall tell her the good news."

"Ay. Thank you, Kitty. It would please me to offer you a place at Pemberly as well. Kitty— you are closer to my sister in age than Mary. Mary is instructing her in the scriptures and helping with her pianoforte— but she really needs a companion who shares some of her interests. Lizzy told me you love to draw, as does Georgie. You will have many things to do together if you choose to come to live at Pemberly with Mary and Georgie." Kitty jumped up and threw her arms around Darcy. "Oh! Thank you, I thank you! A thousand times thank you, ay, I shall love that so very much. When may I go?"

"Kitty," he said, looking into her sharp eyes, "When Bingley and I find Lizzy and Jane, we are planning on asking your sisters to become our wives. If Lizzy agrees, she shall live with us at Pemberly. But you may leave immediately. The four of us shall join you as soon as possible. We must find them, and then if they agree, we shall marry."

"Oh, Lizzy will agree! You were all she spoke of while she was here. She told me she loves you with all her heart, but she is worried because she has not heard from you. Oh, Lizzy has not put a claim upon you, but she spoke only of her high regard for you. I could tell from her face that she is worried that you do not feel the same. She did not say so, but I could tell that she fears you have found someone else and you have forgotten about her. Lizzy is very brave and she tells me that our current trials will just make us stronger. But her encouragement to me, does not fool me. Lizzy is worried over you, Mr. Darcy and she is very worried about Jane because we have not heard one word from her in such a very long time. However, Lizzy acts as though all is well with Jane. I know she does it for my sake."

At this, Charles turned white and became very quiet. Darcy left him with Kitty while he sought the butler. He wished to receive Kitty's full severance pay, call for her belongings and complete the arrangements for her to leave her current employer. With these issues resolved to his satisfaction the three were soon standing at the curb preparing to enter the Darcy carriage.

Suddenly Darcy felt a firm tug upon his coat. He quickly turned his head around and met the earnest eyes of a young boy of about six or seven years. He was of a small stature. Darcy bent down so that his face was level with the child. Kitty seemed to know the lad and called him James.

"James, is it?" Darcy asked kindly. He smiled at the boy.

"Ay, sir. James Parker. I am the proud son of Mary and Thomas Parker. Me papa is somewhere at sea, and just last year mama fell asleep with the angels. The cleric, Mr. Tubbs sent a letter to me papa, to say where I am, an' the terrible news of me mama. Mr. White owns this proud mansion, sir. I heared sir that you got the money for 'er," he declared, pointing at Kitty. "I wondered if yer could please tell me 'ow I might get me mine, sir?" Darcy was shocked. He liked the boy's pugnacity which was tempered with the right amount of self-restraint and respect. This was a bright boy, indeed. Holding his gaze he asked, "Ay, James Parker. Have you a dispute over your own wages?" The boy nodded his head, "Ay, sir. Me an' all the other children who work 'ere for Mr. Evans, the butler. He feeds us regular, the house laundry does up our togs an' we 'ave a sound roof over our 'eds, yet none of us got any money, sir. Most been 'ere for ye'ars, sir." "Do you trust me, James Parker?" Darcy asked. Bingley understood the fire in his friend's eyes. He knew he meant to somehow right this wrong. Bingley nodded to encourage James. "Ay, sir. I do." James smiled with pride. He knew this powerful man was taking his case and that help was on the way, for him and all the other children as well. "Rest assured you will be assisted in getting what is rightfully yours. Tell the other children that soon things will be set right." Darcy handed Kitty up into the carriage. She was followed by Charles, with Darcy climbing in, after taking one last look at James. The boy smiled. "Thank you, sir, and thank you Kitty." The child stood waving and speaking out his thanks until the carriage was out of sight. He did not know the man's name, but he would never forget his face, or his friend Kitty.

Once at Darcy House, Fitzwilliam requested that Bingley take Kitty into the salon, and order a hot meal for her. He requested Bingley to keep the girl company, but in truth, he hoped to give some type of industry to Charles. He was a man with too much time on his hands. Kitty needed the fellowship and Darcy thought they should get better acquainted. Kitty's travel plans would be done, and a lady's maid would be acquired for her journey. Anything the girl might need, must be purchased before she left town. All tasks would be performed quickly. Darcy was eager to have Kitty join Georgiana and Mary as soon as possible.

Soon all was accomplished and travel plans were set in place for Kitty to join Mary and Georgie. An express missive was sent to Mrs. Reynolds informing her that Kitty was on her way, and a letter was sent to Gracechurch Street informing Mr. Gardiner that both of his younger nieces would be installed at Pemberly. He advised both Mrs. Reynolds and Mr. Gardiner of his trip to Scotland and his intentions to wed as soon as Miss Elizabeth Bennet could be located. The Gardiners were asked to send any information about Monty and Hannah to his address in Scotland.

Darcy felt relief upon getting Kitty and her maid off to Pemberly in one of the Darcy coaches. Reflecting upon both girls, he thought it exemplary and praiseworthy that each had demonstrated patience in their suffering. Showing no resentment or anger for their unkind circumstances— each girl had only thanked him and spoken of a willingness and happiness to serve Georgiana. He was convinced they would be the best of sisters and the kindest of friends to their new sister, Georgiana. He knew they would do well at Pemberly.

He had words with his butler Wentworth who agreed to inquire as to which servant had refused to answer his door and speak with Elizabeth Bennet. Darcy had not been able to locate any missive outside his front door. Wentworth had no information about any such note found thereabouts. There was no excuse for this failure. Wentworth pledged to set things right at Darcy House.

Collot was requested to meet with Darcy and Bingley as soon as possible to organize an urgent journey to Scotland. Darcy requested the services of his man Cooper to ride on horseback and follow the carriage. Cooper knew the area of their route and might prove helpful. Spencer would join Collot as soon as he returned from Pemberly, and as usual, the two would make the trip on horseback. Darcy convinced Bingley to reserve his fears and anxiety until they could meet with Monty and Hannah. Perchance they'd had word from Jane which might assist them in the search.

Darcy referred his own solicitor to the Brightly House problems. James had told them of the numerous children serving the household without wages. It seemed the butler was putting all juvenile earnings into his own pocket. The London magistrate would be contacted by the solicitor, and urged to press charges against Mr. Evans, the butler. Darcy and Bingley agreed that Kitty's mention of her lack of wages was the rescue all those misused children needed. It was Kitty's honesty with her future brothers that set the steps in motion. The men wondered exactly how much money was involved, and how many years the evil man had been stealing from his little charges.

Later that evening, Darcy sat down to collect his thoughts and write to Allister. He began by telling him how he had met Elizabeth, and of their courtship. He confessed his love for her and his intentions to wed. Then, he told the entire tragic story of their long separation after Mr. Bennet's death, detailing his own heartbreaks as they unfolded. Omitting nothing, he declared that as soon as he discovered her whereabouts, he would make Elizabeth Bennet his wife. He explained the importance of locating Monty and asked his friend to inquire, and if a result was obtained, to leave word at Killensworth. Lastly, he invited Allister to his wedding and Lady Hamilton, as well, provided she would be in town. He knew Elizabeth would dearly love the older woman and it would be a blessing to have her with them.

Night fell quickly at Pemberly. Georgiana had been sleeping for about an hour and Mary was still weeping bitterly in her room. Caroline had declared Mary unfit to live at Pemberly and harshly told the girl she was sending her away in the morning. Taking her own bags one at a time, Caroline moved herself into Darcy's chambers. She chose to carry her own belongings because she did not want any of the servants to alert Mrs. Reynolds to her change of rooms. Besides, she told herself, all would be well when Fitzwilliam returned home. He would be very pleased at how she had taken things in hand. Dressing for sleep in Darcy's robe, Caroline crawled into the huge bed. She fell asleep quickly. It was exhausting being mistress of Pemberly!

Darcy ordered Spencer and Collot to ride ahead to Killensworth and see that all was in order. It had been two years since he had been to the estate and he must be assured that things were well before he and Bingley arrived. Especially so with Elizabeth expected. Darcy loved Killensworth and he was most eager for Elizabeth to see her Scotland home in the very best light. With Kitty on her way to her sisters at Pemberly, Darcy resolutely turned his attention to Bingley. The usually carefree Charles was turning inward with fear. Darcy would cheer the man if he possibly could. All steps must be taken to reason his friend back into a stronger frame of mind. Seven days after his men began their journey north, Darcy and Bingley set out for Scotland. Their trip began in silence. Something must be done to find Jane; if necessary, Darcy would have his men comb all of England.

Upon five o'clock at Pemberly, the morning chambermaid, Phyllis Green, made an uncomfortable discovery. She entered the master's chambers—knowing him to be away, she wished to perform her daily duties there at an early hour. Approaching the bed she spied what she presumed to be a dead body.

Straightaway the young maid ran to the housekeeper's desk. Shaking like a leaf, she reported her grim findings to Mrs. Reynolds. The powerful woman was still at her desk, drinking a cup of coffee, and going over the day's roster and duties.

"Mrs. Reynolds," Phyllis cried, talking as fast as she could, "the saints help and preserve us all. There is a dead body in the master's bed! I tell you there is, and I cannot go back into that room—to be sure!"

Mrs. Reynolds was calm and collected, as if dead bodies were reported regularly at Pemberly. She put a marker in her log book and reached up to ring a small bell resting atop her desk. Mr. Jenkins, the butler, came running, which was his usual response to the housekeeper's requests. "Mr. Jenkins, Phyllis tells me there is a dead body in the master's bed, do kindly go immediately and learn the truth of the matter. I expect you to bring the 'body' right here to me— if you please. I shall alert Mr. Jones that we may need his assistance." Mrs. Reynolds had spoken and her order was not to be denied nor delayed.

"Pardon?" Confused, Jenkins frowned as he questioned his sober co-laborer.

"Ay! Bring the' body' right here, immediately. No excuses now!"

The man ran off and took a footman with him. Williams was the biggest and bravest as long as Spencer and Collot were off the property. Jenkins wanted support and help—he had been working as butler of Pemberly for eight years, and this was his first call to respond to a dead body, and in the master's bed of all places.

Entering Darcy's room, the men instead found Caroline Bingley asleep, wearing Darcy's bathrobe. Williams reached down and boldly shook her by the shoulder. The sleeping woman awakened and, startled at seeing the men, she demanded, "I order both of you out of this room immediately! As long as Fitzwilliam Darcy is away, I shall be in charge. I believe I made that quite clear upon my arrival, did I not?"

Ignoring the woman's shrill voice, Jenkins reached out and took Miss Bingley by the hair. "Come with me, immediately! You, Miss Bingley, are trespassing upon Pemberly property. You have no authority to be here in Mr. Darcy's bedchamber, and I would just love to hear what the man himself would have to say about you sleeping in his bed and wearing his robe. His staff has been advised that he plans to be married, madam. And may I be the first to inform you that you are not the bride? Be ready to leave the estate within five minutes."

Mrs. Reynolds was gratified to learn the situation with the dead body had been resolved. Steadfast in her beliefs that one's actions lead to resulting consequences she determined to inform Miss Georgiana that Miss Bingley decided to return to London and had departed Pemberly. There would be no need to give her the true intelligence. How could a child her age appreciate the compelling sense of justice that led the master to send an eviction notice declaring the woman "unfit to live at Pemberly"?

Chapter Five

"BUT I WILL ENDEAVOR TO BANISH EVERY PAINFUL THOUGHT,
AND THINK ONLY OF WHAT WILL MAKE ME HAPPY..."
–JANE AUSTEN

Allister laughed so hard he nearly cried as he read his friend's letter. Not only could he obtain the name and address of the mysterious Monty, he had already met the amiable future Mrs. Fitzwilliam Darcy. Elizabeth Bennet had made a most favourable impression on Allister— he quite fancied her. He was especially glad that his friend had told him early enough, because he was already entertaining romantic thoughts about the beautiful young girl and watching her with increasing attachment.

Lady Edith Hamilton was in the main salon. She had just taken her tea when she heard the riotous laughter coming from Allister's study. Rising, she went to him to determine the jocularity. "You absolutely must tell me right now, young man. What the devil has tickled your funny bone?" she demanded, smiling at her favorite nephew.

"It is Darcy! He is to marry the cousin of my associate professor, Monty Knox. Is that not most amusing, Aunt Edith? And we are invited to the wedding, once he finds her."

"I am so sorry, my boy. Did you just say once he *finds* her? What has the boy done to lose her, pray tell? Did she come to her senses and bolt? And do you mean to tell me that your intelligent Monty has a cousin clever enough to trap our Darcy? Nay, I simply do not believe you. This must be a jest! He must be pulling your leg," she decided. "And to go back to my first question—what does he mean, once he finds her?"

Allister told her the entire story. Lady Hamilton listened with interest as he related the part of Catherine's cleric being the heir who tried to leverage his position to get Elizabeth as his wife. She laughed aloud as she heard how Elizabeth denied him. She was proud of this girl and was eager to meet her. Then she listened to the heartbreaking search for Elizabeth. "Oh dear," Lady Hamilton wrung her hands, "now I am sorry I made sport of him. Did you say that this girl is right here in Edinburgh, at the home of your associate?"

"Ay. I have met her several times and was beginning to become quite fond of her myself, Aunt. Upon my first sighting of the beautiful Miss Elizabeth Bennet, she was out walking on her own. I confess, I followed her along the river until she quickly crossed the bridge and lost me in the traffic. May I tell you that I searched for her in the crowds the remainder of the day, until it grew quite dark? That night— I had a dream about the lovely girl and awoke thinking of nothing but her. Later that morning, I was astonished to make her acquaintance formally at Monty's home. Imagine my surprise to learn she was Hannah's cousin from Hertfordshire, come to help the couple. The following day, I asked if I might take her to a lecture at the university. She very politely declined me. Naturally, I wanted to reason that she required a longer acquaintance before granting me the honour of calling, so I waited one week to inquire. During that week, I was at Monty's house daily, several times a day, truth be told. Daily I invented reasons to see Monty at his home. Whenever possible I made conversation with Elizabeth. At every opportunity I offered to provide assistance to her. I accompanied her to the marketplace and carried her parcels. When I learned she loved walking, I made it a point to enjoy my own walks, and I happened upon her, quite by accident nearly every day. Ay, of course I had never walked at any other time, it was all for her. She is delightful, Aunt. I was quite beside myself. I acted the part of the foolish schoolboy, I daresay. My work suffered, I fear. This behaviour continued for seven days. No doubt Monty thought I had lost my mind. When I felt she knew me better, I asked if I might be allowed to call upon her. She most sweetly refused me, in such a way as to let me know that her heart was already taken by another. I might have guessed it would be none other than Fitzwilliam. We were always drawn to the same girl whilst at Cambridge. The man has ever been between a beautiful woman and my fondest desires. Aunt Edith, I most certainly know what he sees in her! Upon my word, if she had been available— or even if she had given me the slightest bit of encouragement— I would have most seriously considered winning her affections. I would have desired to win her as my future wife, and mother of my children. Aunt Edith, wait until you meet this amazingly wonderful young woman. She is all I could ever desire in a wife, I must say. Not only is she a vision in grace and beauty, she is the most intelligent girl I have ever conversed with, Aunt. I wonder, does she indeed have sisters? My, if she does I should move heaven and earth to meet them, should they be anything like Elizabeth. I am heartbroken, Aunt Edith. I do not mind telling you, I fear I shall always keep her fondly in my heart. In truth, I think I shall have a devil-of-a-time removing thoughts of her, even after she weds."

"I am sorry, darling boy," she consoled him, as she patted his shoulder. "You will find a girl of your own. It is good to know you are thinking of marriage at last. It seems I am already obliged to Elizabeth Bennet for showing you there is more to life than your work. Get busy Allister, and find a bride. Apply yourself, dear boy! You spend too much time thinking and working.

"Oh," she continued, "I cannot wait to tell Catherine and Anne that I attended the wedding of Fitzwilliam Darcy and Elizabeth Bennet. What delicious news. Now Allister, do tell me where she is to be found. Lloyd shall take me this afternoon. I shall escort Miss Bennet to my very own modiste and we shall obtain her wedding gown and all of her wedding clothes as my gift to her. We shall become very well acquainted and be the best of friends. Lord, I cannot wait to give the details to Catherine. She has played that one-string violin all these years saying that her Anne and Fitzwilliam were 'formed for each other!' Oh, ay, most delicious. Oh, and I want to be the one to deliver her to Killensworth," she exclaimed. "When does the dear boy arrive? Does he say?"

"Ay, Aunt Edith." Allister smiled at her enthusiasm. "He will be here in six days, so your modiste had better work quickly, indeed."

Elizabeth answered the door when Lady Hamilton lightly tapped. Allister had warned her that a newborn resided there and the new mother needed her rest. Elizabeth was very much surprised to see such a beautiful, obviously wealthy woman of about fifty years of age. Her figure was still slim, as it probably had been all her life. She moved gracefully and easily, defying her age. Her friendly blue eyes were kind, sparkling with pure glee and possibly some mischief. Her dark hair had not yet collected any silver strands, and she had a quickness of spirit that made her seem ageless. Elizabeth liked this stranger immediately and wondered if perhaps she might be a lady of legal title. She was obviously a powerful woman.

"Good afternoon. Please do come in." Elizabeth curtsied as she offered her greeting. "Mrs. Knox is sleeping as is her new daughter, but I bid you kindly wait if you are so inclined. I am Elizabeth Bennet, Hannah's cousin." She smiled in a friendly, warm, and most engaging manner.

"Very pleased to meet you, Miss Bennet, I am Lady Hamilton," she declared, placing her hand upon her décolleté. Smiling at Elizabeth, she waved her hand at a chair and beckoned the young woman to sit. "My dear girl— you are the purpose of my visit. I am the bearer of the very best of news! I am blest to tell you that I am the aunt of Allister Mason, and the godmother of Fitzwilliam Darcy!" Edith Hamilton positively giggled as she watched Elizabeth's eyes light up at the mention of Darcy's name. It touched her heart as the lavender eyes filled with tears at the same time.

"Elizabeth, may I call you Elizabeth? And you shall call me 'Aunt,' please. My dear, I have the great delight to inform you of a letter Allister received from Darcy just this morning. The boys have been the dearest friends all their lives. The missive told of his ardent love for you, and he detailed the difficulties he experienced in his search for you. Elizabeth, the boy has given up his entire life for the past—um, I suppose nearly five months—and upon seeing your sister Catherine he learned you were here with your cousins. He is on his way, bringing your sister Jane's intended with him. Darcy plans to wed as soon as he finds you." Elizabeth placed her hand over her mouth as she heard this amazing announcement. She was unsure what to say in response to this wonderful news! "My dear Elizabeth, you absolutely must allow me to provide the wedding, your wedding gown, and wedding clothes as my gift to you, with my love. I adore that boy! I have known him all his life and his dear mother was a very special friend to me and my family, as is his aunt, Lady Catherine de Bourgh."

Elizabeth was stunned to hear this. She knew Lady Catherine's name and had a dread of the person, but she said nothing. It was a humbling experience for Elizabeth, but she agreed. The shopping would commence as soon as Hannah was awake and could meet Lady Hamilton. Having heard so much about Hannah from Allister, Edith Hamilton felt she was already an acquaintance.

Soon Hannah came into the salon and met the beautiful visitor. Listening to the news, the cousin was thrilled to learn that Elizabeth's nightmare was nearly over. She was very eager to meet her new soon-to-be cousin, Fitzwilliam Darcy. Before the two left, in the care of Lloyd, the three women planned the Bennet-Darcy wedding. Lady Hamilton was buzzing with ideas. She would arrange for everything. Her complete joy in the planning and overseeing all things for Elizabeth was most evident.

In the midst of their discussion, there was a light tap upon the door, and two servants entered. Edith's smile lightened her lovely blue eyes as she gleefully made the introductions. "Hannah, please meet Marie and Mrs. Smith. Marie shall be your maid, and Mrs. Smith shall be your cook. Their services are given to you and Monty as a gift. They shall be with you for the next year. This is through the kindness of Allister. He has been at his wits' end trying to think of what he could do for you and finally he had the good sense to inquire of me!"

"Oh, Lady Hamilton, I do not think Monty—" Hannah began, but Edith put her hand up. "Now, I shall absolutely hear none of this. Allister lives in fear daily that Monty shall be stolen away to another university. This will help him to relax now and complete his project. He has a marvelous mind, of course, but it will not work properly if he is too nervous to think straight."

All Hannah could do was smile and say a humble thank you to her ladyship. They knew, of course, that the "gift" came from her, not Allister.

"Hannah, it seems Lady Hamil—oh do pardon me, *Aunt*—has blest both of us today. I am so thankful to you, Aunt. You are so wonderful, I am quite eager now to meet Lady Catherine as she must be just like you." Elizabeth could scarcely contain her joy.

"Oh, no, dear! Do not count upon that, as we are nothing alike. In fact, let us go and meet your modiste. We shall have much to do and less than a week in which to do it! I shall tell you all about your aunt Catherine de Bourgh as we go, I promise you shall scarcely believe what you are about to hear!"

Alden Mason was most remarkable in that he rather enjoyed talking—to anyone and everyone. His habit of talking was most inopportune. Upon the slightest provocation he would enthusiastically brag about his two genius brothers. Everyone in Scotland knew about the *Virginia Proper*, the first practical steamboat and now, without knowing what he was doing, Alden commenced bragging to the wrong men. He would tell anyone and everyone that his brother Rex Mason was responsible for building the vessel. To Alden, his brothers were his ticket to respect. He had botched his opportunities at Cambridge and earned a revolting reputation as a heavy drinker. As a child he had always wished to become a nabob, but without focused ambition, a strong work ethic, and sobriety, even his connections could not help him attain the status. Aunt Edith had given him many fine boosts into politics, but the lad lacked the wherewithal to sustain each position. Most likely 'twas the problem of getting a foothold on the day each morning and continuing there-on without drinking.

Alfred MacMooney seemed to be a well-respected solicitor and his associate John Glass made a good impression. The two men enjoyed drinking and talking with Alden. The youngest Mason brother was a fountain of the type of information they wanted to hear. They especially enjoyed hearing the young man talk after he had inbibed a few pints. Alden gave more information than he himself had any business knowing. He willingly spouted to these particular men, that his inventor brother Allister had been making good use of his engineer's mind. He had a new invention that would set the whole world afire. Both men were eager to hear more from the young fool who had no idea what he was doing.

Rising at the Glenbreck Inn, Darcy could hardly hide his excitement. Looking at his friend's sad face, he realised the need to temper his anticipation and glee. He dearly wished that Jane was with Elizabeth waiting for them. But— wishing would not make it so, and this Darcy had learned quite well during the past months.

Realising that the two friends had never spent so much time in silence, Darcy spoke. "Bingley, we have a long day of travel but we should reach Killensworth before dark. I am in hopes that we shall have a message from Allister telling us of Monty's address. Tomorrow we shall go together to find Elizabeth. My friend, we do not know what lies ahead, but we shall both of us keep faith that all shall be well. We must go on believing all shall be well for Jane and Elizabeth. May I remind you that my men are using this trip to canvass as much of the area as possible as we travel northward."

"Darcy, I so appreciate your kindness. I am very glad to be on this journey, for it is one thousand times better than sitting at home in London. I know that Spencer and Collot are skillful men and I have confidence in their abilities. It is strange to say but as soon as the carriage hit the Yorkshire Dales, I began to feel more optimistic. In fact, I am feeling better than I have in weeks. I cannot determine why— but my outlook has improved."

"Bingley, it may very well be that Jane is in Scotland, or perhaps even northern England. I promise you, we shall find her, my friend. Bingley, we shall be brothers, you and I. Please keep believing that, will you not?" Bingley nodded his head and looked out the window, as though it would be possible to see his Jane walking alongside the road.

⁊⁊⁊

At exactly two o'clock, Lady Hamilton and Lloyd called at the Knox home to collect Miss Bennet. Elizabeth was so excited to see them, she hugged Hannah twice and kissed little Elizabeth on the forehead. Lloyd gathered her bags, which now numbered four, and two large trunks.

"As soon as Aunt Edith kisses little Elizabeth, we shall be off, Lizzy!" Edith held the wee babe and kissed her on top of her head. "Oh my, girls, 'tis a pity that Lord Calvert Hamilton left no issue upon this earth. I would have been a devoted mama. Well, no matter. Until you Lizzy, all I had were my three Mason nephews and my one Darcy godson, and of course, little Georgie. Now, I may boast of and claim as my own little girls Lizzy, my Hannah, and her tiny Elizabeth. What fun!" Standing to walk the ladies to the door, Hannah smiled at her cousin. "The next time I see you, you shall be in your wedding gown with your groom at your side, Lizzy!" Hannah giggled, "Oh, good luck, Cousin. I am so happy for you!" As she watched them away, Hannah was reminded of growing up with cousin Lizzy. It was so wonderful to laugh with her once again. At last Lizzy's nightmare was ending.

Sharing the exciting carriage ride to Killensworth, Edith and Lizzy looked at one another. "Oh, Lizzy, I just cannot stop smiling. I am afraid my face may break, I have such joy!" Edith confessed, as happily as a schoolgirl.

Elizabeth took her hand and smiled. "Aunt Edith, you are so very kind to me. You have shown more care and devotion than my own mother ever bestowed upon me, and I am truly grateful. I desire you to know how much I love your sweet godson."

"Child, I know that quite well. All that is needed to be known can be learned looking into your eyes when you speak of the man. Lizzy, I do not mean to pry, but you are so young. May I ask your age, my dear?"

"Twenty, Aunt. I know Fitzwilliam is seven-and-twenty, is he not?"

"For brides, twenty is young," Edith explained. "I know you are inexperienced. Do you have any questions I may help you with, Lizzy? If you do, I hope you shall be comfortable asking me and I shall try to answer."

"Oh, Aunt, just to see him again will be a miracle. Things that might have bothered or concerned me if I were still in my father's house are no longer in my head. I must and shall accept that he has had—probably two-and-ten years of ah—experience— whilst I have had none. I am accepting of the experience, but I have a dark corner of cold fear in my heart. Would you tell me please, did he have a past love? Is there perhaps someone who may suddenly show up, socially, or otherwise for whom he may, even now, have some feelings? I understand, one cannot help having feelings."

Lady Hamilton patted her hand and smiled. "Lizzy, I have met most of the young ladies who were somewhat hopeful that they would marry Fitzwilliam. I begin by declaring that none compare to you. Now, I do not say that to calm you or make you feel better. 'Tis a fact, my dearest. You are superior in every way, my Lizzy."

Lizzy took her hand to hold, and squeezing it, she smiled. "Thank you, Aunt. I wonder though, may I please ask you—what do you know of France?"

"Oh, he told you about Suzette?" Lady Hamilton realised her error the moment she said the name aloud. Elizabeth nearly dodged the impact of that name, as it seemed to ricochet off the roof of the carriage, and crashed downward having a powerful result upon her.

"Nay," Lizzy answered, suddenly looking at her hands, which were now folded in her lap. "He told me nothing, except that he learned to kiss in France."

"Well, I suppose that is true. He took a grand tour after Cambridge. Allister was with him. I believe he met Suzette somewhere in France. He came home alone. However, about two years ago she showed up in England. He brought her to Scotland, then, just as suddenly, she went back to France and Fitzwilliam has never mentioned her since. I would think if there was anything there, it died two years ago. And how old were you two years ago, Lizzy? Were you even out yet? Let me see, Fitzwilliam finished Cambridge six years ago. That would have been when he met Suzette. You were four-and-ten at that same time."

"Point taken, Aunt, I am grateful that you told me. It felt like a spear of ice and fire piercing my heart when I heard the name and the other details. Yet it happened, and I cannot change the past. That is one of the biggest lessons I learned when I was put out from my home. I am just happy and thankful that he told Allister that he wishes to marry me. I do adore him, with my entire heart Aunt."

"Lizzy, just one word of advice. It would be best if you do not mention the others. He will be thinking only of you. After all, the man has given up his entire life for months just to search tirelessly for you—you, Elizabeth Bennet. You, Lizzy! He did not go to France after Suzette. Please tell me you hear and understand me."

Lizzy stretched over to Lady Hamilton and kissed her cheek. "Thank you, Aunt. You want me to use wisdom and enjoy my life with my husband. Her name shall never be spoken by me. However, I should not think I shall ever be disposed to travel to France!"

At that, both ladies laughed.

"This is Killensworth, Lizzy. Take it in, child. We should reach the mansion in about three minutes." Elizabeth held her breath. It was so completely beautiful in its situation, to her mind it was a wonder that Fitzwilliam ever left the property. "Once we are inside, I shall give you a tour. You may decide which rooms you will use as your own."

Elizabeth frowned at her Aunt Edith and begged, "Oh, Aunt, please do advise me. Where shall I be situated? Do you have rooms here? I should like to depend upon your wisdom in this matter. Please direct me, Aunt."

"Ay, and I do have rooms here, I shall show you," Edith offered. "Perhaps you should select a seldom-used guest room. Keep in mind that he is bringing your sister's intended, so let us select your rooms first."

Alfred MacMooney and John Glass met Alden Mason at the tavern. Upon this occasion Alden was already intoxicated when he arrived. He was angry with Allister and without thinking he told the men that his brother had invented a powerful steam engine that would be put in a locomotive design to bring a railway to Great Britain.

Buying more drinks for the lad, the two determined Allister's address and learned that he did indeed work at his home study. They were told he worked all alone with no assistants and no secretary. The files and all items were stored in Allister's study. Using intelligence he had obtained from his Aunt Edith— he told the men that Allister and his aunt would be out of the residence on the morrow, at ten o'clock. There would be a prodigious price to be paid for this disclosure.

Lady Hamilton had much enjoyment in helping Lizzy dress. She hovered over the lady's maid she had sent ahead to serve Lizzy whilst she was in Scotland. Edith personally selected the gown Lizzy would wear to greet Fitzwilliam and even choreographed where they would be and what they would be doing when he came into the room.

"Aunt, you are nearly as excited as I," Lizzy giggled. "Honestly, I do not know what I would have done without you. Please understand, it is not the clothing and the jewellery I am speaking of, it is your company, your wisdom, your wit, your knowledge of human nature. You have the experience that gives you knowledge but your very nature makes you wise and so very kind. I wish to thank you— but I simply do not know how. I have known such joy these past six days spending time with you. If only I had been blest with your guidance my entire life long. You have been such a benefit to me. How would I have fared without your assistance these past six days?"

"Darling Lizzy, we shall one day go arm in arm to meet Catherine. The expression on her face shall be my reward, but you, my darling, wonderful Elizabeth are my prize. When I said you are the daughter I have longed for, I was quite serious. And, somehow I feel, I may very well be the mother you have felt yourself needing, am I not?"

Elizabeth nodded her head and opened her mouth to speak but before she could form an answer, Mrs. Boyd rushed excitedly into the room. Edith and Lizzy looked at each other. "He is here, Lady Hamilton. He is here, and a handsome gentleman with him! Oh my, he looks so very tired."

"Thank you, Mrs. Boyd. Kindly tell him I—only I, Lady Hamilton—am here and would like him to join me in the library. Would you?" Rushing off, Mrs. Boyd had a charming smile upon her lips, for Lady Hamilton had told the entire staff that Elizabeth would wed the master on the morrow!

"Bingley," Darcy asked, when he was given the message, "shall you not meet my wonderful godmother?"

"Darcy, I beg to be taken to my rooms, if I may. May I perhaps meet her at dinner?"

"As you wish, old friend, Mrs. Boyd, shall show you to your rooms. Rest well, Bingley."

Darcy turned down the hallway leading to his rooms. He would refresh himself, then see to his aunt. Odum had already taken his bags to his rooms and his valet was in the process of putting things away, and setting other items out for cleaning. With one slight nod of his head, he sent the valet from the room and stretched out on top of his huge bed. Too tired to nap, he gazed around the room. All was in order, of course. It looked exactly like it had when he was last there. Beautiful, serene and filled with peace. Peaceful now that Suzette had gone back to France. He remembered the last time he had been with Suzette in that very room. They had quarreled over Georgiana. Darcy kept insisting that he would in no wise send his sister to any boarding school, much less one in Germany! Suzette, using her wiles and all her power against him, threatened to return to Nice or Paris. Darcy took out his cash and gave her funds to leave him. He paid for tickets for Suzette, and her lady's maid to return to Paris, and he included in that sum, a very liberal amount for travel expenses. Suzette took no time in packing and when he returned to his rooms, after her departure, he'd found her calling card. Rising from the bed now that he remembered— he crossed the room and opened the dresser drawer. Taking out her scarf, he held it close and buried his nose in it, to catch her scent. He closed his eyes, and very faintly he could smell the gardenia notes. He thought she had simply overlooked the scarf, but when he gave it more thought, he realised. She had placed it directly upon her side of the bed. He was sure she had saturated it in her signature scent perfume— gardenias. Briefly, he wondered where she was… A firm knock upon his door ended his thoughts. He put the scarf back into the drawer, and opened his door. Odum had a message from Aunt Edith. She was tired, and required him to kindly hurry to her side.

Overtaking Odum at the door, Darcy's long legs carried him quickly down the hall.

Entering the library, he laid eyes upon his godmother, and saw a well-dressed girl with her. He could not see the girl clearly as she was more than a quarter turned from him and he did not see her face. He approached Edith, hugged and kissed her, then turned a puzzling look toward Lizzy. Edith could scarcely contain her excitement.

"Fitzwilliam— I have a surprise for you, godson!" Lady Hamilton said excitedly.

Turning as planned, Elizabeth smiled at Fitzwilliam, lifting her hands toward him. They flew into each other's arms. He began kissing her and speaking her name at the same time. She tried several times to say his name— but emotion overtook her at each attempt and she could only cry as she smiled at him. Holding each other tightly, neither one breathed for the excitement of their reunion. Aunt Edith held her breath as she watched them.

Edith Hamilton cried as well for a few moments. She walked to the couple and simply stood silently with her arms around both of them. They turned and kissed her on the cheek. As she began to quit the room, Lizzy called out, "Thank you, Aunt, from all my heart!"

"Aunt?" Darcy asked, with a frown and a quizzical smile dancing upon his face.

Lady Hamilton stopt and said, "Darcy, I feel more like the dear girl's mother than an aunt. She has taken my heart, son. You are so blest, my boy. Be good to her!"

"That is my plan, Aunt Edith!" he answered, turning to kiss Elizabeth again. Edith Hamilton was a very happy and satisfied woman. She could not remember ever having a better time in her life. And tomorrow— the wedding! Edith happily headed for her rooms to begin a letter to Lady Catherine. She wanted to record the exciting reunion of Fitzwilliam and Elizabeth so she would not forget the smallest detail.

Darcy and Elizabeth held each other so tightly she thought she might faint from lack of oxygen. She could not breathe, and he had no intentions of releasing her. With not one inch of space to separate them, they were experiencing all-encompassing bliss. "Elizabeth, I shall never let you out of my sight again, my darling! I do so love and cherish you! A thousand times I have been angry with myself— for failing to tell you that I love you. It was on my heart so many times at Netherfield, and in your home the night I left you. Allow me to tell you now— I love you, my sweet Elizabeth Bennet. I swear by all I know, you shall always be my very first concern. If only I had delayed my trip to Pemberly until the next morning, you would have told me of your father's death and I would have brought you here and married you! And Bingley said he would have done the same with Jane. Oh— my love— I am so sorry about your papa. I wish I could have prevented your pain and suffering. I have been so angry with myself for not asking your father for your hand in marriage. Had I so done, you would have come to me in Pemberly, would you not? How can you ever forgive me for not taking better care of you...for not finding you..."

Without giving her a chance to speak, he began to kiss her with more passion than he had ever before revealed. She responded with undisguised hunger. Unaware of the passing of time, they held each other and kissed. They did not need to speak, for what they were experiencing was well beyond the usefulness of words. Finally Darcy, with intense emotion, whispered, "Elizabeth— you look so beautiful. Your eyes are still the most lovely and sensuous eyes that I have ever seen. Your appearance is unaltered for all you have endured, my love."

She smiled shyly, touching his face. "Your Aunt Edith rescued me, and rather restored me—just for you," she responded. "I am blest to hear that you are pleased at the way you find my appearance." No longer able to restrain herself, she ran her hands through his hair and kissed him breathless. Fitzwilliam placed her head on his shoulder and panting, asked her to tell him everything she had endured. He bade her begin when he and Bingley left Longbourn. He desired deeply to hear her firsthand account, and he also knew they needed to cool down.

She began by telling him how she discovered her papa's body in his bookroom. It was the first time she had allowed herself to think about the sorrow she suffered upon discovering the lifeless form of the dear man who was her father. She tried to convey her sudden shock, and the sense of loss she felt, as she realised his life had left him. Never again would she hear his voice— or sit quietly in his presence. His smile, and his laughter were gone from her, never to be recovered upon this earth. She confided that her first thoughts were of unbelief. Her grief tempted her to think that if she concealed the news, it would not be true. Somehow her papa would find a way to return to her. Next, she wanted to believe that if she could only hold her tears and not cry, he would not really be dead. With sober eyes, she took Darcy's hand— sighed and told him how difficult it was for her to accept the truth of her father's passing. She described making all the final arrangements before waking Mrs. Bennet. Reminding him of her mother's anger over her refusal of Collins, she disclosed the hateful letter Mrs. Bennet had placed upon her pillow the day Charlotte wed Collins. She told him that no one else knew of that letter, for she was so devastated to receive such a missive from her own mother, she could tell no one. Not her father, nor Jane. The letter warned her to fear her mama on the day her papa died. Darcy held her tightly as she related the painful memory.

Reliving her mother's rage, she told him of being given only minutes to collect what she could carry, after which, she was forced to leave the only home she had ever known and all that was dear to her. Darcy was livid when he heard how she had been sent away, hours after her father's death. Forced to leave so quickly, Elizabeth had not even seen his final resting place. Fitzwilliam could scarcely contain the anger and contempt he felt for Mrs. Bennet.

He tried not to cry as she told him the events of all the months without him, and all the tears she had learned to hold within her heart in order to keep a bold front before others. She confessed her sleepless nights and her deep longing for him. She told of her fears that multiplied, as the weeks and months passed, with no letters from him. She related the feeling of rejection she felt twice at Darcy House, when a servant looked out the window at her— and— each time declined to open the door to her. The message she left for him had been written on her last piece of paper, seeming to her, as if it might also be her last hope. Afterwards, she wondered if she should accept that he had moved on with his life. She felt that perhaps it was possible, that he had instructed his servants to avoid answering the door, if a young woman, unknown to them, should call on Darcy House. Looking deeply into his beautiful blue eyes— she admitted the truth. Even had he rejected her— she would love only Fitzwilliam Darcy for all her life. She would never have had an interest in any other man. At that, Darcy kissed her once more, then murmured his profound appreciation of her.

Darcy began telling his experiences. He told her of his trip into London, one week before the surgeon had released Georgiana from care. He explained that he sought Uncle Gardiner as head of her household, now that her father was gone. He obtained the man's consent to their marriage. Next, he called upon his godfather, the archbishop of Canterbury and obtained a special license for their wedding. He instructed his solicitor as to her settlement papers, having them forwarded to Uncle Gardiner. Then, he sat for over one hour writing a proposal letter to her. He apologised to her for not thinking to use his own private couriers. He admitted that he sent every letter to her by post. It was obvious that not one missive was delivered to her. At the same time, he had not received anything she sent to Pemberly, save the first letter penned on the day her father died. He felt blest to have received that one, as it gave him the vital information he needed to begin his search for her— and later— her sisters.

He filled in his own information about the time he thought her dead, and the girl with the terrible sounding cough, who had occupied the room next to his for an entire week at the Cathedral View Inn. Elizabeth's eyes spilled their tears in two streams when she learned that they had spent seven days in rooms that were separated only by one thin wall. It hurt him deeply to reveal that he had heard her cries, and yet he did not know it was she— calling out for him. She held on to him tightly, as he told her all; becoming concerned for his injuries as she realised he was the lad who had suffered so much pain in his body for the week she was ill. How grateful she was to God, to know that he had been healed of that horrible beating. She ran her hands over his ribs and knee and head, for she remembered how his injuries had been described to her. God had mended him, and he lived! She had prayed for him so often during that week. She recalled that she had wanted to go into his room and encourage him (not knowing it was he) but she felt it would be wrong for her to enter the room of a young man. Their tears mingled as they both cried— for grief in remembering all their pain— and for their happiness at its ending forever.

When he told her that Mary and Kitty were at Pemberly— she could not speak for her relief and joy. All three sisters were a constant worry upon her mind. Wordlessly, she picked up his hand and covered it with kisses. She held it to first to her cheek and then placed it upon her heart. Finding her voice, she looked into his eyes and said, "You, my dearest heart, are the best of men. How shall I ever thank you, my darling Fitzwilliam? Oh, pray, how shall I thank you for all that you have done for us— for me?"

"How shall I thank you, Elizabeth," he questioned, whilst kissing her hand, "for giving my sister and me a family and for giving me all of your love and devotion?" His sincere words, so sweetly spoken, touched her heart. She kissed him, exposing her feelings of arousal and divulging her willingness to offer him as much of her physical expressions of love as he would receive. It was becoming very difficult to conceal their heightened passions and their mutual desire to experience the paradise waiting for them. A short walk down a hallway into a bedchamber was all that kept them from the gratification they both had sought for so many long months. Neither one had much self-restraint remaining and they had little desire to deny what they needed— and wanted.

Understanding her wishes, Fitzwilliam wrapped Elizabeth in his arms and began to nibble her ear. She nearly collapsed at his urgency. They kissed again, and this time their bodies took over. Sensing this new level of passion, Elizabeth lifted her head. "My love," she whispered in a shaky, husky voice, "I am shivering all over my body— yet I feel quite hot blooded. I need you. When I remember all the times I have desired you, throbbed for you— and cried at the loss of you..." She took a deep breath.

"I know," he said as he began passionately kissing her neck, "but we are together now, darling." They were both breathing in short, ragged rhythms.

"Oh, Fitzwilliam, this time I will give myself to you. Married or not, I must have you love me, please. Do not deny me, not after all this time of yearning for you, my love." She begged. "You are the only one in the world who can fulfill me. You are the only one I desire. I wanted you so much the last time I was in your arms— but I did not know how to make it happen. I thought I could sense that you wanted to love me, too. Especially before you awayed to Pemberly."

Looking into her eyes he confessed, "Oh, Elizabeth— I wanted to love you that night. I have wanted to love you since the first day we met— and I have desired you every day since then. I shall not deny you." he promised her, nearly in tears, his emotions were so strong. "Come, my love." He started to rise, but she pulled his hand, and with her eyes, pleaded with him to stay seated a moment longer. "Fitzwilliam, first I must tell you the dream I had last night. May I please just tell you? After you hear it, I shall seek your promise. Is that agreeable with you— please?" Her eyes were filled with tears and he could not deny her. He nodded agreement and told her not to be afraid, she must tell him everything. Sighing deeply, she began. "I dreamt I came to Killensworth, and I was so excited to come, but I believe I had some fears about how you might react to me, after such a long absence. Or, perhaps I feared your response to my being turned out. Please understand," she continued, trying fervently to make him see her point of view. "In all these months— I had not one letter from you— not one indication of your feelings. Remember, I had no idea that you were searching for me. I did not realise all the trouble and inconvenience you had expended on my behalf. Even to the pain and suffering in your physical body, my love. I was unaware of the sacrifices you were making for me. And, may I say, thank you for all you have done for me, beloved..."

He started to speak, but she put her fingertips gently to his lips and whispered, "Please, please, allow me to tell you my complete dream. I need you to hear and understand."

Darcy smiled to ease her anxiety. "—Yes—I know, beloved," he whispered. He knew she needed his love and his acceptance. He was willing to give her anything she needed.

Taking a shaky breath, she continued to share her dark burden. Gazing into his caring eyes, she drew him into the nocturnal drama. "The first part of the dream is so wonderful, I should like us to make it come true. To me, the first part— was a miracle of sorts— I was given a preview of loving you. I have no words to describe my joy, beloved. The second part, became a terrible nightmare. It seemed all my fears came upon me. Fitzwilliam, I believe, fear has the power to turn the most wonderful dream into a nightmare." Elizabeth's earlier happiness was fading, and it seemed she had returned to her pain.

"—Elizabeth— please." He wanted to remove the darkness, wishing her joy to return. "Please, have no fears about my rejecting you, and no fears about anything, ever again!" He was impatient to shift her behaviour toward a more positive stream.

"Yes— I thank you so much," she said. "Yet— I beg you to know that I must share this with you. Please indulge me, beloved, for just a few more moments."

He inventoried the grave emotional afflictions she had endured over the past months. The burdens and the anguish of her pain, he reckoned, would be deeper than he could know. Satisfied that he should allow her to speak of one tormenting nightmare, he ceased his efforts to quell her fears. Holding her close, he kissed the top of her head. "Go on, of course, Elizabeth."

Choosing her every word with care, she continued. "I dreamt that we went into your bedchamber. It was a large room with a standalone mirror in the corner. You moved the mirror over, to about four feet from the side of the bed. Then I asked you to disrobe me, and you did. I was unclad and you were dressed. After I turned around, about two times, for you to look at my body, you knelt in front of me and said you would be so happy for the morning when we would be married. I told you I was happy, too."(She could sense that he was beginning to relax and listen.) "I requested that you kiss me, and you started to rise, but I held your shoulders down, and said, 'Nay darling, I mean kiss me there. Kiss that part of me that wants you— please. That powerful part I told you about in the passageway at Netherfield.'"

As she related this portion of the dream, he began to smile his acceptance. He thought he would be only too glad to make this part of her dream a reality. "Fitzwilliam, you looked so happy. You kissed me, you loved me so spectacularly with your mouth and your hands. You said you enjoyed using the mirror, and looking at me in a standing position. Then, I stood in a dancer's wide stance and touched the floor. You were delighted and said you had never seen a woman from that perspective, not even at Cambridge, viewing class models. You loved me again in that position, and we were both so pleased."

Upon hearing this portion of the dream, an eagerness began to build in him. Truly this was the most exciting and pleasurable idea he had ever heard. In all his experience, he had never encountered, nor expected anything of this nature— so different— so intimate.

Excitedly he asked, "What happened next, dearest heart?" She squeezed him and continued to relate the good part of her dream. "Next— I said it was my turn. I asked you, if it was it not customary for you to disrobe, as well. I began to remove your clothing. Oh, I wish I had words to tell you how the sight of your spectacular naked body excited me, beloved! My— oh my— but you evoked such stirring stimulations in me! I was overwhelmed at seeing you. I told you how beautiful you were and then I held you with one hand, and proceeded to kiss every inch of you. You were enormous and it took a wonderfully long time to achieve my delightful ambition. Then, something happened to me, Fitzwilliam. It is hard to put into words. As I kissed you, suddenly I wanted to lick *all* of your manhood. It was an overwhelming desire, and I could not help myself. For a brief moment I worried what you might think of me. But beloved, I was compelled to show my devotion to you with my mouth. I began kissing your velvety sack, containing your seed. You were pleasured and you told me you enjoyed my affections. Finally— I kissed your tip and took as much of you into my mouth as I could and began to suck you. Oh, my darling, it was so wonderful. May I say, I could not have resisted doing such, even if you had told me to stop. But, happily you did not stop me. You were very pleased, and we were both so happy together. Darling, before this dream, I did not know such experiences were possible. I wanted to remember to ask you if this type of loving is done by other women. It was all— ah—very new to me—um—as I have never before seen a naked man— in my life. It was an astonishing dream, to be sure! Darcy was captivated by her account of the dream. He dearly wanted to hear more.

Elizabeth's delightful smile faded and a deep furrow appeared between her eye brows. "Then the nightmare began." She related this portion of her dream with very slow speech. Putting one hand upon his arm, she fought back tears and continued. "You said, 'now we shall get into the bed, Elizabeth, and we shall join.' I was filled with such excitement and joyful anticipation. But, those were the last words you said to me— because— before you entered me— you began kissing me. At first it was wonderful— just like our first kisses at Netherfield— then, suddenly it seemed the room was filled with gardenias. I could smell them, although I did not remember seeing them. It seemed that with this strong scent, you completely lost interest in me. For a brief moment, I thought to look around the room for the gardenias; but there were no flowers in the room. After that, it was as though your mind began to travel, and kept going until you were a world away from me. You left me— even though you were right there beside me. To me, it was as if the bed caused the loss of you. I felt I was very much alone. In truth, I had never felt more alone or more terrified. Not even when I had no home, no money, no family or friends, and no place to go for help. Death would have been kinder, because after all these months, and then the thrill of knowing you wanted to wed, you rejected me."

Darcy tried to stop her from speaking. "Elizabeth, please say no more. What a terrible thing. That could never happen, my love. I would never treat you thusly."

Her discomfort caused him to seek tranquility for both of them, but Elizabeth was firm in her resolve to tell him all. Strongly pressing her hand against his chest, she said, "Please, beloved, just a few minutes until I finish this horror. I shall feel better when I get it out of my head." She rushed on, recounting the crushing rejection, loneliness, and isolation she experienced in her nightmare. It oppressed her, just as if it had really happened. "I began to cry and beg you to tell me where you wanted me to go, because I knew you did not want me to be with you. I saw a sofa in the room, and without a cover, I lay down upon it. I did not know where my bags were, and I could not leave in darkness. I slept— and during the night— you lifted me into the bed and said, 'We belong to the Church of England and so I must worship you with my body, Elizabeth. I shall enter you just this once, and I hope I shall give you a child.'" After telling this part of the dream, she broke down and could no longer speak.

"Elizabeth," he said, clearing his throat, "Do not do this to yourself. You had a nightmare because of everything you have been through. Please do not cry, I promised you that I shall never leave you again. Believe me, my dearest heart, I shall never, ever leave you!" Darcy was stupefied at hearing her dream. He had never spoken of art classes at Cambridge or of their use of live models. Elizabeth had no access to such intelligence and her accurate descriptions of oral love would be unknown to a virgin such as she. With all his experience, he had never thought of using a mirror. He thought her dream most unusual and of necessity must consider both parts valid. Her stunning reference to smelling gardenias made him feel weak. He would always remember what she told him of the dream.

"Now, let us go and move that mirror. I shall see that the good part of your dream is performed by us. We shall enjoy each other, and then we shall get into bed and love to completion. And, if we have a child— I shall never leave either of you. Do you trust and believe me, Elizabeth?"

She nodded her head and then kissed him, showing him her fervor. Standing to her feet, she smiled and took his hand. He kissed her hand and led her to his rooms.

"Tomorrow we wed!" he said, showing his enthusiasm. "But I cannot wait, and I am so pleased that you cannot wait, beloved."

She squeezed his hand, lifted it to her lips, and kissed it gently. "Oh, thank you for hearing my fears," she said, nearly singing the words, feeling so much relief in having shared the dream. "I love you so much. Please, let us go quickly. I am throbbing for you, right now!"

Darcy stopt and asked, "Elizabeth, did you say you were throbbing for me? Is this what you were telling me about in Netherfield?"

"Ay," she answered, giving him a shy smile. "I shall show you when we get to your rooms, my love."

Suddenly he felt an intense warmth spread over his body. He led her quickly to his bedchamber and moved the mirror, just as she had dreamt. Standing in front of the mirror, Darcy dropped one pillow from the bed onto the floor. Slowly he kissed Elizabeth, as his experienced hands began to remove her gown. Weeks of eating well at Hannah's home had filled her body out again. Gone was the gaunt look, caused by several lean months with little to eat. "You," he said smiling, as he surveyed her unclad body, "are beautiful, my darling." Darcy thought about all the dreams he'd had, in which he saw his beloved, *au naturel*. But, the reality of her nude form, in front of him now, far exceeded any previews he had envisioned in his dreams. "Oh, Elizabeth, you are more wonderful than any naked female form I have ever viewed. Even the statue of *Venus de Milo* does not equal your perfection. You, my lovely Elizabeth, are flawless, ay, you are perfect. In all my studies of art—and even after going to Italy to see the masters' works—I can say— you are the ultimate form of supreme excellence. Artists would kill to paint or sculpt your contours. All your lines are so beautiful, so clean and regular. Oh, what a model you would have made for the masters. Your body is superior to all I have ever seen!" He could not stop stating the distinction of her perfection. Wrapping his arms around her, he continued to gush his admiration. "Oh, beloved, I am so blest. Here you are in your flesh, my beautiful Elizabeth! We are together, at last."

She smiled at him and said simply, "I am grateful you are pleased with me, Fitzwilliam."

"Oh, nay, Elizabeth, I am far beyond being pleased. Tomorrow, I shall show you the sketches I have made of you. Perhaps you shall model for me, my darling."

This took her by much surprise, she was unsure that it was a jest, but thinking it to be so, she thought to tease and play along with him. "Tomorrow I shall promise to obey you, so my being your nude model, shall be rather your decision, not my own, I dare say."

"Precisely," he happily agreed. "Upon my word, I thank you for reminding me. Indeed, we shall consider this. Now, love of my life, please show me where you throb for me. I long to worship you with my body, as I shall promise before God on the morrow, shall I not? 'Tis a vow I shall keep, daily, my love. Here, put my hand upon that part that throbs, we shall start there, beloved." Darcy was thrilled to feel she did literally throb for him. In truth, he had never heard of such a thing in his life.

Their acts of love were more exciting than she had described. Elizabeth was scarcely aware that she was standing, as she had no fatigue. Both positions were even better than in her dream. It was all so much more exciting and far more pleasurable than she remembered feeling in her dream. In fact, she could never have imagined anything ever giving her as much pleasure.

"Fitzwilliam," she gasped, between kissing his responsive lips, "I have never had such joy! Thank you for making the good part of my dream come true. And," she continued, as she panted to breathe, "for promising to keep the hideous nightmare portion away. I loved watching you in the mirror. Were you pleased, my love?" she asked him.

Truly, he had found it quite stimulating. Looking into her lovely lavender eyes, he said, "Perfect girl, it was breathtaking, and so very wonderful. It was so sweetly intimate, my darling Elizabeth. Ay, in truth, I was much more than pleased, my love." Fitzwilliam had never experienced such a stimulating situation. All during his years at Cambridge, he had never viewed a female model in an inverted posterior position. He never would have thought of such on his own. Perhaps he would request this type of love making again in the future.

Satisfied with his response, she began to disrobe him, watching him closely to see his reactions. Darcy eagerly placed his hands upon her shoulders. Shaking her head, she removed them to his sides. "Please relax, my beloved," she insisted. "Allow me to take my time appreciating your beautiful body. Remember, I have never seen a naked man, except when I saw you in my dream, and you are the only man I shall ever see in the nude. Please show me patience, dearest. Do you recall what I told you about the powerful feelings I experienced upon seeing your unclad neck and your chest hair? I was most taken with seeing your muscles as revealed through your linen shirt. Now, I shall see you for myself, in the flesh and I shall have very strong feelings about you. I do not know what I might be compelled to do to you, my love."

They smiled at each other. Darcy spoke, but did not touch her, "Do what you will, my dearest heart. I shall not fear."

She looked at and felt his body, every inch of him. She kissed him in places that embarrassed him, and she occasionally bit and sucked him in places no one had ever even touched. Darcy was shocked at her devotion— never had he been the object of such keen interest, nor had he ever received such adoration. It nearly made his heart ache to be loved so elegantly; he was utterly preoccupied with her exquisite attentions to his body. He found it absorbed all his concentration. He thrilled to her touch and was held in rapt appreciation of her devotions. He loved each sensation as she fondled him. Delighting to the gentle swaying of her breasts as she massaged his muscles and nearly squirming as she gently palpated his genitalia— he affirmed to himself that no one had ever loved him in this manner. Her soft hands worked seductively over his hands and so stimulated them, he could scarcely resist applying them to her curves. Even her attentions to his feet set forth a series of shudders up his spine. Her every movement and act upon him was hypnotic. He could scarcely wait to see what she would do next, and at the same time wished she would never stop her current devotion. Fitzwilliam was mesmerized. He had but one thought: on the morrow this fascinating woman who had captured his heart and imagination would be his. He was enthralled by her, she held him spellbound. There was no one like her in all the world, and he knew it.

At last, he trembled as her tongue showed a genital interest. Precisely as she described from the dream, she did indeed taste every part of him, several times. Her fingers displayed such talent for teasing him, while her eager mouth savored him. She caressed him as she kissed him. He was nearly overcome. He watched her in the mirror, as she took him into her mouth, again and again. He closed his eyes and enjoyed the massage. The seductive repetition of this behaviour so indulged his sensual pleasures, that he desired her to continue this in-and-out teasing, yet he desperately awaited the pulling suctions. He felt his knees weaken. She noticed and asked him to kneel down. Holding him with one hand, and with the other delicately rubbing his scrotum, she licked her lips, drew him into her moist mouth, and sucked him at last. He could feel one soft breast gently touching his thigh. Taking her time, she showed an obvious appetite for him and the sense of gratification that she found in this particular act. Darcy was thrilled to the core. This voluptuous and highly suggestive work upon his body was more than he had ever hoped to gain in the marriage bed. He had a strong craving for this activity, a longing, and very private yearning for its exclusive enjoyment. The thought of her fulfilling his fondest wish, and with frequency, stirred him. Here he was, experiencing it all, just as she saw it in her dream. Although Fitzwilliam's desire was to use quite tight self-control, he became much excited. Sensing she should help him regain control, she slowed down and looked in his eyes. This cessation seemed to disappoint her. She kissed his plump, blunt tip again and then she stopt. Turning her face up to his, she smiled lovingly at him.

He was bewitched…body and soul…

"Oh, my Elizabeth, where did you learn to do all of this?"

She looked at him blankly, "I am sorry, I do not have the pleasure of understanding your question." Narrowing her eyes, she studied his face trying to learn his mood.

"This?" he repeated the single word, as a question. "Elizabeth, all of the things you have been doing. How did you know to do them? From books, my love?" he suggested.

"I suppose," she began, suddenly shy, "that I do not understand why you ask me such." She searched his eyes for clues to comprehend. Believing he was demanding more information from her, she sought a way to explain her actions. "I have not studied for this, nor did anyone tell me about what I was doing. I sincerely hope I did not make a mistake and give offense. Oh, Fitzwilliam, my darling love, do you not understand what I am trying to do? I am simply loving you from my heart. If I feel inspired— or I experience an irresistible urge to do something to you— then I simply abandon myself to that urge. I release myself to loving you. My thoughts and feelings follow my heart— in an effort to please you— and show you my love. I want all of you; I desire your desires, my love."

She took a moment, hoping he would speak and reassure her that he was pleased, and that all was well. He spoke not, so she continued. "—I want all of this— because I want all of you." Elizabeth paused. She cautiously asked, "Do you not already know this, because of your—possibly two-and-ten years of experience?" Seeking helpful information from his knowledge, she inquired once more. "Has it not been the same with others you have—well, have you not—?"

Stunned at her boldness, and remembering she had promised Aunt Edith she would not speak of any others, she felt a sudden stab of pain, and feared the worst. She touched his chest as she spoke to him. Her eyes were pleading with him not to be angry. "Fitzwilliam, I am sorry, I foolishly made such suggestions, please forgive me and forget my unfortunate choice of questions. I am still an impertinent and ignorant country girl."

At the words "has it not been the same with others," his heart froze. Truth suddenly occurred to him. He had always begged his lovers for fellatio, and not one would oblige him. Even the two candidates he considered strongly for wedlock flatly denied him his secret delight. Furthermore, he remembered, none would spread their legs for him to taste of them. He had always paid for these services. It never entered his mind that perhaps those he had loved had not loved him. He thought he had loved Suzette, and most likely he did, but even though she was French, she would not love him like this. Neither did Ellen, yet he thought they each had loved him; nay, he was sure they had loved him.

"Oh, my Elizabeth! You have helped me to understand a great truth, my darling. Thank you for your love." Standing up, he took the pillows off the bed and removed the top sheet. He put the sheet on the floor and arranged the pillows for their heads. Then, he gently positioned Elizabeth under him and began kissing her breasts and stimulating them with his tongue and fingers. He gave her so much pleasure she was lost in a storm of sensations. It was a new and exciting experience for him, as he learned for the first time it was possible to bring a woman to her heights by stimulating her nipples. Silently, he wondered why he had never known this before now. Continuing their mutual enjoyment, he reached his finger into her ring, delighting her epicentre. She thrilled to the jolting pleasures he was creating in her.

Waiting until the last possible moment, he withdrew his digit collecting her sweet lubricant. Smiling at her, he rubbed it on his tip, and whispered softly, "Your body is ready for me, my darling. Are you ready, Elizabeth?" he asked her with so much tenderness, she nearly cried. She answered by guiding him into her portal. He watched her in amazement.

"Please—" was her whispered answer. He loved her with tenderness. Her virgin hips began to move, matching his as she worked as hard as she could to possess all of him. Because of her rising ardor, she nearly yelled at him to plunge deeper inside her. He obliged but he did not last long because he had invested so much of himself into their preceding acts.

Displeased that he had so little control and angry with himself, he spoke his displeasure. "Darling, this shall get better. I am so sorry that I—" he began.

Hearing his apology she realised his disappointment. She caught his head with her hands and demanded, "Nay! I shall not allow you to ruin this beautiful experience for me, Fitzwilliam. You were wonderful. Our joining was so beautiful, even if somewhat painful."

He was startled by what she said and became filled with self-loathing. "Forgive me, my love. I should have asked about your pain and been more caring with you. I think I forgot you were a virgin. I know it is not an excuse," he said with no little embarrassment.

Looking into his beautiful eyes, she smiled and sighed deeply. "You did? You actually forgot I was a virgin? How wonderful! I suppose that means that I was not terrible with my first attempts at sensual affections. It must mean that on some level, I was able to bring a degree of pleasure to you, my darling."

Darcy smiled at her, forgetting his embarrassment and self-reproach. Resolving to take better care of her, he asked her with concern, "did you bleed much, my darling?" They both examined the sheet for evidence. The pair rose as soon as they saw it. There was more blood than either of them had expected. Elizabeth was concerned about her body and the condition of his expensive looking rug, which was under the sheet. Quickly she snatched the sheet from the floor and scanned the rug for stains. She was thankful it was clean. Holding the bloody portion of bed linen up for his inspection and relying upon his experience, she asked, "Is this too much?" She questioned him with anxiety, thinking that something might be wrong.

He considered it for a few moments, then peering deeply into her eyes with tender compassion, he slowly shook his head. Placing his hands upon her ivory shoulders, he spoke his answer softly. "Darling Elizabeth, I am so sorry. I do not know. I have never—ah— that is to say, you are the first and only virgin I have ever, ah—well, I do not know, my love. Do you think the bleeding has stopt? Are you well?"

Elizabeth threw her arms around him. "Oh, Fitzwilliam, it is so obvious to me that you, love of my life, are far less experienced than I first thought!" She gazed into his eyes, and nearly laughing, told him, "Excuse me whilst I visit the water closet. I shall assure myself and return quickly."

He reached out and grabbed her hand, she stopt and turned around to face him. "Before you leave, I must tell you that your first efforts at sensual love displays were so astounding that I am amazed at you and wonder if I shall be strong enough to survive your devotions as you become practiced. I am blest above all men, my sweet Elizabeth." He drew her hand to his lips and kissed it, maintaining a seductive gaze into her lavender eyes.

Elizabeth smiled at him, and found she had to slow herself as she quit the room. Her excitement and newfound happiness in sensual lovemaking overpowered her.

Darcy looked at the bed and remembered the two women he had taken there in fornication. Each woman, he had thought he would wed. He was so certain it was right each time. But both of those women had betrayed themselves with ill treatment of Georgie. It had been very hard to deny Suzette. She came all the way from France, years after they had been together in Paris for one year. He fancied himself very much in love, but she was not mindful of Georgiana, suggesting they send her to a German boarding school. It was the same with Ellen; she had wanted Georgie gone, as well. Now, with the lesson Elizabeth had just taught him, he realised that neither had loved him. They were pretending for their own gain. Each of those women was cold to him when compared to Elizabeth. Elizabeth, *ne plus ultra*!

Thinking briefly of the second part of Elizabeth's dream, he nearly felt weak as he realised that being in that bed and kissing her the way they kiss, the way he had kissed with Suzette, just might have caused his mind to drift away from her. Knowing what a disaster that would have been, Darcy felt blest indeed. He resolved to listen carefully to all her dreams whenever she wished to share one with him. It was remarkable that her dream taught her to use a mirror and exactly how to please him. Elizabeth's mention of the smell of gardenias also startled him. In the future, she might keep him from the pitfall of errors, which he believed she had just done. Ay— he would always listen to her dreams and heed them as well.

A very happy Elizabeth returned to him and removed his thoughts of the others. "I am well, it has stopt and I need you again. May we? Is it too soon?"

Helping her down to the floor once again, he looked into her eyes and said, "Ay, Elizabeth, we certainly may. Beloved, from now on we may love as many times a day as we wish." He patted the pillow and she put her head down, next to his. Their kisses started a fire within their bodies and their lovemaking was with more power. To their delight, Darcy lasted much longer the second time.

When they dressed and were ready to quit the room, he inquired where she had put her things. She told him the rooms and he smiled. "We shall go back to your rooms after dinner. Tomorrow after we wed, we shall choose a brand-new room and select from the furnishings. Or, you may redecorate, if you would like. I am sure Aunt Edith would be most pleased to assist you, my darling. One thing we shall most certainly do is purchase a new bed. I think we shall require elegantly scrolled iron work, to be placed attractively into the headboard, and we shall need a footboard, of the same design. This shall provide places for our hands to hold. I think that would be beneficial, do you not agree, Elizabeth?" he asked, smiling. "It would have helped your dancer's position to have had a place on which to hold."

Understanding this, and thinking it good to change, she smiled and agreed.

"Excellent!" he declared. "I shall order the very same for London, Pemberly, and Ireland. Darcy summoned his butler and ordered the bed to his specifications. He asked the man to write to his other housekeepers, directing them to obtain the same. Silently he thanked God that he had given a good excuse for changing the beds they would use at all four of their homes. He wanted a clean, new start.

Later that evening, Fitzwilliam and Elizabeth sat in the grand salon awaiting Aunt and Bingley. Having a few moments alone, Darcy told Elizabeth of Bingley's sad state.

As Charles entered the room, just ahead of aunt, it was obvious that he was very unhappy. It was a tearful reunion with Bingley. He became very emotional upon seeing Jane's dearest sister. Dinner was spent speaking of Jane and talking about any and all family connections. Elizabeth could think only of the MacDougals, her father's uncle, Albert MacDougal and his wife Elsie who lived on a small farm somewhere near Trickby Landsdale, in the

Yorkshire Dales. Although Albert was her father's uncle, he was younger than Mr. Bennet. She felt the couple would still be living. "I believe their farm to be somewhat near Morecambe Bay," Elizabeth remembered.

At hearing the area mentioned as their home, Bingley nearly shot out of his chair. "Darcy," he blurted, "do you remember my saying I suddenly felt optimistic? Where the devil were we when that flew out of my mouth?"

Darcy thought a moment, and responded. "Bingley, it might have been along the water somewhere, I cannot recall for a certainty. Do you have a feeling about it?"

"Well," Bingley answered, "it is strange that no one has heard from her, as we can all confirm that we have no reason to believe she took employment with anyone. So, we should ask ourselves—how has she been living? Is it possible she went to them? Lizzy, how would the postal service be from such a farm, do you think?" Bingley asked her, using the name his angel had called her, and it touched Elizabeth's heart.

She considered his question very carefully. "Charles, you might have something, the farm is quite isolated, postal service may very well be difficult. I fear simply finding the farm shall be most challenging. Jane and I went to visit with Papa one time. I may have been around five years of age, Jane would have been closer to nine. I remember Papa taking us to the bay. Jane loved it there. She cried all the way home and told Papa she would run away as soon as she got back to Longbourn because she so loved Uncle Albert and Aunt Elsie.

Darcy looked at his friend. Bingley seemed to be feeling better, he become more animated, more like Bingley.

"Oh, good heavens!" Elizabeth shrieked. "I just remembered Jane hugging me good-bye and saying she wished we could both live in the Yorkshire Dales on the farm. I do not think I even heard her at the time, as I was mortified to be leaving Meryton and my home. I was just about to board the post wagon, a thing Papa would never have allowed me to do without a servant going along with me!" Edith reached over to Elizabeth and gave her an understanding little pat on the hand. The wise woman had realised that Elizabeth was recounting a most painful experience. Of course she wanted to shed light on the mystery of Jane's whereabouts, but her own hurtful history was still very fresh in the beautiful young girl's mind; even if her outward appearance reflected her joyfulness.

Lizzy looked up and smiled, no words were spoken but she caught Edith's hand and held it firmly in her own. Darcy saw the quiet gesture of loving support and smiled at both of them. He was thankful for the obvious help Aunt Edith was giving to his beloved. Suddenly he remembered Aunt Edith holding his own mother's hand. Anne Darcy had been quite ill and Lady Hamilton had come to Pemberly. He thought the wonderful woman was a treasure, indeed. He understood the love and support she was giving Elizabeth. Edith Hamilton was a very wise and loving person. Fitzwilliam saw a special bond between the two of them. Perhaps it was quite like that of mother and daughter.

Darcy became very interested in this idea of the Yorkshire Dales. "Perhaps Jane did go to her uncle and aunt. She most certainly would have written letters to you, darling, and to the Gardiners, and of course to you, old chap. It would be very possible that she would be unable to get her letters out of a remote area. Even Elizabeth and I found that we were unable to send and receive letters from each other." Darcy seemed to be speaking to himself and no one in particular, as if he wanted to listen to his ideas. He continued, "Jane may well have written to everyone, having no idea that her missives were never delivered. Tomorrow after our wedding, we shall ask Mr. and Mrs. Knox what they think."

Bingley could hardly bear to look at Darcy and Elizabeth. He was happy that both his friends were together at last, but it was a grim reminder that no one had seen nor heard from his angel in months. Anything could have happened to her in such an amount of time.

Sensing his pain, Lady Hamilton patted his hand and said, "Charles, do not fret, just enjoy an evening with a friend you have not seen nor heard from in many months. Tomorrow we share in their joy as they wed, then every one of us shall meet and discuss a plan to continue the search for dear Jane. I, especially, am eager to meet an angel."

This lightened the mood and Charles became a bit more lively after dinner. He talked of Netherfield and the week the Bennet sisters stayed under his roof. He told Lady Hamilton it was the happiest time of his entire life.

Darcy took Elizabeth by the hand and led her to her rooms. He felt a sense of relief that it was one of the few rooms in which he had never held a physical encounter. Fitzwilliam's youth was spent in skirt-chasing. Many times he and Allister brought girls here, and sometimes, he shamefully remembered, he would seduce the servants when he had an urgent need. For all of this, the man was truly sorry and had deep regrets about the pain he caused. He was frightfully arrogant and prideful in those days and ascribed it to a feeling of entitlement. Life had not yet taught him to value others. Trying as best he could to remember, he thought of two servants each in London and Pemberly who would have to be dismissed with pay. He must not have those four women around Elizabeth. His life would now be clean before God. He would *honour* Elizabeth Darcy, but he would never tell her. He would be ashamed for her to know the truth. It was an embarrassing and sad truth.

Hand in hand they entered the room that had always been used to lodge Aunt Catherine. This was why Darcy never used the room. At one time he thought it a kind of honour, an arrogant private jest, to have had a woman in every room—and this included the dining- room. But a room used by his fierce aunt? Never. He thought it odd that Elizabeth should have selected these rooms.

Hannah was pleased with the arrangements for the wedding. Flowers, food, and even an elegant cake were appearing in the Knox home from out of nowhere. An entire case of very expensive champagne was delivered to her door, and four men arrived with cases of china, silver, and serving dishes. A note written by Lady Hamilton advised her that these were not used in her own home, and she would be delighted if Mr. and Mrs. Knox would put them to good use, perhaps when they entertained faculty members. Lady Hamilton's cleric and his wife came early. There was time enough for the helpful woman to assist in the decorating. Planning to help, she possessed a handwritten list that Lady Hamilton had penned.

Hannah was dressing with Marie's assistance. She would stand up with her cousin, Bingley was to stand up with Darcy, and Monty would take Mr. Bennet's place.

At last, ten o'clock struck, and the bride and groom entered the home. Hannah nearly ran to Elizabeth's side, she was so excited to see her cousin's dream come true. Elizabeth looked like a completely different person from the shell of a girl who had knocked upon their door a few weeks earlier. She was beautiful in her pale lavender gown. No one seeing the bride today would guess the heartbreaking difficulties of her recent past. It was wonderful to meet their new cousin, Fitzwilliam. In truth, she and Monty felt they knew him already, Elizabeth had told them so much about him. Aunt Edith and Allister sat next to each other, both missing Alden. Darcy's men Spencer and Collot stood by the door.

As Monty walked Elizabeth into the room he was thinking of Uncle Bennet and wishing he could have lived to see this day. Elizabeth was so very happy. This was not an occasion for tears, even though she had missed her father when Monty placed her hand in Fitzwilliam's.

Darcy had never looked happier. Allister could not get over the transformation of his appearance and demeanor. Fitzwilliam Darcy was, at last, a very happy man. Allister tried to remember when he had last seen the man's teeth as he smiled. It must have been at about age two and ten, before Darcy's mother passed away. It was bittersweet for him to watch Fitzwilliam receive Elizabeth's pledges. His heart could not deny that he had fallen in love with her. With all considerations, Allister knew that Elizabeth Bennet was so much in love with Fitzwilliam that she would have denied all others even if Darcy had rejected her. Elizabeth was Darcy's love, now and forever.

The cleric began the Solemnization of Matrimony as the couple looked into each other's eyes. They took their vows, meaning every word. She thanked God for such a wonderful husband, and he was grateful that he had not made a mistake and wed Suzette or Ellen. He thanked heaven that he was marrying the right woman, at last.

As Fitzwilliam recited, "With this ring, I thee wed," he surprised Elizabeth by presenting her with a five-carat, nearly perfect, clear, and beautifully cut diamond ring. He told her it was her engagement and wedding ring. He had purchased it when he was in London, at a time when he had no clue as to how he would find her. He bought the ring completely on faith. Excitedly he slipped it on her finger. He had guessed at the size, but it was a perfect fit. Elizabeth whispered her appreciation in his ear, and he kissed her in his excitement. Watching from her chair, Aunt Edith cried for joy, and smiled. Bingley decided he would purchase a ring that very morning in Edinburgh, before he set out for the Yorkshire Dales. By faith, he too, believed he would wed his angel.

After the service, the cleric's book was signed. Lady Hamilton produced a wedding certificate her cleric had devised. They all signed it, and she kept it to show Lady Catherine. She would prove that she was indeed present when Darcy wed. Following the wedding breakfast, the newlyweds sat down with Monty and Hannah, Edith, Bingley, Spencer and Collot to discuss their plans to leave at first light for the Yorkshire Dales. The search for the MacDougal farm—and for Jane—would commence as soon as they crossed back into England.

Hannah could not remember too much more than Lizzy. Both were younger than Jane and it was thought likely that Jane did remember how to reach the farm. Mr. Bennet may have spoken of it often, as Jane enjoyed drawing her father out on the subject. It seemed everyone had reasons to strongly believe that, indeed, Jane, might be in the Yorkshire Dales, living on the MacDougal farm. A young woman would be quite a help to an older couple. They would show her likeness, yet be sure to mention that she might have been seen often in the company of an older couple. Remote areas should not be overlooked. Darcy ordered his men to meet in his study by six on the morrow. They would start out as soon as daylight afforded safe travel. Darcy would involve his men, and spend his resources, but foremost in his mind was spending time with his adorable and wonderful Elizabeth Darcy. She was his wife, he had promised her they would love each other as many times a day as they desired. He would be attentive only to her. The Darcys planned to focus upon each other, each and every day.

When they arrived back at Killensworth, Darcy found an urgent missive from Allister. He was very sorry to intrude upon the newlyweds, but he had an emergency and wished to come and speak with both Darcy and Elizabeth. He wished to see Edith and Bingley as well. Everyone assembled in the study when Allister arrived. Monty was with him, and the two appeared frantic. Both men were genuinely regretful to intrude. "I apologize, Elizabeth. I hate to obtrude upon you and your husband at this time. Please know that Monty and I would not be here if we did not need immediate assistance." Elizabeth smiled and nodded at Allister and her cousin, but she let her husband speak for both of them. Fitzwilliam would conduct all their family business. Elizabeth would defer to Darcy on all matters. Her complete faith had been placed in her husband. Darcy was most pleased that his wife looked to him in this situation. Although she had been addressed, she chose not to respond but allowed her husband to provide an answer for both of them. She was beginning to learn how to captivate Fitzwilliam.

"Allister, we are more than happy to be of assistance to you both, and we are pleased you have such confidence in us." Darcy declared, wishing to rush him along. Spencer and Collot stood quietly in the corner. Nodding at them, Darcy continued, "Allister, I have asked my most trusted men to join us. They are discreet and have certain specific skills which are useful in all types of needs. How may we all help you?" Darcy asked, wishing the man would come out with the problem. He was anxious to get to the solution so he could attend to more important essentials. He desired greatly to be alone with Elizabeth. They had not loved since early that morning.

"Darcy, as Aunt Edith knows, I have invented a highly performing steam-powered locomotive engine which will run on independent rails, pulling several cars. Such will transport anything from human passengers, animals, produce, or any other materials from the interior to ports of call and then load up on goods sent from overseas and transport them to the interior. It can move the military, and it may be used by businessmen to travel about the nation quicker. There will be no end to the benefits. With these cars pulled by my steam-powered engine, our entire economy shall flourish. As a nation we shall be the established leader in ground transportation, which will eventually be found in all modernized nations.

"Monty and I are preparing to apply for the patent. We know it will take much time to build the prototype. 'Tis a long project, but we are now preparing to approach investors. You and Aunt Edith are at the top of my list."

"Congratulations my brother," Darcy exclaimed jumping to his feet. He loved progress and was always eager to be the first to invest in new inventions. He had been a major investor in the *Virginia Proper*, and made a very handsome profit.

Allister wrung his hands and continued quickly on, eager to be heard. He agonized, "I thank you, brother, but the problem is that I was robbed during the wedding! My home was broken in to, my butler and my valet were knocked unconscious. All other servants were tied and put into the attic. As you may have guessed, Monty and I worked at this project from my home. Ay, now I see the folly of my home workshop. The design and all plans for this invention were taken. We have not as yet applied for our patent. Someone knew exactly where to find these plans, and what time to strike." Allister looked down at the floor as if a solution might be read upon the lush carpet.

Darcy could sense Allister's anxiety and knew his friend felt responsible because he had failed to provide adequate security for the project. Working at home was indeed a very bad situation. Darcy wanted to help him through this crisis. He looked at Elizabeth but spoke to Allister. "Allister, this is most disturbing." Turning to look at his men, he nodded to Spencer and put him on the spot. "Spencer, what are your thoughts?"

Not being one to rush with his opinion, Spencer looked at Collot. The men seemed to silently agree with one another. Spencer turned his gaze back to his employer and said, "Because of the time of the theft, we feel that perhaps the younger brother may have had something to do with this crime. We noticed he did not attend the wedding, which makes it look as though he could have played a part. I have two questions for you, Mr. Mason. First, did your brother have any knowledge that you were working on such a project? Perhaps he did not have full details or even know what type of transportation invention it is, but did he have even partial information?"

"Ay, he did. I tried to keep it from him, but he had an annoying habit of arriving when I was working. He would try to engage Aunt Edith and stay somewhat near me at the same time, would you not agree, Aunt Edith?"

"I believe so," she answered, very embarrassed and sorrowful to implicate Alden.

Spencer looked at Collot again, and as if by mental transfer of thoughts, the two seemed to agree once more. Spencer went back to his inquiry of Allister. "My second question, Mr. Mason, does your brother frequent taverns?"

"I suppose so, I do not spend much time with him on a social level. Aunt Edith, do you know how to help me answer this question?" he asked his shocked aunt.

Lady Hamilton voiced her thoughts, "Allister, it is a well-known fact that Alden is quite a drinker. He has not held a steady job for over three years. I would say he is living on his inheritance, my boy." She looked down at her hands, as if avoiding the truth. "Ay, he often comes to your house talking of taverns. Let me see if I can remember any by name. Give me a moment, please."

Everyone looked nervously around the room as Lady Hamilton thought about any names of taverns her youngest nephew might have mentioned. There was a general sense of embarrassment at the possible involvement of the little brother, but the time to pine over his character had long passed.

"Ay! I think he often talks about Rooks, or Nooks. Something like that. Is that of any use, Mr. Spencer? He has at times spoken of Beaver Creek and Old Bridge Crossings. Whether these are locations or the names of taverns, I am afraid I cannot say. Now, names of men. He has talked quite a lot lately of lawyers. Ay, he is quite proud of these two men—especially mentioning them upon several occasions. Let me remember, the first was a very Scottish-sounding name, somewhat lyrical, what was that now?" Answering her own question, she blurted out, "Alfred MacMooney! Indeed. That is it. He is an attorney, and the second, I believe, is an associate or perhaps an assistant in his firm. Glass, oh, of course, John Glass, those are the two most recent names he has mentioned and repeatedly discussed."

Allister sadly added, "I know he is quite fond of talking about his two brothers. I have heard him call us genius brothers. He rides upon the *Virginia Proper's* coattails, telling everyone his brother was the builder, and that he was onboard for that maiden cruise in March."

Spencer put his hand up and said, "Professor, one last question. The plans that were stolen, are they the original and only plans in existence? Or are they copies, with additional copies stored in a vault, or a safe?"

"Ay, copies, of course, my originals are in a vault. However, should these plans be sold, anyone may put their names upon them. I am ashamed, but as I told you, I have not yet applied for a patent for this invention. If we can recover or even destroy the plans they stole, it shall not harm me. I shall certainly process my patent request with haste. I shall begin the process this morning, but it shall not be prepared for the patent office before six months hence. However, should these thieves find a buyer, it may be too late for me to prove the invention is my own." He finished this sad confession, then looked to his aunt for comfort.

"That is most helpful," Spencer replied. "Collot and I shall away. We shall act quickly, never fear. It is most likely they are for sale now, and going to the highest bidder, should they already have interested buyers. However, if your brother only recently told them of the invention, they may not have had time to locate a buyer. We would like to work on them. It would be well if Collot and I can offer to act as middlemen and locate a buyer for them, asking for a percentage of the sale price, of course. Then, take the buyer to them, along with another engineer, who will discredit your plans and convince them they are worthless. It would be well for them to destroy what they stole. We shall complete our investigation quickly, for it must be done with haste." Spencer nodded his head briefly at Allister and the two men turned to depart.

Before they could quit the room, Allister called after them, "Say, Spencer, shall I alert the magistrate and enlist his assistance?" Darcy's voice joined those of his men in a resounding, "Nay!"

At once the two men awayed, and Darcy took Elizabeth's hands. "Darling, I am so sorry for all of this. How can I make amends? I need to know what you expect of me, Elizabeth. You told me to go to Pemberly and remember how that turned out for both of us. Now it is my good friend and Cambridge brother and our cousin in need of help. What are your feelings, dearest? Say the word and I shall step back and allow my men to take care of everything and stay out of the situation."

Elizabeth wanted to panic. It felt like the same type of urgent press that had taken him from her nearly five months earlier. Seeing Lady Hamilton across the room, she relaxed. Her mind stopt spinning and she was calm. "Aunt?" Elizabeth called out to her. Edith looked up, "Ay, Lizzy?" she answered as she made her way to the girl. Edith left a very upset nephew behind to come to Elizabeth's side.

"Thank you, Aunt," Elizabeth began, taking her hands and looking into her eyes for help. "I need advice and you are the wisest woman I have ever known. What shall I say to my beloved husband? I am in a near panic thinking of him leaving my sight for even five minutes, yet I know that your nephew and my cousin are in a terrible situation. Doubly so, for it seems Allister's own brother may have had some part in this wrongdoing. Men have been injured, and I know that with high finances involved, these thieves may stop at nothing in their efforts to sell those plans. Pray, what shall I say to Fitzwilliam?"

Edith brushed a stray strand of hair from Elizabeth's face. She briefly held her hand against the young girl's cheek. Looking directly into her eyes, she declared, "Lizzy, you are the bravest young woman I know. You have come through adversity beyond anything I have ever had to face. I say, with your courage, make him devise a solution that shall allow him to take you along with him."

Startled, Darcy disliked what his aunt told his bride. "Damn it to bloody hell, Aunt Edith—" he began.

Lady Hamilton stopt him. "Darcy! I forbid you to speak that way in front of your own godmother, much less directing such remarks to my face! You calm down and think. If these men are looking for a buyer, what about the wealthiest young man under age thirty? He has just married this morning, and what could be more natural than taking his beautiful bride with him, to what he thinks is just a routine business venture appointment?" Lady Hamilton was somewhat proud of the solution that she had just devised for them. She stood awaiting his answer.

Darcy thought about it. He motioned for Allister, Monty, and Bingley to join them. "Say, Aunt has suggested something which may work for us. It seems these men are looking for a wealthy buyer. How about Fitzwilliam Darcy? As far as Alden is concerned I have no knowledge of anything Allister has invented. In fact, I scarcely know Alden. He might not even be with them any longer, now that they have no more use of him." The three men looked at Darcy thoughtfully. Allister glanced at Elizabeth, trying to gauge her confidence level. He dared not ask her what she thought, yet he was concerned for her safety. Darcy continued. "I could go to these men with my bride. What could look more like a legitimate business meeting, than a man, newly married, taking his bride along on a shortly timed, first-come, first-served business opportunity? Such a man would have no expectation that any type of crime had been committed."

All heads nodded agreement as they considered the scheme. Allister looked at Edith. She seemed perfectly at ease with the plan. Glancing at Allister, Edith caught his eyes and smiled reassuringly at him. She knew he wanted to confirm the idea that Elizabeth would remain safe, without revealing his level of care and concern. Edith spoke out, nearly as if speaking only to herself. "Ay, a perfectly safe plan for all concerned. Lizzy, your presence will virtually guarantee a safe meeting. Absolutely no groom would knowingly take his bride to a meeting with dangerous thieves."

Darcy heard her and added his agreement, "Yes, we agree, Aunt Edith. I would be allowed to think these men held honest ownership of said plans, would I not? The fact that I have brought my bride into the meeting will absolutely confirm my confidence in these men. They shall be well convinced of my earnest and honest interest."

All agreed. Elizabeth smiled at Darcy and took his hands. "Husband, I am well pleased with Aunt's scheme. I shall be very happy to stay by your side and follow your directions at all times. I have complete confidence in you darling, and your men as well. Please, everyone be at ease for my sake, for I am far better satisfied going, than I would be staying behind."

Darcy smiled at Elizabeth, then looked at Bingley to size him up. He had never seen his friend under pressure. Bingley was untried in situations of adversity, and Darcy had no idea as to what his reactions would be in times of danger. He thought to take a chance.

"Bingley, if you choose to help, you could play the part of the engineer who has been hired to confirm the authenticity and effectiveness of the plans." Looking at Allister, Darcy said, "I am sorry, Allister. If indeed Alden is involved with this theft, or if he is present at the sale of the plans, Monty would be of no help. In fact, his very presence would spoil our efforts." Allister looked down; sadly he nodded his agreement.

Everyone was silent as each one considered the plan. Bingley spoke, "Darcy, I am not an engineer, but with my factories, I do have some working knowledge of fuels—and especially of steam. I am no expert but, if the professor and Monty would enlighten me, I could speak convincingly."

Allister warmed to the plan immediately. He believed that Bingley could do the job. "Bingley, I have copies of this design. All that is needed is the destruction of the plans stolen from my home. If I tell you what to say, would you be able to repeat it to them in a convincing manner?"

Bingley straightened to his full height and responded, "I say, let us give it a try, Professor. I was a thespian at Oxford. I am certain I shall be able to play the part of a visiting professor. I could be from Oxford, on assignment to Glasgow University, could I not?" Bingley finished what he thought was a most confidently spoken part that would include him in the intrigue.

The three men huddled around a paper as Allister made a hasty drawing. In a few simple and easy-to-remember phrases, he taught Bingley how to make his plans sound faulty. He would convince the thieves that the design was not workable and in fact would cause great physical injury.

After their strategy was devised, and Bingley showed great proficiency as Darcy's hired consultant in the steam industry, Spencer and Collot returned. Not only did they discover the tavern, Rooks, they had met Glass and MacMooney. It seemed these men proved the point that most crooks are very stupid individuals. They had already put the word out about the sale of a highly successful invention they desired to sell on the open market. This they foolishly noised abroad in the tavern.

"We approached them and asked for a cut if we could deliver a certain very wealthy young man who has a keen interest in making money. Collot told them that you were just married this morning. We said that you were always looking for a sound investment, and we felt sure we would be able to bring you to meet with them. Spencer seemingly let it slip that you have a home here and said the name, Killensworth. Both greedy bast—I mean, gentlemen—knew that name and were eager to hear more. We then told them that you invested in the *Virginia Proper.* Upon this report, they were invigorated and nearly asked to come with us to see you. If you agree, we have already set the time within the hour. Is that too soon?" Both men looked eagerly at Darcy.

Almost laughing, Darcy asked, "how did you know I would participate?"

Their answer came without delay, "because you could do no less, sir."

Upon hearing this exchange between Darcy and his men, Edith began thinking back to the time and circumstances when she learned that her godson was highly trained in the use of weapons. She became aware of his skills the night Lord Hamilton was kidnapped. Fitzwilliam was visiting his godmother when the thugs arrived at her home with their ransom demands. Taking over for Aunt Edith, Darcy claimed to be Hamilton's son. In minutes, he formed a plan to rescue Calvert. Edith remembered Darcy kissing her and telling her all would be well. She was aware that Fitzwilliam had arrived with two of his men, yet she was riveted to the sight of him leaving her house with two highwaymen. Amazingly, Darcy brought her husband home, within the hour. As they entered the house, Edith met them, demanding to be told what had happened. Her husband held her hands, and frankly told her that her godson had— spilt much blood— to set him free. Calvert looked her in the eye and said, "Edith, if Darcy ever helps you with a serious problem in the future, never ask him what he did to resolve it." Edith gratefully gave her promise.

Suddenly Edith Hamilton was jolted from her remembrances as she heard the loud clapping of hands, and Darcy's stern voice demanding everyone's attention.

Darcy announced that they needed to run the entire scheme past his men, who had just set-up a meeting for them, within the hour. His men listened carefully, asking questions as they went along. All that was needed was for one of the thieves to either tear up the plans or cast them onto the fire. Spencer proudly reported an enormous fireplace that was lit and warming the tavern nicely when they left. It seemed everything was ready.

Bingley approached them. "Darcy, Lizzy, I am ready to go, let us get this behind us, shall we? Afterwards, would the two of you assist me as I purchase a ring for my angel? Doing a good deed is a good thing. May Heaven bless us in our plan and then reward all of us by giving us back our Jane!"

"Amen!" the Darcys chorused. The three of them laughed and set out for the tavern. Bingley carried Darcy's valise. He wanted to look authentic even though he would not open the case. He was set to discredit the design, just as he had been taught.

Once underway, Bingley reached over and patted Darcy's leg. "Have no fear, my friend," he said reassuringly, "I am an Oxford-educated man. Oxford, the oldest educational institution on the planet earth, therefore, the best! You are about to see that I truly am an educated man. Not an intellectual such as yourself, but educated, none the less."

Chapter Six

The carriage arrived in front of the Rooks tavern. Spencer and Collot were the mounted escort. Unbeknownst to Elizabeth and Charles, the men were armed and well trained. They would not hesitate to take a life in protection of Mr. and Mrs. Darcy or even Mr. Bingley.

Dismounting, Collot opened the carriage door, and taking the place of the ready footman, moved aside as Mr. Darcy stepped out and looked around at the area. He wanted to be certain it was safe enough, before handing Elizabeth down. Bingley followed along, staying three steps back, as he was already assuming the role of Professor Bingley of Oxford on visitation to Glasgow University.

Darcy let Collot and Spencer enter the tavern first. He put his full attentions upon his bride and kept his lips very close to her ear. She smiled demurely, mindful that they were in a public room. In reality, Fitzwilliam was whispering that he very much enjoys her loving him with her mouth as they awaken and hopes she shall continue to do so every morning. To this she returned a whispered message that she fully intended to do so, and it was therefore a very good thing that he so wished her to continue. They whispered questions about which acts of love they enjoyed most, and what each one desired to do to the other as soon as they arrived home. Each message delivered and received was bolder than the previous as both became more aroused. Every eye in the tavern was locked on the young couple. They were striking—she very beautiful and radiant, and he extremely handsome and obviously very wealthy and powerful.

Spencer and Collot approached the two men at the exact time arranged. "Mr. MacMooney, I have secured your appointment with Mr. Darcy. You shall note that he has brought his bride as they have only just left their wedding breakfast. Accompanying Mr. Darcy is Professor Bingley of Oxford University. He has been on a temporary assignment at the University of Glasgow. We have secured his services to authenticate your plans and certify their effective claims, because you told me you have not yet acquired a patent. If you gentlemen are ready, Professor Bingley will look at your design now and advise Mr. Darcy.

MacMooney could hardly wait. He motioned with enthusiasm for Bingley to join them. Spencer and Collot stayed next to MacMooney, but their eyes constantly searched the tavern for potential threats against Mr. and Mrs. Darcy. Putting his case upon the table, Bingley took the plans offered to him. He studied them in the manner in which he had been coached and took quite some time in reading them carefully.

All the while, the Darcys continued to privately whisper explicit suggestions to each other, much to their own entertainment. They were very effective in ignoring every other soul in that tavern. Both were becoming more and more mentally aroused. Every man in the tavern could imagine what they were saying and guessed by their clothing that they had just wed. It was obvious that they were deeply in love.

MacMooney and Glass were pleased. In their greed they could hardly wait to obtain the young man's money. All went well until Bingley began to draw his hand up and repeatedly stroke his chin with his thumb and forefinger. After a few minutes, he began to slowly shake his head. A few seconds later, he developed an acute frown between his brows. Spencer pretended to take note of something negative in the professor's behaviour and approached him with a nervous question. "Is everything quite right, Professor?" Spencer inquired.

Taking his time to be convincing, Bingley slowly shook his head and spoke with regret, "Well, I am so sorry to say this, gentlemen. I have seen a very similar design. The plans I have viewed were quite like these. It was James Watt of the University of Glasgow, who was repairing Newcomen's design on the 1769 patent." Turning to MacMooney, Glass, and Spencer, he said, "Do you see this?"

This was Darcy's cue. He looked up and listened, placing a scowl upon his face. Bingley continued, "This is a separate condenser; it is connected to a cylinder by this valve. Now that looks proper, but see that you have mistakenly used too thin a sheath on your cylinder. By the numbers, you have selected inferior materials. Nay, that shall not do, gentlemen. I say, next week I shall expound upon this very error in lecture. Nay, this shall overheat and the steam in your engine will explode, I should say causing injury." He stood considering his words. "Indeed," he corrected himself, "grave injuries."

Sensing the right moment, Mr. Darcy, took Mrs. Darcy by the arm, and not lightly. He hastened to their table and abruptly jerked the plans away from Bingley's hands.

"This shall not do! Did I hear you say 'explode and cause injury'? Nay! You gentlemen interrupted our wedding breakfast, bringing us to hear about an inferior invention!" Turning quickly, he ripped the papers and threw them onto the roaring fire. It happened before MacMooney or Glass could make a move. Darcy looked back at them. He gave them a brooding stare and spoke to them as servants who had just disappointed him. "Such nerve! In the future should you want my time and expect my attendance, do your homework. I do not put my money and my name, to say nothing of my reputation, on inferior products. I dare say I should bill both of you gentlemen for taking my time and attentions away from my beautiful bride. Professor, my apologies to you, sir, my driver will deliver you back to the university."

Looking at Spencer, he ordered, "Kindly collect twenty pounds to pay the professor. These two gentlemen must learn to pay their own bills. When they offer inferior plans to prospective buyers, they must pay the consequences of their poor judgment!" Turning his back on them, he took Elizabeth's hand and kissed it gallantly. "Please forgive me, my dear. What an unfortunate turn of events and a gross waste of our valuable time, my love. He placed her hand back upon his arm and walked her quickly away, with Bingley following close behind them, valise in hand. "Come, darling, allow me to make amends for this insufferable and insupportable excuse of a meeting." Darcy consoled his bride with enough volume to be heard by all in the tavern.

John Glass looked as if he had just been told to stand in the corner. Spencer and Collot approached Mr. MacMooney, who seemed to have been in charge of the fiasco. "Mr. Darcy requests that you remit full payment to Professor Bingley in the amount of twenty pounds. I shall require cash, if you please." Not in a position to offend Mr. Darcy further, Mr. MacMooney removed his wallet from his coat pocket and withdrew the paper notes in the correct amount. Looking especially annoyed, Spencer held his eye contact and said, "Next time, do not bother to inquire of us for Mr. Darcy. We shall both suffer his anger and reproach for stopping his celebrations. No doubt, he is doubly angry that his bride witnessed an unsuccessful meeting, when both of us promised, upon your word, that he would be rewarded with a handsome profit from your excellent invention!" Quitting the tavern, Spencer and Collot mounted and rode towards Glasgow.

The Darcy carriage made its way to Camshron Jewellers on New Heights Street. The three passengers were in extremely high spirits, celebrating the convincing performance of Professor Bingley and the outrageously daring destruction of the plans by Mr. Darcy. Elizabeth could not stop praising them, especially her husband. She made mental notes of what to say to him when they were alone.

Once Bingley made his selection, guided by Elizabeth's knowledge of Jane's ring size and personal taste, the three happily headed back to Killensworth. "Oh, Charles, Jane will be so thrilled with her engagement ring. When do you plan to wed?" she asked, as though Jane would be found on the morrow. Elizabeth had complete confidence in her husband and his men.

"As soon as we reach Gretna," he answered her, frankly. "Then, with your patience, I hope we can return to Killensworth with the two of you. That is, if you will have us."

Darcy answered for both of them, "My friend, we shall be delighted to have the two of you at Killensworth. I think Jane would very much enjoy time with the Darcys, do you not agree?" Fitzwilliam thought it would be wonderful for Bingley to have his angel, but his constant attentions would always be focused on Elizabeth.

Bingley smiled and nodded his head in agreement. He was nearly overcome. "Darcy, Lizzy, I want to thank you both for allowing me to be of help this morning. It did me good to do something for someone. I believe I made a difference. For a few moments, I was able to take my mind off my own problems."

Darcy slapped him on the knee and laughed, "It would not have happened without you, old chap! Indeed, you made more than a difference, Allister and Monty can continue work on their project, and you and I shall be offered an opportunity to invest. Think it over, Bingley. It would be sound, however, not a rapid return upon your funds."

"Darcy," Bingley retorted, " I am beginning to think that nothing I do has an immediate return!"

❦

Always the professionals, Spencer and Collot wished to complete the subterfuge. They were men who knew the importance of doing a job with meticulousness, and care. Should certain insipid thieves begin to have questions about the spoiling of their best laid plans, the pair were thoroughpaced. Mr. Darcy would tolerate no less of them. The announcement upon the bulletin board at the University of Glasgow stated simply, "All lectures previously scheduled for Professor Bingley have of necessity been cancelled. Professor Bingley has been called to become chancellor of a new university in America. Inquiries after his appointment may be presented to the president of Glasgow University." Spencer and Collot approved the communication. They felt Mr. Darcy would enjoy knowing that his expert advisor had been so celebrated in two countries.

The men smiled. The announcement met their high standards. Collot slapped Spencer on the back. "Not a bad morning, eh Spence? Less than three hours work, scarcely a forenoon." Spencer smiled and agreed, "Ay, and ten pounds each for our efforts. Amazing, how Mr. Darcy always sees to it that we come up on top, eh?" They laughed as they mounted their horses and headed back to Killensworth.

❦

Returning to Killensworth, Mr. and Mrs. Darcy barely made it into her chambers before they engaged one another in an urgent attempt to express and satisfy their hot-blooded responses to their experience in the tavern. Closing the door behind them, Darcy took two steps, and putting Elizabeth against the wall, pinned her shoulders. Their eyes darkened with desire as they held each other's gaze. Their breathing, in unison, was ragged and rapid. Licking her lips passionately, Darcy began a wild and very seductive series of openmouthed kisses. Moaning his urgent need, he felt his heart racing faster than he could remember. Elizabeth tried to speak through the kisses, but her husband's steadily rising ardor caused him to hold possession of her mouth. He displayed a somewhat rough treatment in his haste and sensual excitement. It was a side of his affections she had not yet experienced. In truth, it was a side he had never displayed, nor felt, prior to this very moment.

Elizabeth found it very stimulating; it had an aphrodisiac affect upon her. She responded with like fervor and shocked him by breaking the kiss to demand, "Fitzwilliam, I need you inside me immediately!" He continued his hungry excursions over her mouth, and pressed his body so tightly into hers, she felt a rib might break. "Now!" she begged, "I need you this moment. I am ready! Oh, I dare say I am quite ready!" Her words were now coming in short bursts, as her breath was not adequate for a continuous phrasing of speech. "You were so confident, commanding and authoritative in that tavern. And, the way you whispered into my ear, and the *things* you said! Oh, my darling husband, I cannot wait for you to enter me. I must love you—now, right here, please, I beg you, dearest!" Her intensity was demonstrated in this new, impatient solicitation. Her thirsty mouth found his again. She renewed her interest in kissing him with mounting erotic passions, which he felt instantly.

It was he who broke their kiss this time, his chest heaving forcefully, his hot breath warming her face. It took a few moments for him to realise what she had been requesting of him. Once he fully understood her sensuous demand, he was most eager to oblige her. "Remove your undergarment, my dearest," he requested in choppy-sounding words.

Excitedly, she gave him a momentary shock. "My love," she thrilled to his request stammering breathlessly, "—I have not— worn such— all day!"

He struggled to grasp her meaning. The announcement electrified him. He was transported to an even greater feeling of excitation. Mentally he pictured his bride taking her vows with a bare bottom and thought about her going into the tavern without her undergarment. He was now intensely desirous of her. "Had I known this in the tavern—Oh God— Lizzy— whatever shall I do with a wife like you?" He stammered somewhat as he opened the fall of his trousers. She quickly lifted her skirts and laughed at his words. Darcy smiled as he watched her, shook his head, and said, "I do honestly think you will very well kill me with your loving arts, my lovely girl." He was awed at the sight of her beautiful, silky, dark curls. His hand instinctively reached for them, and he began to fondle her. Lost in her audaciousness and sensual daring, he asked her hopefully, "Was this just a wedding gown accommodation, being married with a naked bottom, or have you made a decision to continue such practice? Please advise me so that I may know how to plan." His eyes sparkled as he inquired, whilst skillfully sliding one finger inside her wet ring.

She smiled, then quickly placed her hungry mouth over his once more, capturing his lips and preventing his wishful questions. She was impatient for him to take her. Breaking free, she begged him again. "Oh, p-l-e-a-s-e!" she gasped, drawing out each letter of the word. "Now! And with that same position you started us in, I beg you. Hurry, my love." She was near to tears, her intense physical need of him was so great.

Once more, he placed her against the wall, then pinned both her hands above her head with his left hand. She found this position very exciting, "Now! Please, I beg you," was all she managed to say as he smothered her mouth with his passionate kisses.

He penetrated her with unyielding force, hard, fast, and steadily. She welcomed him without flinching and held him tenaciously, matching his determination to give and receive satisfaction from their union. They were powerful together, stunned at their urgency and their abilities to love in any position and at any time. Their minds were so sensually kindled in the tavern, having all those men watching them, knowing they were newlywed and talking seductively. It excited both of them to have been observed, understood, and unblushingly envied. Being aroused by those unusual circumstances somewhat shocked them. And now, their urgency, the entrapment of her body, and the rugged strength he was using, brought their loving to a new level. It was exciting and new for both of them.

Elizabeth gloried in having her powerful husband handle her in such a manner. They thoroughly enjoyed loving each other in a standing position. She told him she took pleasure in his dominance and the increased power of his penetrating force.

Darcy's passion was inflamed, with the consequential excitement of his bride's omission of her undergarment. He told her that it greatly heightened his desire for her. He was delighted at her using such a powerful element of surprise. By this, he knew she would never be predictable. He said it made her even more desirable.

Withdrawing after reaching mutually timed heights, Darcy picked her up in his arms and turned them around and around. Both were laughing at the top of their lungs. Taking her to the bed, he tossed her atop the counterpane and then stretched out beside her. They were ebullient. Reveling in their extreme, intense gratification, he began to recount his own feelings about their tavern experience. "Oh, to know that every man in that tavern could see that we were fresh from our wedding and surmise the things I was whispering into your ear. Your very satisfactory responses to my suggestive whispers were exhilarating. I knew every man there wanted to be me, so he could have his way with you, my precious wife!" Darcy took hold of Elizabeth and rolled her over on top of him.

"Sweetheart, you are Fitzwilliam Darcy. Of course every man there wanted to be you," she corrected him, lightly tapping his nose with her index finger.

"Nay. They wanted to be me so they could bed *you*, Elizabeth!" he laughed.

At that, they sat up, removed their wedding clothes and joined again. This time in a side lying position that allowed them to touch each other freely, amusing themselves whilst enjoying coitus. Darcy's new found awareness of his power to bring his wife to her heights made him relentless in stimulating her breasts. This he did skillfully and artfully giving her exquisite ecstasy. He said how much he loved watching her enjoy her raptures with each elated bliss. Again and again he took her to her own paradise. Enfolded in that warmth, she closed her eyes and stretched her arms above her head. "Have you always liked this especially?" she asked dreamily. Catching herself, she quickly pulled her hands down, and covered her mouth. Wincing as if in pain, she apologized for asking such a question, begging him to forget it and not answer, for she had suddenly remembered her promise to Aunt Edith and feared his reaction.

Darcy's response took her off guard. His entire face lit up with a delightful smile, and cheerfully he said, "Elizabeth, I have never done this before, because I have never cared enough about a woman to want to be as generous as you see me now. Truly, I have never thought to perform anything like what I am doing. Before you, it never even occurred to me to give a woman her own pleasure, or even to think of a woman's pleasure whilst joining. Only with you, my dearest heart, Elizabeth Darcy, do I wish to play. I could spend hours, playing with your perfect body, my love. I desire to take my time with you, my wife, to ensure your delectation in all of our joinings. I want to give you heights that make you dizzy and cause you to wish for your next delight. I long to watch your responses to the heights I give you in our play and in our joinings. It is my fondest joy to flirt with your breasts and to caress all of your perfect curves. My fingers eagerly fondle you and manipulate your most sensitive places to arouse you to greater gratification. My eager mouth so willingly adores your entire body. Oh, Elizabeth, I desire to bring you to your very own pleasures over and over again. I long to give you thrilling sensations and hope you shall crave my attentions just as I crave yours. As soon as we finish loving each other, I desire you once more. Darling, this is brand-new to me. I adore loving you, my sweet wife, my own precious playmate."

"I feel the same, my husband," she sighed, looking deeply into his eyes. "Thank you for giving me all this pleasure. I want you to know that it is intoxicating to me. It makes me so happy to know you enjoy being with me in this way, beloved. I do adore and love you, and I wish you to be fulfilled." Kissing his shoulder, she closed her eyes.

"Elizabeth, it is invigorating and completely refreshing to love you like this. Not only is it stimulating for me, but seeing you at so many heights is renewing me. I feel like I am just starting to have a sexual life, even if you do keep pointing out my age and calculating my experience." He said this in jest, to tease her, but he could see that she was stricken with conscience. She seemed genuinely sorry for the times she had spoken in such a manner. "Darling," he explained," I am older and have—well, let us not dwell upon that, but what may I do to persuade you that your love is a tonic to me? Shall I tell you the truth of all my past loves? What you and I have had together in less than two days, is better by far, than my entire experiences over the years. Believe this of me, just as you must believe that you are the most wonderful, beautiful, and perfectly formed woman I have ever known much less joined with, for you, Mrs. Darcy are the only woman I have truly loved with all my heart. Elizabeth, you make me feel alive!"

His words reassured her. Her eyes began to sparkle and she smiled with an expression he had never seen upon her face in all their acquaintance. She began to kiss him with such devotion and love, he felt it ushered them into a new understanding. "What was that, Elizabeth?" he asked her, with both corners of his lips turned upward, and his eyes filled with wonder and eagerness. He felt a sense of urgent excitement. "You must tell me now! What has happened to you, love?"

"Oh, my husband," she answered, trying to suppress joyful laughter as she spoke. "I believe it to be confidence. I do not know how to share this feeling with you. It is as if we—you and I—have stepped out of a deep shadow and now we are in the pure bright light of the sun! Suddenly, I do not have an icy spear in my heart nor a piercing blade of worry and doubt over some ghost of your past loves." Putting her finger over his lips, she quickly added, "oh, please do not be angry with me, because I said such. Let us simply say you now have a confident wife. I shall not be a victim of doubt about your past or fear of what may break us apart in the future. I know you love me, and I most certainly love you with my whole heart!"

Darcy laughed. "Be assured that I also love you with my whole heart, Elizabeth. Nothing from the past, nor of the future, can separate us. You and I, my darling wife, are destined to be the happiest couple on earth."

"Ay, and, I think we have just set a record for our longest joining, my love," she giggled.

Elizabeth was thoroughly exhilarated. She put all her fears and anxiety behind her and was confident as Mrs. Darcy. Fitzwilliam loved the change in her. He believed he could tell that her torment had left her. Needing sleep and rest, the newlyweds napped. As they slept, wrapped in each other's arms, a beautifully written note was slid under their door. Darcy woke first, and could not resist stroking his bride's silky dark curls. Feeling very much at home with her body, he took as many liberties with his wife as he desired. Elizabeth awoke joyfully. She reached down and waggled her husband's erection playfully. Giggling, she asked, "How early must I rise to find you without a fully erect member, love? I want to have my way with you whilst you sleep. Would you mind, awfully?"

"My darling Elizabeth, you may do whatever you wish with me at any given moment. I live for your sweet touch, my love."

"I feel the very same, dearest heart!" she whispered, "I adore your touch, beloved. Thank you for your consent. I shall not forget." She giggled, then soberly asked a pressing question. "Shall we not dress for dinner and take care of our guests, Fitzwilliam?"

Agreeing they must be the first in the salon to greet their guests before dinner is served, Elizabeth went to her dressing room to prepare, and Darcy was required to return to his rooms. Approaching the door, he saw the note for his bride. He read it and laughed, saying, "Darling, I fear Aunt is planning on missing you terribly when we away. She is asking for a private talk with you before we retire. Shall you see to her before dinner, my love?" Elizabeth knew his question was a request. It revealed how much he loved Edith and wanted her to know that she would always be important to both of them. Elizabeth dressed quickly and presented herself at Edith's door. The older woman hugged her as she bid her to enter.

"Lizzy, girl," she began as she crossed the room to pick up an envelope. "We did not have much of a 'mother-daughter talk' before your wedding. I especially want to give you these powders, keep them with you. When I was first wed, Lord Hamilton and I had a very agreeable sensual life. We were quite vigorous in loving each other and I soon developed a slight condition. They call it bride's disease. It is not really a disease, it is just more pain than you might believe possible whilst peeing. I have heard it reported that the larger the husband's member, the more opportunity for the occurrence. Should it afflict you, Lizzy, simply dissolve one spoonful of the powder into a cup of water and drink it. It will put you right. If you feel it coming on, by all means, take the remedy, child."

Standing up to put her arms around Lady Hamilton, she kissed her cheek and said, "Thank you, Aunt. You are too kind to me, and I do love you! You helped me so much today with the Allister crisis, I have so much to thank you for already. I do so value my health. Pray, what is the first sign, Aunt?"

"Burning when you pee, or possibly a backache or a general feeling of illness. Lizzy, if any of these signs show up, begin dosing and continue until you are well, child."

"I shall, and I thank you. I shall miss you, Aunt, we away very early." Taking a deep breath, Lizzy continued, "I should like to confess to you, I have mixed feelings. Of course, I want to find Jane, but I am worried that she may have another man in her life. Oh, may I please speak the nagging fear of my heart, Aunt? How shall I share my burden, and allow you to know that Jane is completely wonderful, and innocent?" Elizabeth looked at her hands as she spoke. It grieved her to speak of Jane in a manner that might cause Lady Hamilton to misunderstand and think poorly of her beloved sister. Elizabeth suddenly felt torn. She was overwhelmed with a need to speak out her deepest concerns, yet she wanted to honour her dear Jane, and protect her character. Above all, Elizabeth desired Edith to love Jane, as she was so worthy to be adored by all who made her acquaintance. She offered a silent prayer requesting the right words to release the pain and worries of her heart. She wished to have the wisdom of Aunt Edith applied as a soothing ointment to her fears of what the uncertain future may hold. She felt the need to form some type of plan should a difficult situation face them in the Yorkshire Dales. Lifting her head, one stealth tear coursed her cheek and held in perfect balance on her jawline, as she waited for Aunt to speak.

"Really?" Edith asked, "I am all curiosity now, Lizzy. Please tell me why, child."

Taking a shaky breath, Elizabeth looked deeply into Edith's compassionate eyes. "Because," she began, "Jane follows others too easily. If the MacDougals have a neighbor who helps them, Jane may feel she owes him something. She may show him kindness. This could lead to trouble, as you know Jane is very beautiful, and I fear that a clever man may attach himself to her before she has a chance to keep him at bay. Her own kindness is often an enemy. Poor Charles, I know Jane loves him, but honestly, I also know what it is like to endure over four months passing without one word from the man you love. Jane has not heard from anyone for nearly five months; therefore, I know she is lonely. Oh, Aunt, do you not see my point? Please advise me, what shall I do if this be the case? Oh dear, is there anything to be done?"

Edith looked Lizzy in the eye, "Child, have you told Darcy your fear?"

"Nay. I suppose I do not want to cast my beloved sister in a bad light, insofar as my husband is concerned. Jane is a most wonderful and worthy lady, I wish Fitzwilliam to think only the very best of her at all times. Now that you ask me that question, of course, I feel I certainly must tell him my fears.

"Ay," Edith answered. "You must share your concerns with Fitzwilliam, just as you have explained them to me, he shall understand. When you find Jane, if you feel she has made a promise to a man and she does not wish to keep it, you must tell Darcy immediately. He will know what to do." Looking Lizzy in the eyes, she warned, "Child, do not ask him what he did to solve your sister's problem. If, on the other hand, Jane does love another man sincerely, that is her choice and Charles must learn to live with the crushing disappointment."

"Oh, Aunt, please pray that neither shall be the case but that we shall find Jane, and she shall be waiting to return with us."

"Lizzy," she countered, "that is a perfect-world prayer, but I shall try. Now, shall we go to dinner, child?" Joining hands, the two ladies set out for the grand salon. Elizabeth was glad to have a plan in mind. Should Fitzwilliam's help be needed, she would remember never to ask him how he assisted Jane.

In the opposite wing, Darcy had given instructions to his valet. He was very clear as to the preparations for his trip. Satisfied that his clothing would be packed and readied, Darcy made one quick tip of his head towards the door, and the valet made an immediate exit. Fitzwilliam wanted to spend a few moments alone before going to the grand salon. When the door closed, he crossed the room to the dresser against the far wall. He opened the top drawer and withdrew the scarf he had kept there as a memento. The scarf Suzette had planted on her side of the bed. A *souvenir*, left as a trophy, perhaps? He took it in his hand, and held it up to the light as if some message had been inscribed, and left for him to discover, and decipher at a later time. He thought it was indeed a trophy, yet the winner of that contest had been Suzette. Loving Elizabeth for the past two days had given him the truth. Elizabeth had helped him see the truth. He had love in his marriage. He loved his wife, and he certainly was loved by his wife. At last he had *given* love, not just received— nay— *taken* satisfaction from a woman. Laughing at himself, he quickly crossed the room and wadding the silk into a ball, he dropped it upon the flames of the fire. Watching the scarf yield its colours and its powers to the flames, he began to smile at the ashes. The man was once again proud of himself. He felt free… He was free to love Elizabeth. Elizabeth Darcy the woman he knew to be right for him. He congratulated himself on his correct choice. Elizabeth, best for him and best also for Georgiana. He would be happy with Elizabeth.

He opened the door and stepped joyfully out into the hallway. He set his feet to the grand salon. He would meet Elizabeth and they would wait for their guests to join them. Darcy was ready for his first family dinner as a married man. He was gratified that the meal was to be in Scotland, as he loved Killensworth. Even as a lad, Darcy developed a fondness for the estate. True, it was sad circumstances that led Elizabeth to Scotland yet he was pleased for their ultimate good fortune. Marriage was quicker in Scotland, less complicated without the presence of his sanctimonious relatives, and Killensworth was not as grand as Pemberly. He thought it good to rather break his wife in gently. He feared she may have a difficult time accepting the ostentatious magnificence of Pemberly. A palatial home, offering unrestrained plenteousness—he had a slight dread of her reaction to such superabundance. They had never once discussed his holdings. He simply knew Elizabeth loved him, not his wealth. Having the ability to give his wife and family anything their hearts desired was not troubling to him. He fancied himself that their life in Derbyshire would be agreeable. He was untroubled about taking Elizabeth to Pemberly. She was a woman who would fit into any situation. He was certain that she would do well there. He would keep their lives the same in Pemberly as they had been in Killensworth.

Entering the grand salon, Darcy was much surprised to see that everyone was there and seemed to be waiting upon him. As they entered the dining-room, he briefly wondered how long he had been musing over burning the scarf. Dinner was spent in merry time, recalling the scheme Aunt Edith had devised. Bingley was touted as the most talented of actors, and Darcy as the most audacious of would-be-investors. Edith was much amused and the four could not remember ever enjoying a meal so very much.

After hugging aunt and saying their farewells, the Darcys went hand-in-hand to Elizabeth's rooms. In actuality, they were still occupying the guest quarters of Lady Catherine, as the day had yielded no time to select their rooms. Inviting Elizabeth to be seated upon the bed, Darcy removed a leather sleeve from atop one of the dressers. He withdrew the contents and began to spread the papers, one-by-one, atop the counterpane. Elizabeth's reaction could not have pleased him more, as she was completely speechless at her first viewing. She stood and bent over the bed, holding her slender hand over her open mouth. "Most of these were drawn when you had no idea I was sketching you, darling. Nay, I should be correct and say, these were accomplished during the time you wished little to do with me. And, I daresay, you had even far less interest in any activity which might have engaged me." She looked at him and frowned, as she had forgotten the past pain of his harsh words. Darcy put up his hand and continued, " Nay, I quite remember my harshness, even though you are so generous as to have dismissed my ill manners. No doubt though, you had very little interest in my activities, at the time I drew these. My biggest concern, was keeping my endeavours secreted from the ever-present Caroline. I dreaded her reaction to my obsession, and feared an outburst from her should she discover that I was an artist, heartily in love with my beautiful subject. Even upon the pain of such supposed penalty, I could not stop myself. I continued to draw you on paper, and then plotted as to how I would paint your nude body. Ah! I very well knew— my challenge— was" he said slowly, "how to obtain your permission. He gave her a rakish look, presenting a sly smile and quickly lifting his eye brows.

Elizabeth picked up one of the sketches and smiled brightly at him. "But darling, these are so perfectly wonderful, and very flattering of the subject I must say. Nay, might I instead declare that I have never seen this girl? I know not such a person. What amazing talent you possess, my love. If I had such skills, I can only suppose I should wish to use them daily." He looked at her and smiled. "Ay, my lovely subject. This is my exact plan for us. I shall sketch and paint, and you shall be my model. We shall begin at a later date, but for now may I suggest a certain pose we shall entertain. Kissing her lips tenderly, he began to skillfully remove her garments. In moments, she found herself reclining upon the pillows with her nude husband stretched out beside her. Entwining his arms and legs around her, he began to kiss her again. Between kisses he whispered, "I feel this pose shall make a good start, my love…"

The Darcy carriage awayed at dawn. Heading south, the three decided to see how far they could travel before sundown. The goal was to reach the Yorkshire Dales as soon as possible. Spencer and Collot were well underway. After riding for a few scant hours, the Darcy carriage reached Gretna, very near the border. Darcy was pleased and announced, "I cannot believe we made it to Gretna in such good order. Bingley, I think it best to overnight before we get too far into the wilderness. If memory serves, there should be a small village with an inn just over the Esk. Perhaps we could stay on the road longer, yet it may be best to obtain lodging in a proper establishment each night, even if it means retiring early. I desire to keep us in safety. Does this plan suit you, old chap? Agreed?"

"Ay, Darcy. That sounds fine to me, I thank you." Not knowing that the Darcys had not slept even an hour before rising to depart on their journey,

Bingley remarked, "Riding in a carriage is exhausting, is it not?" The couple answered not. Lizzy put her head on Darcy's shoulder and began to sleep. She had slept very little since beginning her exciting life as Mrs. Darcy, and even the night before their wedding, if the truth be told. Darcy smiled.

Spencer and Collot rode separately into England. They split the area into two parts and took in as many hamlets, villages, and farms as possible. Together they had canvassed as many souls as accessible, and no one had responded to the sketch of Jane. It was agreed that Spencer would be responsible for reporting to Mr. Darcy. His task was to locate the inn, report on the day's work, and receive any new assignments. Rightly did Spencer estimate the carriage's travel time. He had no difficulty finding the place the Darcy party had spent the night.

Preparing to depart just after daylight, Darcy paid the bill, and the clerk handed him a message. His man Spencer awaited him in the common-room. "Mr. Darcy, we split our route and each of us can-vassed as many people as we could encounter. We have even asked children, as they sometimes observe more than adults. Together, we interviewed about three dozen people, and no one has reported seeing Jane. If you do not have additional, or any new directives, I shall away, sir." Dismissed with Darcy's gratitude, Spencer agreed to check in the following day. He claimed his horse, and headed once again into the remote areas. No acre would be left unexamined, per Mr. Darcy's orders.

As soon as the three were in the carriage, Darcy shared Spencer's report. His men had covered the area around Solway Firth. No positive responses were given when Jane's likeness was shown. His men hoped to reach Morecambe Bay by afternoon. Darcy suggested they follow the roadways which were more inland. As Elizabeth felt the farm was near Trickby Landsdale, that area should be their first targeted search. The route they traveled skirted around the Lake District, which Lizzy pined to see, and Darcy promised they would indulge her on the way back to Killensworth. Darcy wanted to locate Jane, but his focus was on his bride. They would visit the Lake District as they returned to Scotland, only because it pleased Elizabeth.

Just before sundown, the carriage stopped at a small village called High Point. There was a charming little inn, and Elizabeth was happy to stop and rest. Charles began showing Jane's likeness to everyone, yet no one reported having seen her. Elizabeth sat watching the process. After a few minutes, she joined Darcy. Silently, she tugged on her husband's elbow. He leaned his ear toward her lips and she whispered excitedly, "Darling, do you see the way that man in the black coat is looking at Charles, watching him with his eyes? He scarcely glanced at the sketch, yet, he certainly is showing a lot of interest in Charles, is he not? Darling, do you see what I am seeing?"

Whispering in her ear, he told her he wanted her to go to their rooms right away. Calling for his footman, he squeezed her arm, told her he loved her, and that he would be up shortly. Elizabeth quit the room, praying for her husband and Charles to stay in safekeeping. The footman escorted her quickly upstairs, then returned immediately to his employer.

Darcy approached Bingley, speaking within earshot of the man in the black coat. "Professor, why do we not call it a day, and you can explain that steam engine error to me, if you would. Mr. Spencer is needed for that emergency, but I feel we should discuss it ourselves. Do you not agree?"

Understanding this quickly contrived code, Bingley nodded. He followed Darcy into the common-room and the two sat down at a table. The man in the black coat also entered the room, and occupied a table near the door. Darcy kept his eyes on him yet maintained his conversation with Bingley. He continued without interruption. Cooper entered the room, and in an unusual move, the footman sat down beside Mr. Darcy. It was an indication that he was making himself available, should he be needed in an emergency. The men talked of the indications for good weather on the morrow. Darcy suddenly arose and walked quickly to the man in the black coat.

"Friend, you seem to take an uncommon interest in us." Darcy towered over the seated man. "You followed us into this room, you are listening to our conversations, and your eyes have not left my friend since he showed you a likeness and asked if you had seen that lady. Pray, stand and tell me your name. I would have you know, I am in no mood to be trifled with, sir. I would suggest, that you speak the truth, for I have the greatest dislike in the world of lying. If you have the slightest inclination of telling me a contrived story, you will have brought an unlucky remedy to your evil."

The man, about forty years of age, with a large frame and a slightly balding head stood slowly to his feet. His eyes darted around the room but he faced Darcy, who was much taller. The three men watched him and awaited his answer. "Ian O'Toole," was his only reply.

Darcy stared at him. "Indeed. Pray tell me, Ian O'Toole, where is your home?"

"Glasgow," he answered.

"What is your purpose here at the inn?" (Silence) "Come, come," Darcy urged him, "you are keeping me waiting and I warn you, I am not a patient man." The two men, stood facing each other, the stranger silently scowling. "Pray, how do you earn your living?" Darcy demanded.

"I work to earn me own way and no wealthy papa has left me anythin'. But the way I earn has naught to do with ye, nor yer friends."

"Ay," Darcy spat, "but what does have to do with me is the way you looked at my friend and followed after us, to listen to our business. It was observed that you scarcely looked at the drawing of the lady, when you were asked directly if you had seen her." Darcy gave him a moment to reply, if he wished to explain himself. (Silence)

"Do you deny my charges, sir?" Darcy hurled the words of his inquiry. His patience with the man was growing thin. He was becoming eager to take him out of the inn and beat him to a pulp. He knew the man was acquainted with Jane, and probably knew her whereabouts. With the right encouragement, Darcy felt they could have their answers tonight and actually see Jane in the morning. "It is my considered opinion," Darcy continued," that you looked so briefly because you do know the lady, and you do not wish us to have that intelligence! Am I not correct in this?"

The man in black maintained his stubborn silence when questioned. Darcy could not but feel the man would have the ability to stave off this verbal inquiry all night. Fitzwilliam had more than a hunch that this man was protecting someone near to him who might be a malefactor against Jane. He looked deeply into the stranger's eyes. The man showed obvious fear of Darcy, yet it seemed he perhaps feared someone else much more. He did not behave as one who was protective of a weaker person, but perhaps he had a deep dread of someone much stronger than he. It was becoming clear to Darcy that this local man would keep his secrets. Such stubbornness irritated Darcy beyond words; he was done with questions.

Bingley started to rise from his chair at the thought of the man actually knowing Jane, but the footman, Cooper, placed his strong hand upon his shoulder to keep Bingley seated. Clearly out of patience, Darcy used his right hand to grab the man's left lapel and with his left, gripped the man's right arm. He began to push him towards the back door, which opened to a pathway leading to the stables. Cooper went immediately to Darcy's side in a show of strength.

"What shall it be, friend?" Darcy asked, with his eyes narrowing and his nostrils flared. During his childhood, Fitzwilliam had been raised with a bully who tormented him. It left him with little patience for contrary men. An excellent swordsman, marksman, and fighter, he was ready to use his skills when necessary. Neither could he see a problem with punching the man to obtain the needed information. "Cooper," Darcy ordered, "we away to the outside." At that, the three men moved slowly towards the door, which Bingley was in the process of opening. Once outside, Darcy hit the man squarely in the face. Bingley was stunned at Darcy's force. The one who had called himself, Ian O'Toole, staggered backwards, then quickly struck back, but his blow merely glanced off Darcy's right arm.

"Ay," the man pled, "Stop, and I shall tell ye. I have seen the lass, a pretty thing, somewhat lanky. It may have been about a month ago. But I know not where she is, and 'tis the saints' truth of it. I only watched ye because I was curious and listened for reasons of the same. Go on then and beat me if that shall help ye find her sooner!"

Darcy shoved him to the ground. "Get up and find your mount. It is time for you to go back to Ireland, or wherever you are from—and I know better than Glasgow, for there is not a trace of the right accent in your voice. Let me be understood, I know you lied to me about where you are from, I highly suspect you also lied about your name, and should I learn you are lying to me now about the lady, mark that it shall not go well with you! I have no concerns for your wellbeing, stranger. Do not make the mistake of thinking I shall not find you. Now that we have seen you, we have the ability to find you, whenever we please. Away with you, and be thankful that we allowed you to leave in one piece."

No one noticed when Cooper left them, and walked to the stables. He saddled his horse and prepared to follow the man. Hearing the crunch of gravel, Cooper spun around to look at the owner of the feet approaching him. It was Bingley.

"I shall take that horse, Cooper. Tell Darcy I have chosen to follow that devil." Unable to argue with Mr. Darcy's guest, but knowing it to be a grave error, he released the animal to Bingley. The pounding of hooves sounded, and the black coat flew past them at an alarming rate. Charles mounted and attempted to chase the man into the darkness. Too late to stop Bingley, all Darcy and Cooper could do was struggle to watch the stranger in black disappearing on a grey horse into a backdrop of ink. The general area of his ride was known, but it was too dark to see details. Bingley, a less than expert rider, was able to do little more than mount Cooper's big bay. His start was too late, and his speed too slow.

Realising his inefficiency, he decided to return to the inn. The bay bucked at his abrupt pulling of the reins whilst attempting to turn. The decision to about-face was correct, yet his unskilled hands caused the horse to jump smartly and start stomping the ground. In short order he lost the reins, and within seconds the horse unseated him. A humiliated Bingley flew through the air, landing upon a large rock. The bay returned to the stables as Darcy and Cooper rushed out to retrieve Charles from the face of the boulder.

"Are you hurt, old chap?" Darcy asked, already knowing the answer to be affirmative.

"Ay," Charles whimpered. "More than the extreme pain in my leg, I now realise that all I did, was lose the first solid lead we have had, that might have taken us to Jane!"

Knowing that it was impossible to answer him in such a way that would provide any type of comfort, Darcy and Cooper simply carried the man up to his rooms. They called for a surgeon, but Darcy did not need a medical man to tell him what he already knew: Bingley's leg was broken. He ran his hands along the limb to see if there were any bones sticking out through the skin. It seemed the bone had not splintered. Darcy thought it to be a good sign.

Taking a few minutes to see Elizabeth, he suggested that his wife take a bath. He would return and they would talk, but he wanted to love her while they spoke. Smiling broadly, Elizabeth knew what he was suggesting and the idea had more than a little appeal to her. Darcy quit their rooms and returned to Bingley.

A light tap upon the door was Darcy's announcement. He entered and saw his friend. "Old chap, I think we shall be looking at a few days of rest for you. We shall plan on remaining at this inn for at least a week. It would be wonderful if this hamlet had a surgeon. However, it seems doubtful. If not, we shall obtain one from a larger village."

Looking his friend in the eyes, Darcy put one hand upon his shoulder. "We shall not slip into despair, Bingley. Spencer and Collot arrive tomorrow evening. They will aid in finding the man. I am going to go and sketch his face now whilst it is strong in my mind. Do you require anything at the moment, old chap? Cooper is downstairs obtaining some port for you. He will stay with you until word of a surgeon is heard. Do not attempt to walk upon that leg. Allow Cooper to help you. With his hand upon the door, Darcy turned back to his friend and said, "To console you, Bingley, even an expert rider such as Cooper would have lost that man. A dark night with a dark rider, how long can a grey horse remain visible when the rider wants to be concealed? We do not know this area."

Bingley attempted a smile but in his intense pain it appeared more a of wince. "Thank you, Darcy." was his only reply. He wanted to be left alone to concentrate on controlling the pain. He hoped the break was not life threatening. Bingley had never felt such sensations of physical agony nor emotional despair.

Entering their rooms, Darcy heard Elizabeth happily splashing in her bath. He smiled at the thought of her, and took out his artist's materials. He quickly sketched the man in the black coat. It was a good likeness, he thought. He would show it to his wife to seek her agreement. Quickly he made an additional copy, he wanted one for Spencer and Collot.

Going into the dressing room, he reached into the tub waters and fished out his bride. Wrapping her in a towel he began to sensuously dry her beautiful body. He carried her to the bed, quickly removed his clothes, and stretched out beside her. Turning Elizabeth onto her side he kissed her and gave intoxicating pleasures to his lover. When she was ready, he slid into her. Darcy thought the touch and feel of Elizabeth was like heaven. It was a heaven he had never known before she came into his life. Just the thought of her filled his heart with much sweet desire. He was amazed at his own need of her, and her need of him. She was so generous to him, always giving herself to him in the sweetest surrender. It caused him to wonder, if it would always be so with them. He had never before received such devotion. Elizabeth was correct in her calculations, he'd probably had hundreds of women before her, thinking each time that he had received good pleasure and enjoyment. They had all shown him great attentions. He always thought coitus was coitus, yet Elizabeth had taught him otherwise. No matter what his experience had been, it was true that only his young wife had set his soul on fire. With Elizabeth, he had a shared intimacy. Elizabeth was precious, one of a kind; his one and only. He promised himself that he would devote his life to her safekeeping, and each day would be spent with the goal of bringing her happiness. To Darcy, Elizabeth's happiness was his joy. He thought himself devoted to her. Elizabeth had become his reason for living. And their two lives, lived together, brought him assurances of happiness.

Elizabeth very gently told him of the fears she held about Jane. He understood, and readily agreed. It seemed that without judging Jane, he had observed those facets of her nature. Omitting the small skirmish from his account, he told Elizabeth of their questioning the man in the black coat, the back-door escape and the over-zealous actions of Bingley. He praised her for her excellent detective work. Gently giving her the news of Charles's injuries, he explained that it was possible there would be a delay in leaving. A surgeon's examination would prescribe proper rest. Spencer and Collot would join them on the morrow, and new plans must be made.

Turning their thoughts back to their loving, he smiled at his obviously happy wife. "Are you enjoying yourself, Mrs. Darcy?" He asked, with a sly smile. Taking her lips into his, they began to love each other with their mouths. Neither one was in a hurry to end their lovemaking. Not since Netherfield had they had allowed their tongues to dance together, and delight one another. Elizabeth answered his question, without the need for words.

$$\text{Ε7τ}$$

Under the cover of darkness, the lone rider continued to look over his shoulder. He did not hear approaching hooves and felt a surge of relief to be on the road alone. This sense of calm allowed him to slow his horse and begin to relax. He would not permit himself to feel fear, although he knew that the big man was a force to be reckoned with, and he wondered if they were about to receive their comeuppance.

Arriving at the farmhouse, he took the animal to the barn and removed the tack. Spiking some hay with the fork hanging nearby, he fed the mare and patted her neck. Heading to the house he determined to sit alone in the darkness and wait for his brothers to return. They must be told about the men with Jane's likeness. He did not know who they were, but he could tell they were powerful and influential men, possibly wielding some kind of authority. No matter who they were, it was clear they were bringing trouble for him, and his brothers. His sainted mother had always threatened her boys with a thing she called consequences. Once, when he was a lad of about ten he had asked her what they were and she told him, "They be that which ye bring upon yeselves, son. Yer own evil compels 'em, me boy."

$$\text{Ε7τ}$$

The surgeon, Crowley left some powders for Bingley's pain. He wrapped the upper leg securely between two lightweight planks. "A broken femur is always a worry," he told Charles. "Only time will tell. The body needs time and rest. There 'tis not much to be done, except to wait and see what miracles the body itself will bring." Instructing his patient to remain in bed for the next week, he promised to check in on him from day to day.

Taking the powders on an empty stomach, Bingley amplified the drug's power. The medicine worked best with food, but the pain was too insistent for him to wait to eat. He spent the night tossing and turning. In the tumult of Bingley's mind, there was a continuous nightmare. It was of Jane, running from a man in a black coat. His anxiety on his angel's behalf was his prevailing concern.

⁊⁊

Morning broke in splendor. A bright new day dawned and the Darcys celebrated the newness of their union once more. True to her word, she loved him most passionately just as she had done every morning since their wedding day. The two were in no rush to leave their rooms, as they were so delightfully occupied. They reveled in their contented joy and were so happy being together. Fitzwilliam and Elizabeth were thankful for each other. Darcy was so pleased that his bride concentrated her focus upon their combined lives and their wedded tranquility. He knew she had concerns about Jane, just as she had confided in him, but her excellent and lavish gifts of her sensual attentions to him, continued to confirm her extravagant love.

⁊⁊

Cooper set out on his horse, in the general direction the stranger had gone. Cooper was very well trained and a man of action and loyalty. There was no need to attempt to track the horse, he simply wanted to see if a farm, cottage, or other dwelling could be spotted within a reasonable distance from the inn. He would not attempt to go near such a place, he simply wished to obtain a general idea of where the stranger might have gone. Riding for about ten minutes in the general direction of the man's departure, he stopt in the road. A small farm stood about a furlong from him, with a barn and a small cottage. Tied near the house was the grey horse.

Turning slowly so he would not draw attention to himself, he returned to the inn. As soon as possible, he would inform Mr. Darcy. No doubt, the stranger would not be returning to the inn anytime soon. The farm and the cottage were going nowhere, and there would be plenty of time to deal with the situation.

⁊⁊

Hand in hand, the Darcys knocked upon Bingley's door. They kept their tapping light in the event that he was still asleep. Elizabeth felt that sleep was the very best medicine, no matter what ailed the human body. Bingley moaned softly. Elizabeth whispered that she would wait in their rooms, and Darcy entered alone. Looking at his friend, he said, "Old chap, you look like you fought against the champion and lost. Is it possible that the horse fell upon you?"

"Darcy, do not jest, if you please. The surgeon was here and left me some awful medicine. I had a frightful night. I think I shall call for some breakfast, coffee enough to last me the morning, and then take more of that dreadful powder. Where are you off to, please?"

"Bingley, I do believe this is a first! I am cheerful and you are brooding! Can this be a reversal of roles, my friend?" he said, laughing at his own jest. Then, sorry for his words, he tried to encourage the man. "We have a lead, Bingley. Elizabeth was very shrewd to notice the man's reactions, both to his slight interest in the drawing and his keen watch of you. We saw the general direction in which he departed, and if I know my men, even now, Cooper is out looking for a nearby dwelling with a grey horse in the barn. Once Spencer and Collot arrive, we shall devise a plan. I feel more encouraged than ever, old chap. You just rest and mend that break, will you not?"

"Thank you, Darcy. Please tell Lizzy that I shall look forward to seeing her later. Best wishes as you go out today. I know you will tell me what you learn."

Cooper stood in the back of the common-room whilst the Darcys were seated for their breakfast. He made no moves except to keep his eyes upon Mr. and Mrs. Darcy. He would relate the intelligence to Mr. Darcy when he could see him alone. Keeping a lighthearted conversation with his wife, Darcy's eyes were drawn to his man, Cooper. He knew the footman had information for him. Elizabeth was happily telling her husband about the lunch she ordered for them. As she spoke, a servant delivered two hampers. Per her orders, they also brought one blanket and two large containers of water. Cooper took delivery of them and quickly relayed them to the driver of the carriage. Returning to the common-room, he once again waited to be received by Mr. Darcy.

Elizabeth begged to be excused to speak with the clerk about the care of Charles. She desired to order his meals and have fresh coffee sent to him throughout the day. In her absence, Cooper sat with Mr. Darcy and told him all he had learned. Smiling, Darcy said, "We shall leave a message at the desk for Spencer and Collot in the event that they arrive before we return. They will know what is to be done."

❦

The older man entered the cottage and looked at the sleeping form of the middle brother. He considered waking the lad, but fearing his occasional ill temper he thought better of the plan. He would go perform the lad's chores and allow his brother to awaken on his own. There was plenty of time; their baby brother was already at his employment, a good lad in his eldest brother's eyes.

He headed for the barn and commenced his morning duties. He quite often did all the work. It seemed fine to him if his younger brother rode off alone. It fell to the eldest to look after the younger two—he thought that was right and just. Besides, he knew the lad would be ill tempered when he learned of the men looking for Jane.

❦

Spencer and Collot both reached the inn around noon. They were beginning to feel that Jane was nowhere nearby. As they inquired of the clerk they were given an urgent missive containing a sketch and a map to a local farm and cottage. Spencer read it silently, then, nodding his head to Collot, handed him the message. Collot read it, folded it, and placed it within his breast pocket. The two ate their meal in silence, and then quitted the inn. Outside they devised a plan to approach the cottage on the farm.

❦

It was around twelve o'clock when Elizabeth heard her husband's stomach growl with hunger. Laughing, she teased him that they should stop for their picnic upon spotting the first few trees. The land there seemed quite flat and dull but some few trees were to be enjoyed. "See, darling," she giggled, "there! There is a very small line of trees. Shall we stop and have our meal?"

"Ay, Elizabeth. You are aware that we must needs walk to the trees, are you not?" he asked, wishing they could drive up closer. "Our carriage will not make it over such rough terrain. I estimate a twenty minute walk is required to reach those trees." This he said to discourage her, but she received the information with joy. She smiled sweetly at him and touched his arm. He felt a warm sensation and smiled. "How wonderful," she sighed. "I have been desiring to stretch my legs. Let us go then, shall we?"

Setting out with his wife on his right arm and the blanket and basket in the left he marveled at her good nature. He knew she wanted to find her sister, yet her constant focus was upon him. She did not speak of Jane or Charles all day. Elizabeth seemed to have no worries about the process involved. She trusted her husband, and he knew it quite well. Darcy wanted to find their sister, but foremost on his mind was his honeymoon with his beautiful Elizabeth. She had been his reason for living, practically since the very moment they met. He was thankful that the two of them could keep their focus upon each other. The more time he spent with her, the more captivated he became. Elizabeth Darcy was, he believed, the perfect wife.

Following the map drawn for them, Spencer and Collot easily reached the farm and cottage. Tying their mounts they went afoot, keeping to the shrubs for cover. It was decided that Spencer would go inside, as Collot kept watch outside. The cottage was empty. Three men were seen working in a far off field; one of their horses was a grey.

Spencer worked swiftly. He had been well-trained, and he knew with sharp instincts where such men kept secrets, stashes of weapons, and all other manner of contraband. In the second place he searched, Spencer found a rather dirty box. Opening the lid, he saw many letters. They were banded in rough straw-type strings and the outsides appeared grubby. All the envelopes were unopened, and in the same handwriting. The sender was Miss Jane Bennet. Setting the box outside, he signaled to Collot, and then he returned inside the cottage to look for weapons. He found them easily and removed their bullets, carefully replacing the guns in their original positions. It did not take long to find an entire box of ammunition. This he also removed and placed outside. Careful to leave all things as he found them, he quit the cottage. On his exit, he noticed a carved announcement over the door: ORAN BRESLIN AND BRONA BRESLIN—BUILT IN 1782. Under this was a crudely carved list: SONS—NOLAN, KIERAN, AND DORAN.

Concluding the search and securing their finds upon their mounts, they returned to the inn. The cottage was left as it had been found and its returning occupants were none the wiser. There were no indications that their provisions and possessions had been reduced.

The Darcys enjoyed their lunch. The day was clear and bright and Elizabeth encouraged her husband to sketch the area. He did so as his wife watched, admiring his work. It was a very pleasant diversion. Next he sketched Elizabeth, requesting her to remove her cloak and lower her neckline. Once completed the sketch revealed her bosom as if she had posed nude. A stunned Elizabeth forced his promise to keep it in a vault, and Darcy agreed only when she would commit to being his model sans clothing in the very near future. Her face crimsoned, although she did find the idea quite titillating. Looking at his watch, Darcy insisted they return to the inn and check on Charles. The truth was, he was eager for the return of Spencer and Collot and to hear of the results of their search thus far. He wondered if they had reached the High Point Inn, received the sketch of the man in the black coat, and map to the farm cottage. It was possible, he thought, for them to have had enough time to investigate the farm cottage, and perhaps question the man in black.

Just before dusk the Darcy carriage rolled back into the driveway of the inn. Once inside the couple went straight to their rooms, and ordered a bath before dinner. Elizabeth was thrilled remembering the ride back when she slid to her knees inside the carriage and surprised her husband by loving him most passionately. It had long been his fantasy and he obviously enjoyed her spontaneity. His young wife knew, quite instinctively how to make him happy.

Waiting for his bride, Darcy opened a book to pass the time, and startled when he heard one quick tap upon his door. Knowing this to be Spencer, he went quickly to Elizabeth. Seeing his wife's half-dressed form, he kissed her shoulder and told her he was going to check on the horses at the stables whilst he waited. He encouraged her to take her time. True to his word, he did go to the stables.

Spencer and Collot told him of their find at the Breslin cottage and the identities of the men. Relating all they had recovered, they showed Darcy the box of letters from Jane. "Mr. Darcy, these men are very dangerous," Spencer began. "If your family is indeed on that farm, it is best to take Jane, and her uncle, and aunt out of the area; rather than approach her and obtain her permission to leave. In short, sir, Collot and I feel it might be best for you, Mrs. Darcy, and your friend Mr. Bingley to leave in the carriage. Perhaps make your way back to Scotland through the Lake District as tourists. Dealing with these men might become very treacherous, sir."

Darcy related Bingley's accident to his men. Mr. Crowley would need to be consulted as to when Bingley could be moved. His friend's well-being must be considered. Darcy took the box of letters from Spencer's hands. "I shall take these with me," he declared. "Excellent work, men! As always, I am in your debt."

Both men looked worried; it was troubling that he would show them to Mrs. Darcy and Mr. Bingley. They were afraid things would get out of control. As if reading their minds, Darcy calmed their fears. "Bingley can go nowhere with such a badly broken leg, and while my wife is eager to see her sister, she will follow my lead. After nearly five months now with no word from Miss Bennet, I feel it is only fair that Mrs. Darcy be allowed to read the letters addressed to her. We are to dine now. Come to our rooms with the letters in one hour. It is my desire that the four of us read them. Perhaps they give clues as to her whereabouts. We can learn the state of health for all three, and perhaps additional information which may help us decide how best to extricate her."

These ideas calmed the men, and they readily agreed to meet in one hour. Both saw the wisdom in reading the letters to learn as much as possible about Jane's situation. Mr. Darcy gave his word that it would be well for Mrs. Darcy to read her letters. He knew best, both men understood his intelligence and his ability to accurately address the situation. Truth be told, they had each learned much from working under Mr. Darcy's direction.

❦

Darkness fell upon the Breslin cottage and farm. Three men were weary from their long hours in the field. None suspected their home had been visited, none missed their ammunition or a particular box of letters. Eating a meager meal, they drank crude whisky until it finished their day. The Breslin brothers did not light a fire, nor did they use candles. They considered it wasteful to burn candles or wood, just to see better in the darkness. Darkness was just the absence of light. It would be light enough upon the morrow.

❦

During dinner, Darcy prepared Elizabeth for the news. He cautioned his bride not to allow her imagination to run wild. Explaining that his men had discovered some items, he stressed their need to slow down and use great wisdom in their next moves. "Oh, darling, Aunt told me not to ask you any questions. She said you would know what to do. I depend upon you. You have wisdom in this and all other matters. I shall trust you to make the correct decision for my sister." She touched his hand and smiled.

"Thank you, Elizabeth. Pray for me, that God will give me wisdom, I am afraid there may be some disreputable men involved with our family. Let us reserve judgment until we know but proceed with extreme caution, my love."

They returned to their rooms and waited for the single tap upon their door. Finally it came, and Darcy admitted his two most trusted men, who took the chairs he indicated. He handed Elizabeth the box of letters, and she began to sort them by recipient, making a stack for her letters, Bingley's, and the Gardiners'. Her lovely lavender eyes filled with tears as they beheld her stack of letters. Ever pragmatic, she arranged hers in the most sensible order, by date. Opening the first letter, she began to read and was at once lost in her dearest sister's company. Silently she experienced the life and times of the writer and opened her heart to the emotions Jane meticulously expressed.

The three men whispered amongst themselves. Darcy kept his voice low, "Of course, Miss Bennet has no idea that the one she trusted to post these letters betrayed her. Possibly we should keep them together and show them to her as evidence that she has misplaced her trust."

Collot boldly interrupted him. "Mr. Darcy, it may be that she knows of that betrayal quite well by now, sir. If one of those men has entered into an intimate relationship with her, she is unsafe. We cannot know what such a man might do to her if we attempt to remove her. Mr. Darcy, I strongly feel it is best that you and your wife leave the area without seeing her. Trust us to rescue Miss Bennet along with her uncle and aunt."

Darcy slowly nodded his head. Staring at nothing in particular, he considered the best course of action. In his view, that would be keeping his wife well out of harm's way and staying close by her side. Elizabeth had already experienced enough danger and trauma for one lifetime.

"What course do you favour, Collot?" he asked bluntly.

"I would have Mrs. Darcy write a missive, very brief and to the point," said Collot. "Trust us, we are able to help her and her uncle and aunt. Once we see the location of the farm, we can best determine what action to take. I hope they can make it to the shore by wagon, without attracting attention. We are fortunate that the lazy Breslins are now busy about their fields. If we can get your family to the bay, we can take them by boat. Those bast—ah, men have not the means to pursue on water. It is providential to have Cooper with us. He served in the navy before entering into your service, sir, and he can obtain a vessel and pilot the thing."

Darcy nodded, but was silent. Clearly he was weighing the matter.

"It will be a carefully orchestrated dance, Mr. Darcy. We shall need to determine the location of the MacDougal farm first, then, hitch our horses to a wagon, putting our tack in the back. We shall go to the farm at first light on extraction day and take your family to the bay where Cooper will be waiting in the boat. Spencer and I shall see them safely off to Scotland, and then away to see to the Breslins." Collot looked at Darcy's face to read his thoughts. He and Spencer had served the man for seven years and there was no one they respected more than Fitzwilliam Darcy. Both wanted to do the right thing for his family.

Darcy began to slowly nod his approval. He was deep in thought, but he quickened to the sound of his wife, weeping. He gave a slight nod to the door and his men quit the room. Rising, he joined Elizabeth on the sofa and gently comforted her. He placed her head on his shoulder and dried her tears, waiting for her to speak.

"Oh, Fitzwilliam, it is so heartbreaking. She feels so empty, sad, and alone. She fears she committed a grave error in going to the MacDougal farm. Uncle and Aunt MacDougal are now also in the clutches of three men who are robbing them nearly every week of cash, goods, and even food! Jane feels responsible because the middle brother, Kieran, is attracted to her. She fears she shall be forced to marry him, as his attentions are more physical each time he sees her, which is nearly daily. This man must be illiterate, darling, for none of the letters has been opened," she reasoned aloud. "Let us count them."

There were ten for Bingley, twelve for Lizzy and ten for Uncle and Aunt Gardiner in London. "Oh, she must be so despondent," Elizabeth whispered. "She does not know that we did not received her communications. She does not realise we knew not her whereabouts, and we were not able to write to her. Fitzwilliam, is it not heartbreaking?"

To reassure her, he spoke quickly of the next action needed. "Elizabeth, we must read every letter. We need to know their general state of health, and their finances, if she mentions such things. Are your uncle and aunt able to walk? Will you help me, love? Take paper, we shall write down anything Spencer and Collot must know. I wanted them to read as well, but I could see your discomfort. It would not do to cry before our servants. Do you understand you are a Darcy now, Elizabeth?" He spoke the words gently, not to hurt her feelings but to help her begin to comprehend her new and elevated station in life.

"Ay," she answered. "Should you desire to have them return, I shall contain my emotions, Fitzwilliam. Please do not allow my poor reactions to hinder the important work you require of your men. I shall not blunder again, upon my word, I shall control my feelings, my love."

He regarded his young wife with respect and admiration. She accepted his gentle corrections and was eager to pledge her confident deportment should he recall his men. Smiling warmly at her, he kissed her hand and said, "I thank you, my wonderful wife. Indeed, we shall resume as you wish. You do me honour, Elizabeth."

Smiling, she said, "I shall call for some tea and coffee, beloved." Elizabeth arranged for refreshments, and Darcy requested his men to return. In two hours they had read and made notes on Jane's letters. When they finished, Spencer handed all their notes to Darcy. He read them quickly and compiled them on a single sheet. Jane and her uncle were in good health. Her aunt suffered in her joints and walking was sometimes difficult, although she did not depend upon the use of a cane or a crutch. In one letter to Lizzy, Jane had given directions to the farm. Upon seeing it, Darcy was convinced that finding the farm would have been impossible without the map.

Elizabeth wrote a brief missive to Jane.

Yorkshire Dales
26 October 1801

Dearest Jane, I have only just read your letters. The one you trusted to post them kept them all. I am now Mrs. Darcy. These two men are Fitzwilliam's most trusted. Do everything they tell you, promptly and without questions. Have no fear about leaving goods, and animals, etc. Fitzwilliam will see to everything. We shall meet you when you three are safely away. Bingley is with us, he is as much in love with you as ever. He has been searching for you daily for nearly five months. Oh, Jane, he wants to wed as soon as you reach Scotland. We shall be together soon. Please burn this after reading.
All my love, dearest Jane, Lizzy.
PS—Fear not!

She handed the missive to Darcy who read it quickly and flashed a brilliant smile at her. The men approved her letter and Spencer folded it and placed it in his shirt pocket. It was nearly midnight when the two departed. Darcy went to check on Bingley and found him sleeping. The news would keep until the morrow.

While her husband was out of their rooms, Elizabeth dissolved one spoonful of Aunt's powders into a cup of water, and drank it down quickly. She folded the envelope and placed it back into her bag. It was a bitter-tasting fluid, but anything would be better than the urge to urinate with no result but a burning dribble, and pain in her low back. "Thank God for you, Aunt!" she said aloud.

The door opened and her weary husband entered the room. Taking one look at him, she said, "Disrobe and get into bed my sweet husband, your body needs sleep. Fitzwilliam, you are the best of men. I shall never stop thanking you for all you are doing for Jane, Uncle, and Aunt. Wrapping their arms around each other, Mr. and Mrs. Darcy slept soundly all night.

Fitzwilliam left a note on his pillow for Elizabeth. He was meeting with Spencer and Collot and would return as soon as possible. He wished her to rise and prepare to travel very shortly. Mr. Crowley would be consulted as to Bingley's abilities to make the journey by carriage.

Elizabeth awakened feeling cold and lonely. Silently she prayed for her husband and his men. She took a dose of the medicine and hurried on to prepare for the day. She dressed in traveling clothes and put their things in order. Once ready, she sat down to read Jane's letters again. Although quite hungry, she would not leave their rooms without Darcy, for she realised that evil men were not far away. She could sense the danger.

When Fitzwilliam returned, the sight of his young wife's travel prepared-ness pleased him. Their belongings were set out for the driver to store in their carriage. Knowing she was as hungry as he, breakfast seemed a good idea. As they entered the hall, the two saw Mr. Crowley. He had been expected early to advise them on Bingley's ability to travel. Looking very upset, the surgeon asked Mr. Darcy for a private consultation. Elizabeth looked first at one man, then the other. She found herself in a state of confusion.

"Mr. Crowley, I am going to ask that you allow my wife to join us, as I shall absolutely not leave her unescorted in the hallways."

"Mr. Darcy, my wife is having breakfast in the common-room. May I offer to accompany both of you and make the introductions? Bertha will enjoy Mrs. Darcy's company, and I assure you, sir, the intelligence I proffer is for your ears only."

Understanding the urgency of the request, both Darcys went quickly downstairs, where Elizabeth met and broke her fast with Mrs. Crowley. Darcy returned to their rooms with Mr. Crowley, who wasted no time in disclosing the matter at hand. "Sir, there has been a development this morning. When I examined my patient, I noticed a very accurate drawing of Miss Jane Bennet on his bedside table. Upon that excellent likeness was a wedding ring. Knowing Miss Bennet to be unwed and the same of Mr. Bingley, I put two and two together. I knew immediately he had been searching for her. Just to be certain, I inquired. He said he had been remiss in not asking me if I had seen her and took the opportunity to do so.

"Mr. Darcy, I excused myself, stating that my wife needed my brief attendance and that I should return in moments. I understand Mrs. Darcy is Miss Bennet's sister, and you, therefore, her brother. Sir, I do indeed know Miss Bennet, she has been my patient on two occasions. I should first tell you, that I informed our local law official of her ill treatment, and nothing whatsoever was done on her behalf. I am sorry to tell you, Mr. Darcy, that Miss Bennet was on the first incident beaten into an unconscious state. She suffered numerous bruises, and there was evidence of rape. Our local law enforcer is afraid of Kieran Breslin, the guilty party who has terrorized her for months."

Darcy ran his hands through his hair and breathed heavily. He was visibly angry and nearly lost control. "What of the second call, Mr. Crowley?"

"The second treatment was for a miscarriage Miss Bennet suffered—again from a beating she sustained. Sir, do you wish me to relate this information to your friend? He is not a family member, so I desire to have your consent. I know this is terrible news, the worst sort of news, I am sorry to deliver it to you, Mr. Darcy. Miss Bennet is a fine Christian lady, very gentle and kind, quite undeserving, of course, of all the evil she has been rendered."

Uncertain of what he should answer, Darcy asked a question instead. "Mr. Crowley, is Mr. Bingley well enough to travel by carriage through the Lake District and into Scotland? Our final destination is Edinburgh."

"Ay, provided he continues to stay off the limb." The man kept a keen eye on Darcy.

He knew he was giving the matter careful consideration.

"And the last time you examined my sister, pray, what was your opinion of her state of health and mental outlook?" he asked with genuine distress.

"As good as can be expected, on both concerns. She will make a full recovery, and especially now that better care and conditions will be obtained. I assume you are going to take her home with you?"

Darcy made a hasty reply, "Mr. Crowley, I am sure you understand the need for extreme caution and secrecy concerning those plans. Her very life is at stake, sir."

"Indeed," Mr. Crowley answered. "You are very correct, Mr. Darcy."

"Mr. Crowley, one more question concerning Mr. Bingley. Would hearing such news about the woman he intends to marry cause a set-back of his health and general wellbeing?"

"Mr. Darcy, I do not know your friend's temperament and character. I suppose I must answer by asking you what it would do to you to be told such news, following a terrible ordeal of searching month after month and sustaining a life-threatening injury in the process. Suppose you take him to Edinburgh first, then give him the news in better surroundings and after more healing has taken place. I would suggest to you, more critical for Miss Bennet, is that you tell your wife. Mrs. Darcy will provide a great comfort and give understanding and acceptance to the young woman. Mr. Bingley will survive the news, but depending upon the man's values, their relationship may not. I believe you have some very difficult decisions to make, sir. I shall, however, tell you this without hesitation." Looking straight into Darcy's eyes, he declared, "Had you not come now, I doubt the young woman would have survived another month out on that farm. I know for a certainty that her elder uncle and aunt would have perished. "

"Mr. Crowley, you have just made up my mind for me. Please say nothing to Mr. Bingley. I shall accompany you to his rooms to tell him we shall leave immediately for Scotland through the Lake District. I shall tell him the rest later, when I feel the time is right. As for my wife, I shall deliver the tragic report to her immediately. May I ask you one more question, about Miss Bennet? I have often heard it said that following rape, it is not possible for the woman to have a child. Is this true in Miss Bennet's case, sir?"

Mr. Crowley looked Darcy in the eyes. Holding his head level he said, "Mr. Darcy that is often the case with violent rape. Yes, Miss Bennet suffered violent rape, or should I say multiple rapes, yet I feel fairly sure that she shall be able to have children. In fact, she herself has questioned me on that same topic. I told her I did not see any existing condition that would prevent her from having a future family. She is a healthy woman, sir."

Darcy looked very relieved. He knew Elizabeth would ask that question straightaway.

He was pleased to have even the smallest ray of hope to shine upon a very unhappy situation. Although Fitzwilliam dreaded telling his wife, he felt that bad news was best given immediately. He suddenly thought of one more question his wife would ask of him. "Mr. Crowley, would you tell me the date of her first rape, and also the date of her miscarriage, please? I am certain my wife will want to know those details. I want her to know that I have been diligent where our sister's health is concerned."

Crowley scratched his head with his right hand, then he patted his coat pocket with his left. Reaching to the inside pocket, he withdrew a small book. He carefully opened the leather bound volume and touching his right thumb to his tongue to moisten the digit, he thumbed the pages until he reached the desired leaf. "Mr. Darcy, her first call for my assistance occurred four months ago, on this very day, sir. Returning to his book, he thumbed once again until he found the page detailing the second visit, regarding the miscarriage. "My second call to assist Miss Bennet was just three weeks ago. She told me she knew it was for the best, as the child's father was nothing more than a monster. Mr. Darcy, it is difficult for any woman to lose a child in miscarriage, even under Miss Bennet's horrible circumstances."

Fitzwilliam hung his head upon hearing the sad news about Jane. He took a few moments to think about what he had just heard, and making sure he had no more questions, he thanked Crowley.

Crowley put his hand upon Darcy's shoulder. "Mr. Darcy, be very careful about the way you provide this information to your wife. Miss Bennet needs her support, but take care that you do not tell you wife so much that she becomes engulfed in sorrow for her sister. It is perhaps best to give her the good news that Miss Bennet will be able to have a family someday, and leave the grim details to yourself. Think about telling Mr. Bingley the entire story. Sometimes it is good for a man in his shoes to realise that his beloved was simply an innocent victim of a very violent crime against her person. I can assure you that her attacker had absolutely no regard for her pain and suffering, or for the murder of his own unborn child."

Darcy slowly shook his head. He extended his hand to shake hands with Crowley, then he withdrew a thick envelope of cash from his inside coat pocket and silently handed it to the man. Darcy was thankful that he had been very liberal and provided a very large compensation to the surgeon. It was enough to cover his two calls to Jane as well as his current assistance to Bingley. He felt that Crowley's attempt to notify and interest the law in taking Jane's part was exemplary.

The two men quit the Darcy rooms and visited briefly with Bingley. Darcy waited for Crowley to leave and then told Bingley that the farm had been located. The three of them would away to the Lake District and then go on to Scotland. Spencer and Collot would go to meet Jane and her uncle and aunt, if indeed they were on the farm. There would be plenty of time later to tell Bingley of the extraction. In truth, Darcy himself had no proof that Jane and the MacDougals were indeed on the farm. As to Jane's sad history, the right time for disclosing that intelligence would announce itself, just as Bingley's letters from Jane must wait for an opportune moment. Darcy felt it was not the proper time to present the letters to Bingley. He deserved to have them when he could concentrate on their contents, and reflect upon his angel. The vital need at present was to away immediately.

He would send a man to help Bingley dress and prepare. A servant would deliver breakfast with coffee. Darcy would see to Elizabeth's needs.

❧

Cooper donned the apparel of a common fisherman and set out to the bay. He knew where to find men who may be willing to sell a fishing vessel that would give sufficient room for their immediate need. There would be no cargo, as no one would be bringing luggage. He knew well how to store the minimum provisions needed for sailing to Scotland.

Approaching a father with his young son, Cooper greeted them and asked if their pram, an old Danish flat-bottomed fishing boat, might be for sale. He said he was new to the area and had recently come into a rather respectable amount of money. He could pay well for the vessel, but he had an immediate need. Stepping back, he examined the sail, and remarked that it looked in order. The overall appearance was acceptable, and he asked them to name their price. The fisherman quoted his asking price, thinking it to be a fortune. Just for show, Cooper pretended to balk but at the last minute acquiesced. He told them he had to go and get the money and asked them to wait. Agreeing, they returned to their work and Cooper set out to tell Mr. Darcy and set a timeline with Spencer and Collot.

❧

Darcy joined Elizabeth and Mrs. Crowley, then escorted his wife to their rooms. Sitting on the sofa very close to her, he locked his gaze on her beautiful lavender eyes, dreading the look of pain he would soon bring into them. As gently as possible, he told her all of Mr. Crowley's report. "My sweet girl, Elizabeth. How I wish you could be spared this pain, but you knew it was very possible that Jane had met with evil. She herself told you in one letter that she feared physical violence from Kieran."

This news, while terrible, was not a shock. Elizabeth took Fitzwilliam's hand and kissed it. She said not one word, but he could see she wished to cry. Very bravely, she allowed him to continue speaking and held her questions. He told her of Crowley's initial call to Jane, three months to the current date, then he related information about the miscarriage, omitting the beating. Taking Crowley's suggestion, he reassured his wife that Jane will be able to have a future family.

"We now know our mission is life-saving for our sister," he told her. "Time is of the essence. We must act now." Darcy kissed her cheek and drew her closer. "You have already gone through so much fear and torment. The sooner we end Jane's nightmare, the better for you, and for her, of course. We both know that we shall provide the very best of care for Jane, and we shall bring her back to health and to herself. "For now my love, I need you to act completely normal. I know I am asking much of you, darling. You are feeling like a good cry would help you, but unfortunately, it will not help Jane. It is most important that we execute our plan as tourists and take Bingley to the carriage. We must set out for the Lake District immediately. There is no time to tell Bingley, and we have no idea how the lad shall react when he hears of Jane's unfortunate history. We must wait until our next inn is secured and there is sufficient time to reveal all to him. Do you not agree, my love?"

"Beloved, I shall follow your lead entirely. We shall away as cheerfully as if she is waiting for us in Scotland— as she may well be— after all. Fitzwilliam, I trust you in this matter, and in all things. I am but a newly married bride— happy with her husband and very much in love with him. Let us enjoy the Lake District, love. We shall pray silently for Jane and dear Bingley. Let us trust God to set things right."

Darcy slowly nodded his head in agreement with Elizabeth. He carefully explained, "Perhaps reading Jane's letters will give him a clue of what is to come. Please allow him to read your letter as well, Elizabeth. I feel it will help him understand how dire her circumstances were." He gave her a slight smile and gently rubbed her back, "There is my brave, wonderful girl. Just keep praying for success, this morning and in the days to come, love."

❦

Spencer and Collot hitched their beautiful mounts to a humble farm wagon that showed years of honest wear and tear. Putting their tack in the back of the wagon, they sat upon the seat. Consulting Jane's map and directions, they set out to find the MacDougal farm. Dressed as humble farmers, the pair were very well armed, concealing their lethal weapons beneath their coats. In truth, they were well prepared for the three Breslin brothers, and on the strength of the surgeon's report, which had been related to them, they were eager for the confrontation. Spencer and Collot were indeed men who quite enjoyed the challenge of bringing justice to those whose actions simply provoked judgment from willing providers.

Fortuitously, the men spotted Jane leading a cow up the path towards the barn. Unaccustomed to seeing strangers, she regarded them with trepidation.

Collot pulled to a stop, and Spencer called, "Miss Bennet, I have a letter for you from Elizabeth. Kindly come and read it quickly."

Upon hearing this good news, she released the cow, and ran to the wagon. She took the letter and read it through quickly, eager for any news from Lizzy. "What do you want me to do? Tell me and I shall act quickly," she offered soberly.

"Who is at the house?" Spencer inquired sharply.

"Only Uncle and Aunt. The youngest Breslin brother is at work on his own farm this morning." Jane trained her eyes upon the men and awaited their instructions.

"Miss Bennet, we must tell your uncle and aunt to come quickly. Are you able to persuade them to leave with us immediately? Mr. Darcy shall take care of their property needs, they must not concern themselves with deeds or other documents, and there will be no time to bring anything other than coats. Do you understand?"

"Ay," she answered. "Shall I walk to the house and get them and meet you and your wagon?"

"Precisely. It is vital to make haste, Miss Bennet."

Jane turned on her heels and ran to the farm. She wasted no time in reaching the house. Stunned but responding quickly, Mr. and Mrs. MacDougal followed instructions. The three got their coats and climbed into the wagon. Collot noticed that none of them looked back nor expressed any interest in taking anything with them. It was confirmed that the weight of this outcome was life and death, indeed.

Cooper sat in the pram. He had inspected the vessel and was ready to make way the moment his passengers were on board. He scanned the distance for the wagon and was at last rewarded with the sight of them. Cooper quickly jumped out and made ready to help the two ladies and the elderly gentleman board the boat. Spencer and Collot had a straight roadway large enough for the wagon to unload the passengers at the dock. In precious minutes they were settled. The rescued family quickly thanked the two skillful men who had delivered them, and the pram was off. The winds were right and Cooper set their course to the open bay. He was pleased with the boat which had been recently built, following an ancient pattern. It was better than sufficient and Cooper felt they would sail very well. Perhaps they would make camp somewhere near Whitehaven. He reckoned it would put them a little better than half-way to their destination.

A look of relief spread over Mr. MacDougal's face. He had greatly feared that Kieran would come upon them and do "God knows what to Jane," but now they were off shore. He was certain that Kieran could not come after them on the water.

Collot turned the wagon around and headed for a clump of trees where they could unhitch their horses and saddle them for the next part of their job. Before they could away, Spencer saw a grey horse and rider galloping towards the shore not far from their location. "This must be the bastard, Kieran, that Mr. Darcy told us to see to, for the benefit of the beatings and evil done to his sister," Spencer announced. They were not surprised to see the man. He was the reason they had need to rush the evacuation of those innocents at the farm. It had been their experience that this type of individual, possessed an evil ability. Somehow he knew when Jane was about any activity that threatened his hold upon her. Both men had encountered this type of monster. They had met his kind many times, in many places. He did not care about Jane, she was only his victim. Kieran simply wanted to control her, keep her in his evil clutches, use her without mercy, and beat her within an inch of her life anytime he pleased. But, there would be hell to pay if someone dared come to her rescue. He would hate anyone who might dare to depreciate his pleasures. If possible, he would stop them. Finally, if he could not stop the rescue, he would stop Jane. If she could not be his to do with as he willed, she could not live. He simply would not allow her to be free of his total control.

Realising the man did not know them, they took their time and watched to see what he would do. He dismounted without tying his horse, and rushed to a modest little dock. Tied to the dock was a drifter, a small vessel used for fishing. Once inside he untied the boat. The pram was in his full view. As they watched, Kieran pulled out his gun and took aim. He attempted to fire the pistol, not knowing the weapon had been emptied by Spencer. Fortunately, Jane, her uncle, and her aunt sat with their backs to the shore. The pram, under the capable hands of Cooper, was well underway. None in the pram saw Kieran in the drifter, nor his attempt to shoot Jane in the back. The four continued their trip to Scotland across the peaceful water.

"Spence, did you see that man stealing the drifter? That craft is someone's livelihood. Those boats are used by fishermen, and not the successful kind. What think you? What should be done for such an offense upon the high seas, lad?"

"Collot, that is a vile crime, indeed, to say nothing of the attempted murder by shooting a woman in the back. I say, should the tides wash him back to us here upon the shore, we should impose a pirate's punishment for him. Have you heard of 'tying to the mast'? Pity there are no masts here abouts, yet yon tree has a nice big limb way up there. Do you see it? 'Tis parallel of latitude, is it not?"

"Ay, Spence. That limb is perfectly grown to align with the ground, yet so high up as not to be easily seen from here. Enlighten me as to its use, please. We have time, the waters must return the bastard to us first, and I know for a fact they will. Tell me all, my friend."

"A gag will do nicely," Spencer began. "Then we shall wind a rope about him, in a tight coil. You are limber and a good climber. You shall ascend that tall tree, taking a rope with you. Next, you will toss the thing over the branch, allowing both ends to fall to me, below. I shall tie one end around his useless person, and tie the other to my saddle. I shall lead Rusty away and as my horse walks, the bastard shall rise up to the tree limb, where you shall tie him securely along the limb. Face up will justify, I should think."

"More than fair!" Collot replied, nodding his head in agreement. "'Tis a more sporting chance at survival than he gave Miss Bennet or her unborn child. More sporting also than leaving a family of three to slowly starve to death."

Sooner, rather than later, the drifter was pushed back to land nearly at the same place it was loosed. Kieran looked in a foul mood. He came to land cursing and spouting one oath after another.

The two men got to their feet and slowly approached him. "Say there," Spencer began, "we noticed the tides were against you this morning. Did you manage a catch anyway? What type of fish were you after?"

Not wishing to speak to them, he puffed out his chest and swaggered past them. Both men were at least one hand taller than Kieran, and he did not wish to fight them.

"Collot, I do believe he thinks he can steal a boat and then attempt murder without giving an answer to anyone. Would you not agree?"

Kieran whirled around with his fists flying. Looking like a gnat attacking two bulls, the man, of about thirty years, tried to engage Collot first. He attempted one right cross to the face, which the agile Collot easily avoided, smartly returning a sound blow to Kieran's face. Breslin went down onto the boards with a loud *thwack*. It nearly sounded like a gunshot, it was so loud. "My," Spencer said in disgust, "I suppose my friend here is a little tougher to fight than Miss Bennet. The surgeon said you beat her unconscious, but we shall not do so to you. We wish you to be awake so your punishment is of full benefit." Kieran struggled to get to his feet. Although he was scrappy, he was no match for two highly trained and extremely skilled fighters. Knowing that efforts to resist would be ill-rewarded, he bolted, making for his horse. However, since he had failed to tie the animal, the grey mare was on her way back to the farm, leaving her owner afoot. Deciding he could run away from the men, Kieran ran as fast as he could towards his home.

The pair allowed the man to exhaust himself. Spencer grew tired of watching him and mounted his horse. He took off down the roadway to apprehend the vile offender. Spencer loathed woman-beaters and rapists. It would be a pleasure to gag this puffy, tough-acting little man, bind him, and then hoist him along a branch in the tall tree. Cantering behind him, Spencer grabbed his shirt collar and scooped him up off his feet. Although he resisted as best he could, Kieran was powerless against the horseman.

Spencer turned Rusty around and headed for Collot. Reining in, Spencer dumped Kieran at Collot's feet. A gag quickly stopped his profane lips and the evil they uttered against Jane. Spencer bent over him and spat, "You shall finally know what it is like to be helpless, just like your many victims."

Only one man was required to coil the rope around the dizzy and exhausted Kieran, and it was done in short order. Collot climbed up the tree and using his strong arms, propelled his body out on the thick limb, straddled it and put his rope over it dropping both ends upon the ground. Spencer tied one end to his horse's saddle, and the other he fastened firmly to the coils holding Kieran. He was careful to place the evildoer facing upwards as he hoisted him alongside the waiting limb. Collot secured the coiled body to the branch and in moments tied him securely with his head facing the sky, so the vile evildoer could keep a careful watch on the crows and other large, hungry birds that are not too choosy upon whose flesh they feast.

Collot and Spencer were satisfied with the punishment and believed it set things right, considering the three men were slowly starving three souls. "Kieran violently tortured Miss Bennet, at least two times that the surgeon confirmed, and we saw him try to kill her—and according to my canvass, there were many others," Collot said.

"I say 'tis a more sporting chance than he deserves, Collot. We know many folks have told us of the Breslins taking their stock and demanding their money. There is no way to know how many souls they have starved to death, or just killed."

❧

Bingley was happy to be in the carriage and underway. Elizabeth worked hard to remain cheerful, and Darcy cast his mind upon his men and their progress. He was edgy and concerned, and his heart was as heavy as Elizabeth's. He knew that once they were installed at their next inn, he was required to tell Bingley of Mr. Crowley's report on Jane, a task he faced with a fierce dread. He could not guess Bingley's reaction to the account of Jane's difficulties. In truth, Darcy worried about the impact upon Jane, should Bingley turn his back on her in her time of need. He knew that Jane would eventually be well, because Elizabeth would not rest until Jane would be restored. Darcy was concerned that Bingley would lose Jane forever, if he shunned her over these violent attacks. He reasoned that Jane would not give him a second chance, should his initial reaction be a poor one. He pondered what he might do to help the couple.

Spencer and Collot returned to the MacDougal farm. They searched the farmhouse and found only the deed, which had been hidden fairly well for persons who had no training in methods of concealment. There was nothing else of any value in the home. The pantry was nearly empty. It was determined that these three people were barely clinging to life. Perhaps only weeks were remaining for the three souls.

Two men, riding double on the grey, approached the MacDougal farmhouse. Their chatter was heard from afar and Collot remarked that it sounded very much like whisky talking. The Breslins were angry at their brother, and one of them wished to take a lash to him. Sitting in the parlor, Spencer and Collot knew they had only a few minutes more to wait before they could tidy up, balancing the scales of justice for the MacDougals and Miss Bennet. If the law for this part of England was not able to face these evil brothers, someone else needed to remove the vermin. Knowing the Breslins would not be able to use guns against them, Darcy's men took their guns out of their belts and headed outside without their weapons. They would not need weapons to see to these evildoers.

There would be a bit of a mystery, the disappearance of the three Breslin brothers and Miss Bennet, along with her elderly uncle and aunt. Mr. Crowley knew a little something about the MacDougals and Miss Bennet, but he would not be inclined to speak on the subject. Neither would the folks who would find the numerous animals that strayed away from the Breslin farm. Two horses, two cows and one goat. The chickens would most likely become prey for either strangers who wander the dales, neighboring farmers or even large cats or dogs. It would most likely be years before anyone would come near the Breslin or even the MacDougal farms. In truth, no one for miles around would care to ask many questions at all about those Breslin brothers…

Cooper inspired the complete confidence of his timid and silent passengers. The weather was mild and the winds were obliging. At this rate he calculated they would need to spend only one night camping. He would be sure to select the area long before dark for safety's sake.

Breaking the silence, Cooper addressed all three passengers. "As I told you when you boarded, Mr. Darcy instructed me to take you into Scotland. He and Mrs. Darcy will meet us at a place called Eastriggs. The trip to his home near Edinburgh will be completed by carriage."

Upon hearing the name, Jane's eyes flashed at Cooper and she blurted, "Pray— how is she? Mrs. Darcy?"

"Madam, she is in excellent health and very eager to be with her family, I am told."

"I thank you, sir," she answered, lowering her eyes.

"If you have any questions, I shall be pleased to answer. We shall continue on for about four hours. Please drink the water I have given you. It is very important to drink when you suffer such intense exposure to the elements." At his encouragement, they all drank eagerly, showing great thirst. He wondered why they had not troubled to quench it on their own accord. It struck him as very odd.

The Natural Splendor Inn was inviting, cheerful, and well-staffed. A mountainous man was ready and able to assist Bingley, and he was most eager to be installed in his rooms. Mr. and Mrs. Darcy were quite taken with the charm of the inn. They both wished this could have been a honeymoon destination for them without the all the torment. However, both Fitzwilliam and Elizabeth were determined to enjoy the perfect inn for the evening. For the newlyweds, it was a romantic little hideaway with lovely rooms and pictur-esque views from every window. Their dinner was delicious, the music was splendid and the Darcys were filled with desire. Fitzwilliam would have liked nothing better than to join his beautiful wife in their very private rooms. He would have loved to shut out the reality of Jane's sad history, which would soon torment Bingley's future.

Entering Bingley's room after dinner, Darcy saw his friend seated in front of a cheery fire, looking as if he had the use of both legs. Darcy crossed the room to pour two glasses of port. As a rule, the beverage would be the perfect after-dinner accompaniment, yet tonight nothing would be perfect.

Darcy reached into his coat pocket and withdrew the stack of letters. Thinking the best way to open a difficult subject was to launch out and speak plainly, Darcy simply said, "Old chap, we have much to talk about, but first I must give you letters that Jane wrote to you, over the past months. My men discovered them in the farmhouse of the person she trusted to post them for her. As you can see, they are all unopened. Elizabeth and I realised that the entire family must have been illiterate. Take your time and read them. I shall go see Elizabeth and return to you in one hour."

Bingley received the letters with a trembling hand. Instantly his eyes brimmed with tears. "Darcy, I hardly know what to say. I shall read them."

As Darcy quit the room he thought he saw a quizzical expression upon Bingley's face. It was as if he had been trying to determine why Darcy did not give them to him when they were discovered. As if answering the unasked question, Darcy turned slowly to face his friend. He shook his head and tried to offer a slight smile of encouragement. "Bingley, I brought these to your room late in the evening, on the day of their discovery. You were sleeping when I entered your chamber. The following morning, events moved quite rapidly and I felt it best to wait until this moment to give them to you. I desired you to have sufficient time to read them, and reflect upon their sentiments. Do forgive me, old man." Feeling a sudden rush of cold, he closed the door and hurried away to the warmth of Elizabeth.

Darcy held his wife for an hour. She did not cry; she had told him she would not, and she kept her promise. Tears would not help Jane or Bingley. Darcy was proud of her and praised her for her strength. Reluctantly, he rose from the bed. Bending over her, he kissed Elizabeth and asked her to pray that he could find the right words for his dear friend.

Suddenly Elizabeth rose up from the bed and rushed to him, throwing her arms around his neck she leaned into him, whispering, "—Darling— when you return— would you like to love me? I shall desire you— I shall miss you whilst you are away from me."

He exhaled his response into her ear, and nearly let his body go slack as he answered, "Ay!" It sounded somewhere between a hoarse whisper and a soulful sigh.

"Good, I shall await you, my love. Are you pleased?" she asked eagerly.

"I am so happy, dearest heart! Ay, I am more than pleased; I live to love you. Elizabeth, I did not think you would feel—ah, so inclined, perhaps because—"

She placed her index finger firmly between his nose and chin. "Shh," she said, "You are my world, Fitzwilliam. We are newlywed, and of course I cannot be without loving you every night. I live for your attentions, and pray you feel the same of mine. Jane is my sister and I love her, but we cannot undo her past. When the time comes, we shall help her, and Bingley, too, if he wishes, of course. Yet we shall always live for each other, only. We shall keep the whole world away, and hold our eyes and attentions upon each other."

Feeling intense relief about his wife's attitude toward the problem, he grabbed her and kissed her most passionately. He felt such ease, as if a burden had lifted. Placing his lips against her ear he whispered, "If I find that you slumber, I shall awaken you, beloved." He smiled; then he turned and quit the room.

Darcy returned to Bingley's rooms, and lightly tapping the door he entered before the man answered. He refilled their glasses and sat down in the chair facing his friend. "Darcy, I do not know what to say. She never knew her letters did not post, she kept writing. Finally, she told me she had to face the fact that I had moved on and she wished me happiness and all the best in this life." He stopped to wipe his eyes on his sleeve.

"Bingley, I asked Elizabeth to allow you to read one of her letters. This tells of her fear of a certain man. An evil man with two malefactor brothers, the eldest of whom we met at the inn, the man in the black coat. Please read it, my friend." Bingley read it quickly, then reread the missive. He dropped it on the floor and looked blankly at Darcy. Finding his voice, he lowered his head, and looking deeply into his glass of port asked, "Tell me the truth, was she raped by this man? Ruined?"

Darcy was stunned. He could not believe his ears. Was this the man who had pursued his sister for nearly five months? Did he just call her "ruined" as though he no longer had any interest in her at all? "Pardon, please, Bingley? I am quite at a loss. Would you not rather ask me if she is well? Was she harmed? If so, how seriously? Is that not the place a man in love would begin his inquiry?"

"Damn it to bloody hell, Darcy! I fail to see how this could happen. Why Jane? I honestly do not know how I feel now that I hear this news. This is a disaster!"

"What is a disaster, Bingley? Your attitude toward Jane? She is a victim, much like Elizabeth, who endured a near rape. It would not have been her fault had he succeeded. Jane is still Jane. She is still your angel, Bingley. When we see her she may be more lean, appear more frail, but she will fill out with the proper care and good food. Just being with you again will be a tonic for her."

"But, she is ruined, no longer a virgin; therefore, no longer an angel, Darcy!"

"Are you so shallow, Bingley? Not a virgin, a victim of rape? Do you think she willingly allowed this? Nay, I have information that she fought so hard she was knocked unconscious. Your angel did not give herself to another man, he took her! He stole her body through a very violent act, and cared not whether she lived or died. Now the question is, do you care? Do you care about her at all, my friend? Would you seriously let a little thing like loss of a hymen keep you from true love? It could have broken in a riding accident, or during her childhood. By God, man, the first time I joined with Elizabeth, I was so overjoyed and lost to my own passion that I completely forgot she was a virgin. Not until afterward when she innocently remarked on her enjoyment, regardless of the pain, did I remember and face my own embarrassment as a husband who thought more of his own satisfaction than to have concern for her. I would have cared not about her lack of virginity just to have her as my own forever. Had that surgeon succeeded in rape, I would have married the girl and been thankful to heaven for the life that still resides within her. Then I would have loved her with patience, kindness, and tenderness until she was healed of all that hindered her.

"Bingley, this is not a disaster. Jane will recover. She will be Jane Bennet once again. She is a very beautiful girl, and as you told me that night in your study at Netherfield, she is everything you want in a wife. I well remember what you said of her. She was 'accommodating in nature, beautiful of face, and beguiling in her figure.' Bingley, I admonish you to think it over carefully. Many who meet her will want her. They will have compassion upon her for this very sad history and not care one bit that she is not a virgin. You should keep that in mind. Had she been a widow when you met her, would you think her to be ruined? Good God, man!"

Darcy looked at his friend as if to determine his thoughts. He rushed on to continue. "In fact, I warn you about Allister. Aunt Edith told me he had feelings for Elizabeth and inquired about any sisters. He is actively looking for a wife. Aunt said my letter of intent arrived just in time. I went to Cambridge with him. He is charming and will waste no time once he sees your beautiful angel. Think hard on this, my friend. I shall leave you.

"Rest well, perhaps tomorrow you shall see things differently. We should meet with them in two or three days. They may very well make Eastriggs before us. Eastriggs on Solway Firth, Bingley, is but four miles from Gretna, my friend. May God help you make this decision. Sleep well, brother."

Bingley wrung his hands. He kept staring at the door and wishing his friend would return. He would rather talk, or listen to Darcy, than think. Anything would be better than being alone with his thoughts. He rang for assistance from the mountainous manservant. He wished to bathe and go right to bed. This was something he could not decide in one evening, perhaps not in a week, a month, or even a year.

Bingley's thoughts tumbled. He began to murmur, "What would Caroline think or say? What of Louisa and Mr. Hurst? Surely they would find out, and then all of London would know. I would be shamed, how could I then rise above my father's class? Perhaps Darcy was right at Netherfield when he counseled me to wed only a woman of breeding, position, wealth and high class. Not a turned-out girl from Hertfordshire whose body has been ravaged by an Irishman!" Bingley raved aloud as he awaited his helper. At last, the mountain of a man loomed over him and assisted him. Soon he was in bed, and the port helped him go right to sleep.

Alden Mason could not stop. He rode day and night towards Dover. He wished to cross into France. He would live in Calais, well away from his family. Allister knew. Two of his servants were injured, and his plans for the design were stolen. By now they were sold to another, all due to his own fault. Alden Mason, failure in life, failure as a brother.

Stopping at the inn just outside London, he bought two bottles and then climbed back onto his mount. For a moment he thought to stop at Darcy House. He wondered if the man would remember him. Thinking it possible that Allister had written to all he knew and told them of his evil deeds, Alden pressed on through London. His horse was weary, but he needed to get out of the country.

Opening one bottle, he quickly drained the contents. His stomach growled from hunger, but he fed it only liquor. He would eat in France. Tossing the empty bottle aside, he eagerly opened the second. Drinking it empty, he tossed the second bottle and began to feel somewhat improved, ay, mellow and rested as though his rigid body was finally beginning to relax. Nodding his head, he began to sleep.

Cooper watched over his charges with an eager eye, each sleeping soundly in their hammocks. The weather was mild, their blankets were sufficient, they were in good health. His only concern was watching for thieves and mischief makers who sometimes roamed these shores.

Jane allowed herself to feel safe. It was the first time since her father's funeral that she had a glimmer of hope for a good future. Bingley had been searching for her. The intelligence thrilled her very soul. Her hopes soared, and she felt thankful to God at being given a second chance at life. Elizabeth had given her the good news. She would become Mrs. Charles Bingley.

Exhausted from their lovemaking, the Darcys slept wrapped in each other's arms. They were sound asleep when each one began to fondle the other. In his sleep Darcy climbed upon his young wife, spread her legs, and entered her for a second time that night. Elizabeth, as though wide awake, responded to him, and both quite enjoyed their wordless nocturnal joining, although neither one was aware of its happening. Reaching her ecstasy, Elizabeth clutched her husband's shoulders and cried out, "Oh, Fitzwilliam, Ay!" thus waking her husband, and, herself. Both now fully awake, were awed. Continuing what their soundly sleeping bodies began, they could not stop laughing in their delight!

"Beloved," he chuckled as he rolled to his side, "Is this not unbelievable and truly excellent? I must tell you that I have never heard of a couple loving whilst both were completely asleep. Oh, my precious wife, what love we experience for one another. I so fondly remember telling you in the butler's passageway that we have a strong physical attraction for each other."

Elizabeth could hardly control her pure joy and laughter. It lightened her heart and took away some of the anxiety she felt since her husband returned from his talk with Bingley. She knew Fitzwilliam wanted to spare her feelings. His silence on the subject when he returned from Bingley's rooms told her all she needed to know. Charles was most likely put off Jane. Elizabeth knew not to question Darcy. He would tell her his thoughts when he felt it was the proper time.

Contented and seeking sleep once again, Elizabeth whispered in the darkness. "Darling, do you remember the brief missive I wrote to Jane? I am quite angry with myself for telling her that Bingley was with us and wished to wed the moment we all entered Scotland. Oh, why did I so write?" she agonized.

Taking her hand in the darkness, he said, "Elizabeth, I require you to stop this trend of thinking. You honestly told her exactly what the man himself has been saying for months. Let us both agree right now— Bingley shall make his own decision in this matter. He alone shall decide either for or against marriage with Jane. 'Tis up to Bingley whether he exposes himself to the censure of the world for caprice and instability whilst also offering up dear Jane to its derision for disappointed hopes. Only he can make that decision. He has but a very short time in which to solidify his own mind. May God help him, for should he reject her, I fear he will not ever have a second chance." Snuggling close to him, his young wife yawned her agreement.

※

Elizabeth entered the carriage after the mountainous man had placed Bingley inside. He required much room to keep his leg in comfort. After riding several miles he asked Darcy how they would manage three more passengers, as space was somewhat limited already.

"Old chap," Darcy smiled warmly, "you raise an interesting question. The answer requires some discussion amongst the three of us. Two days ago, whilst plans were being made, I sent an express missive to Pierce at Killensworth. The second Darcy carriage awaits us at Eastriggs. My original thought was for you and Jane to occupy this carriage, and Elizabeth and I would accompany Uncle and Aunt in the second carriage. This was before I listened to you last night. Our transportation, I believe, depends upon your decision, my brother."

Before Bingley could clear his throat to respond, Elizabeth turned to her husband and asked sweetly, "Fitzwilliam, I wonder if I may have a word now?" Her husband nodded approvingly, guessing at what she was about to say. He felt it would do his friend good to hear her before he made a decision. "Charles, do you recall that night at Netherfield when your sister Caroline told a servant to falsely summon me to your study?" She waited.

It took him a moment to get the courage to look her in the eye. "Ay, Elizabeth, I do." He looked pained at the remembrance.

"I told you that night that I thought you were everything a young man ought to be, and I was very sincere. I have not said thank you for all the time, effort, resources, and emotions you have given in helping to locate my most precious sister. Mr. Crowley told Fitzwilliam that it was good she had been found because he felt she would have lived no more than one month had she been left in her current circumstances. You were a help in bringing us to this area. It was your intuition or instinct that compelled you to persuade the rest of us that she was in the Yorkshire Dales, near the water. You were correct. Please do not let me make you uneasy, but I must tell you that all of the letters Jane wrote to me contained words of respect, friendship, and love for you. In that, she was—and I am sure, is—unchanged. However, I feel certain that she is changed. My experiences changed me, and I have not suffered as she."

Bingley maintained his position as Elizabeth spoke. He occasionally looked up at her, and often held his gaze upon his hands which were in his lap. He did not reveal his emotions. She boldly continued, "Fitzwilliam's men requested that I write a missive to her, instructing her, Uncle, and Aunt to follow their lead to safety and to join us." She paused here, waiting to give him opportunity to speak if he wished. He was silent, so she concluded. Looking at her husband for courage, she said, "Charles, I wished to encourage her, yet I was told to keep my message short. I told her you had been looking for her for five months, and you wished to wed as soon as we arrived in Scotland."

Bingley jerked his head up quickly and appeared as if he wished to speak. Darcy quickly intervened. He cleared his throat, as if reminding Bingley he was in the carriage. "Old chap," Darcy began, "my wife did you no harm by telling her sister the truth. I would advise you to settle back and think. Perhaps your affections and intentions have changed, but even that cannot undo your affections, intentions, and your actions of the past. 'Tis true, you did search daily for five months, and you stated to all our family, even her younger sisters and Uncle and Aunt Gardiner, that you wished to wed Jane.

"If today you have changed your affections and intentions, I desire that you expose that to us, right now, if you please. Soon, Elizabeth and I shall be taking care of three new guests, we shall offer our homes and resources to them. They are family and in need of care. Elizabeth and I shall happily provide all they need because we love them. They will live with us at Pemberly and be blessings to us. Jane will be welcome also, should you have no desire to love, honour and keep her unto yourself, my friend. Are you prepared to tell us? Shall we be your brother and sister, or not?"

Tears welled up in Bingley's eyes. He looked at his hands, still clasped firmly in his lap. "Darcy, I cannot find my mind in this thing. You, of all people, know what strong emotions she evoked in me. I told you that my wife was brought to my doorstep at Netherfield. Now, I cannot bring myself to think of marrying her after her...problems, yet I cannot think of living my life without her."

"Bingley that shall not do, what think you of marriage? Did you not listen to the service when you attended me? The third reason to wed is to become a community with your wife and help her as she requires, and she to assist you when your needs arise."

Elizabeth spoke one last time, asking Darcy, "Darling, may I add something, please?"

Darcy was filled with pride. His wife respected his relationship with his best friend and did not intrude upon them. Should he decline her request, he knew she would not be angry. Admiring her wisdom, he invited her words. "Please my love, feel at your ease to speak. We know you greatly value Charles and are devoted to your elder sister."

"Thank you, my husband. I simply wished to speak to a practical matter. Quite obviously Charles shall require space in a carriage. We must address his need for proper healing and his comfort, of course. I do, however, wish to point out that dear Jane has suffered greatly. We do not know her physical condition. And, as I am beginning to understand, even without your saying it, Charles, Jane's rescue will not have the happy ending of her dreams. She is the most forgiving of women. She will be the first to wish you comfort and happiness, think only the very best of you, and make it easy for you to be in her presence. However, just at the moment of meeting her and taking her to Killensworth, I hope, Fitzwilliam, we could offer her transportation that does not make it necessary for her to suffer the agony of being with Charles. I am sure she will feel embarrassment and would not wish to think she is forcing Charles to be kind to her. Fitzwilliam, please consider our travel needs and come to a decision. I somehow feel that Cooper has nearly arrived at his port, and we shall be reunited very soon."

Seeing an inn ahead, she asked, "Fitzwilliam, shall we stop for a hot meal? It would be heavenly to stretch my legs, and I am sure our friend Charles would enjoy some time to himself. A hot meal would do us all good, would it not, my love?"

When they stopt at the inn, Elizabeth turned to Charles before being handed down from the carriage. "Dear Charles, you are still everything a young man ought to be. Your decision changes your life forever, not our affection for and devotion to you, dear friend." Smiling, she headed for the inn, holding her small reading and writing box. She had an important and urgent missive to send.

Elizabeth entered and requested some time to write an urgent letter to their aunt. Darcy thought it a very good idea and she sat down at one of the small tables. He stood behind her chair as Bingley was being carried into a private room to tend his needs. They would all meet together in the common-room shortly.

Lake District
28 October 1801

Dearest Aunt,

My, I have sorely missed my surrogate mother. I have many times tried to imagine what your words of wisdom would be for me. Knowing that we shall see you very soon, I shall wait and eagerly hear you for myself.

We spoke of two possible outcomes for dear Jane. I fear a third horrible event has occurred. When I see you, I shall disclose all, but for the shortness of this missive, may I ask that you come to our assistance now, please?

I must enlist your help in the planning and the preparations of rooms for three very important guests. Jane will require her own rooms, Bingley will remain in those he previously occupied. Our great uncle Albert and great aunt Elsie will require rooms. In addition to this, might we ask that you have a surgeon at Killensworth as we arrive? If possible, the man should plan to attend for a few days, so he will need rooms as well. I am also afraid I must impose upon your modiste for our sister Jane and our great aunt. They and our great uncle were compelled to leave their home with only the clothes upon their backs.

Fitzwilliam has approved my requests, Aunt. He sends his love along with mine. Thank you for all you do for us.

God keep you safe, F. D. and E. D.

PS—I am well and very healthy. You are so wonderful!

Darcy smiled as he read the letter. Elizabeth fit so very well in his family and lifestyle. He approved of her words and actions, and although he was curious about her postscript, he thought it best not to inquire.

Darcy sent the express and returned to escort his wife into the common-room. Just as they approached the door, he spotted Spencer and Collot finishing their meal. It was not unusual that the two on horseback arrived at the inn before the carriage. Extremely eager to speak with them, and to hear of all the events, he installed Elizabeth next to Bingley and excused himself. Along with his men, he quit the common-room and went out to the horses, tied behind the inn. The topic and related details they would discuss must not be overheard.

Cooper was amazed at the progress they had made. Landfall was close, yet his passengers were breaking his heart; they acted as if he would beat them at any given moment. It made him wonder what the three of them had endured for so many months. Proud to have a part in their rescue, he held it an honour to have been a help to Miss Bennet. Surely she was the most beautiful woman he had ever seen, much less spoken to, although he must tell no one his thoughts. "At the rate we are moving, Cooper said, "We should make Eastriggs by late afternoon. If we continue, we could have our meal there as soon as we arrive and set up our camp. Or, if you are hungry now, we can stop and eat, making our camp along those trees."

Albert MacDougal found his voice, "Mr. Cooper, I think it best if we reach Scotland as soon as possible. We are a family eager to put the past behind us, sir."

"Ay, well enough, Mr. MacDougal. Please remember then, drink the water, will you not?" The three drank eagerly, but once again would do nothing until Cooper gave them permission.

⁂

Darcy told his men there would be a bonus for them, he was so pleased to hear their report. He asked them to rush to Eastriggs and watch for the craft to come to shore. He also requested that Spencer obtain rooms for them and secure the carriage being sent from Killensworth. He ordered him to hire lady's maids for Jane and Aunt, and a man to serve Uncle. They were to purchase whatever was needed for the three. A few new articles of excellent clothing and new coats must be had; Elizabeth would see to the rest when she arrived. He advised they use the best modiste and purchase beautiful gowns for the two women and several new suits of clothing for Uncle.

Darcy was in the best of moods when he returned to the common-room. Elizabeth felt a sudden rush of relief and could not wait to hear all. Eagerly he told them the good news. The solutions reached for the Breslin men would never be revealed to Elizabeth or anyone else.

"How soon should we arrive at Eastriggs, darling?" Elizabeth asked most eagerly.

Darcy smiled at her. "Spencer told me we shall be another four days. Carriages move slowly, my love. We must employ our patience and be thankful they are safe."

Elizabeth began fidgeting in her chair. She watched her husband's facial expressions, and listened with great interest, yet she remembered Aunt told her strictly not to ask him how he solved her sister's problem.

Her beautiful sparkling eyes displayed her gratitude and respect. She could not hide her complete admiration for her beloved husband.

Taking pity on his wife, he offered, "Shall I tell you the basic story?"

"Oh, please," she said. Bingley remained silent, looking quite embarrassed.

"Very well, Spencer told me they never would have found the farm without the benefit of Jane's directions." Bingley looked up and acted as if he would speak, but dropped his head once more.

"Upon reaching the lane leading to the farm, they spotted Jane leading a stray cow towards the barn. They were grateful to have a few moments to speak with her before they saw Uncle and Aunt. Collot remarked upon the beauty of the farm; however, he related that it needed care. He mentioned the house seemed as if there was something amiss." Squeezing his wife's hand, he smiled at her and continued. "The men were also glad to have your missive, Elizabeth. Jane read it and then inquired as to their requirements of her. Spencer said she acted quickly and was more than a competent help with Uncle and Aunt. Both men remarked that all three left hurriedly and did not make one request to take anything with them, nor did they object to leaving everything. All three climbed into the wagon without difficulty, even Aunt. They made it to the pram with haste and Cooper was ready to make way as soon as they were aboard. Spencer and Collot watched the pram get underway very quickly. Jane, Uncle, and Aunt sat with their backs to the shore. None looked back."

Here, Darcy debated about whether he would tell of Kieran. He searched Bingley's face and continued. He knew Elizabeth would hear without difficulty and would never tell Jane. She had proved that to him months earlier in the library at Netherfield. Elizabeth would do nothing to cause Jane distress. Darcy continued, "what happened next was shocking. The second brother, Kieran, galloped to the dock upon the grey."

Bingley looked into Darcy's eyes here, and Elizabeth gasped sharply and squeezed his hand. Her eyes grew wide with fear.

Darcy hastened on, "He leaped off his horse, forgetting to tie the animal. Running to the small dock, he jumped into a drifter."

Elizabeth stopped his narrative. "Sorry darling, what is that, if you please?" she asked.

Darcy smiled at her beautiful face. "'Tis a small fishing boat that uses only the tides to move about," he answered. "The little boat moved very slowly. Kieran then pulled a pistol from his pants and extended it over the water to shoot. There were no bullets in the gun, for our men had previously removed them all at the same time they recovered the letters."

Bingley's face revealed shock and relief. Gasping, Elizabeth looked down, unable to fathom anyone on earth wanting to kill her precious sister.

Her husband put his hand gently upon her shoulder, in a quiet gesture of comfort. "When the tide returned the drifter to its place, Kieran stepped to the dock and made to pass Spencer and Collot. They detained and questioned him. He confessed that it was he who had beaten Jane. He spotted her in the village upon her first month at the farm. He then forced Uncle to pay him fairly large sums of money to ensure that he would leave Jane unmolested. Uncle continued to pay this extortion until all his savings were exhausted."

"How horrible!" Elizabeth nearly cried out, she caught herself and kept her voice low. Bingley looked at Darcy but made no comment. Darcy continued, "Collot canvassed the neighboring farms and learned that these evil men extorted monies from numerous families. It seems that Jane was not their only victim, darling."

Darcy slowly shook his head and said, "During this time, the youngest brother began to 'work' for Uncle. This means he came to the farm every day and spied upon them. Each evening when he left he would 'pay' himself a wage by taking something from them. Food, clothing, candles, and whatever else he could procure. Kieran came about once a week. When the money was gone, Uncle gave him livestock. All the horses and cows were given, the pigs went next, and at last the chickens. Spencer said they had taken nearly everything and in his view, the three would have lived about a month more without assistance. Collot questioned many neighbors, and no one would help our family against those evil brothers. Even the magistrate refused to provide protection and would not prosecute the men."

Elizabeth took her husband's hand and kissed it. She did not care that they were in public. "Oh, my wonderful husband, you are the best of men. You and your men have saved three lives. And, thank you, too, Charles. Without you, she would not have been found. They all would have perished. What a cruel and senseless death they would have suffered." Looking at Fitzwilliam she cried, "Oh darling, we never would have known what had become of them. I am so thankful to God for saving them."

"Darcy, that is an amazing story, your men are skillful. What happened to the three brothers?" Charles asked passionately, suddenly caught up in the horrible drama.

Elizabeth spoke up. "Charles, I feel it is not important to ask that question. Is it not enough that our family is saved? I would rather we never speak of those terrible men. They do not deserve the breath we spend with our inquiry. Let us use our breath to praise Mr. Spencer, Mr. Collot, and Mr. Cooper. All three are heroes."

Darcy was extremely pleased with Elizabeth. He very much admired her response. Her protection of his methods filled him with pride. She knew the perpetrators deserved any punishment that was given, and she safeguarded the secrecy of his methods. Quick thinking caused her to speak the praise of his men who had saved Jane and her Uncle and Aunt. They returned to their carriage and pressed on with rested horses and rested minds, all but Bingley—his mind was not at ease with itself.

Sergeant Hunter was getting sleepy. He had been called to duty when Sergeant Post took ill. It was Hunter's job to check off property listed and attempt to send it to the next of kin. His eyes fell upon the next name: Alden Mason, deceased. Cause of death, fall from his horse. He had been riding during the dark of night. Having no funds upon his person, the army would keep the horse and saddle to pay for his burial. Finding a partially written letter in his coat pocket, they sent notification of his death to the addressee.

Georgiana, Mary, and Kitty giggled as they watched the old bed being removed from Fitzwilliam's room. They had heard the story of Caroline Bingley's shameful removal from Pemberly after a maid found her sleeping in Fitzwilliam's bed. All the girls wondered little at the installation of a brand-new bed.

Looking at the letters they had just received that morning, Georgiana offered to read hers first. Thinking it was from Fitzwilliam only, she squealed with delight when a missive from Elizabeth fell out onto the floor. Mary and Kitty were ready to read their letters next. All of the missives told of the wedding, Allister and Aunt Edith, Hannah, Monty and baby Elizabeth. They told of their plans to find the MacDougal farm and search for Jane. Read together, they told a wonderful story. Mrs. Reynolds prepared a party celebrating the newly connected sisterhood of the young ladies. They were all jubilant knowing that now they were, indeed, real sisters. Now they awaited the return of the Darcys and Jane and Charles.

It was noon at Eastriggs. Cooper watched over the camp and kept an eye out for Spencer and Collot. He knew that the men would reach him before Mr. Darcy, and within minutes of his first watch, the two rode into camp, with a Darcy carriage following them. Jane greeted the two by name and Mr. and Mrs. MacDougal stood. Spencer thought this was a very good sign. He had feared that Jane would be suffering emotionally.

The carriage collected the three of them. They offered Cooper heartfelt thanks and then eagerly embarked upon the short ride to the inn. It was a small yet very accommodating inn. To Jane and her uncle and aunt, it felt like heaven.

Once in her rooms, Jane threw herself upon the bed and wept. She was so grateful to be rescued after her five-month-long nightmare. A slight tap upon her door brought her back to the present and she happily admitted the lady's maid into her room. An offer to go to the modiste and obtain a few new gowns and a new coat was more than she could refuse. Jane and Aunt went happily to the shop and each received three beautiful gowns and a new coat. Uncle was taken in hand by a valet and received three new suits and a new coat. They looked very handsome and prosperous. No one new to their acquaintance would guess their recent tragedy. The delicious fare provided at the inn was nourishing and helped them to recover their strength. It took some effort for the three to realise that the food was available to them at any time. They had been forced to nearly starve for several months. The following days passed quickly and all three slept deeply and dreamlessly each night. The nightmare was over.

Chapter Seven

"I MUST NOT DECIDE ON MY OWN PERFORMANCE."
–JANE AUSTEN

As the Darcy carriage finally arrived at the Eastriggs Inn, Elizabeth could scarcely contain her enthusiasm. She nearly pulled Darcy by the hand. Upon entering the salon she spotted Jane seated by the fire next to a handsome couple who could have been a couple of fashion. Uncle and Aunt MacDougal were thankful for the clothes; both knew the only clothing they had possessed was shabby and horribly behindhand.

Elizabeth rushed into Jane's arms. The two held each other for many minutes. Neither girl cried, instead they laughed. This was Lizzy's doing—she told Jane to laugh, not cry, for that was her plan. Jane joined her laughter. Elizabeth turned Jane toward Darcy, "Here is your new brother, Jane. Is he not wonderful?"

"Mr. Darcy, how shall we ever thank you for saving all our lives?" Jane began.

Darcy cut her off, "My dear sister Jane, you must call me Fitzwilliam now—we are family."

Jane smiled at this, and simply said, "Brother, my thanks forever!" Jane looked extraordinary, indeed. Her lady's maid had revived her beauty, and the new gown was perfect. She looked as flawless as she did when Bingley last saw her. Still unable to bear body weight, he called out, "Jane! My darling angel, Jane, I am not yet able to walk but would you consent to come to see me, please?"

This took Darcy and Elizabeth by surprise. Both thought it was Jane's appearance that persuaded him to propose to their sister. They watched Jane cross the room to Bingley. Then the Darcys joined Uncle and Aunt, allowing some privacy for the young couple as they reunited.

Elizabeth approached the MacDougals. "Do you remember the little imp, Lizzy? It is I, your Lizzy, the little girl who would not milk the cows but wanted to ride them." All three laughed at this, even Darcy who was now bowing to his new uncle and aunt. They were very attractive people and made a handsome couple. Darcy was most impressed to hear Uncle talk of his farm. They spoke with energy and knowledge on many farm related topics. Before all the trouble followed Jane into their lives, Uncle was a very successful farmer, using modern methods.

A manservant moved Bingley, and the six went into the common-room to enjoy a family dinner. Elizabeth could not take her eyes off Jane, and Darcy could not take his eyes off Elizabeth. Jane seemed to be fully recovered and even Uncle and Aunt were mending from their ordeal. Charles could not stop looking at Jane. He smiled at her, asked after her comfort in all things, and kept apologizing for his broken limb. She was attentive to him, and her eyes sparkled at his attentions. At the conclusion of the meal, Bingley looked at everyone, then said, "My darling Jane, my angel, I cannot get on my knees, but, forgiving me that, please say that you shall marry me tomorrow in Gretna." He pulled a small box from his coat pocket, and opening it, gave it to Jane. In a most pleasing voice, Jane looked into his eyes and said, "My darling Charles, I confess before my family that I adore you, most ardently. You consumed my daily thoughts and not one night was spent without dreaming of the day I would see you again. Nothing would make me happier than to say 'ay' immediately, yet I fear we must discuss many things before we should take such a step as you offer. Oh, Charles, my answer breaks my heart." Jane's voice trailed off and she looked as though she might faint.

Each family member quit the room to give them privacy, knowing that Bingley was unable to leave the table on his own. The Darcys, along with

Uncle and Aunt, went into the salon and used the opportunity to become better acquainted.

Once they were alone, Charles began, "Darling Jane, Mr. Crowley attended me when I broke my leg. Someday I shall tell you of the events that caused the break." Reaching into his pocket, he withdrew her likeness and showed her, explaining that Darcy had drawn it, as he did of each sister. She held it for some time, wondering how many people he had shown it to and asked for their assistance.

"One morning, Mr. Crowley saw your likeness, with your ring sitting on top. He guessed who I was to you."

Silently Jane looked into Charles' eyes. He started again, "Dearest Jane, I know all. How I wish with all my heart I could go back in time and take you from Hertfordshire to Pemberly with me. Darcy and I have both declared it hundreds of times. Oh, that I could have spared you everything you suffered. But, I cannot, and I have not the power to change your past. Yet I do have the power to offer you a good future, a better and a brighter future, my Jane. I beg you to allow me to make each day better than the previous. Please be my wife, spend all of the days to come with me. It is my vision to buy an estate, we could purchase in Derbyshire and live near the Darcys. Shall we not marry in the morning, my lovely Jane?"

Tears coursed down her beautiful face. "Charles, were it only that simple. Are you sure you could forgive me my sufferings? Would I not bring shame upon you?"

"Jane, my angel, how could beatings and acts of violence bring shame upon us? You are innocent. Those evil acts of a selfish man shall not keep us from living a happy life. How can we give him power over our lives? You and Uncle and Aunt are safely away now, and nothing more can harm you. Please say that you shall be my wife tomorrow morning. We shall be married whilst sitting in chairs, because I cannot yet stand. In fact, I suspect it shall be several weeks before I can worship you with my body, my dear. Would you forgive me that?"

"Ay," she whispered into his ear, "if you shall be patient with me as well."

Bingley wasted no time in taking the ring from the box and placing it upon her finger. "I should like to kiss you, if only we were not in public. Please come to my rooms with me."

Jane nodded. "I shall of course. Shall I call our family to rejoin us and celebrate our good news? Tonight, when all retire, I shall join you."

Elizabeth was the first to reach the couple. She threw her arms around Jane and told her how happy she wished the two of them in their life as man and wife. Darcy shook Bingley's hand and said how wonderful it would be to have him as a real brother. Uncle and Aunt were pleased and felt honest relief to see their favorite niece so happy in her new circumstances. It was consoling, that Bingley would love Jane. They felt they knew the man, she had told them so very much about him.

***

Cooper completed the sale of the pram. He was pleased that the price he settled upon brought a profit for Mr. Darcy. Meeting Spencer and Collot, he mounted his horse and rode with them into Gretna. The three would make certain all was well for the ceremony. A cleric of the Church of England was notified and the time of service was reserved. Collot also arranged for a wedding breakfast at the most luxurious banquet hall in town. Spencer sent an express to Pierce at Killensworth detailing the wedding and requesting Lady Hamilton be informed immediately. All was done as Mr. Darcy directed.

***

Elizabeth and Fitzwilliam almost raced to their rooms! They had so much to say to each other, they were ready to burst forth with an explosion of verbosity. "Mrs. Darcy, your words to Bingley in the carriage, and your willingness to defer to my permission to speak to him at all, pleased me quite well. You, Elizabeth Darcy are the perfect wife for me! Your letter to Aunt, with your gentle directives to her, yet under my authority, were all quite pleasing. Your staunch prevention of Bingley's inquiry about the application of certain punishments was completely brilliant, my love! You understand me, you approve of me, and most important, you love me, sweet Elizabeth Darcy. You are perfect and I cannot deny that I am so in love with you, Elizabeth that I quite fawn over you. You captivate me, darling!" He placed his arms around her and drew her near.

She smiled knowingly, yet it turned to laughter, she was so pleased with his praise. "Now, it is my turn to tell you what an excellent husband you are, Mr. Darcy. Your expert understanding of how to solve each problem causes me to give you my unending trust and total appreciation. I admired the words I heard you speak to Bingley, and can only imagine the wonderful wisdom you gave him whilst in the privacy of his rooms. You kept me safe during our trip and saw to my total comforts and well-being. You keep me in a perpetual state of craving your love and thrilling to your affections when you bestow them. To look at you is to hunger for you to love me, and I live for each morning when I awake to loving you most passionately!

"You directed your men to make our inn accommodations secure and you ordered the engagement of the lady's maids, a valet, and approved their shopping for the wonderful clothes and coats. The three of them looked fetchingly beautiful and well-rested. Our dear sister Jane, looked as lovely as she did the last time Bingley saw her, and I feel certain that was more than a little responsible for his reaction to her." Elizabeth finished her lavish praises and laced her fingers around Darcy's neck. She took his lips into her own and kissed him with much passion. Mr. and Mrs. Darcy communicated quite easily with each other, and words were no longer necessary.

Jane lightly tapped upon Bingley's door, then entered. Her beloved was lying atop his bed, wearing his breeches and a linen shirt. She took a moment for her eyes to become accustomed to the firelight in his room. He called to her softly, and she turned toward the direction of his voice. "Charles? It is so dark in here. My eyes are not yet adjusted to the firelight. Please speak to me again, my dear." Following the sound of his voice, she located the bed, just as her eyes were able to focus and see his face. She went immediately to his bedside and asked if she could sit without disturbing his leg. She did not wish to cause him discomfort.

Charles patted the bed where he wished her to join him. She removed her slippers and climbed onto the bed beside him. "Is this what you wanted, dearest?" she asked him sweetly.

He smiled at her and said, "Please be at ease, Jane. I shall not be ungentlemanly with you. In fact, I am quite certain that even tomorrow I shall be unable to love you. I must have at least six weeks for healing. Apparently one's femur is an unfortunate choice of bone to break. It is quite large and healing takes some time."

Understanding, she said, "Please tell me if I do anything to cause you pain, Charles. I should like to help you, not hinder your healing, my dearest."

"Oh, Jane, please allow me to kiss you," he begged with such devotion in his eyes. At once Jane was back at Netherfield. She was not ill at ease; she relaxed and allowed Bingley to take control of her person. They kissed, tenderly, gently, and sweetly. Both became lost in their affection. Jane felt not one trace of Kieran's touch. She felt only her Charles. Charles thought only of his beautiful angel, in his arms at last.

Quietly they planned the next few weeks and then discussed buying an estate in Derbyshire. Jane slept soundly with her head upon Charles's shoulder. Bingley was persuaded he had chosen wisely.

Down the hallway, the Darcys settled between the sheets on their bed, both feeling very pleased with their loving. Elizabeth asked Fitzwilliam what she could do for him to show her appreciation for all he had done, and was currently doing, for her grateful family. Supporting herself on one elbow, she looked into her husband's eyes and saw them shining with excitement. "Do you mean this, Elizabeth, or is it just a casual question?"

"With all my heart, I desire to do something special for you, darling. Just name what you would enjoy, please Fitzwilliam?" Considering what she might think of him if he told her, he decided to risk her good opinion of him. Yet he took his time answering, so much so that she became impatient.

"Fitzwilliam? I am waiting to hear. We shall plan immediately unless, of course, it is something I may do now." She offered in sincerity. "Please, my love?" "Darling," he began, "we have a charming little fishing lodge at Killensworth. It is a small, two story lodge with about twenty rooms. It is located on the estate about six miles from the house." He spoke all this slowly, watching her facial expressions with great care. "I have a fondness for it because I designed it and supervised all of the construction. It is about nine years old. There are ten fireplaces, it is warm and cozy and each room is cheerful. I am sorry to say it has had very little use at all."

Trying to help him get on with his wishes, she offered, "Oh, darling, of course I shall stay there with you. Do you desire us to fish?"

Gathering his courage, he continued. From out of nowhere, he found the pluckiness to say, "Nay, my charming Elizabeth, we shall not fish. 'Tis too cold outdoors now, I desire for us to remain inside and spend one week alone together, my love."

Elizabeth smiled widely at her husband. He was beginning to relax. She reached over and kissed his cheek saying, "That sounds so wonderful, Fitzwilliam! I shall adore one week to ourselves. Due to my family's trials, we have suffered and been denied time alone. How wonderful, darling. I am so eager, how soon shall we go?"

"Elizabeth, I must finish my request," he said slowly, with a particular sweetness to entreat her. "I wish for the two of us to spend one week together at the lodge and be completely naked day and night. I wish us to copulate as much as we both desire, and perform any and all other acts of love, as we both consent, of course. Do you think your husband eccentric, my bride?"

Elizabeth shocked Darcy. She began to laugh, she kissed him hard on his lips and nearly shouted, "Darling, I would love that! I can hardly wait to look upon your beautiful body for an entire week. I shall memorize its planes, the shapes of your firm masculine muscles and of course, your manhood. What a wonderful opportunity to look upon you day and night without cumbersome clothing, to touch you and handle you whenever I am inspired to do so. And you have already given your permission for me to do whatever I desire at any time of my choosing. Oh the advantages of our bareness! However did you think of this, beloved?"

He could not tell her that she was the third woman he had thus invited. The other two women about whom he was serious thought him an impractical lunatic. With each woman, he had been certain they would accept the offer, but neither did. He had suffered so much ridicule from Suzette and Ellen that it was difficult to summon the courage to ask it of Elizabeth. Once again, her love and devotion was proved to him. In addition, also confirmed were their evenly matched sexual appetites.

With much joy, he took her in his arms and whispered in her ear, "It has been a long standing fantasy, beloved. It will be just the first week of our honeymoon. I am honoured and so pleased that you wish to make my dream come true."

"Fitzwilliam, I thought you knew, I wish to make all of your dreams come true."

Chapter Eight

"THE PERIOD OF EXPECTATION WAS NOW DOUBLED."
–JANE AUSTEN

A lbert and Elsie MacDougal got down upon their knees by their bed. The two thanked God again for releasing them and their precious Jane from the clutches of evil. The couple asked blessings upon Fitzwilliam and his wonderful men. They agreed to pray for each man every single day for as long as God provided them with life. The two looked forward to the trip to Pemberly which would take them to the new life Fitzwilliam and Elizabeth had described to them.

It was four o'clock in the morning and the Darcys had been sleeping soundly. Elizabeth gave a start and sat upright, weeping bitterly. Fitzwilliam sat straight up in bed, "Are you well, Elizabeth?" he asked, thinking perhaps she'd had a bad dream.

Staring directly at him and shaking from head to toe, she asked, "Oh, beloved, may I tell you my dream, please?" she begged with tears running down her cheeks. "It had three parts. The first part was completely wonderful. It was the wedding of Charles and Jane. We were all six seated in the chapel and the cleric, Mr. Brown, conducted a beautiful service. You stood up with Charles, and I with Jane. Uncle gave the bride away, and we were all so very happy."

Trying to calm her down, Fitzwilliam, said reassuringly, "That sounds beautiful, Elizabeth. There is nothing to fear, my love. It will be a beautiful wedding, dearest."

"Husband, there is more. After the ceremony we went to a place that was prearranged for us. There was terrible violence. The owner, a Mr. Young, had agreed with four men in white coats—they were acting as though they were servers, but in reality they had guns under their coats. And as we sat eating, they took their weapons out and shot all of us! We trusted them, we thought they were there to serve us, and they shot us. Oh, Fitzwilliam, it hurt so terribly. I was shot in my stomach, and it was so painful I knew I could not live. One of the men took my ring off my finger. Just after that, I saw Aunt Edith and Allister. They were holding a black-edged envelope, and they were crying because Alden was dead. I cried, too, because I knew that they were about to get another envelope telling of our deaths."

Fitzwilliam tried to console Elizabeth. She would not allow him to hold her, or tell her it was only a dream. She looked him in the eyes, "Darling, I know just because the dream I told you about at Killensworth did not come true, you think this dream does not have any validity. I do not know how I know, but it is a warning to us. At the end of the dream, I was flying and looking down, I saw birds picking the flesh of a man tied to a tree limb. It was an awful dream warning me of the feast of the birds."

Fitzwilliam did not know what to say. He remembered how her dream kept him out of trouble at Killensworth. This was a disturbing dream, to be sure. Again, the first part was wonderful and they desired it to come to pass. But the last parts were calamity. Most of all, the last vision of the man being eaten by birds whilst tied to a tree limb rang true. There was no way that Elizabeth could have known about Kieran. He was beginning to look upon this dream as a warning specifically given to avert disaster. He silently wondered if Aunt and Allister had received a death notice. Not wanting to take any chances with their security, he said, "Darling girl, I shall dress right now and call for Collot and Spencer, they shall alert Cooper as well.

Please be patient with me and detail the dream once more, especially the part about Mr. Young."

Elizabeth sat up and dried her eyes. She threw her arms around her husband and whispered, "Oh, you are listening to me, thank you so much, my wonderful husband."

"Yes, my sweet girl, I shall always listen to you. The things that are serious to you will always be serious to me. Now, slowly from the beginning, tell me the dream again, take extra care to remember everything about Mr. Young."

Elizabeth retold the horrible crimes. She remembered that robbery was the motive but all were shot. Their family along with his three trusted men. Hearing all he needed, he dressed quickly and set out to find his men. The time was now five o'clock. His men were dressed and having breakfast in the common-room. The three stood to their feet when Fitzwilliam entered the room. He nodded for them to sit and eat and ordered a coffee. He inquired of Spencer to tell him of the day, starting with the plans for the wedding, the breakfast, and the balance of the day.

"Mr. Darcy, all is happily arranged for a wonderful day. The cleric for the Church of England at Gretna is a Mr. Brown. He is a friendly and helpful man, very professional. All will remain seated during the service, as he understands Mr. Bingley's special needs. Darcy felt a shock as he heard the name of Mr. Brown. Elizabeth named the man from her dream, one completely unknown to her in this life. Darcy nodded, and Spencer continued. "We have contracted for a wedding breakfast with a wonderful man named Mr. Young. Interestingly enough, sir, he seemed to know your name and that of Killensworth. We looked at his premises and he has ample room, and told us he would have sufficient help. We informed him it would be a party of nine but he insisted that he take on an additional four men to ensure your complete satisfaction. Be assured that his establishment is the most luxurious in Gretna. After this, we travel home to Killensworth, sir, reaching there just before sundown."

Looking at his men, Darcy took a deep breath. Without revealing his source, he began to tell them of certain disturbing intelligence he had just received. He related that two names had just been given to him. Mr. Brown, the cleric, who has been declared harmless; and Mr. Young, who was named as a deadly threat.

Collot and Spencer looked at each other with skepticism, they wondered who this source might be and doubted the reliability of this intelligence. "I have it on the best authority," Darcy declared, "that Mr. Young has four men who will serve in white coats, under which will be concealed weapons. Their motive is robbery, yet their plan is to kill all nine of us. I shall disclose that this report is genuine and valid. I am afraid that I am not at liberty to reveal the source, yet upon your investigation, be assured it shall be verified as accurate in its exact detail."

Spencer and Collot exchanged glances, and Spencer spoke, "Mr. Darcy, tell us what you wish from us, sir."

Looking at his men he smiled and explained, "You men are my experts. I rely upon your judgment in all matters. We certainly have the expectation of surprise where these unsavory men are concerned. They have no reason to presume their plans have been made known to us. Therefore, take a few moments to confer and offer your plan to me. I intend to support you vigorously."

Darcy stood and walked out to the salon. He stretched his arms upward and then stood a few moments in prayer. He thanked God for Elizabeth's dream. He went back into the common-room and took a sip of his coffee.

Spencer leaned towards him and said in a low voice, "Mr. Darcy, we shall ride to Gretna and check out these men. There is time to do a silent inquiry, learn of their quarters, and then question the men themselves. Experience has taught that men of a certain ilk have similar habits. We shall get to the truth of this threat. Shall we dispense the regular resolution, should we find they are planning events as you stated? We should not allow them to resume their plans upon another day, sir. Do you not agree?"

"Ay," Darcy affirmed, "Do all that you deem best. We shall divert our wedding breakfast to the Gretna Inn. This shall be without notice upon that establishment. There is no reason to open ourselves to additional risks."

Rising to leave them, he suddenly thought to inquire, "Spencer, what news from Killensworth and Edinburgh? Is all well with Allister Mason and my Aunt Edith?"

Instantly blanching, Spencer apologized, "Mr. Darcy, please forgive me, sir, that I allowed this to slip my mind. I take full responsibility for the lapse. I regret to inform you that just yesterday morning her Ladyship received a black-bordered envelope from London. It seems that His Majesty's Army has recovered the body of Mr. Alden Mason and buried him. He had not the funds for burial upon his person, and in lieu of this payment, the army retained his mount and tack. He took a fall from his horse whilst riding at night, sir. This is all I know of the matter, Mr. Darcy."

Darcy wore a look of shock, which his men believed to be bereavement. He slowly shook his head and then told them, "I warn each of you. Do not take my information lightly. The intelligence I have given you is true, and these men are very dangerous. Take extra caution as you approach and deal with these malefactors. They are not servants, as they wish you to believe. Their deadly weapons are concealed, yet at their ready. I can spare none of you, and I promise you will want to live to enjoy your bonuses!" With that he quit the common-room and hurried up the stairs to deliver the news to his wife.

Jane awoke before Charles. He was so content; he looked as though both legs were sound. His face no longer wore the look of intense pain and suffering. Charles had his angel at last and he had held her tightly all night long.

Not knowing the time, yet wishing to quit his rooms and go to her own, Jane kissed her beloved's cheek. She whispered her love and devotion to him and said she was eager to become his wife in just a few brief hours. As she attempted to roll out of bed, Charles caught her hand and pulled her back towards him. He smiled at her and wished her a good morning and a happy wedding day. He kissed her lips before she had an opportunity to respond. Finally able to speak, she explained that soon her uncle and aunt would call on her for coffee. She had to go prepare for the day. Uncle and Aunt were early risers and would be up early for a head start on the day. She kissed her fiancé and set out for her own rooms.

Darcy had just entered the hall when he caught a glimpse of Jane leaving Bingley's room. He smiled and bit his lip to keep from laughing aloud. He could hardly wait to tell Elizabeth. It was a confirmation of the good work the two of them had done to keep the pair together.

Spencer, Collot and Cooper rapidly covered the distance to Gretna. The men quietly entered Mr. Young's banquet facility by the back door. They could hear many voices, sounding together, quite like those in a tavern. Soon a most interesting oration began to take place in the kitchen. Some of the voices seemed familiar, possibly even identifiable.

A deep voice was beginning to underscore the several other male voices talking together. "Bartlett," the bass voice was commanding, " you shall act as the head servant. All will be as usual during the first two courses. Take your time, do everything right. The last thing we desire is someone becoming nervous, making a mistake, and alerting them to the fact that you are not servants. Next—just as the dishes are being removed from the table, the four of us and Mr. Young will open fire upon the nine. Be sure to go for the trained and armed men first. You have the element of surprise in your favour, take your time and aim for the forehead, follow that with one shot straight into the heart. Include Mr. Darcy in that group— the man is lethal. If you did not know, Darcy is trained in all the arts of self-defense. He is always armed and is an expert marksman. Once you have removed these men, be sure you get a clean kill on the others. We do not need to have anyone acting as witnesses for the magistrate, and then later for the courts. Take your time, use your heads, and do the job the right way. You are professionals, after all. One more thing, I need to determine which of you will shoot and kill Mrs. Darcy and her sister. These are beautiful young women so if any of you has a problem with putting a bullet into such a forehead, let me know now. We cannot afford one moment of hesitation. A voice from group spoke up: "Ay, leave them to me. I have no problem with killing such women. No character— never done a day's work in their lives— they have no idea what it is to be hungry— ay— it will take me no time to shoot both of the worthless ladies, lad." There was some course laughter, then the bass voice answered, "Ay, and do you best, Douglass. I thank you. Now, to finish up so you can all go and prepare for a successful day: Remember that Pierce at Killensworth will have his part as well. At exactly the same time, eleven o'clock, Pierce will enter the house and bring all those present into the grand salon, shoot them, and take as much of the wealth as he and his men can carry. If Lady Hamilton is on the property she will be taken hostage. Her nephews will pay a large ransom for her release. That money goes into the pot, too." This brought much laughter. Many voices began uttering curses to emphasize the large amount of money which would be divided between the men. They laughed at the fact that the wealthy always became a target for those who are smarter and better. The men listened to their leader, who continued with his instructions for the day. "Mrs. Darcy has a very valuable wedding ring. Douglass, be sure to get that off her finger after the kill. Do not forget."

Darcy's men listened, knowing that their lives, and those they protect, depended upon this opportunity to gather intelligence. Spencer and Collot thought the speaker sounded like a footman called Martin who was employed at Killensworth. They estimated that there were five armed men in the kitchen—too many for them to rush. Spencer put one finger in the air and then pointed to Collot. He motioned for the man to go around to the front of the establishment and hide by the door. Collot did as he was directed. Cooper was sent to the back door and stood silently as indicated. Spencer pulled his knife and waited in the dining-room. He was not disappointed. One man came through the kitchen door and entered the dining-room. As he did, Spencer placed his hand over the man's mouth and silently slid the blade of his knife under the sternum and into his heart causing him to bleed to death rapidly and silently. Then, Spencer quietly rolled the body under a table, and concealed it with the floor-length tablecloth.

Cooper stood quietly at his post, and within minutes a short, stocky man came out the door. Just as Spencer had done, Cooper put his hand over the short man's mouth to keep him silent and then using his knife, he drew the point from ear to ear. With his throat cut, the man slumped to the ground, where he bled to death. Cooper rolled his body behind a hedge. A moment later, a third man came out. He seemed to be looking for the first, but he did not call out. Shorter than Cooper, he was handled in a similar manner and placed behind the same hedge.

Collot crouched with his knife drawn, and did not wait long before he saw someone approach. He was about the same size as Collot, yet not suspecting any difficulty he was not alert to any danger. Collot easily slipped up behind him, covered his mouth, and plunged his knife into the man's heart. The hired killer slumped to the ground and Collot placed the body behind a wall dividing the garden from the entrance. Slipping back to Spencer, Collot indicated the number of men he took down, Cooper approached and reported likewise. Spencer did the tally and indicated that all four assassins had been eliminated. Next, the three of them went to Mr. Young in the kitchen.

Young was about his cooking, having no idea that the four killers had been eliminated. Hearing conversation, he presumed it to be his own men. He was alarmed to see Spencer, Collot, and Cooper enter his kitchen. Acting as if he took it in stride he greeted them, "Good morning. Are you coming to assure yourselves that all is as scheduled?"

"Something like that," Spencer answered him. "Shall you tell us now how you made your evil plans, considering the bride and groom did not know they would marry until yesterday afternoon?" He put Mr. Young in a wrestling hold with his arm bent behind his back, and kept twisting it until it nearly snapped off. Soon, all the answers came.

Young confessed that Martin, assistant to Pierce (Mr. Darcy's longtime and trusted steward of Killensworth) had approached him two days earlier; he had been sent when the request for the second Darcy carriage had been received at Killensworth. Martin told Young that his pay would be Mrs. Darcy's ring if he would allow for the killing of the Darcy party at his place of business. Young had a well-earned reputation for being a Gretna criminal figure. The scheme was presumed possible when Spencer innocently sent a missive detailing the wedding plans and their expected arrival time at Killensworth. Young's banquet hall was selected because it was the best in Gretna, and it was well-known that Mr. Darcy would have only the finest establishment to host the wedding breakfast. Young seemingly had no prior relationship to Martin or Pierce.

Quitting the Young establishment, the three men discussed their four fellow footmen and the involvement of Pierce at Killensworth. They would make haste to tell Mr. Darcy in the event he did not already know. The man's resources never ceased to amaze the three loyal employees. Their abiding respect for Mr. Darcy continued to increase.

Elizabeth put her head on Darcy's stomach and reached her hand up to touch his cheek. She had just loved him and was feeling relaxed and happy.

Fitzwilliam chose that moment to give her his news. "Sweetheart, I have two things to tell you. One will make you laugh with glee, the other will make you cry, I fear. The first, I saw Jane as I returned from speaking with my men. She was coming out of Bingley's room and headed to her own. Darling, she had an enormous smile on her face and looked quite happy, I must say."

At that, Elizabeth laughed and hugged her husband. "Oh, I am so happy for them, my love. Does that not make you so very pleased? We did help them, did we not, Fitzwilliam?"

"Indeed," he answered, hugging her. Then, pulling her up to his chest, he held her close and told her that Spencer had just informed him that Aunt Edith did receive a death notice about Alden Mason. He gave her all the information he had and reassured her that she should see Aunt Edith very soon and have ample time to comfort the woman she had learned to love as if she were her own mother.

At that moment, a single rap came upon their door. Darcy jumped to his feet and fastened the fall of his breeches. Elizabeth wrapped the counterpane around her nude body and went quickly into her dressing room.

Opening the door, Fitzwilliam read the look on Spencer's face and observed the condition of his clothing under his coat. He went into the hall and Spencer indicated they needed to speak in private. Taking a moment to tell his wife he was going to the stables, the two men set out to meet with Collot and Cooper. Recounting their activities exactly as they occurred, Spencer also informed him of Pierce's planned attack on Killensworth and the identity of the four Darcy footmen from Killensworth who were posing as the servers in white coats at Mr. Young's. He was shocked but had no time to reflect upon his feelings. There was not one moment to lose. Spencer asked permission to take Collot and Cooper and ride hard to Killensworth. He felt certain that they could reach the estate before eleven. Darcy gave them leave to go. Had he been single he would have accompanied them, but his first duty now was the protection of Elizabeth.

Spencer's plan was to tell Pierce that the wedding was cancelled and the two carriages were about twenty minutes behind them. (Mr. Young had revealed that Pierce had been plotting such an attack for quite some time, they were unsure of the number of men involved.) By eleven o'clock, Pierce would think Mr. Darcy's death had been accomplished. He would then boldly execute his plan at Killensworth. But, if Pierce heard that Darcy had never gone to Young's and would return to Killensworth within minutes, he would not proceed with his plan, thus giving Spencer time enough to apprehend him.

Darcy asked that Pierce and all accomplices be detained in the basement. He would speak with them upon his return. Especially important was the opportunity to talk with Pierce, for the man had, he thought, earned his complete trust and confidence. It was a terrible blow to Darcy to lose his loyalty and longtime friendship. Pierce and unknown others had betrayed him. It was difficult for Darcy to believe. He gave full permission for Spencer to execute whatever force was needed to subdue the men. These were traitors who had actually dedicated themselves to the destruction of Darcy's own family.

Fitzwilliam returned to Elizabeth and the two prepared for the wedding and packed for their travel home. Elizabeth was in high spirits and very happy. She felt safe and very comfortable.

Calling for his driver, Darcy gave orders to pack the carriages and ready them for the short trip into Gretna. He sent Elizabeth to fetch Jane as early as possible. He used the excitement of the day for the schedule change. Uncle and Aunt were up, dressed, and packed for the trip to Killensworth. They made Darcy proud with their agreeable manners and willingness to fit into the family. He was convinced they would do very well at Pemberly. Uncle was eager to resume his farming, and Darcy had decided to give them one of the house farms as their own for as long as they lived and were able to farm. After that, they would be cared for, of course.

Darcy knocked once upon Bingley's door. He could scarcely contain the amusement he felt at the remembrance of seeing his sister leave the man's room just two hours earlier. With much mirth, he began to toy with his friend. "My brother," he cried with exultation, "what a grin you have this morning. Did you sleep well, old chap?"

"Agreeably, and you, Darcy?"

"Ay, Bingley, thank you. Upon my word, you look quite spry. Perhaps your leg is mended quicker than expected, eh?"

"The leg is tolerable, Darcy." Bingley looked at his friend and smiled broadly.

"I must say Bingley, you seem to feel fit this morning. What a delightful and happy mood. Have I missed a special occasion? Your birthday, perhaps? "

Bingley smiled, but made no answer.

"Oh good heavens, man!" Darcy declared, "I saw your fiancée leaving your rooms this morning. She did not know she was observed, but my, she did have a glorious smile upon her face!"

Bingley laughed and looked not one bit embarrassed. Good-naturedly he said, "Darcy, I must thank you and Lizzy for setting me straight. I was such a fool. I have no idea what made me such a coxcomb over the news of her sorrow. She is quite remarkable, my brother. I must say, we did quite enjoy ourselves last night! Would you ring for my servant? I should like to get up and get going. I should like to be early for my wedding, Darcy."

"Bingley, I would ask that we all get going. I should like us to be at the church by eight of the clock, rather than ten. I need you to trust me in this matter, brother. Do you think you can make it? After the service, we shall breakfast at the inn at Gretna, and later Elizabeth and I will host you with something much more special at Killensworth." Bingley smiled, he was in high spirits. "Of course, Darcy, there is no need to explain."

At eight o' clock, the two Darcy carriages pulled up before the church and Mr. Brown came out to greet them. He had received the message that the couple wished to wed earlier than had been expected, and was very happy to oblige. The chairs had been readied the evening before, his wife was prepared and in minutes everyone took their places. Uncle came in the door with Jane on his arm. She looked beautiful in a pale blue gown and carrying a bouquet of flowers. Bingley sat in his chair, and watched her come down the aisle. She took her chair next to him, and Uncle placed her hand in Bingley's at the proper time. Elizabeth and Darcy sat in their chairs as well, and the service was beautiful, if not a bit different with each one being seated throughout the ceremony.

Following the service, the two Darcy carriages made haste to the Gretna Inn. They were seated in the common-room and breakfast was ordered. The service was very quick, accommodating the large number who come for marriage ceremonies. Many meals are served daily and the staff was excellent at rushing the diners through, so that more may be served. A fact that would annoy Darcy on any other day. At exactly eight-fifty o'clock, the two Darcy carriages departed for Killensworth.

They arrived only six and one-quarter hours later, and all looked well. Darcy alighted at the gate and asked the guard if all was quite in order. The man handed him a sealed missive. Darcy walked to the side of the carriage to read it:

'Mr. Darcy, all is secure. Please come to the basement at your pleasure, sir. Lady Hamilton is well and unaware of the recent events here at the property. Spencer.'

Darcy noticed the guard dispatching a rider to the house, no doubt headed for the basement to inform Spencer that he had arrived. At last the tension left his body and Darcy became festive. Opening the carriage door next to his wife, he poked his head inside, smiled at his bride and asked, "Elizabeth, shall we dress for a celebration and serve our family our best champagne? We shall have Cook prepare a very special dinner for all of us. Please send a missive to the Knox home, darling, and invite all three of them to come and help us celebrate. Do let Monty and Hannah know that we shall send a carriage for them. You decide the time, my dearest heart."

"Ay, Fitzwilliam, I shall." Elizabeth could not contain her happiness. "I shall speak with Aunt and determine if she feels it proper to celebrate with us, given the loss of her nephew. She shall advise me as to extending an invitation to Allister as well," Elizabeth said.

"Oh, of course, I completely forgot. Please do forgive me, love. Naturally do what you feel is best for them, Elizabeth." Jumping onto the seat next to her, he closed the door with a snap and soundly rapped his cane on the carriage top to send the driver to the front door. Once inside the beautiful home, he greeted Mrs. Boyd and asked her to see Uncle and Aunt to their rooms. Then he took Elizabeth by her hand and led her into the rooms they had been using. Behind the closed door, he held her close and told her that her dream had saved at least nine lives and possibly more. He would explain all later when they had more time to be alone. He kissed her passionately and then set out for the basement and Spencer. He would confront those enemies he had only known as trusted servants.

Elizabeth went back to their guests. Bingley and Jane had already gone to his rooms. Uncle and Aunt MacDougal were being installed in the rooms Aunt Edith had selected for them. Seeing them settled, she turned her thoughts and her direction to Lady Hamilton. Elizabeth prayed as she walked towards Aunt's rooms. Edith was now so dear, and Elizabeth wanted to have just the right words for her, yet never had she felt so amazed at her own discomposure. She feared she would be a poor comfort, and she dearly wished to be of some cheer to the woman who had done so much for her, in her own time of dire need. Edith was more a mother than an aunt.

ᔦᔨ

Allister was not one to bow to ceremony, and the whole idea of mourning his brother did not appeal to him. He was sure some would censure his improper behaviour, yet he was compelled to continue his work. It was his spirit in general that seemed to suffer. The loss saddened him, and the way the lad died was very unfortunate. No one knew where he was headed, he never finished the letter he had begun to Aunt. It may have been the drink. His thoughts were disorderly and incomplete. It was unfortunate— yet they would know nothing— but that Alden confessed to his part in the robbery.

ᔦᔨ

Elizabeth dried her eyes as she left Edith's rooms. Her love and devotion for Lady Hamilton greatly increased as she listened to the older woman's fond remembrances of Alden; and heard her grief over his lack of character, and the lowly station in life he had assumed. Somehow she found the words to speak to Aunt. They must have flowed from heaven, for Elizabeth had not the slightest inclination of speaking on behalf of a lad she had never even seen. The kind words she dispensed were for the benefit of Aunt. Lady Hamilton seemed comforted and told her she was so happy they had returned.

At the close of their conversation, Elizabeth extended an invitation to come to Pemberly. She was most eager for Aunt to become acquainted with the Bennet girls, and their newly rescued great uncle and aunt. Not wanting to disclose all the trouble the MacDougals and Jane experienced, she simply told Aunt that her wonderful support was needed by the entire Darcy family. It was enough for Edith, she knew Elizabeth would share her heart at the proper moment. Embracing Elizabeth, she indicated her happiness in joining them at Pemberly, to encourage her new family. She would begin her support by attending their celebration, which would include the Knox family and baby Elizabeth. She thought it would be a tonic for Allister as well.

ᔦᔨ

After speaking with Pierce, Darcy nodded to Spencer and Collot, communicating that he wished to meet with them. The three went to the house and entered the library. Darcy nodded to the conference table, and his men were seated. Darcy himself poured a glass of port for each man. He did not want to be attended by a servant. "I found the root I was looking to find." Darcy declared. "Pierce has long wished to rob me. Young revealed that information, and it helped prepare me. Yet, hearing it from Pierce himself, I own to feeling sorrow. How could he do it? I always had a fondness for him, trusted him, and relied upon him. Now, I trust only three upon these grounds—yourselves and Cooper. Too long has Pierce been a rotten apple in the Killensworth barrel. No telling which men he has infected with his poisonous greed. Would you not agree?"

"Ay," both answered. Spencer spoke up, "'Tis a risk to trust any others. Where seven are involved, numerous others knew and possibly approved the plan. What shall be done, sir?"

Darcy spoke out of duty. He loathed saying that all must go. Finally he announced his thoughts. "Sadly, everyone but Odum, the butler, and Mrs. Boyd, the housekeeper, must be dismissed. I shall promote my assistant steward from Pemberly to Pierce's position. Winter approaches. This is a blessing, as fewer staff will be necessary until late April or even May, depending upon the weather. Murray will journey to Killensworth immediately, and I shall request that he bring two assistants with him.

"Household staff will be on loan to us from Bounty Faire, Ireland. Collot, I will need you to go and bring back household staff as Mrs. Boyd indicates she has need of, and let each one know it is of a temporary nature. They will winter in Scotland and return to Bounty Faire, in Dun Laoghaire, by May at the latest. This should get us through the winter. I am thankful it broke when it did. Spring would have caught us completely off guard, with too much required.

"Spencer, it falls on you to go to Pemberly. Inform Murray, and the two men of his choosing, that they are on temporary assignment for me. No one must know of the recent plots or any names. I have just wed, and I shall indicate that due to my new status I must make many changes. We must never allow the intelligence of the plot to be made known. What think you of the Kirkwall Heights Assurance Services?" he asked his men. Neither had heard a bad report. Darcy decided to bring them in to examine the background of all new hires. Thanking his men, he announced a meeting with the three of them for the morrow at six o'clock. Each man would receive their bonus money and travel pay, and then they would go on to their new assignments. Cooper would be the one to ride with their carriages when they awayed to Pemberly, which should now be much sooner than he wished. His week with Elizabeth at the fishing lodge would need to wait until spring. This was a great disappointment to him.

Sitting at the desk in his study, Darcy wrote a letter to his cousin Colonel Fitzwilliam. He related his good fortune in finally locating Elizabeth (he had previously told his cousin of his quest and had even enlisted his help for a time) without telling of the present difficulties, he asked for names of men, trusted and well-screened, trained in military skills, disciplined, of exceptional judgment and loyalty; men whose time commitment to the Crown was near an end; men who might wish to enter his employment in an occupation to their liking.

Next, he sent a servant to request that Elizabeth join him. He had much to share with her, and they needed to make immediate plans. He did not feel he could guarantee her safety anywhere in Scotland at the moment, certainly not at Killensworth.

Chapter Nine

"THERE IS A STUBBORNNESS ABOUT ME THAT NEVER CAN BEAR
TO BE FRIGHTENED AT THE WILL OF OTHERS. MY COURAGE
ALWAYS RISES WITH EVERY ATTEMPT TO INTIMIDATE ME."
–JANE AUSTEN

G uests for the celebration dinner began to arrive. Allister was first. Fitzwilliam was grateful for an opportunity to spend some time with his friend talking about his loss. As soon as Monty arrived, the two sat in a corner and spoke only of steam engines. Darcy presumed it was the man's method of dealing with his loss. Hannah enjoyed reuniting with Jane and with their great uncle and aunt, all of whom loved baby Lizzy. Charles enjoyed seeing Jane so happy, and having received a good report from the surgeon, he felt nearly healed; even though he could not as yet, put his weight upon his broken leg. The evening's marriage celebration for Mr. and Mrs. Bingley, and also the happy reunion, was a wonderful success. Dinner lived up to the elegant meal Elizabeth had ordered, and everyone was well satisfied.

Elizabeth took the opportunity to whisper in Fitzwilliam's ear. She requested that he accompany her to his study for five minutes. Looking around the room, he felt they would not be missed. Taking his hand, she led him inside and closed the door. "Darling, I am your wife, and I shall obey you in all things," she said most seriously.

"Ay, I know, dearest Elizabeth. Is that what you called me in here to tell me?" he asked, hoping she had a more sensual plan in mind. Reading his mind, she answered, "I wish to say that we cannot leave for Pemberly until we have spent our week in the fishing lodge, Fitzwilliam. According to your schedule, we cannot depart for another four days. Why would we not extend the time three days? Would the danger increase in just three days?"

"Elizabeth, I am afraid I must deny you this. We shall have our time in the lodge when we return in the spring."

"Very well, yet how about tonight, might we not go just for this evening and spend one night? Ay? Please?" She ran her hands up and down his arms and looked into his eyes. Seriously tempted, Darcy thought it over. He could see no harm in spending one night. He had a planned meeting with his men at six in the morning. He acquiesced and told Cooper to prepare the phaeton and pony for their six mile trip to the lodge. He directed Mrs. Boyd to see to provisions for them at the lodge, for one evening. They would away at ten. Cooper would alert Spencer and Collot to the plan.

At seven, Cooper himself went out to the lodge and prepared it for the Darcys' arrival. He lit a fire in the large fireplace and set up candles. He also set out food, wine, and even coffee, then he returned to attend those within the mansion.

After the very successful celebration dinner, Fitzwilliam and Elizabeth drove the little phaeton to the fishing lodge. Elizabeth was excited to see it and stay for one night. She knew they were not going to be sleeping.

Upon their arrival, Fitzwilliam showed his wife through the house. He was very proud of the comfort and enjoyment it provided. Passing the tray of food Cooper had set out, Fitzwilliam noticed that a large amount of meat appeared to be missing, the wine was half gone, and he thought he could smell coffee. Silently he motioned to the tray, and then indicated that Elizabeth remain quiet. He took her to the kitchen and bade her crouch underneath the butcher table. Her eyes widened as she saw him draw a gun from the back of his belt. Until that very moment she had not been aware that her husband concealed a weapon upon his person. In some undefinable way it made her feel somewhat in awe of him. She wondered what other information about Fitzwilliam Darcy should be made available to her. Perhaps he will tell her why he is armed.

Darcy slowly walked down the hallway, towards the salon and its fireplace, which was warming the room. Entering there, he saw a man reclining upon the sofa, sleeping so soundly his mouth had fallen open. Reaching for the twine in his pocket, he made ready to wake and tie the man.

He saw no one else present, so he walked over to the sleeping man and put his hand firmly upon the man's upper arm. "Wake up and tell me who you are and what you are doing here?" Darcy demanded.

The man startled, sat up, and tried to focus on Fitzwilliam. He had been sound asleep. "Is there not a meeting tonight?" the groggy man asked. "Say, you are new. I do not know you yet. I am Fred Thompson. Do you work for Mr. Darcy? I have not seen Pierce yet but sometimes they are late."

"So I have been told, " Darcy responded. "This is my first time. How many are coming?"

"About eight, I think. There's me, Cook, Barnes, Douglass...let's see, that is four. Mr. Pierce, of course, Martin, Bartlett, and Walters. Ay, eight, but with you it will be nine. I hate to see the number get too big, that will make our cut get smaller."

"Ay, but I heard it is a lot of money," Darcy said, baiting the man.

"You are so correct about that. I understand he has millions. I saw them come in this afternoon, so I guess that means we shall need to make another plan."

"Did you remember everyone? Just eight?"

"Ay," Thompson said, "they tried to get more but some fools are too loyal to Darcy to be trusted. Only the eight of us, and now nine with you, are willing to turn against him. They are very late to the meeting. Whatever do you suppose has happened to them?"

Darcy calmly pulled out his gun and leveled it at Thompson. "I think they were delayed, Thompson. You are about to be delayed as well, for I have another plan for you. Stand up very slowly, Thompson. Put your hands behind your back. I would not wish to shoot you, for my wife will be angry with me if I spill your blood upon her carpet. She has great plans for this room, you see."

Pulling the man's arms behind his back, Darcy grabbed Thompson's sleeves with his left hand. Then, winding the twine around his wrists, he secured both hands together. Darcy tied them so tightly, they began to turn purple. He held his gun on Thompson's back and instructed him to walk out to the phaeton. He had walked to the lodge, as Pierce had been the only one to ride to and from the meetings.

With Thompson tied to the back of the phaeton, Elizabeth drove while Darcy kept an eye on him. He would be delivered to the basement to be interviewed by Spencer and Collot.

Once they arrived at the basement door, Darcy asked Elizabeth to wait in the phaeton.

For a few minutes he spoke in very low volume with his men and gave them the additional names. The remaining men would be apprehended before sunrise. The meeting for six o'clock remained on the calendar for Darcy, Spencer, Collot, and Cooper. A report would be given to Darcy at that time. Spencer, Collot, and Cooper would receive their well-deserved bonuses, for they were of great value to the Darcys.

"Darling, you are such a brave girl. I am so proud of you. You were instrumental in our apprehending this man, and learning the names of other dangerous men. I do not want to take your courage for granted. I wish with all my heart that this plot had never existed. I desire to provide only safe residences for you, my love. I also feel I must explain that I have been wearing a weapon upon my person since my father suggested I qualify as an expert marksman. I have also been schooled in the arts of self-defense. 'Tis a pity that our wealth makes all of this necessary. I pray I may be able to make amends to you, my darling."

"Oh husband," she said, " I daresay that I trust you with my life. I quite understand the necessity for you to be armed, and it makes me feel more secure, not less, beloved. I am happy you are proud of me, now please take me back to the fishing lodge. I should like to be benefited with the other 'arts' in which you are proficient, my love." Elizabeth demanded this with a broad smile. Darcy put his arm around her as he drove the phaeton. Elizabeth reached over and nibbled his ear. "Am I to understand that now we may spend an entire week there, as planned?" She did not take the time for him to respond. Biting her lower lip she ran her hand up and down his leg. " Tonight is just a bonus because you must attend your men in the morning. I shall go back to the house with you on the morrow, and then, tomorrow night we shall set out for our week of sensual nudity, my love." Darcy laughed and squeezed her hand. He was only too happy to oblige.

The trip to Pemberly was underway at last. Located nearly in the heart of England, Pemberly was closer than London. The Bingleys planned to remain on the estate until they could enjoy a more comfortable journey to London. Weather was colder, and everyone feared that winter might perhaps be setting in early. Upon spring, Charles and Jane would travel to Bingley House. Until that time, Jane along with Elizabeth would renew their friendship with their sisters, and become acquainted with their new sister, Georgiana. Whilst in Derbyshire, the Bingleys would search for an estate to purchase.

𝕰🦌

Mr. Quincy and Mr. Talbot left Longbourn after two hours of filling their wooden crates with hundreds of glass bottles and pieces of strange looking equipment. Mrs. Collins was very pleased to have the two men take all the debris away, and at no charge. She insisted they take all the books, and all the dried flowers as well. It seemed she was most eager to be rid of all Mrs. Elizabeth Darcy's herbal oils and supplies. The men felt she behaved as though she had actually been expecting them. It was a slow trip back to Pemberly, but they had good weather and very passable roads. They knew the master would be very pleased, indeed. They recovered all the materials on the list Miss Mary and Miss Kitty wrote out for them. There was no sign of Mr. Collins, and Mrs. Bennet did not come to inquire. Happily, Mrs. Collins was friendly and obliging.

𝕰🦌

Elizabeth, Jane, Uncle and Aunt MacDougal had not seen Pemberly or Derbyshire. They took in the scenery very closely, yet Elizabeth tried to memorize each landmark she encountered. Her excitement at seeing her new home caused her to bite her bottom lip so hard she drew blood. Darcy enjoyed every moment of the journey over their lands. Her first view of the mansion caused her to panic, and it took some time for her to adjust to the grandeur of her new home. Truly, she would need time to feel comfortable living in such a mansion.

A reception line was organized for all of the servants—there were over one hundred. Fitzwilliam and Elizabeth arrived first, they disembarked from their carriage and the two walked the entire length of the line, hand in hand. The process took over half-an-hour as they acknowledged each person individually. As they entered the mansion, Elizabeth reached for Fitzwilliam's hand. She was shocked and hurt to see him look down and step ahead of her. She called softly to him, but he acted as though he had not heard her, and bolted up the steps to the second floor, leaving her on her own. She was so shocked at this strange behaviour, her eyes filled with tears. The stunned faces of the startled servants who had observed them, nearly made her release herself into a loud wail. Never had she felt more embarrassed, rejected, and humiliated. Elizabeth was at a complete loss to understand her husband's behaviour.

Entering the salon, Darcy was met by Georgiana, Mary, Kitty and, surprisingly, Colonel Fitzwilliam. The young colonel was most eager to meet Elizabeth and of course, her sister Jane. Having the letter from Fitzwilliam, which gave him the date of their arrival at Pemberly, he had planned his leave accordingly. He wished to meet his new cousins. At last entering the salon by herself, Elizabeth held her head high, and forced a smile upon her face. She fought the desire to weep. Shocked and scarcely able to breathe, she acknowledged the cold fact—she was unwelcomed by her husband. He had made it most obvious to her. The girls were eager to see her; Georgiana was most happy to become better acquainted. Even Colonel Fitzwilliam held Elizabeth in high esteem, yet something was changing in her husband's behaviour. Elizabeth reasoned that the unexpected change seemed to occur almost the same time he entered his house. *His* house, indeed. Her unfortunate entry made her realise, that it was indeed, his house. At best Elizabeth felt like a houseguest. Silently she wondered if anyone would show her to her rooms. It seemed doubtful that she would be invited to share Fitzwilliam's rooms. Pemberly was most certainly not like Killensworth. How she longed to be back in Scotland. Well she remembered her exciting introduction to Killensworth. Aunt had given her a tour of her home in Scotland— she had been welcomed there. She began to search her memory for any offense she might have accidentally given her husband. She would inquire of him, as soon as an opportunity presented itself.

Bingley fearlessly ascended the stairs without putting weight upon his broken leg.

It would be another three weeks before Charles could have freedom from his crutches. Cooper followed closely behind him and Jane held her breath. She was relieved when they made it to the second floor. Charles led Jane to the rooms he had always used at Pemberly. They would be very agreeable for the two of them. Upon entering, he saw several letters that had been sent on to him from London. One interested him especially. Upon close examination he saw that one missive was from his solicitor in London. He sat down, opened the letter, and began to read silently. Looking at Jane, who was talking to the lady's maid Mrs. Reynolds had sent, he said, "Darling, would you mind if I go and see Darcy? I would like a little chat with him in private, if I might?" She smiled and nodded prettily to him as he quit the room.

Elizabeth begged Fitzwilliam to give her a tour of the gallery of the Darcy family. Many of the paintings dated back over two hundred years. It was difficult for her to imagine such wealth as evidenced in the portraits. He began his introduction of the Darcy family with his arm around her shoulders, then almost as if a spell had been cast over him, he removed his arm and put a pace between the two of them. It struck her as quite odd, and put her in the same frame of mind as when they had originally entered the house. Elizabeth fought back tears, and a sudden chill settled upon both of them.

"Darling— are you well?" She asked him with some measure of concern in her voice. She reached out with her right hand to take his arm but he pulled it away from her. "Have I given offense?" She asked, looking at her hands as he sharply moved to the opposite side of the hallway. Bravely she took a quick step towards him and reached for him, but then—she stopt— changing her mind about offering such a gesture. She stood in silence, for he had successfully intimidated her and she feared saying something wrong.

"Of course not, Elizabeth." He scoffed. "Why would you say such a thing? Please think before you speak such nonsense to your husband." He scolded her without looking at her. "Thank God no one heard you utter such a foolish thing." He turned towards her to give her a brooding stare. She could feel his intense displeasure. It frightened her very much. "—Fitzwilliam— I am only wishing to do all the right things here at Pemberly. You will tell me if I make mistakes— will you not?" She leaned her head away to hide her tears. He did not answer, but turned as his butler approached to ask if he might meet with Mr. Bingley. Without a farewell, Darcy left Elizabeth standing alone in a darkening hallway, surrounded by austere faces. She fancied they looked upon her very disapprovingly.

Within minutes the two men faced each other across Darcy's desk. "Bingley, sit down my brother! What may I do for you, old chap? My— but this is grand, is it not?" Looking at his good friend and brother, Fitzwilliam's mood was quite light. His spirits were high.

"Darcy, have you a bottle? I think we should have port or sherry. I know it is early but we have a matter of some importance to discuss." Rising to pour the two glasses of port, Darcy talked over his shoulder. "This sounds somewhat mysterious, brother." Handing him the glass,

Darcy sat down behind his desk and looked Bingley in the eyes. "Pray, whatever is on your mind? Please be at ease to tell me anything."

"Do you remember the conversation we had in London, the night before we saw Kitty?"

"Ay, many things were discussed. Please refresh my memory, Bingley."

"We were talking about our loves being left with only fifty pounds. You directly asked, what if Mrs. Bennet instructed her brother Phillips to 'say' it was only fifty pounds, and then award the four girls in that amount," Bingley reminded him.

"Ay, I recall it quite clearly. What of that talk?" Darcy now was very curious. His eyebrows shot up as he stood from his chair.

"I wrote to my solicitor that very night and asked him to look into the matter," Bingley recalled. "Remember we felt that the courts would have a record of such a document as a last will and testament? After several hours of research, my man Mr. Bell discovered not only the instrument, but the attorney who wrote it as well. There are five letters, and legal awards each written by Mr. Bennet. This was all arranged six months before his demise. Darcy, the man must have known he was dying."

"I see," Darcy sat down at his desk, and brought his hand to his cheek. Suddenly his mind flashed back to Mr. Bennet, trying to help him declare himself—"Go on— please."

"I shall skip the whereas and hereafters, and get right to the amounts bequeathed. After each sum is a comment. Are you ready? Brace yourself, Darcy! *'To my five daughters I leave the following: Jane Bennet is to receive fifty thousand pounds. This is for your recent fondness, Jane. Elizabeth Bennet is to receive seventy-five thousand pounds. You have always loved me no matter the treatment I gave you. I am sorry for my neglect and the times I hurt you, dear Lizzy. You have been my heartbeat, my dear little girl! Mary Bennet is to receive twenty thousand pounds. I never felt your love, dear Mary, yet I loved you. Catherine Bennet is to receive five thousand pounds. I believe your mama will take care of you for the sake of Lydia. I loved you, Kitty, but I did not feel you loved me. It made me very sad, my dear. Lydia Bennet is to receive five thousand pounds. Your mama will share her funds with you. Each time she told you to do an evil to your papa, you complied. I loved you through all the pain, Lydia. To my wife, I leave five thousand pounds.'* Do you believe this, Darcy? What shall we do?" Bingley began to chew his nails.

"Good God, man!" Darcy jumped up to his feet. "Do you realise we each married an heiress? What might that money have done for our wives and their sisters? Elizabeth told me several times that if they had inherited enough money they would have purchased a little house in London. Good grief, they could have done so and never needed to work one day in their entire lives! My own cousin, the colonel, has not such an inheritance as Elizabeth!"

"Ay, Darcy. That is the point, is it not? They actually do not have such because their uncle was an accomplice. He and his sister scarcely gave them enough money to get out of Meryton."

"Did your man Bell send the letters Mr. Bennet wrote to his daughters?"

"Ay, Darcy," he said patting his right pocket. "Shall we give them to our wives? What action is to be taken? True, we do not need their funds, but what of our daughters and sons in the future? One never knows what life may send our way. Look at the ill fate my darling angel suffered. That never would have occurred if she and Lizzy had inherited. They never would have been turned out and sent into cruel circumstances. Lizzy nearly raped, and Jane…"

Darcy sprang from his chair. "Ay, and what fate might sweet, timid little Mary have suffered had Spencer and I not encountered her at the exact moment needed for an intervention? Or, the sad circumstances of Kitty at the Brightly Street employment where she was being robbed by the selfish thief of a butler. A robber of children, no less Bingley. Brother, I think we should have a meeting with our wives. You must read this to them, and they should have their letters. They will advise us as to what action they wish to see taken. I feel the final decision rests with us. We could prefer charges against Mrs. Bennet and easily win. My men who retrieved Elizabeth's oils told me she still resides in the dowager house. Is it possible that her brother, Phillips, stole the funds and even Mrs. Bennet does not know about the money, or was he her accomplice? Should they be co-defendants?"

Both men took a drink of their port. Darcy ran his fingers through his hair and said, "Time will tell the story, Bingley. Time and a lawsuit will tell." Darcy completely forgot that he had left his wife standing alone in the great hallway and without one thought of Elizabeth's care or comfort, he simply continued to enjoy the fellowship of his brother Bingley. Sadly, he troubled himself not one moment about his wife's whereabouts. Truth be told, he gave Elizabeth not one thought.

Realising that her husband had no plans to return to the great hallway, Elizabeth walked towards the grand salon. She was in hopes that Darcy would reason that she might be waiting for him in the company of others.

Entering that beautiful room, she sat very much alone on the large sofa. Mercifully she heard the rustle of a long skirt approaching her, and she was filled with much relief and happy expectations to see Aunt Edith enter the room and join her. Edith smiled and sat quietly beside her Lizzy. She made no conversation but took the girl's hand and simply held it in her own. The wisdom of Lady Hamilton allowed her to be comfortable just sitting in the company of another when necessary. Edith knew the girl would share her heart in her own good time. For a certainty, she was now assured that she loved Elizabeth with a mother's own love. Lady Hamilton could not love Lizzy more had she given birth to the girl. It was true, that Elizabeth looked upon Edith Hamilton, with the love of a devoted daughter. Seated in that room, Edith remembered the many times she spent in quiet prayer and contemplation. Lady Hamilton had visited Pemberly many times to care for Anne and provide her comfort during her illnesses. Edith spent many hours in prayer, seated in that very room, offering petitions for Anne and the Darcys, and also asking God to send her a child, a daughter. She had often asked for a loving, thoughtful daughter who would bring her great joy, and grandchildren in her later years.

⚜

Lord and Lady Matlock read their letter in shock. Their son had taken a week's leave to go to Pemberly and become acquainted with Darcy's wife. Impossible! Darcy would never dare wed without the family approving his marriage and attending the wedding. The couple packed their bags with great haste and awayed to Pemberly. No matter how long he had been wed, they would force an annulment. How dare the boy marry a nobody? The older couple agreed to go unannounced and put an end to what they called a 'little game of playing house with a girl of ill circumstances.'

⚜

After the men finished the bottle of port, they quit the study and looked for their wives. Darcy beckoned to Elizabeth from the door of the salon, and Bingley went to their rooms to find his wife. The four of them headed to Darcy's study and closed the door behind them. That door opened fifteen minutes later and Darcy went out to look for Aunt Edith. He brought her back to his study and seated her next to his wife who immediately whispered into Edith's ear. Lady Hamilton nodded and Darcy closed the door. He gazed upon her and said, "Aunt Edith, apparently my wife needs to have you present before she can make a decision." Darcy made no attempts to hide his frustration. He could not understand the deep feelings Elizabeth held for Lady Hamilton and he was beginning to experience feelings of jealousy. He remembered the many times Elizabeth relied upon his wisdom, and the close relationship they had enjoyed. This current request to include Edith in their private family meeting irked Darcy. He was angry that his wife did not defer entirely to his wisdom in this matter.

Taking five minutes for Bingley to read the abbreviated part of the will again, all eyes were upon Edith. Darcy spoke to her in a no-nonsense voice. "Well, Aunt, we appear to be waiting upon your vote." Elizabeth whispered something more to Edith.

Lady Hamilton rose from her chair and floated across the floor. "Godson, a word in private if you please." The two smiled at the others and stepped out into the hall. Edith took Darcy's hand and said, "Come with me, Fitzwilliam. We shall duck into the library."

Lady Hamilton's reputation was known all over the kingdom for being a very wealthy, extremely powerful woman. Lord Hamilton's connections—and Edith's own—had been a force for over forty years. Fitzwilliam Darcy listened to the woman when she spoke, and he recognised she still possessed power even now, without her husband.

Closing the door to the library, she commanded, "Sit down, Fitzwilliam! I am speaking to you now as your godmother and your own mother's best and closest friend. I have two words of admonition for you: Stop it! What in blazes has happened to you? You have changed, little by little, ever since we crossed your threshold into Pemberly. Your change is not for the better, my son. You are cold to your wife and short tempered. I promise she has done nothing to deserve it." She raised one hand and added, "Nay, she has not complained to me about it, nor to anyone else. She loves you too much ever to say anything against you. She would never wish to have anyone look at you except in the very best light. You know that to be true, do you not? Be aware godson, those of us around you have eyes and ears. Your harsh treatment of the girl is not unnoticed, even the servants have observed. I often remain in silence in order to be an observer, my boy. You know that is also the God's truth."

Edith took a moment to give Darcy an opportunity to rebut if he desired. He was silent. "The only reason she wanted my opinion about the lawsuit was to be certain she had decided correctly. By the way, she agrees with you. She whispered her agreement moments ago. Let me be understood, Fitzwilliam," she continued, maintaining eye contact. "I most strongly advise you to drop the master of Pemberly routine. You married a flesh-and-blood woman. She does not need your cold shoulder she needs the hot-blooded man she married. If you think you can be he, then by all means be so immediately!

"While I have your attention, have you asked after her health lately? Do you know that she vomits after most meals? Nay, probably not, because it does not affect you, does it? Although you most likely have noticed that her breasts are fuller. Men!" Rising from her chair, she said, "I have begun work to officially make her my legal daughter and of course, my sole heir." She grabbed him by the ear and led him out into the hall. "That will make me your mother-in-law! How does *that* sit with you, Mr. Darcy?" Walking back to his study, Darcy's thoughts tumbled. He tried to make sense of what his aunt had just said to him, but he felt confused. He would inquire as to Elizabeth's health and perhaps ask if she had noticed any changes in him. But, to grasp the idea of Lady Edith Hamilton becoming his wife's mother, would require a period of adjustment, to be sure.

Returning to the others, Darcy said, "Then we are agreed that Bingley will have his solicitor initiate a lawsuit naming Phillips for fraud against four victims and Mrs. Bennet for theft of her four daughters' inheritance." All heads nodded agreement.

Elizabeth stood. "I feel I must make an announcement of sorts, if you please?" She looked around the room and all faces seemed in ready agreement, save that of her husband, which displayed confusion. Undaunted, she continued, "If indeed my father bequeathed to me the sum mentioned, and the courts shall deliver such unto my hands, I should like it to be known—" looking at her husband, she rushed on, "—should Fitzwilliam agree, I would be inclined to use a portion of my funds to begin charitable work in London. It has been upon my heart since my first day as a homeless girl to do something to provide some measure of support to those in my same situation. Should you agree, my love, I wish to establish a sort of agency where those who wish to volunteer may help women who have been put out of their homes. It would give assistance in finding work, safe shelter, and aid in communicating with lost loved ones. I wish to help provide hope and peace of mind, to say nothing of safety in a dangerous world where women may so easily become prey to wicked men."

Here she stopt and looked at Fitzwilliam, who was stunned at such a generous and benevolent vision. Finally he found his voice in the matter and declared, "Darling, I am overcome at your sentiment and your goal. After months of feeling such fear for your welfare, I can well imagine what such an institution would mean to the homeless women, and for all those who love them. What great assistance it would have been to myself and Bingley as well. I wish to contribute to such a project."

Edith rose and embraced Lizzy. "Child, I desire to assist you in this most worthy cause. I believe many others in London's society might feel so disposed as well. It would give me pleasure to join your efforts."

Seconds later Jane and Charles rose and declared their wishes to be a part of such a plan. Edith returned to her rooms and began a letter-writing campaign which would solicit assistance and contributions from the elite in London. She would wield her power to be an amazing blessing.

As they began to quit the study, Darcy stepped behind Elizabeth and leaned down to whisper in her ear. "May I take you for a short walk, my love?" A look of confused pleasure spread across her lovely face and she smiled at him. "This is a pleasant change, Mr. Darcy. Whatever is the occasion? We have had so little time together just to talk, or for almost any other activities—" her voice faded as she rose from her chair. He placed her hand upon his arm and escorted her to their front door. A servant anticipated their needs and met them with coats. Darcy helped Elizabeth with hers and the two stepped outside.

It was cold, a slight breeze was rising, and the clouds looked heavy. Elizabeth felt a chill but she did not allow herself to admit to anything that would shorten their time together. Darcy began by asking her a pointed question. "Elizabeth, tell me truly, have you noticed any changes in my personality since we have arrived home? You are my wife; I expect honesty. Have you seen a shift in my deportment?"

"Perhaps I have," she answered quietly, not wanting to confirm his ill behaviour.

"In what ways, please?" he questioned her with sincerity.

She told him. "I perceive you to be much colder to me, distant, and somewhat…perhaps disapproving of me in a general way. Possibly as though I embarrass you in some manner. I am not really sure what I should say, or how much you wish me to tell you. You are my husband— my life— and I love you ardently. You have done so much for my family, I should not speak in a negative manner. Please forgive me if I have spoken poorly."

"Nay, I want and need you to speak to me thusly. Is there a difference between us? Pemberly is not Scotland, things are more formal here, I have more demands on my time. Are you unhappy?"

She did not answer. Turning her head away from him, she fought back tears. Quickening her pace, she commented upon the cold weather and asked if they should not perhaps return to the house. She started to turn, but he grabbed her hand. "Elizabeth! Please, I need to understand what I have done so I can make amends. Will you not help me?"

"Very well," she responded sadly and with much reluctance. It gave her great pain. "We spend very little time together. Of course I realise the house is full of people, my family, and with all you have done for them— for all of us— I feel I must not speak even one word against your behaviour or attitudes. I suppose I should just say I miss you loving me. I feel lonely and shut out away from you, as though you are no longer pleased with me and no longer desire my company. It is said, that this is the type of behaviour that comes right before the husband takes a lover. Nay," she corrected herself, nodding her head slowly. Then she continued. "I quite forgot secrets; indeed, keeping secrets from the wife, then the lover is taken. Fitzwilliam, if you are unhappy with me, please, I beg you to tell me what I have done wrong, and I shall change. I promise I shall stop whatever is making you dislike my company, and I shall seek to improve myself. If I do not please you in loving you, tell me what you wish me to do and I shall do it for you. Only please," here she finally broke into tears, "do not stop loving me, and I beg you, do not shut me out of your life."

"Elizabeth, are you well? I have not shut you out of my life! In what manner have I so done?" She looked at him as though he'd just told a lie and gasped. She shook her head at him, much confused that he did not know his own behaviour. Carefully choosing each word she said, "We used to love several times a day, now perhaps it might be one time a week. Do you not see a change, Fitzwilliam? I see you in the evenings. No matter how early I rise, you are already gone from our bed. I do not understand how you do that. Each day I arise earlier and earlier, and still you are gone from me, leaving no notes, love or otherwise. It feels cold and indifferent to me. You were angry with me when I asked if Aunt Edith could please listen to our situation and offer her opinion. You have never shown me that side of your personality. Never have I felt your disapproval before, except when I heard you telling Charles that Jane and I could never marry anyone as good as the two of you. Perhaps you now regret not having married a woman of influence. I know not what, but there is something within you that is not peaceful. If it is I, and my behaviour has been poor, I apologize, Fitzwilliam. Now, please do let us go inside. I was wrong to be excited about this walk, for I dare say, it did absolutely nothing to warm or comfort me."

He followed her inside. There may have been other issues he desired to raise, but he felt he'd lost control of the conversation and wished to end it as soon as possible. Elizabeth went to their rooms and called for a bath. She sat therein and cried for the space of one half-hour. Darcy played at billiards with the colonel and Bingley.

Following her bath, Elizabeth turned the counterpane and blanket down on their bed.

It was only one o'clock in the afternoon, but she felt as if she could go to bed and sleep forever. In truth, she wished to sleep and never rise. Everything made her feel sad, and the urge to cry was overwhelming. She loved her family, but upon their wedding day, Fitzwilliam and Elizabeth had made each other their only focus. She was lost without him. Getting comfortable in their bed, she closed her eyes just as she heard his voice speaking to her. Without opening her eyes, she knew he was standing over her. A great excitement began to rise in her, and a strong desire to love him began to overtake her. She opened her sensuous lavender eyes and smiled at him. "Darling, what a wonderful surprise, please join me." He looked stunned and confused. "Elizabeth, are you ill? What are you doing in bed during the middle of the day? Pray, tell me at once. How can you possibly explain this— insupportable behaviour? What of our guests? I am at a complete loss as to explain your severe neglect of our family." Elizabeth was instantly hurt and confounded. Was it possible that he did not understand that she was offering herself and her love to him? She took a few moments to think of what she should say. Reaching her arms up to him, she offered, "Darling, I was going to sleep awhile, just to rest, but upon seeing you, love of my life, I would rather spend the afternoon in sensual love making. Please remove you clothes and let me love you, Fitzwilliam. I know you will enjoy it."

"Elizabeth, this is not proper behaviour. What would our guests and even our servants think, should they know what we are doing in our rooms?" She blinked her eyes and asked: "Pardon, Fitzwilliam? What are you saying to me? Do you honestly think anyone would think our behaviour improper, and it is most unlikely that anyone, save the two of us should know what happens behind our closed and locked door. Please have the courage to be honest with me. Will you not rather tell me that you do not desire to love me? How can I be ignorant of your feelings? You make your feelings plain in your treatment of me—why will you not express them to me. Tell me now that you no longer love me. Your very actions, confirm your lack of caring for me. You depart from our bed early in the morning, so that I cannot love you as I once did. You come to bed late into the night, after drinking and playing games with your cousin and brother. I long for you, as a wife who has been forced to release her husband to serve his country far away in the wars, yet you are still here under your own roof. The army has not called you away from me. You simply chose not to love your wife, or to spend time alone with her. I cry into my pillow for you, yet I keep a cheerful face and pleasant smile for you whenever I see you. And, I see you rarely, Fitzwilliam. It is heartbreaking to see you avoid me daily. It is humiliating to know that the servants see your avoidance of me, as well. You have made it plain to everyone. I worry because I do not know your thoughts, although I can guess at them. You spend hours and hours out of my sight. Whose sight are you in, and in whose company? Will you send me to Ireland to live alone in your home there, and will you leave me there for several years? Shall I see my husband only a few more times before I die? You once told me that I was the perfect wife for you. Was that a lie? I thought you loved me— you said you loved me. Is this love, Fitzwilliam? No,' *this is Pemberly and Pemberly is more formal than Scotland.'* So you said. I desire you, I offer myself to you, I throb for you, and you prefer to find your satisfaction elsewhere, not with me. But where might that be, Fitzwilliam? A servant? One of your past loves? Or, your own hands? Husband— I am rejected— you have made it quite plain to me. I understand—and I am heartbroken…" She turned her back to him. He rose quickly, and quit the room in a storm of anger. Reaching the door, he pulled it open and then slammed it shut with such force, the noise could be heard throughout the entire floor.

Elizabeth put her head into her pillow and wailed.

Feeling much unsettled herself, yet desiring to put everyone else at their ease, Elizabeth sought to arrange a pleasant evening. She asked Georgie and Mary if they might play the instrument, and perhaps sing after dinner. Georgie, ever looking to ensnare Lizzy into a duet, agreed as long as they might play together, and Elizabeth would promise to sing. After the commitments were secured, the evening's prospects appeared brighter. Eleven souls were seated in the salon, awaiting the call to dinner and looking very much forward to a wonderful evening's entertainment.

Peterson appeared at the salon door. But rather than announcing dinner as everyone expected, he pulled himself up to his full height and with his head towards Darcy, although not looking at him directly, he announced, "Sir, Lord Matlock and Lady Matlock." Looking vastly unhappy, the couple stepped into the salon and into a firestorm of their own making. Both seemed to be focused on Fitzwilliam.

Colonel Fitzwilliam shot to his feet, expecting trouble from his parents. He was stunned to see them there. "Father, Mother whatever are you doing here?" he asked anxiously.

"Good heavens, what a way to greet your parents! We live in London not four miles from you, yet we must track you down all the way out here in the country. Is it a sin to wish to see our boy, and do we require an invitation to visit our own nephew?" Looking at Darcy, she pouted, "Fitzwilliam, we are most disappointed in you, nephew. You and Georgiana have neglected your Aunt and Uncle Matlock of late." Elizabeth looked at Aunt Edith. Edith calmed her just with the sparkle in her eyes. "Aunt and Uncle," Darcy was saying, a little louder than Elizabeth thought he should, "I am so pleased you came." His voice rose one full octave. He sounded like a choir boy, and appeared as nervous as a guilty little child, caught stealing pies.

"Ay, my boy," Eleanor Fitzwilliam replied with a sneer, "—and who are all these— these…people? I cannot recall ever seeing so many rag tags in my entire life. Are you beginning a charity work at Pemberly, nephew?"

Darcy crossed the room to where Elizabeth was sitting. He placed his hand upon her shoulder. Nervously patting her, he said, "May I present my wife, Elizabeth Darcy." "Indeed?" Eleanor mocked, failing to acknowledge or speak to Elizabeth, "and who are these kinfolks? Attached to the wife's skirts, I presume. Hungry mouths to be fed from the Pemberly troughs? Is this to be the regular tribe to receive lodging ,and all the finer provisions of life from the Pemberly treasure house? I see you have included the elderly members of the clan, as well. My! Fitzwilliam— you are a generous man— are you not?" Elizabeth stood and frowned at Fitzwilliam, who appeared to be willing to remain silent. He seemed fearful of the woman and the fat, short man by her side. This was unbearable. Squaring her shoulders, she said, "Your ladyship, I was born and raised in Hertfordshire, the daughter of a gentleman. We were taught manners and a most gentle conversation. However, we also had animals upon our farms. When the occasion arises, I have learned to communicate either way. If it please your ladyship, I should like to be gentle with you. However, these lovely individuals require your respect, and as mistress of Pemberly I am afraid I cannot and shall not, allow you to insult our guests. I assure you, madam, no one from Hertfordshire would so behave. However, I clearly see— by your failure to greet me upon the occasion of your nephew introducing me as his wife— and your neglect of wishing newlyweds well— that you were raised elsewhere. I must say, however, *most shocking* to me is your complete disregard of Lady Edith Hamilton, who I am certain is well-known to you, is she not?"

Apparently Eleanor had overlooked the presence of Lady Hamilton. Edith stood to her feet. Nearly laughing she locked eyes with Lady Matlock, tipped her head and openly declared, "Eleanor, it does my heart good to see someone stand up to you!" Adopting a more serious tone— she asked, " Who do you think you are— insulting us in such a manner? Have you taken leave of your senses? Elizabeth has just saved her husband the trouble of drawing your errors to your attention. I feel certain that you desire to be more polite and speak with civility to all of us, do not you?" Pausing briefly to catch her breath, she continued to cast daggers with her blue eyes. "And, to save you the trouble, Elizabeth is an heiress, her father having left her more money than you and John have set aside for your own daughter. Now, if you have any outrageous thoughts about annulling this marriage, you will have to go through Darcy and then myself. I have it on good authority that Darcy has wed for love."

An awkward silence crept into the room. Certainly this was the time the man should have spoken up, both to confess his love for his wife, and to command authority over his uncle and aunt. Finally Edith got his attention and her eyes told him to speak. Darcy stepped closer to Lord and Lady Matlock. All his life he had feared them, as well as his fierce Aunt Catherine de Bourgh! In truth, Darcy had dreaded this very moment. He had dismissed the idea of pleasing his family when he wed Elizabeth, because at that time he was consumed with finding her and making her his own. Yet somehow being home at Pemberly he began to fear and dread the moment his family would learn of his unsuitable match. After all, no one had so much as heard of the Bennet family. God help him, once back at Pemberly, he had even begun to wish he had married Suzette when he had the opportunity to do so. Her influence would have gained the complete respect of his entire family. For a few beats of his heart he wavered…

Finally, he found his voice. "Thank you, Aunt Edith. Well-spoken indeed!" Smiling at Elizabeth, he took her hand. "Darling, I also admire the sentiments you expressed. I quite agree. Aunt, should you ask me, I shall most happily introduce you to this wonderful group of fascinating people. I am so proud to call them my family. For years Georgie and I have been each other's family. Now all that has changed. Aunt Edith is correct, I love and adore my wife. Elizabeth has been my reason for living practically since the moment we first met." Looking directly into Elizabeth's eyes now, he continued, " I have determined that nothing and no one shall keep me from showing my love and devotion to her. She is my world." Bending down to place his lips on her ear, he whispered, "you are my world, please forgive me my darling." Standing straight and looking at his uncle and aunt he said, " Both of you and Aunt Catherine must know that we shall never part." He smiled at Elizabeth, and then in front of all their guests, he put his arms around her and kissed her lips tenderly. Everyone present was shocked at the display, yet no one dared to stop them or comment.

Lady Matlock humbled herself and asked for the introductions. Fitzwilliam took up the civilities. Elizabeth stepped back and smiled. She thanked heaven that he had spoken up at last. And, he had given her a clue as to what had been troubling him. Was it possible that he was living in fear of what his family would say about their marriage?

After dinner the men separated to the library and the ladies gathered in the music room. Georgiana went over her sheet music with Elizabeth, and Mary looked through books to find something she wished to perform. Aunt Edith sat beside Jane, the two were deeply involved in a quiet conversation. Kitty sat beside Lady Matlock and quietly hoped the intimidating lady would not ask her any questions. Lady Matlock sat in silence, and Lady Hamilton made no efforts to ease her discomfort. She had come into the Darcys' home and attempted to separate two young people who loved each other. She should think about her actions. Truth be told, Edith thought nothing could have helped Fitzwilliam find his bearings faster. She was thankful that Eleanor was herself and had actually forced Darcy to look at what had been troubling him since returning to Pemberly. Edith hoped the boy would confess it all to his wife.

The men joined the ladies in the music room, Fitzwilliam stood behind his wife and wrapped his arms around her. He whispered his love for her in her ear and told her he had some things he wanted to say to her, but he wanted to love her as they talked. Instantly she whirled around and put her arms around his neck. She cared not who was in the room watching them. "Oh, darling, you have made me so happy. Thank you so much. I can scarcely wait!" Not caring who was watching, he kissed her lips. She turned around facing the pianoforte, and Darcy kept his arms around her. It was their home and they would do as they wished, propriety be hanged.

Lady Hamilton was very pleased with the evening. This was the first time she had heard Elizabeth sing and accompany herself on the pianoforte. She selected a beautiful new love song, and everyone in the room spoke about her performance being equal to those they have heard upon the stage. Elizabeth performed two duets with Georgiana, and they sounded as if they had played together all their lives. Even Lady Matlock had to admit they made a very talented family.

Fitzwilliam went into Elizabeth's dressing room. She was excitedly splashing in her extra-large bathtub. Singing as she bathed, she did not notice her husband enter the room nor did she know when he got into the tub behind her. He spoke her name and touched her back. Startled, she nearly screamed. Quickly she turned around to face him. She smiled her relief, and held his eyes. Taking her sponge, she applied the soap she herself made.(It smelled of oranges and mint.) Darcy loved the scent and relished having his wife wash him, slowly and seductively. She smiled and said, "Just lie back and close your eyes, my darling, I shall lave you and you will relax. These essential oils will both ease and revive you. May I apply special body oils after we bathe? I should like to massage you. I think you will enjoy it very much."

All he could do was sigh, and Elizabeth took that as his consent. She finished his bath and he took the opportunity to wash his wife. Looking into her lavender eyes, he said, "Oh, Elizabeth, I do not deserve you. You are too good for any man, and that I know. When my aunt insulted you and demonstrated her great displeasure at our union, I immediately realised I had been treating you differently. I knew it was because I feared them. 'Tis so absurd, and yet it is the God's truth. All my life that lunacy about marriage to the right person was drilled into me. I was living in fear of what those ridiculous people would say and do when they found I had made a love match. Here am I, a full-grown man, married and with responsibilities of a man. Why should I have tried to put you aside, fearing the moment when they would discover us, as though I had done wrong? May God forgive me, and especially you, my wonderful wife. I pledge I shall always give you the respect, love, devotion, and companionship you deserve, my lovely Elizabeth Darcy." Elizabeth simply smiled at him. She felt they were on the road to recovering their special relationship.

"Please kneel now, Elizabeth." She did as he requested and Fitzwilliam slowly applied soap, beginning with her silky curls. Much time was spent in washing her, and then even more in rinsing. When he began kissing her, he noticed chill bumps on her arms. Reaching for her towel he carefully lifted her from the tub and dried her, then he led her into their sitting room where a large fire blazed in the enormous fireplace. Tossing a blanket and several pillows onto the floor next to the hearth, he turned to see Elizabeth holding two small glass bottles containing her oils. Smiling, she gently pushed him down upon the pallet, then kissed him sweetly, taking his lips slowly into her own and sucking them very softly. Carefully she poured a small amount of sandalwood oil onto her palms and slowly rubbed them in a circular pattern around his stomach.

Straddling her husband's legs, she rubbed the masculine scented oil up and down his chest, massaging his shoulders each time she reached them. Darcy moaned. He closed his eyes, and mumbled about how heavenly it felt to him.

Putting oil into her palms once more, she rubbed his inner thighs starting just above his knees. Reaching his groin, she began to squeeze his flesh on either side of the root of his penis. He shivered with anticipation, but her hands slid back to his knees each time. He opened his eyes and watched her breasts sway as she continued to rub his legs from his knees to his groin—and back again. Without halting, she persisted in the tantalizing massaging of his thighs, teasing him. He swallowed and began chewing his lower lip, his eyes eagerly following her every motion, trying to determine her next move. He wished she would place her mouth on his tip and suck him, but she did not. She straightened up and held his gaze— licked her lips— then caught her lower lip between her teeth. Halting for a brief moment, she lifted the second bottle to her palm and poured. Darcy could smell her signature scent, roses and sweet almond oil. It was unmistakable.

Slowly she pressed her palms together and to his utter delight, began rubbing the oil onto her own breasts, all the while maintaining eye contact with him, and continuing to hold her lower lip within her teeth. Fitzwilliam stared in wonderment. He marveled at the sight of his wife's hands seductively caressing her own breasts. It aroused his ardor and he found himself fascinated with the image. She held his level stare. He knew this provocative act was just to heighten his enjoyment of the erotic massage. He laced his fingers together and put his hands behind his head, and watched this awe-inspiring display of seduction with great pleasure. Never in his imagination would he have conceived of this sensuous demonstration. In truth, he would have requested this display long before now, had he thought of her doing such a thing to herself. How the artist in him wished to paint her or even sketch this scene. She looked so beautiful in the firelight. Her lavender eyes were dark with passion, her skin so perfect with the dew of youth upon her. Her cheek bones were perfection, her classically formed neck and shoulders inspiring artistic appreciation and her lover's fondest desire. Her shapely arms had the well-developed look of an active person, muscles that were well-formed and highly defined, yet delicate. Her form was gorgeous and seemingly symmetrical. Her breasts were endowed with an elegant shape; they appeared extraordinarily developed, ripe, and delicious looking. He adored their shape, not simply because they were large. He thought them gracefully sized, very ample and embellished with an astonishingly well-rounded and rather large areola, surrounding youthful nipples, quite perky and whenever he was near her, they were peaked upwards, revealing her arousal.

Holding his eyes, she arched one brow and poured more oil onto her palm. Smiling at him, she placed it between her breasts. Slowly bending forward, she pushed her bosom on top of his penis and pressed firmly onto him. Moving her body in a small circular motion she began to grind into him, wiping the oil onto his shaft. She repeated this process two additional times, each time more sensuously than the last. Finally, she applied her talented fingers upon his genitals, as skillfully as she had played upon the pianoforte. On and on she played him, until he was nearly in pain from his increasing desire. She ignored his state and continued her pleasurable palpations. Sliding onto her side, she reached for his tip, and touching it with her tongue, she lingered there for a few moments. Her tongue began to quiver with anticipation, Fitzwilliam put his hands on her head and begged her in a low raspy voice, "—Oh— Elizabeth— *please!*" Hearing him, she lifted her head and gave him a glorious smile, then lowering her lips she drew him in, reminding him of what he had been missing for weeks.

Finally able to stand to his feet, Darcy took his wife's hand and led her to their bed. Pulling down the counterpane he enticed her to lie down upon her side. Lifting her top leg over his own, his hand reached out to her silky curls. Squeezing her mound, his intensely desirous fingers spread her ring and discovered her sweetness. She encouraged him, and he slowly yet deliberately entered her, hearing her sigh and watching as she closed her eyes. She smiled and told him how much she had missed their loving each other.

"Tonight— I realised exactly why I have been frightful since returning to the place I was raised. The ghosts of my father and mother telling me it was critical that I marry a certain type of woman gave my mind no rest. I was taught from an early age that I had responsibilities and must ignore my heart. I honestly believe it was frozen in that time and place when I met you. Oh, Elizabeth, how can I ever thank you for loving me? When you fearlessly stood up to my Aunt Matlock, you made me see my problems and gave me the courage to break free. Do you know how frightened I have been of those people all my life? And you— my lovely girl— you spoke to her as she needed to be spoken to— just the way you reproached me at Netherfield, through your speech to Bingley."

Elizabeth, looked up at him, and saw he was suddenly staring at her breasts. She smiled and wondered if he would notice the difference. He seemed pleased, but because he had held her so infrequently of late, she doubted he would notice their increase.

"Can you forgive me, Elizabeth for acting as if I wished you away from me and from Pemberly? I can admit it now. I realise that was what I was doing. I think it was unconsciously done— yet I admit to doing so nonetheless. Unforgivable of me, my love. Please let us go back to the way we were in Scotland— I wish to be *that* Fitzwilliam Darcy, not the frightened little boy scared witless by his powerful relatives; and not a pompous cold-hearted arse of a husband, abusing his wife with shameful neglect."

"Of course, Fitzwilliam, I am just so happy that you have come back to me. Promise me you shall never leave me again. I was so lonely for you and longing for your love and attentions." Kissing her and teasing her nipples, he felt a sudden sense of warmth. Releasing her mouth, he said, "I cannot believe I denied myself this love, Elizabeth. What a fool I was allowing myself to slip back into that pompous man who spoke such utter nonsense to Charles, that night at Netherfield!"

She kissed him, passionately just the way he had taught her to kiss him. Elizabeth Darcy required no words to communicate with her husband. In truth, she still had much to say to him.

§⚬⚬

Lady Hamilton sat at her writing desk. She was most comfortably installed at Pemberly as well as she was at any of her own homes. Tonight she was well satisfied with her godson. Taking a pen and paper she began a pithy letter to her friend, Lady Catherine de Bourgh. Boldly she told of her love of Elizabeth Darcy, boasting about the recently discovered inheritance and revealing her high regard for the girl. Forecasting their traditional visit for Eastertide, she requested that the Darcys share one bedchamber, as they did at Pemberly, and that their rooms be near her own.

Smiling to herself, she left the letter open so she could add any other rich details as they might occur to her. She would be very careful to keep the biggest news to herself until she stood directly in front of Catherine with her new daughter by her side. Ay, she wanted to see Catherine's face when she heard the best news. Sliding to her knees, Edith thanked God that Darcy had returned to himself, and that Eleanor had been the help that was needed.

Chapter Ten

"THERE ARE FEW PEOPLE WHOM I REALLY LOVE, AND STILL
FEWER OF WHOM I THINK WELL."
–JANE AUSTEN

Charles and Jane put their money down upon a charming estate only ten miles from the back entrance to Pemberly. The couple planned to move in right after the first of the new year. The afternoon post brought an official envelope addressed to Bingley. Seeing the sender was Bell of London, Darcy urged him to open it immediately and put an end to the suspense. Indeed, it was a letter informing him that all documents concerning Mr. Bennet's last will and testament, and the conducting attorney, had been secured. The case was ready to move to court. The date was set for March twelve, in London. It was decided that the couples would away to their homes in London on the first day of March.

Mr. and Mrs. Edward Gardiner read the letter from Lizzy twice. They could scarcely understand the evil done to the four girls. Had the proper inheritance been given at once upon Mr. Bennet's death, neither Jane nor Lizzy would have suffered such ill, and Mary and Kitty would have been spared their grief and sufferings as well. Letters from Jane and Lizzy, detailing the violence done to them, persuaded the Gardiners that the lawsuit was correct and necessary. Gathering her writing supplies, Aunt Gardiner wrote to Jane and Lizzy of their support and understanding. Should Fitzwilliam and Charles request his presence, Uncle Gardiner would be willing to accompany them to the court. Both girls felt a sense of relief to know that their wonderful uncle and aunt agreed that they were taking the correct course of action.

❦

Elizabeth marveled at the grace and beauty of Darcy House. It was enormous and she adored it. Even the staff impressed her with their efficiency and friendliness. She quickly took control as mistress of the home. Darcy gave her a tour of the house, and she readily selected rooms for themselves and for Aunt Edith. Fitzwilliam understood immediately when she requested they take new rooms, change furnishings and linens. Their new bed was installed to their satisfaction. Although quite young, Elizabeth realised that her husband had been a bachelor, living in the house. She was unwilling to allow him to maintain his memories, or to allow either of them to be confronted by them.

Darcy understood when Elizabeth requested that Aunt Edith go to London with them. She and Jane wanted the woman's support during the hearing. Happily, Lady Hamilton agreed and planned to use some of the time to work on their soon-to-be-founded charity.

❦

Aunt Edith requested the pleasure of the Darcys' company for afternoon tea in her private sitting room. The couple entered at the precise time. Darcy kissed Edith on her cheek, and Lizzy embraced her fondly. When they were seated and served, Edith drew paperwork from a leather sleeve that had been upon the sofa beside her.

"Child," she began looking fondly at Lizzy, "do you recall my telling you, that you were the daughter I had always wanted?"

Elizabeth slowly nodded her head. Her eyes were filling with tears as she said, "Ay, and my telling you that after less than one week you had already shown me more kindness and showered more love upon me than my own natural mother had in my entire life. I do so love you, Aunt."

"Lizzy, child, I certainly know that quite well. I should say I am as certain of your love for me as I am assured of your constant love of and abiding faith in my godson. I also told you it was a pity and great disappointment that Lord Hamilton left no issue upon the earth, for I knew I would have been a devoted mama."

Lizzy began to speak, but Edith put her hand up and continued, "I believe I know what your answer will be, my girl, and so therefore I boldly tell you both that I have had all the necessary papers drawn up to settle claim upon you, Elizabeth Bennet Darcy, as my one and only adopted child and therefore my one and only legal heiress as I leave this earth. Oh, and by the way, that will not be for a very long time, for I must and I shall enjoy all my grandchildren. I certainly shall be present for all their marriages as well as those of my little Georgie, Mary, and Kitty."

Darcy was speechless and sat in awe as he watched the two women. Elizabeth threw her arms around Edith but was unable to say a single word. Edith held Lizzy in her arms and gently smoothed her hand over her hair.

Finally Elizabeth found her voice. "Oh Aunt—I mean, Mama! You wish to be my mother? I am so overwhelmed it is difficult to find the words I require. I cannot find the way to thank you sufficiently for all you have already done on my behalf, and now this—" Lizzy shed more tears and this time Edith joined her.

The older woman held Lizzy at arm's length and looked into her eyes. "Lizzy, should you wish to become my daughter, you shall be required to take up the legal name Elizabeth Bennet Hamilton Darcy. My solicitor has left your maiden name as your middle name, child. Does that meet with your approval? Please look at the pages of my last will and testament. Someday you shall inherit my four homes and the combined fortunes of both Lord and Lady Hamilton. Perhaps you would consider giving the homes to each of your children, should you have five. Your eldest son will have Pemberly and all of Fitzwilliam's holdings, of course." She smiled at Lizzy.

Elizabeth returned her smile but with tears of joy spilling from her eyes. Then she said, "Oh, I do not have any words to answer except to say how much I love and admire you. I wish to call you *Mama*, yet as Lady Hamilton, perhaps you prefer *Mother*?" Elizabeth nearly giggled as she asked.

Edith Hamilton did giggle, "Oh Lizzy, you have made me so very happy, you may certainly call me anything you wish, except Lady Hamilton, Edith, or Aunt!"

Darcy stood to his feet and finally spoke to the two women in his life. "I shall certainly call you Mama. And may I say I hope this shall not put me in the position of facing you as my mother-in-law! I have already had a small taste of that, Aunt—*Mama*!" The three laughed.

Elizabeth looked at Darcy and said, "Tell me, am I dreaming?" They laughed again, and Edith looked at them and said, "I suppose I have a son, too! Children, I ask only one thing of you. Please say nothing until Easter at Rosings. I shall have so much to share with dear Catherine, and I wish to dwell upon the satisfaction that is mine." Looking at Lizzy she said, "Now, daughter, you have several pages that require your legal signature."

Elizabeth began the process. Seated at Edith's desk, and with her new mother standing behind her, she signed her new legal name for the very first time. Edith had never been happier, and Elizabeth had never felt more loved. Darcy sat quietly trying to determine the financial windfall this would be for his children and his wife. He knew Elizabeth would need time to adjust to this wonderful news. Her love and respect for Edith had been obvious from the moment he first saw them together.

❦

Jane enjoyed touring her new London home with her husband as her tour guide. Pleased with Bingley House, she could scarcely wait to show it to her sister and Uncle and Aunt Gardiner. The Bingleys planned a dinner party for that purpose, inviting all their family for the following night. Jane had much to do to organize the happy event. She had settled in as mistress of Bingley House quite well, even though Louisa Hurst had considered herself for that role, upon Caroline's absence. Although Jane was a gentle person, Louisa soon learned that the new Mrs. Bingley was indeed, capable of assuming her authority. Her husband was very well pleased with her abilities and was eager for his first family dinner as a married man in his own home.

❦

At Darcy House, the couple enjoyed their home, and it was a pleasure to share it with their new mama. The newly selected rooms were very beautiful and spacious. Fitzwilliam relished the comfort of the sofa in their cozy sitting room. Removing his shoes and jacket, he opened his shirt halfway down, and taking a pillow from the bed, made himself comfortable for a nap. Within minutes he was sleeping soundly.

Elizabeth seeing him, thought it would be interesting to join her husband. Taking off her gown, she stretched out on top of him. In his sleep he wrapped his arms around her, and soon she was sleeping most peacefully.

After half-an-hour, Darcy awakened and smiled at his slumbering naked wife. He sat up and swung his legs out to plant his feet upon the floor. He stood up, taking his sound asleep wife with him. He moved them to the bed where he began to caress her. Elizabeth's responses were quite pleasing and more than a little welcoming to his overtures. He pondered the delicacy of this situation which was clearly within his discretion. Fitzwilliam had to search his mind for information related to entering one's sleeping wife without her consent. True, they had enjoyed copulating whilst both slept, but he was fully awake. With the decision to wait being made, the man contented himself with playing with her breasts and sucking her nipples. Suddenly, he stopped to examine and ponder them. Could their size be increasing? He wondered. Perhaps she was filling out. It was true she was only twenty years of age. Also true, they ate extremely well and it was logical that she may still be developing. As he debated this issue within his own mind, she stirred and seemed to be chilly. He pulled the blanket from the foot of the bed over them. This did not seem to warm her as she had folded her arms and was holding them close to her chest as she slept. Occasionally she would rub her hands up and down her upper arms as if trying to warm them. Tossing her head to and fro on the pillow, she appeared to be agitated, uncomfortable or perhaps extremely angry.

At last she gasped loudly and bolted upright. Tears began to flow from her lovely eyes and her lush lashes closed upon her cheeks, as if to provide privacy to the eyes or to prevent looking at someone. *Him?*

"Elizabeth? Are you well, my love? What is it dearest?"

She looked at him strangely and then attempted to move away from him as her tears increased in a solid flow down her cheeks. She did not answer him.

"I believe you have had a dream. Is that correct?" he asked directly. She made no attempt to answer him and did not wish to look upon him. "Dearest, are you angry with me? Does it have to do with your dream?" he inquired.

Looking at him with anger in her eyes, she said, "I had a dream, and right now I do not believe I can discuss it with you. Yes, I am quite out of sorts." She averted her eyes.

"Please," he begged, "tell me what you dreamt. If I have done any wrong, I shall make it right, I promise you. Upon my word, I can think of nothing I might have done to upset you in this manner."

Realising he was right, she calmed down and began to disclose the dream. "I am sorry, darling, of course you are correct. You have done nothing, I realise the dream was a prediction, perhaps, or a warning. I was so very angry with you in the second part of my dream, and then terrified for you in the third."

"Please, Elizabeth tell me immediately. I cannot endure this emotional disturbance when I have not one hint of my own wrong-doing." He pleaded his case with conviction. It touched her heart and she favoured him with a slight smile.

Placing several pillows in an upright position, she sat up straight and patted the bed where she wished him to join her. "We were so happy in the first part of my dream. It was the most wonderful dream I have ever experienced. Darling, I was sad when it changed into a terrible nightmare!"

"Indeed? Pray, do share the wonderful part." He smiled, happy to see her returning to herself again.

"I dreamt it was Jane's birthday, August ten, and we hosted a fabulous picnic upon the lawn at Pemberly. We had musicians from Lambton and the staff prepared a wonderful meal served under a beautiful canopy. Suddenly, I grabbed your hand and said, 'Darling, it is time! I have just felt my waters break. Thankfully we brought our midwife to occupy her rooms here at Pemberly. I think this is two weeks early!'

"You were so excited you could not tell anyone where we were going. Georgie got up to follow us and you asked her to wait with her sisters and Bingley. Darling, we were only in our labour room for a little over two hours when our son arrived! It was a fairly easy delivery and you watched the entire procedure, commenting on how much my body stretched for the baby's birth! Just when we were deciding on his name, my dream changed scenes. Like a play, going from mirth to conflict, my entire being shifted into such unbearable sorrow and fear. It was very hard to leave the first dream. I wanted us to continue to enjoy our son together. I believe I tried to return to my first dream, but I could not and I was forced to enter the second, sorrowful part.

"We were here in London. I had just returned from shopping with Mama and bought a very special gift to surprise you. Wishing to put it on your desk, so you would encounter it as you worked and be charmed, I stepped to your desktop. My eyes fell on an outgoing envelope waiting for the post. It was addressed to a Madamoiselle Suzette Simoneaux, ten Front Street, London, England. My heart stopped. It could not be. I stared, then shut my eyes tightly, wishing it to be gone when I opened them, but it was still there. When I looked up, you were standing next to me, asking me what I was doing looking at your private correspondence. I was so hurt and shocked that you— my own husband— were not only communicating with an unattached woman, but you described the missive as *'your private correspondence'* and you were angry at me, for seeing such in your outgoing post.

"We had very angry words. You told me to open the letter and prove to myself that it was harmless. You had only answered her missive, which had come that morning whilst I was out shopping. You brought out her letter, which you kept in your desk. This was insupportable. You had actually retained her letter, concealing it in your desk drawer. What could I presume but that you wished to read it over again at a later date, or perhaps you desired to re-read it several times? I tried to leave the room, but you caught my arm and forced me to stay whilst you opened the letter and read it to me. She acknowledged you to be married and asked if the two of you could meet. She was still in England, never having left two years ago, and was now somewhat down on her finances and needing your assistance. She said she wanted you so very much.

"I broke free and fled. Racing away from you, I went to the sofa in our sitting room, clutched a pillow, and buried my face in it. You pursued me and told me that it was all innocent and I was acting childish and silly. But I could not stop myself from weeping. I felt betrayed and worried that you would begin an affair with her. Then you tried to get me to go with you to visit her, thinking that I would be persuaded that you had no feelings for her. It was so horrible. I became violently ill, and a physician was called to attend me."

Concluding this second portion of her dream, she looked up at Fitzwilliam. He was silent, even though her suffering was very apparent to him. He had no words to offer her, and he made no gestures or attempts to provide her with any comfort. Elizabeth had paid an emotional price to experience the dream and he knew it. She had felt a very real pain as she disclosed the contents to him, and yet he allowed her to suffer the cost of the dream alone. He felt a momentary pang of guilt, as a result of his cold indifference to his wife.

"Well?" She phrased the single word as a question for him. He maintained his silence. "Fitzwilliam, I am waiting to hear if the name in the dream is one that you know. Perhaps, someone from your past? Have you anything to say to me about this person?"

"Elizabeth, I suppose I forgot that you are the dreamer of the dream. Of course, I should own to knowing the person. Your own emotional outpouring tells me that you must surmise that I do know her, just as your dream indicated. I have no idea where she is— and if I had received anything from her, you would have been the very first to know. I want no evil thoughts in that beautiful head of yours, darling. Elizabeth, I love you with my whole heart and have no room for any others." After somewhat admonishing her in this manner, he marveled to himself that she had said Suzette's full name, along with a London address. The two had never met, of course, and he had certainly not told her of Suzette's existence or of their relationship. In truth, it is a name he had wished his wife would never hear. He did not want to discuss Suzette with Elizabeth. It was a remarkable dream. If a letter was coming, he would like to read it. He also wondered at the specific street address written upon the envelope. Was it indeed a current address for Suzette? He briefly considered sending Spencer to verify it as hers. Darcy had to force his thoughts away from Suzette and her portion of Elizabeth's dream. He was unhappy about his lack of self-control over his ruminations of the woman.

Elizabeth turned her head and lowered her lashes. She was uncertain of what to think about his actions in her dream. He confessed nothing, did not say he was sorry and he maintained an innocent position about his acceptance of the woman's letter. She felt he was defensive in her dream, and somewhat defensive now. Elizabeth was not pleased with his response to the second part of the dream. She did not feel anything had been resolved between them. Sitting with her hands folded in her lap, she held her eyes upon her fingertips. Unknowingly, a sigh forced her shoulders to rise abruptly, and then lower. Fitzwilliam took a particular notice of her now. He was becoming somewhat concerned.

Uncertain about any additional conversation on this topic of Suzette, she thought of Mama's earliest cautions about Fitzwilliam. She had suggested that Elizabeth never mention any *others*. All at once, she came to realise that he, himself, had not said her name −*Suzette*! Her husband did not say his past lover's name! Now it suddenly seemed remarkable to her. Fitzwilliam did not pronounce the name, *Madamoiselle Suzette Simoneaux*. Elizabeth lifted up her eyes and looked at her husband's face in complete wonder. So much so, that he was distracted by her close gaze.

Shaking his head slightly, Fitzwilliam's forehead produced a momentary frown as he said, "darling, your dreams are very special, indeed. You indicated you feared for me in the third portion of the dream. Please enlighten me, Elizabeth. I am quite concerned."

Elizabeth was most uncomfortable with the way her husband requested to know the third part of her dream. She was not satisfied with leaving the topic of the second portion. She looked deeply into his eyes. He held her stare, but it gave him an uneasy feeling. Elizabeth did not smile at him, instead she pressed on at his request, and watching him closely, she began to unfold the final portion of this most uncomfortable dream.

"Next, a third and final nightmare, I entered the breakfast room as you were reading the *London Times*. On the front page was a story with a large headline telling of a man who had been found guilty of fraud, and before he left the courtroom he implicated his business associate and chief investor, Mr. Fitzwilliam Darcy. The reporter left little doubt that you would be found guilty as well. I read the headline, WILLIAM HUXLEY OF BENTLEY, OXFORD FOUND GUILTY OF TRIPLE EXTORTION AND EMBEZZLEMENT. MAJOR INVESTOR OF THE PROJECT, FITZWILLIAM DARCY TO STAND TRIAL AS CO-CONSPIRATOR AGAINST THE CROWN."

Fitzwilliam turned white and began to nervously pace the room and stammer. "Bloody hell— everyone told me he— he was so well recommended. There was no one to warn me. Father always said I trusted too easily…" He ran his hands through his hair, leaving him with most of it standing up and away from his handsome face. He sat down in a chair, only to rise abruptly and continue his pacing of the room. All at once, he remembered his wife. Rushing to her side, he lifted her hands and began kissing them. Tears filled his eyes. "Oh Elizabeth, God sent you to me as a most special and wonderful gift. You are a treasure, and you do not know your worth on this earth! How I thank you for telling me the dream, and how I thank God for sending it to us. Without this warning— I would have been hanged— Elizabeth! Do you realise the fate from which you have saved us both? Remarkable girl! I do most ardently and sincerely love you with all my heart and forsake all others!" He wrapped his arms around her and drew her close to him, squeezing her so tightly she could hardly breathe. He kissed her lips, but not gently as his tears flowed down his cheeks, and mingled with her tears. After many minutes, he led her to a sofa and sat down, pulling her onto his lap. Turning his head to one side, he placed his cheek on her head and inhaled her signature scent. He closed his eyes and whispered. "Darling, once again you have given me a warning with enough time to extricate myself from evil, and a resulting punishment that I wish to avoid, with all my heart." She reached up and touched his cheek. "I am so thankful my husband. God has saved us once again, love."

Taking her hand in his, he began to request more information from her. "Please let us talk more about this dream, and be patient with me, as I ask you many questions."

Elizabeth nodded. She smiled a faint little smile at him and ran her fingers through his hair. Smoothing a stray lock back along his head, she offered. "Tell me what you would like me to do, my love."

Fitzwilliam began with the first part of the dream. He wanted to be gentle with his wife. Feeling somewhat guilty at the thought of his rather keen interest in Suzette's portion of the dream; he was stricken with a need to focus on Elizabeth. He regretted his immediate interest in Suzette, and now he wished to concentrate on the dream of a baby. He knew this is where Elizabeth's interests would be centered. It was right to put her feelings and needs first. She was a wonderful wife and he did love her with all his heart. Of course the third part of the dream was most urgent to him, but he needed to be sure that all was well in his relationship with his young wife. He smiled and said, "My wonderful girl, the first part of your dream was a good part and perhaps someday it will be true for us. We are happy as we are, and we are willing to wait for a baby, are we not, beloved?" He smoothed his hand over her hair, and kissed the top of her head.

She smiled at this. She wanted to wait for the best time to tell him, and so she did not confirm her condition.

"As to the second part," he continued, " I am happy to say that I believe this is also just a dream. Please know that I would tell you immediately should I receive any type of communication from that woman—or—any other woman, my love. Be at ease to ask me any questions about that woman. I want you to be comfortable in knowing that I wish to be completely open and honest with you. She is of the past, and please recall my words to you, *'nothing from the past can tear us apart.'* "

He looked into Elizabeth's beautiful eyes and smiled at her. Slowly, he continued… "Now, I feel as if I need a drink to tell you that the third part strikes terror and fear into your husband. Let me pour some wine for us, beloved." Darcy stood up and walked on shaky legs to the sideboard. He poured the wine then rejoined his wife on the sofa. Slowly, he began to explain his connection to Huxley, as Elizabeth climbed onto his lap.

"Elizabeth, I have had my solicitor looking into writing papers for Mr. Huxley. I was expected in Mr. Marshall's office on Friday to sign the papers and arrange for the bank draft. I had no idea anything was amiss. It is just like the wedding breakfast with Mr. Young. I did not suspect anything was wrong with Huxley or his business venture. Oh, Elizabeth, I thank God for you! I am so thankful for your dream, my love. For whatever reasons, God Himself has chosen to send dreams to you that are life-saving. I do appreciate you and your dreams, more than I can say."

She sat in his lap and laced her fingers around his head. Kissing his neck, she said, "I am so happy you are safe and will not face any problems associated with that man, my love. Ay— God protected us."

He smiled at her. She was obsessing over his neck, kissing him and licking him, then she began to suck him there. He found it rather stimulating, holding his naked wife who was showering such attentions upon his neck. He knew that his open shirt, and the sight of his neck and chest aroused her. Then, remembering to be considerate of her feelings about not having a baby, he said, "Elizabeth, I hope you are not too disappointed about the dream of a baby boy's birth. We are happy to wait, are we not?"

Involved with her devotions to his neck, she answered between kisses, and did not even look up at him. "Nay, I am not disappointed in the least, beloved," she answered.

Proud of her excellent attitude, he began to kiss her hair, and rub her back. Suddenly she leaned back and took his hand, placing it over her stomach. She smiled at him and waited. In just a few seconds, he quickly pulled his hand away from her and demanded, "Elizabeth— what was that?" She laughed. Placing his hand over her stomach again, she said, "I believe it is the result of a week of sensual nudity at our fishing lodge, my husband. What did you think would happen, when you planted your seed inside me, with such frequency?" She studied his face. "Are you pleased, my love?"

Darcy looked confused as he tried to adjust to the idea that they would have a child. "Do you know when the baby will come?" he asked, wide-eyed and staring in disbelief.

"Our midwife says August twenty, but my dream says August ten," she answered matter-of-factly. Then she asked again, "are you pleased, Fitzwilliam?"

"Are you well? Do you feel ill, is everything as it should be? Are you pleased, Elizabeth?"

She could not stop smiling at him, "Ay, quite well, I thank you, I am over the illness. For a few weeks I would vomit every time I ate. Ay, everything is as it should be. We shall need to have some talks, and I am hoping we shall love whilst we talk. We may love as often as we wish— it is good for me— and for our child. Oh, my wonderful husband, I am so happy. I have never been so thrilled. I only waited to tell you because it is advised to wait for the quickening." Seeing his confusion, she added, "Oh, I am sorry, that means when the baby begins to move about in my womb, giving clear indications of his life. If you only knew how many times I wished to tell you early— but— I did not want you to suffer disappointment should anything have gone wrong. Are you happy, Fitzwilliam? You are beginning to frighten me. I have asked thrice if you are pleased."

"My darling Elizabeth, this is such wonderful news! I have thought of it so many times. I have never felt closer to you, my love. We are going to have a child! Of course I am pleased— I am so very happy." He stood up with her in his arms and turned her around and around. Placing her on their bed, he stretched out beside her and began kissing her with great feeling. She began to understand his joy. Fitzwilliam was beginning to communicate with his wife, without the need for words.

Suzette Simoneaux was certain she could get Fitzwilliam back around her little finger anytime she wished. She wished it now. Her finances were low since her most current lover had sent her away. Living in London on her own was very expensive. She had been forced to sell nearly all the fine jewellery Darcy had given her. So many fine gems set in the purest of gold. They were very expensive, too. Well she remembered that he took no notice of the cost. He had only wanted to make his Suzette happy. There would be plenty of time to shop for new jewellery and clothing as soon as they reunited. Darcy was even more wealthy now, according to the London Times. He had more money to spend upon his lovely Suzette. Smiling, she took paper and pen, and then she crafted as skillful a letter as possible. She reminded him of all they had been to each other and invited him to come to her. Suzette was careful to use poor English and she skillfully inserted just the right amount of French into each line. After all, Darcy thought she had been living in Paris all this time. She knew he had married, and the idea of being his mistress was very appealing. To be the affirmed and favoured mistress of Fitzwilliam Darcy, was an absolute honour. Suzette would be sure that all of London knew her status. In fact, she would be certain that all of Europe knew. Fitzwilliam Darcy, was a man of profound importance. The whole world would know that Darcy had taken the beautiful Suzette Simoneaux as his lover! She briefly mentioned her finances in the letter. For she must be careful, that he knew she desired him, not his money. She would be willing to accept residency at Darcy House. His wife was young and would be easily managed. Suzette began to daydream about sharing Darcy's rooms with him. If the child he married did not like it, she could go back to the chickens and cows at Pemberly, and live there with the brat Georgie. Addressing the missive to him at Darcy House, she wrote "personal" across the back of the letter, and sprinkled some of her gardenia perfume on the envelope. Smiling to herself, she gave it to her only servant to post.

Court appearances were as highly charged as expected. Jane and Elizabeth, of course remained at Darcy House under the comfort of Edith. Their husbands and Mr. Bell stood before the judge, who had read the will and then the single letter attached. It was the missive to Elizabeth from her father, intended as an example of the gentleman's love and devotion to her. Judge Whipple was a man who had experienced life and was ready to retire from the bench, this was to be his last decision. He held the rapt attention of Darcy, Bingley, Bell, Mrs. Bennet, and Mr. Phillips.

Looking at all of them, Judge Whipple began to speak. "One cannot stress too strongly the power of a last will and testament. Mr. Bennet was of a sound mind, and he expressed himself without errors. It is clear that he had given much thought to the dispersing of his monies. His fortune is to be given as *he* directed. In keeping with his last requests, his *female heirs* shall receive his divided funds. This court orders that his directive be honoured immediately. There has already been too long a delay."

He directed Phillips and Mrs. Bennet to rise and addressed them. "I have no desire to entertain a shouting match or a session of finger pointing. I find you both guilty of fraud and four counts of theft. I am appointing Mr. Bell as the new executor of Mr. Bennet's concerns and sentence the two of you to five years in prison. Mr. Phillips, you are removed as an officer of the court and are no longer qualified to practice law within the realm. Mrs. Bennet, you are the sole support of the minor child, Lydia Bennet. I offer you a suspended sentence. You will return to your current residence and receive the amount Mr. Bennet bequeathed to you. However, Mr. Bell will look into your finances and determine whether or not you have already spent beyond those funds. If so, you will repay the money forthwith. Do you understand me, madam?"

Mrs. Bennet took on the appearance of an angry hen. She was swept away in her anger and merely nodded her head without looking up at the judge. She showed no remorse.

"Very well, the magistrate shall check upon your residency each week and Mr. Bell will report your compliance with the financial awards to your four daughters. If you fail to comply, you shall go immediately to prison to serve your sentence. Have you any questions, madam?"

Mrs. Bennet looked at the floor and did not speak.

The judge struck his gavel and declared, "Court is dismissed."

Two men sat in the back of the courtroom. They rose when Mrs. Bennet rose and quietly followed her through the door and out to the street. Their instructions were to keep a close watch upon her until Bell received all monies transferred to the four daughters. Spencer and Collot were thrilled to have a small part of setting things right. They were men who loved justice. Both men believed it was just for the pair to face the consequences their greedy actions compelled.

That afternoon, the post did indeed bring a letter to Mr. Darcy. The sender was a Mlle Suzette Simoneaux, number ten Front Street, London. It was placed in prominence upon his desk. The butler well remembered the beautiful lady and wondered if they would be seeing her again. In truth, he fondly hoped to look upon her lovely face once more. Perhaps she would be calling upon Darcy House in the near future.

After a meeting with their wives and Edith to recount the courtroom events, Bingley and Darcy went to the study to celebrate with a glass of port. Glancing at the stack of letters upon his desk, Darcy's vision fell upon a missive with handwriting he knew quite well. Excusing himself, he took the envelope from his desk and quit the room quickly to find Elizabeth. She was in the sitting room with Jane and Mama. He motioned to his wife to join him. Standing beside him in the hall, she lightly touched his arm and looked at the envelope in his hand. "Darling," he said, "I could not wait one moment upon seeing this. I do not want you to entertain an idea that I am keeping any secrets from you, beloved."

Reading the name of the sender, she smiled at him and asked, "What do you intend to do, my love?"

"I should like to respond in the manner I use when numerous offers of business ventures are sent to me. When I have no interest, and no time, to bother with a response to an unsolicited letter or invitation, I simply write 'refused' upon the back of the unopened missive, slide it into my personalised envelope, address it to the sender, and post it immediately." His response made her smile widely. "What think you, Elizabeth?"

"I think that sounds appropriate, my husband, and it pleases me very much, I dare say."

Kissing her quickly, he embraced her and said "Elizabeth I love you so." He added, "Then I shall do it immediately and send it out today." He heard her soft lilting laughter as he hurried down the hall, back to Bingley and his study. He would execute his plan for the dangerous letter, as soon as he could put a pen to the matter.

Dinner at Bingley House was a success. Even Mr. and Mrs. Hurst were friendly. Louisa was most eager to remain in the good graces of her new sister-in-law, Jane. Now that Jane was a wealthy woman, Louisa could not wait to write a detailed letter to Caroline. She would give her the news of the successfully contested will, and remind her sister that Jane had been wealthy all along. It was a cruel mother— not a punishment of fate –that sent Jane out into the world. Jane was kind, beautiful, wealthy and influential. To Louisa's great pleasure the two were more than sisters through her marriage to Charles, they were becoming fast friends. Louisa would tell Caroline that she now had a closer sister than the two Bingley sisters had ever been. Louisa would include in that missive, news of the very wealthy and beautiful Mrs. Fitzwilliam Darcy. The three ladies had planned a trip to Elizabeth's own modiste, a woman with a waiting list for all of London, except Mrs. Darcy, of course. Louisa had been promised an appointment. She was most eager for Caroline to hear of it. She wished her sister to know of her affections for the whole family, and the warm attachment of dear Jane, in particular. Charles was most pleased with Louisa. Aunt and Uncle Gardiner were thrilled to see their niece installed as mistress of such a lovely home. It relieved Aunt's mind to see that Charles's sister and brother had embraced Jane. Only Elizabeth could clearly see the character and nature of Louisa and her husband. Dear Jane was— as always— far too eager to see the best of everybody. However, Elizabeth was satisfied, knowing that it would be Louisa who would always need to bow to Jane, as Jane's fortune demanded.

Following dinner, Darcy stood before the men went into the library for port. He cleared his throat, tapped his water glass with his spoon, and announced, "Mr. and Mrs. Darcy should like to engage your attendance tomorrow evening at seven o'clock for a dinner at Darcy House. Save yourselves the trouble of refusing. Should you attempt to put us off, Mrs. Darcy shall pay a personal call to inquire!" At that, everyone laughed and readily agreed to attend Darcy House for dinner. Nine for dinner, by Elizabeth's head count, plus Lord and Lady Matlock and Colonel Fitzwilliam, they would celebrate!

Suzette's servant offered the envelope displaying Darcy House as the sender. She was thrilled to receive a response so quickly and happily opened it. A sudden sting stabbed her eyes as she drew out her own sealed letter. Bitterly, she could clearly see it had been sent back to her unopened and unread. Examining the back of her envelope she traced the word '*refused*' with her finger. In her fierce anger, she began to talk to herself. "No doubt the mousy little bride saw my missive, and in her jealousy sent this response to quiet me, and keep me away from her husband. She need not worry, he has money enough for both of us! If she thinks this shall keep me away, she does not know Suzette. Mr. Darcy has not heard the last of his dearest love. I remember quite well that he absolutely adored me, and could not do enough for me. He will pamper and indulge me again, no doubt. I must call in person this time. There will be no refusal once Darcy sees his beautiful French lover."

Looking in her mirror she decided she looked as young as ever. She had never told Darcy her true age. The man was head over heels in love with her. It did not matter that she was nine years his senior. Suzette took good care of herself. She fancied herself looking the five-and-twenty she now claimed to be. Certainly Darcy would look upon her with the eyes of unending love. He would see her as youthful and beautiful as he did upon their last time together. In truth, she rather hoped he would not reflect upon the last conversation they'd had, for he was quite out of sorts with her at the time. He did not like the idea of sending Georgiana to Berlin for boarding school. His attitude took her by much surprise, as she well remembered that Otto Metz, her past lover, had been more than pleased to send his two little girls there. It was far enough away to keep them gone for years at a time. Suzette thought it would have been perfect for the brat Georgie. No matter, now the child he married will see to Georgie. Darcy's little sister will no longer be a problem.

"Tomorrow evening I shall go to Darcy House, and enter the front door without knocking. I shall go at half-past seven, so I shall see him before they dine. Going in unannounced, I may be able to enter his study and find him alone. Ay, he shall be alone and lost in his thoughts of his beautiful Suzette!"

Fitzwilliam and Elizabeth had just entered the salon. Edith sat drinking a cup of coffee and reading the *London Times*. Suddenly she yelled and stood up abruptly, nearly overturning her hot beverage. Darcy and Elizabeth rushed to her side, and all eyes fell upon the headline. "Children, look at this!" She shouted as she spotted her son Darcy's name on the front page. They both read the giant print and then Darcy took up the paper and read it aloud. EXEMPLARY ETHICS EXHIBITED BY FITZWILLIAM DARCY. Darcy, of Pemberly, Derbyshire, London, Killensworth, Scotland and Bounty Faire, Dun Laoghaire, Ireland is celebrated as the preeminent businessman in the Empire for his acuity. He suspected the fraudulent undertakings of Mr. William Huxley of Bentley, Oxford, and directed his accountant and solicitor to report the man to the courts. Mr. Huxley has been arrested on charges of fraud against the Crown and is likely to face hanging. The *London Times* will report the trial. It is expected that the Crown will bestow an honour upon Mr. Darcy, for his assistance."

Darcy sank down into a chair and put his face in his hands. Running his fingers through his hair he stood again. Stepping behind Elizabeth, he put his arms around her saying, "Do you realise what your dream has saved me from? I am positively weak in the knees and shaking all over, my love! To know it from your dream is one thing, but to see it as it 'tis happening, reported in the paper just as you saved me—oh Elizabeth! How can I ever thank you from my heart?" Elizabeth put her arms around him and kissed him. Edith stood from her chair and quietly quit the room. She knew they would tell her all if they wished her to know. Lady Hamilton had the ability to remain unobtrusive whilst maintaining keen powers of observation. Many times her observations told her all she required knowing.

❦

Spencer and Collot returned to Darcy House before noon the following day. Joining Mr. Darcy in his study, they reported the status in Hertfordshire. Mrs. Bennet had made arrangements to transfer the funds to the girls. "Mr. Darcy, Mr. Bell indicates he shall travel to Meryton tomorrow morning. The transfer of funds will be completed before noon, and Mrs. Darcy shall receive her money before dinner tomorrow. Mrs. Bingley shall have her funds at the same time, of course, and the two sisters at Pemberly, Miss Mary and Miss Catherine, shall have their inheritances as well." Spencer smiled.

Darcy thanked his men, then excitedly excused himself. He set out to find Elizabeth. He would share this good news with his wife and their mama.

Darcy House had never been more festive. Fresh flowers were arranged in every room. Beautiful candles were placed nearly everywhere and their light added to the celebration. A string quartet had been engaged, and was well situated in the corner of the grand salon. Their strains of Mozart's Serenade Number 13 in G Major, K 525, "Eine Kleine Nachtmusik": II. Romance Andante— were floating through the air. Everyone was enchanted and eagerly anticipating the delicious meal Elizabeth had ordered. Darcy was very well pleased with his wife and continued to give her expressive looks of admiration, affection and pure wonder at her amazing talents. From time to time, she approached her husband and whispered seductively into his ear. Wishing to maintain proper decorum, he struggled to retain his iconic and effectual manners, whilst trying to avoid becoming aroused in the company of family and friends. It seemed his wife had made a point of whispering that she had dressed hurriedly, and eliminated her undergarment and stays, in an effort to save time. Then she inquired of him, as to whether he remembered the circumstances of his learning that she had omitted the same, upon their wedding day. Fitzwilliam thought his wife had never looked more beautiful, and he very much enjoyed the sparkle in her fine eyes. Servants circulated the room pouring wine into glasses, and each guest was looking forward to the sumptuous dinner. Edith had attended many fine evenings at Darcy House whilst Anne was mistress. She was well pleased to notice that indeed, her daughter had brought the mansion up to a level of refinement that had never been known prior to Lizzy's administration.

Mr. and Mrs. Darcy were eager to share their wonderful news with their family and friends. Only their mama knew about the coming baby. Fitzwilliam had prepared a speech and was very eager for the evening's events. Mr. Bell sent confirmation of the transfer of funds, and Elizabeth was officially an heiress. Her mama could not be more proud of her little daughter, and she was eager to make some new entries in Lady Catherine's letter. How she dearly wished that her old friend could be at Darcy House this evening. It was a triumph, to be sure. Edith could scarcely wait for Darcy's announcement. By seven o'clock, all the guests had arrived. At half-past-seven, the formal call to dinner was heard, and everyone began to move towards the dining-room.

The front door to Darcy House opened cautiously. The staff was so occupied with the dinner, that no one noticed the overdressed, middle-aged-looking woman enter the home. She heard the beautiful music, and soft voices coming from the salon as the enchanted guests began to enter to dining-room. She had never seen the home more majestically decorated and there was a certain air about the mansion. For a moment she wondered if such a gathering would be just the place for her to slip in unnoticed. Deciding to try, she began to enter the dining-room just as Darcy stood to his feet and tapped his water glass with a spoon. She slipped back behind the door and froze there. She listened, as did all the guests seated at the table. Looking from around the corner, she could see into the room quite clearly. Sitting beside Darcy was a very youthful woman, Mrs. Darcy, quite lovely, possibly even beautiful, if met under different circumstances.

He began to speak and Mrs. Darcy looked lovingly into his eyes. "Family and friends, Elizabeth and I wish to thank you for coming. As you know, when a wealthy woman invites you to dine, you do not refuse." Everyone laughed, quite amused at the jocularity. Darcy pressed on, "My wife is now a very wealthy woman with her own fortune, in her own right. I am in the happy position to ask her for a loan should the need ever arise!"

Again, all enjoyed his merriment. It was rare to see Darcy as a joker. Wearing an infectious, gleeful smile, which made him look years younger, Darcy's eyes were locked upon his wife's beautiful face. "More than wealth, more than mere money, I wish to say that the real treasure Mrs. Darcy has given me is the gift of true love. She is the only woman in the world I have ever loved with my entire heart. Elizabeth is my reason for living, she became such at the very moment we first met. It was a meeting that opened up the heavens, did it not my love?" Elizabeth smiled, and the expression grew into her lilting laughter. She nodded her head in agreement, and looked at Jane, who joined in her laughter. Darcy continued, clearly enjoying each moment spent in the spotlight. Looking at Charles, he asked," Bingley, little did we know our gifts that day, did we, old chap?"

"Ay, Darcy!" Bingley cheerfully added. "Hear! hear!"

"My beautiful young wife, with the exquisite eyes that hold my happiness, has shared the best news I have ever received in my entire life. How could I possibly be more blest? We wish to share our good fortune and our most wonderful news with all of you."

Elizabeth stood to her feet. Her elegant gown was tastefully designed, and displayed her bountiful bosom exceedingly well. She stood with grace and style and the calm self-assurance of a mature woman. Smiling at her husband, she said in a melodic voice, "Thank you— for those wonderful words— my darling husband. You have made me so very happy."

Taking her hand, he lifted it and announced, "Sister Jane, I feel you may forever after have needs to share your birthday with your nephew Darcy, for Elizabeth and I are to be blest with a baby, and we are expecting the arrival upon your very own birthday. May we invite all of you now to a glorious picnic at Pemberly to celebrate dear Jane's birthday on August ten? Indeed, we invite all of you to join us this summer at Pemberly. Please come and escape the summer heat of town."

At this announcement, everyone was up on their feet and surrounding the couple. Jane, especially, hugged her sister as though she would never release her. It was a most joyous celebration for everyone, except the uninvited, unwelcome, and unnoticed observer just outside the dining-room door. As quietly as possible, she began to back out of the house, praying to be unobserved. In truth, the butler saw her and remembered the French woman who had tried to snare Mr. Darcy. Although he felt no fondness for the middle-aged Madamoiselle Simoneaux, he had no intentions of interrupting the wonderful celebration. He made a decision not to call Spencer and not to tell the Darcys. They had more important things on their minds. Perhaps, it would be his way of making amends for those two times he'd seen Mrs. Darcy (whilst she was still Miss Bennet) standing outside the front door of Darcy House. He had decided not to allow an answer at the door, and he himself had picked up her missive and tossed it onto the fire in the salon. He had made the wrong decision months ago. He knew it was an action that would cost him his position, should his master ever gain that intelligence. But tonight—and ever after— he would honour Mrs. Darcy and protect her as mistress of Darcy House. She was a well-respected mistress, and worthy of the devotion and support of all her servants. It was fitting that the Darcy celebration dinner continue uninterrupted. He deliberately allowed the trespasser to back out of the house. He saw the woman clearly as she walked through the salon. She was a very tired and quite aged replica of the raving beauty she had been— only a few years ago. Her coming to Darcy House— seeing the wonderful celebration—hearing the news of their coming child was a punishment of sorts. Her actions brought consequences, complete with a good look at the youthful and exquisitely beautiful Mrs. Darcy. This he reasoned, was enough to set things straight for the aging Madamoiselle Simoneaux.

§⁊₹

Suzette Simoneaux threw herself over her bed and wept bitterly. Her plans to ensnare Fitzwilliam Darcy were forever foiled. The man had wed a young, inexperienced woman and now they were to have a child. Suzette wondered how *that* had happened, for she well remembered Darcy was such a failure as a lover and his wife was barely into her twenties, if she was any judge of women's ages. She could certainly feel superior to Mrs. Darcy on *that* topic. She was French, after all, and it was a fact—no one could satisfy a man as well as she. All arts of amour belong solely to French women. Thinking about another possible financial solution to her problems, she determined to go to the Royal Commerce as soon as their hours commenced. At ten o'clock the following morning she would go to see Mr. Angus Bottsworth, chairman of the board. He had seemed an easy touch, exactly what she urgently needed. He would be her final hope, or perhaps she would be required to return to France.

§⁊₹

At nine o'clock on the following morn, Edith and her children quit Darcy House and headed eagerly for their two appointments. The first, with her personal banker and financial advisor Mr. Bottsworth, who would meet with his very important client before commencing his office hours. Lady Hamilton was always to be granted special favors. Their second appointment, with her solicitor, Mr. Richard Burchfield, would be conducted in the same building.

All three were so happy in their new connections that it was difficult to speak without laughing. In the highest of spirits, they recounted the celebration of last evening. Edith was especially thrilled to return the signed documents and to introduce her new daughter to Mr.Bottsworth. Fitzwilliam Darcy, her son needed no introduction; he was already quite well-known. Mr. Bottsworth was more than pleased with his early appointment. Concluding their business, he rose to perform the necessary civilities.

The three were quitting his office through the only access door when an overdressed, overly made-up woman stepped directly into their path. She had been trying to gain access without benefit of an appointment and therefore attempting to avoid all notice of the secretary. Looking in the direction of the secretary, to be certain he was not watching her, she walked quickly towards Mr.Bottsworth's door. It was being opened, to provide an exit for his early clients. She made to allow these very important people to quit his office before she entered, whilst watching the secretary. That bothersome man would eject her from the building, should he see her making an entry without benefit of an appointment. Thinking all had stepped out of the office, she entered quickly, only to step immediately in front of Fitzwilliam Darcy. The momentum each of them gathered, carried them nearly into each other's arms, as they were on a collision course.

Suddenly face to face with the aging version of the woman he had thought himself to be wildly in love with, Darcy was speechless. Elizabeth, of course, had absolutely no idea of the woman's identity, although she was immediately confronted with an errant wave of nausea, due to the assault of an offensive plume of cheap perfume. So much olfactory overload, so very early in the day sent Lizzy's head, and stomach spinning. Elizabeth looked into Darcy's eyes, just as her mama took her hand. Whirling both of them around, Edith quickly led them back into Mr. Bottsworth's office. Edith's quick thinking saved the day. She dipped her handkerchief into the water pitcher, and putting her daughter into a nearby chair, she placed the cool cloth over Lizzy's forehead. Darcy sat beside Elizabeth and taking her hand, he kissed it; all the while inquiring about her health.

Mr. Bottsworth, saw Suzette. He immediately took her hand and led her into his office as well. Then he began to ask about her business and inquired as to her appointment. Embarrassed at the sudden attention, and regretting that Darcy had seen her, Suzette tried to make haste for the door.

Edith stepped in front of her and said, "Upon my word, if it is not Suzette! Are you once again upon British soil, Madamoiselle Simoneaux? Darcy, look here is our old friend Suzette, back from France, I dare say." Looking Suzette in the eyes, she continued her questions. "My dear, how were things in Paris? When did you arrive back in England? "

Elizabeth looked up in surprise. Mr. Bottsworth inserted himself into the discourse and straightway made to correct Lady Hamilton. "Oh nay, your Ladyship, I am afraid you are mistaken. Madamoiselle Simoneaux has been a long time resident of London, have you not, my dear? Mrs. Bottsworth and I have known her since she moved to London some twenty years ago, have we not, Madamoiselle Simoneaux?"

Darcy listened with an intense interest. He was shocked to learn the truth of her residency and wondered what other lies he had been told. Her face certainly revealed the truth of her actual age. She was definitely not his junior. The lines in her once lovely face testified that she was his senior, possibly by many years. He had kept track of her age, year by year, and had calculated her to be five and twenty, based upon the information she had shared with him. His mouth suddenly felt dry, and the smell of her gardenia perfume seemed to make him feel quite unwell—causing him to briefly wonder if she had always reeked of such an overpowering scent. Who was this woman? His mind raced and his heart began to beat wildly. He did not want to speak of her with Elizabeth. He feared the next time he would be alone with his young wife. Elizabeth would have questions. A dread of the coming conversation seized him. Not knowing what to say, in the moment, Darcy made a bad situation worse, with his silence. He was speechless.

Once again it was Edith who spoke up to Suzette. "Oh, I do beg your pardon, mademoiselle. I had understood when I last saw you two years ago, that you had just come from France, and then a few weeks later, you once again departed for Paris. Perhaps I was mistaken. Do you wish to help me understand?"

Suzette coloured but gave no answer. Darcy looked shocked and offered no words. It was his mama who once again spoke to the awkward situation. "Indeed, my dear Mr. Bottsworth," she offered, smiling at the man her business had greatly enriched, " it seems, I may have been misunderstood. I did not intend to give offense to your financial client. Please do forgive me. Perhaps Madamoiselle Simoneaux would like to give a private explanation, just for you, Mr. Bottsworth, she is, after all, your financial client."

Mr. Bottsworth, now looking very uncomfortable offered, "Nay, your Ladyship, we are only friends. Ah, that is to say, she is a friend to Mrs. Bottsworth and me." He earnestly hoped to put the topic to rest. Lady Hamilton was his most highly valued financial client. He sincerely wished to keep her happy, and desired to make a good impression upon her daughter, and the highly esteemed Mr. Darcy.

Edith turned towards Suzette, looked directly into her eyes, and said, "Do forgive me Suzette. In all my questions about the time you left Paris to visit us, and then returned to Paris— I quite forgot to present my wonderful daughter— Elizabeth Bennet *Hamilton* Darcy. What amazing good fortune for me, to have my lovely daughter married to my very own precious godson. That is a very happy ending, fit for a fairy tale, *ce n'est pas?*"

Finding her kinder self, Elizabeth rose from her chair, and holding the damp cloth near her nose to diffuse the vaporous perfume, she offered the expected greeting. Darcy, looking very sober, scarcely tipped his head to

Suzette and spoke a farewell to Mr. Bottsworth instead, saying his beautiful wife was in very urgent need of fresh air.

Elizabeth felt much improved as the three entered Mr. Burchfield's office. Still stunned at the revelation of Suzette's appearance, their business with the solicitor was somewhat stilted. Adoption papers were returned and additional copies signed. These would be filed with the court; an appearance before the judge had already been waived.

The second order of business was to install a Mrs. Blanche Telford, recently of Surrey (a widow and currently homeless) as administrator of the Assistance Agency of London project. Self-educated and capable, strong-minded and yet compassionate, the woman was just what was needed. Mother and daughter were surprised to learn that Fitzwilliam had purchased a large building just outside town and happily donated the structure, which would house fifty residents and include offices for conducting business. All staff members had been selected by Mrs. Telford. As currently homeless women, each had a profound commitment to the project. Darcy wanted to make certain that Elizabeth's dream came true, even if her father's will had not been settled in her favor. With or without an inheritance, her Assistance Agency of London would be a reality. Thrilled at this development, Elizabeth and her new mother were very pleased at Darcy's active role in the project. They would tour the building and meet all the workers before returning to Pemberly.

All appointments completed, the three were once again inside the carriage and headed to Darcy House. Edith looked up saying, "My, I wonder what dark truth surrounds that dreadful woman. So very shocking to see Suzette, was it not?"

They answered not, as both were lost in their own private thoughts about the woman. Elizabeth was more than happy to have seen the legendary Suzette, and was gladdened that her husband had a good look at her. She wondered what age he believed her to be when they first met. Darcy determined a new task for Spencer: to learn all he could about the woman. He had numerous unanswered questions about the one he fancied himself so in love with, not so very long ago. In truth, even as recently as his first night with Elizabeth, God help him. He reached out and took his young wife's hand. Looking into her beautiful lavender eyes he squeezed it, then wordlessly lifted it to kiss. Catching her mama's sparkling blue eyes, Lizzy winked at her.

Chapter Eleven

"Very well...That reply will do for the present."
–Jane Austen

The Pemberly party was caught up in the excitement of the journey to Rosings Park. In truth, this was the first year that Fitzwilliam and Georgie felt any joy in their visit to Kent. The caravan of Darcy carriages conveying the new family of six, now held the promise of taking their own entertainment along. Just last year, it had been only the two of them. Previously, Fitzwilliam and Georgiana had made the trip in frozen silence. Both had a dread in their heart and a fear of facing their Aunt Catherine. Had the truth been told, their last visit to Rosings had taken all the joy away from their celebration of Eastertide, as their terrible aunt had nearly forced poor Fitzwilliam to wed Anne on Easter Sunday. This year, Fitzwilliam, Elizabeth, and Edith were all very eager to see Lady Catherine and give her the good news of their expected baby. Edith could hardly wait to see Catherine react to Lizzy. Georgiana was happy to have her new sisters going with her. She loved living life in their society, and the three girls giggled about Lady Catherine's ill humor. They thought the trip would be an adventure, and the visit would be amusing.

Three carriages arrived at the same time, giving reign to chaos. Darcy jumped out to hand his wife and their mama down. The footmen assisted the girls in the second Darcy carriage, and at last the Matlock carriage was aided. Lord and Lady Matlock were all that was proper and welcoming to the Darcy family. Elizabeth was now an heiress, and the once hostile Eleanor had decided to show her the proper respect as Darcy's wife.

When the party entered the home, all eyes would be on Lady Catherine. Her long-held dream of the marriage between her daughter, Anne, and her nephew was now destroyed. Everyone waited with nerves on edge, because Catherine could behave very poorly when disappointed. Whatever her mood, Lady Catherine was always most dramatic.

As the family entered, the Matlocks were first to greet Catherine and Anne. They took chairs and waited for the introduction of Elizabeth. Edith took Elizabeth's hand, and just as she had promised her upon their first meeting, she introduced her to Catherine.

"Ay, Edith, I have received and read all your letters. I highly suspect they are fabrications and are therefore not reliable." She purposely ignored Elizabeth even though she had just been introduced to the girl. Catherine held her head high, maintained eye contact with Edith, and made a great show of her refusal to acknowledge Elizabeth's presence.

Not being one to back down or be put off, Elizabeth stepped forward to get a better look at the woman. Standing straight and tall, Elizabeth looked at Fitzwilliam. He was watching her with a curious smile on his lips. Elizabeth spoke out so firmly that her voice found an echo in the great hall. "Lady Catherine, at this point in an introduction, it naturally falls to each party the opportunity and the necessity to say some pleasantry. Quite obviously you have decided to omit that civility and now you appear to be speaking unkindly to one of your oldest and dearest friends. As she is my mother in the truest sense of the word, I cannot allow you to do that. I must say, this behaviour falls quite beneath your title, does it not?"

Shocked at the girl's forwardness, Catherine frowned and scowled, "Impertinence! This is not to be borne. Do you honestly expect me to acknowledge that you and my nephew are a couple? 'Tis impossible, because he is to marry Anne! All of this," Catherine screeched as she threw both hands high into the air, "is very untoward!"

"Lady Catherine, nay, I have no expectations that you would acknowledge the two of us as a couple, yet I do desire you to know, that we two are a family, for though you see Fitzwilliam and I, Elizabeth, the third person you do not see as yet is our first child, who shall make his appearance in four months. Madam, it is most certainly time for you to welcome your nephew and congratulate him on his very good progress towards an heir for Pemberly!" Smiling, she squeezed her mama's hand and then looked at her husband.

Fitzwilliam stepped next to his wife, took her hand, and placed it upon his arm. He defied his fierce aunt, by saying, "Indeed, Aunt Catherine! Should you add your well wishes, I shall think you a very generous soul. I have always been aware of your desires, yet never upon this earth would Anne and I have ever wed. Our entire family would welcome the sound of you releasing your hold upon a dream that was never to be."

Georgiana was proud to hear her brother stand up to their formidable aunt. Never before in their lives had he possessed the courage to do so. He was truly a man now, and it was good to see the difference in him. Suddenly she felt safer, more protected, and less fearful of the scary woman who had frightened her every time they met. For the first time in Georgie's life, Lady Catherine appeared to be very old and even somewhat frail. There might have been a somewhat comedic delivery of her words and the way she tilted her head as she spoke. Georgie began to look forward to the carriage ride back to Pemberly. No doubt, Kitty would favour her sisters with a mimic or two. Perhaps even Georgiana herself would join in the merriment. Aunt Catherine certainly provided a broad array of phrases and facial expressions which would lend themselves very generously to a few humourous skits. An impersonation of Aunt Catherine might be added to those Georgie often renders of Caroline Bingley. Georgiana Darcy was becoming most proficient with her performances of Caroline's many sugary and insincere compliments. All the girls enjoyed making sport of the woman sleeping in Darcy's bed followed immediately by her removal from Pemberly… upon comparison of the two women, Georgie felt Aunt Catherine would be as easily imitated as Caroline Bingley. The two women were, after all, strikingly similar in manner-isms and attitudes.

Edith was very proud of Elizabeth. She promptly told the gathering about her legal adoption of Lizzy. Catherine was speechless. Edith took the opportunity to remind her old friend that she was going to be a grandmother in four months. Her eyes sparkled as she reminded Catherine that even though it was thought she would never have a child, her years of prayers had been answered. Elizabeth was the one for whom she had prayed. She told Catherine that it was only Darcy's desire to wed Lizzy that brought her into the the young girl's life. The very girl she had learned to love as a daughter, had at the same time begun to love her as a mother. Lady Catherine was then treated to a most detailed description of the wedding. Next, the woman was favoured with information about the beautiful Hannah, the very intelligent Monty, and their adorable baby girl, named after Elizabeth, of course. Edith called for Mary and Kitty to join them and the many remarkable talents of these lovely young ladies was made known to Lady Catherine. Edith assured her that she would provide all the news of the preparations for the baby's clothing and the redecorating of the nursery during their tea. She assured her old friend that indeed, this was going to be the very best Easter visit to Rosings.

The occupants of the two Darcy carriages were filled with such happiness. The trip back to Pemberly seemed much shorter than the journey to Rosings. Fitzwilliam and Elizabeth and their mama could hear the laughter of the girls all the way from their carriage, which was ahead of them on the road. Lizzy smiled as her head began to bob and weave. She was fighting sleep, but her body was calling for a nap. Soon her head slipped onto her husband's shoulder and her eyes were sweetly shut. Mama watched her daughter sleep. She seemed to jerk and move her head rapidly back and forth. Fitzwilliam noticed and attempted to wrap her in his arms to keep her steady. Suddenly, Lizzy bolted upright, looked him in the eye and said, "darling, we have three people waiting for you at Pemberly. I have just dreamt about them. One is the magistrate, ready to take you to trial in London, the second is a woman three years older than you. Her name is Ellen Simpson, the third is a lad she is calling your son, Fitzwilliam Simpson Darcy. He is a bright boy, very pleasant and well-spoken. He is a rather small lad, but he claims to be seven years of age. He is of your colouring and his hairline is quite like your own. He looks like you, Fitzwilliam. This was an unusual dream for me, in that there was no good portion first. I feel it is a warning, giving us time to prepare.

Lady Hamilton looked as though she would be ill. She took a deep breath and listened.

This was the first time Edith had been a witness to one of Elizabeth's dreams. She was unaware of the *gift* her daughter sometimes received. Lizzy saw the fear upon her mama's face and she reached out to take Edith's hand. "Please Mama, do not let this upset you. I often have such forecasts. All will be well for us." Looking at Fitzwilliam she asked, "darling pray tell me, who is this woman? Have you a son?"

Darcy's mouth went dry and he could hardly speak his answer. "Elizabeth— I had a— relationship with Ellen. Until she made her harsh feelings for Georgie known to me, I— nearly asked— for her hand in marriage." Elizabeth exhaled loudly. She bowed her head, put her hands over her eyes and tried not to cry. Holding her tears, she asked him once more about having a child with Ellen.

He seemed dazed. Elizabeth felt it took him too long to speak his answer. She heard her own voice instead. "Fitzwilliam, your delay in making a denial, tells me that you feel it may be possible. Do you have any information, about such a son? Has a solicitor contacted you?"

"No, Elizabeth. I have not seen nor heard from Ellen since the day she left Killensworth. She lives in Scotland, as far as I am aware. I have not had any such communications from, or about her. Please believe me. Darling, please tell us the entire dream, and be patient with me as I shall ask you questions."

Elizabeth took his hand. She had to remind herself that this woman was in his life when she herself was possibly two and ten years of age. She was a child, not out yet, of course. Still holding her mama's hand as well, she began to tell her dream. "Ellen has my colouring, although her hair is quite grey and she was a bit shy about seeing you. She is wearing a bonnet that she keeps on her head, even in our house. Her *son* is dressed in a very nice suit of clothing, but he seems uncomfortable in them, as though he has never known the feeling of finery. He has an unrefined manner of speech, very unlike Ellen's. His accent is lower class, uneducated English; Ellen's is a mixture of a Scot and of one from somewhere in northern England, quite refined however, and she speaks somewhat haltingly, as though she is thinking what she shall say, before she speaks." Edith's eyes grew wide in amazement, "Darcy, she has her! That is Ellen's manner exactly, my boy." Darcy nodded. Looking at Elizabeth he pled, "please continue, my love."

Elizabeth gave him a slight smile, nodded her head and continued. She wanted to relate everything before they reached their house. She was also beginning to feel quite ill.

"She has papers demanding 50,000 pounds upon the first payment, and she is asking that you escrow 100,000 pounds into an account for your 'son' to be held for his future. The magistrate is clearly on her side; and is not disposed to listen to anything you might have to say. I was shown a most remarkable remedy to the entire situation.

I saw Kitty, entering the room with a small tray. Upon this tray was a piece of cake, and a glass of milk. She took the tray to the boy, placed it upon the table in front of him and said, 'James Parker, this is for you, even though you are being evil to my brother Fitzwilliam, who only was a help to you.' Then, Kitty left the room and the lad began to weep. Ellen gave him a stern look of warning and he ceased his outburst."

Darcy leaned over and kissed Elizabeth on her cheek. "Ay, beloved. James Parker was the lad I told you about from the White mansion in Brightly Street, London. He told me clearly that his father was a man who is at sea, named Thomas Parker. His poor mother, Mary Parker passed away one year ago, and her cleric named Mr. Tubbs placed him with employment at the very same house Kitty served, when Bingley and I found her. The cleric has sent a letter to Mr. Parker, to give him the unfortunate news of his wife, and tell him the whereabouts of his son, James." Edith gave a great sigh of relief, and Elizabeth smiled in agreement.

"Darling, you had your own solicitor work on behalf of this child, and all the others. You have documentation in London. You will need to recall those dates before you speak with the magistrate. Even with this information, the three of us shall have a necessity to get back into this very carriage, and taking Spencer and Collot with us, we shall be compelled to accompany the magistrate to London. Your men will need to locate Mr. Tubbs who will be a witness to the lad's true identity. The magistrate is set against you, because he has been promised by Mr. White, Ellen's uncle, a share of the money. If you stop at the first opportunity before we enter the house, and send a rider to London, the courts may be prepared with your documentation. You shall be spared the embarrassment of this sham of a trial, Ellen and her uncle, are planning to stage."

Darcy was stunned. It was difficult for him to believe that Ellen, sweet and adorable Ellen would want his money. She was quite wealthy on her own, or at least he had been led to believe that she was very well taken care of financially. He nodded his head. "Darling, I am so sorry for this, how can I ever make amends to you? You have just suffered a long carriage ride, and now to London. What may I do for you, Elizabeth? Is there anything that will make you more comfortable?"

"Fitzwilliam, let us just get this behind us, please." He kissed her hand, and seeing the first opportunity to stop and send word to his men, he rapped the carriage top with his cane. Lizzy switched seats and sat next to her mama, as Darcy stepped out of the carriage. Upon his return, they continued to the house. When both carriages arrived, Lizzy stepped out and called for Kitty. Taking a few minutes to tell her sister about the dream, she gave her the instructions she should follow. Kitty nodded her understanding, and went into the kitchen, just as Lizzy had instructed her.

Once inside, a very nervous Mrs. Reynolds met them and disclosed that three individuals were waiting in the first floor salon. It was Ellen's first time to be at Pemberly and Fitzwilliam was very well pleased that she had not been taken to the family floors.

Fitzwilliam, Elizabeth and Edith entered the salon. Edith took advantage of her acquaintance with Ellen. "Why, upon my word, if it is not Ellen Simpson come to see us at Pemberly, all the way from Scotland. And who are you, my strong looking lad?"

Ellen spoke to Edith, but when the boy saw Darcy, he was suddenly quiet and shy. He recognised the very kind man who had helped him, and the other children receive their fair wages. "—Lady Hamilton— indeed— ah— it has been some time, has it not?" Ellen replied very slowly. Edith, nodded and said, "Ellen, I would like to introduce my daughter, Elizabeth Bennet Hamilton Darcy. No doubt you have read of her in the newspapers. Elizabeth is a devoted helper to those who are less fortunate. She was the principle founder of the Assistance Program in London, which will help thousands of homeless women, and some of them with children." Upon hearing this, the lad looked up at Elizabeth, with no little admiration. Elizabeth saw this, and smiled warmly at the boy. Even though he was young, he understood that Mrs. Darcy was a friend, and a help to homeless women, possibly quite like Mary Parker. He was sad knowing that he was somehow a party to hurting these two very kind people. He was not sure what harm he was doing, but the nice man and lady seemed to be in trouble because of him. He knew the clothes were not his, and he well remembered that Mary Parker was his wonderful mama. He hoped the 'bonnet lady' would not call him her son again, and he dearly did not want to call her 'mama—as he had been told.

Before Darcy or Elizabeth could speak, Kitty entered the room with the small tray, just as Lizzy had dreamt. She looked at James, and just as she had been told, she gave the stinging rebuke to her former friend. The lad's eyes filled with tears, and he did indeed weep, just as Elizabeth had been shown in her dream. Ellen attempted to control the boy.

Within a very few minutes, the magistrate related his demands that the Darcys leave for London. Fitzwilliam, Elizabeth and Edith had a united disposition and in all good humour, they agreed and awayed to London, with Spencer and Collot riding escort.

Mr. and Mrs. Darcy and their mama entered Darcy House. All three were in need of rest. Spencer and Collot rode on, following the magistrate's carriage. Just as they thought, the carriage went directly to Brightly Street. Spencer and Collot went to the livery and the back of the house. They were eager to speak with servants. Both men knew there was a story to be learned.

Later that evening, two men entered Darcy House and were shown into the study. The solicitor had already found Mr. Tubbs and brought him along to meet the Darcys. A hearing had been scheduled for the following week. This gave enough time to present a court statement by Mr. Tubbs, and assemble documentation on the services rendered on behalf of young James Parker. By noon the following day, the judge, receiving the evidence, and upon hearing the testimony of Mr. Tubbs, dismissed the case against Fitzwilliam. The courts were not as kind to Ellen. Charges of attempted extortion, fraud and involvement of a minor child as a false witness, leading to perjury— were drawn against the magistrate, Ellen and her uncle, Mr. White.

In a demonstration of mercy, the judge handed temporary custody of the minor child, James Parker to the cleric, Mr. Tubbs. The child would remain in the household of the cleric until his father, Thomas Parker would return to London and claim the boy.

Spencer and Collot reported to Darcy the evening before his planned return to Pemberly. "Sir, we've determined that Mr. White was deeply in debt. Fearing debtors' prison, White contacted Ellen, his niece who was living in London. He enlisted her help, which she willingly agreed to provide. The original plan was to sue you for breach of promise. Perhaps the scheme would be better called blackmail, for a solicitor was asked to approach you directly and arrange the purchase of love letters and poems you'd written to Miss Ellen, years ago. She had saved these items and turned them over to her uncle, Mr. White whose debts were staggering. White's Brightly Street mansion, and all its contents has already been sold, yet the combined proceeds still fell forty thousand pounds short of the amount needed. The money they'd hoped to extract from you, sir was to have been fifty thousand pounds. That would have given Mr. White enough cash to avoid debtor's prison with ten thousand pounds to use for White's personal expenses.

"This plan expanded as Miss Ellen happened to see young James Parker. When she saw him, she reckoned that his physical features would be close to those of yourself. The lad seemed to resemble both of you sufficiently sir, and he was brilliantly articulate. The child was hindered only by his ignorance, yet she felt certain that she could coach him to speak the few words the judge needed to hear him say. The lad was bright, and could be convincing." Collet continued. " Miss Simpson saw new opportunities. Dressed in the appropriate clothing and instructed on elocution and deportment, he would certainly be convincing in the part of a blue-blooded Darcy. She was confident that she could persuade even yourself, sir that the boy was your very own son."

Ellen wished to assist her uncle and help relieve him from his debts, she also deeply desired to damage Darcy. She wanted to extract more money from him, but her true motive was to do him genuine harm. She desired to fill his wife with anger, jealousy and enough resentment to last their lifetime. Ellen hoped to bring perpetual problems of disharmony into the Darcy home, and ruin their chances for happiness. Her goal was to alter their marital union forever. She reasoned that the monies received from Darcy, would give James a better life. Yet, in truth, she wanted to see Darcy brought low. He had his chance with Ellen, he should suffer without her. She would teach him. If no one else would take the high and mighty Fitzwilliam Darcy down a peg or two, she would make it her mission. Why did he turn his back on Ellen Simpson? She never understood it. Reviewing his letters and all the poems, she began to remember the good of the man. Upon thinking it over, Ellen became angry with Darcy for his refusal to marry her. She was livid that he had chosen the care, comfort and company of Georgiana over herself. Upon hearing he had wed, she wished to punish him by a method which would take more than his money. She wished to create problems within his marriage. Her plan was to take his letters and love poems to court with her. She intended to read them to the open court as she testified. She would tell the judge, and all those present about being left alone. She would insist that it was true. She would tell the world that he had taken advantage of her, she became with child, and as soon as she told him, he had refused to marry her. The world would be told that he selfishly turned his wealthy back upon her, and the child she carried. When she was through telling her sad story, there would be not one dry eye in the courtroom. Then, she would offer to sell her secret story and all her personal, and very private love letters, and poems, to the highest bidder. This she would do to increase the publicity. All the newspapers would be eager to publish his letters and poems. She reasoned that when she was through telling her story, Fitzwilliam Darcy would be ruined. His social life in England and Scotland would be over. No one would give him the time of day and Ellen fondly hoped this would include his wife.

Spencer gave Darcy a silver box. He opened it, and immediately recognised the numerous love letters, and poems he had written to Ellen years ago. Darcy took less than one minute to throw the items onto the flames in his fireplace. He quickly gave the box back to Spencer, instructing him to get rid of it in the Thames, posthaste. After his men awayed, Darcy poured himself a glass of port. Staring into the flames of his fireplace, he drained the glass, then poured another. He sat alone at his desk, wishing he had never met, nor loved Ellen. He began to ask himself what on earth he had ever seen in her.

Returning to their quarters, Darcy found Elizabeth sleeping on the sofa in their sitting room. He sat on the floor next to her, arranging the soft blanket that covered her, and watched her sleep. He kissed her forehead and fondly hoped she would be spared more dreaming. He could only imagine how much these dream experiences required of her. While he was thankful that he had been saved pain, and embarrassment, he most sincerely hoped that nothing more from his past sensual life would confront Elizabeth. In truth, never had he expected to hear from Ellen again, much less to be confronted by her, as a real threat to his future happiness. It nagged him that Elizabeth should have been forced to see Ellen. It would have been his wish, that his wife had never heard her name, nor ever had any intelligence concerning her. This was England, and it was unthinkable that a man should be required to give an account of his past, to his wife! The fact that his wife saw Ellen Simpson, and that Elizabeth had an understanding that he had been intimate with the woman, humiliated him, and filled him with remorse. He regretted Elizabeth's taking note of their very similar colouring, and other physical features. They did, in some respects, resemble one another, yet Elizabeth was so much superior in every distinction. Darcy would have given anything to prevent Elizabeth from ever seeing Ellen, or hearing her voice. But, wishing would not make it so— what was done could never be changed. He felt nearly ill from the sickening occurrence. It had been a dagger to his heart, and he could just imagine how ill the entire matter made Elizabeth. After all, it had been only extraordinary good fortune that Ellen had not conceived a child. Thank Heaven that lad was not his seed. What misery that! He now remembered their time in Killensworth reproachfully. He recalled with accuracy, that he had begged Ellen to spend a week of sensual nudity in his fishing lodge. Thank God she took offense and flatly refused. Elizabeth told him that was how they'd conceived. It made him feel sick to think of what might have happened. Ellen might have given consent, they might have conceived a child, and married. Never would he have met Elizabeth, never would he have known true love… He was miserable with a sense of guilt. What a fool. Foolish Fitzwilliam Darcy, blindly in love with such a woman! A woman who would resort to blackmail, a woman who would corrupt an innocent child, force that child to lie and be a party to her crime. Unthinkable! He felt a sense of relief that Spencer had obtained those letters and poems. It was a blessing that he knew they were in ashes and could not trouble Elizabeth. It would be humiliating for his wife to read letters and poems he had written to Ellen. It was embarrassing to remember the way he had all but worshipped the beautiful Miss Simpson. Thinking back, he recalled it to be a one-sided love affair. Darcy being so very much in love with her and Ellen being— truth be told— somewhat cold to him. Although, he did not realise it to be so, at the time. Now, he wondered why he had not been a good judge of the woman's character. For all his high standards, he seemed to have missed the mark with beautiful women, before he met Elizabeth. In truth, he admitted to himself, though somewhat embarrassed; he had misjudged his wife at first. He recalled that he did all he could to resist Elizabeth at Netherfield when he had first made her acquaintance. Even to that blasted speech he delivered to Bingley, within Elizabeth's hearing. He postponed telling her he loved her, and did not make an offer of marriage, even when Mr. Bennet saw his affections and tried to help him on…

She stirred and began to slowly open her eyes. She reached out to him, and touched his cheek. "Hullo darling." She was slow of speech, for she had been sleeping deeply. "Are you well, Elizabeth?" He asked with sincere concern. "I have a question for you, if I may. I dared not ask it of you whilst in the carriage with mama. If I may just ask this one thing of you, I beg that we shall never discuss this particular dream again." She rose up on one elbow and slowly nodded, blinking her eyes at him. She loathed hearing his inquiry. She knew it would be the question she dearly hoped he would never ask. "My lovely Elizabeth, did you possibly omit having seen letters or poems in your dream?" A deep frown creased her brow, a worried expression overtook her beautiful face. She sighed deeply, then began, "—darling man— I beg you not to ask me that." He stopt breathing, for he knew her answer. Then, after taking one deep breath, he demanded, "I fear— I must know— my love."

Elizabeth sat up, putting one slender hand upon his. Looking deeply into his eyes, she answered regretfully. "Why would you ask me? For it seems we both know the answer. You have seen the silver box, have you not? Being acquainted with the talents of Spencer and Collot, I have the assurance that you have seen, and possessed those papers once again. Knowing your heart belongs only to me, I am certain they are now ashes upon the hearth in your study." She held his gaze. He tried to give her a little smile, but it took on the appearance of a painful grin. "Yes, yes. I thank you for the confidence you have in me as your husband. Still— I fear I must know—did you— read anything in your dream?" He hung his head after he made his inquiry, for he could not look her in the eye. Taking a deep breath, she exhaled and told him. "Ay, Fitzwilliam. You, are a very talented man. The one poem I read in the dream was— completely wonderful. It should have been published. I am afraid that I did memorize it— even though it was obviously not written for me— nor— is it about me. I fear that I shall always know the words in my heart, and at once remember the woman who inspired such tender devotions in you." Elizabeth touched his cheek, and continued with glistening eyes, trying very courageously to prohibit her tears. " I am sorry for my mind, my love. I simply cannot forget words that touch my spirit. And you— my darling man— touch my spirit with such ease…" Her response clearly stung him with remorse. This was a wound he knew he had inflicted, with a pain he feared would never depart. He fell into a deeply quiet and reflective mood. Elizabeth stretched out upon the sofa once more. She waited patiently— not sleeping— just watching her husband suffer, in a silence of his own making.

Finally Fitzwilliam found a way to put his feelings into thoughts, and his thoughts into words. "Elizabeth, my own love. I have been sitting here counting my blessings that you are my wife. If I could only make you comprehend, how I love and adore you, and our sweet child. I feel I have somehow betrayed your confidence, and I am suffering as though I have wronged you. I wish only to give you happiness— but see how I have tormented you with this mortifying and incomprehensible evil. We have lost these past few days of our lives, and we shall not be able to ever recover them. My apology to you is useless. I feel I have lost my own dignity in your sight. I am no better than a failed knight, tossed from his mount, stranded upon his backside, without any hope of righting himself! My self-confidence is shattered. I want to give you happiness and every good thing. I want to make-up for the horrible months that were ripped away from you whilst you were homeless, and suffering so greatly. What have I done instead? I have opened the doors to my foolish past, allowed a strong light to illuminate my youthful mawkishness and given you only agitation, grief and insufferable embarrassment."

Elizabeth put her fingertips over his lips. "Shh! My darling husband, kindly stop this talk. I lovingly adore you, Fitzwilliam. I am not a silly girl filling her mind with jealous suspicions, nor am I only infatuated with you. I can naturally fathom, that we each have lives—which are framed by combining both good, and bad events. Some of our friends— have darkness within their persona, and we know it not. Perhaps we choose not to see, or they are able to manifest what they wish us to believe of them.

I freely tell you, I am sorry to have seen Ellen, and to have heard the sound of her voice in my ears, but I am so very happy that she did not give you a child when you gave her your seed. Had she given you a child, you would have married her, lived in Derbyshire and never gone to Hertfordshire. I suppose it is possible you would never have known Charles, and for a certainty you and I would never have met." She placed her hand over her stomach and said, "and—as for this little fellow…" Reaching out to touch his cheek, she gave him a slight smile, then continued. "I would not have my wonderful mama, and— Georgiana—well— I suppose I should simply say— I am thankful to God that she did not give you a child.

"Now her criminal behaviour has been exposed. Certainly there will be a consequence from her actions. Let us go home on the morrow, and with tenderness continue to love each other. We are blest that this attempted horror ended in privacy. The papers will not print the story, the courts will not present the opportunity to lay everything open to a public hearing. We will go home and prepare to welcome our very own son, *your* seed, and your legal heir, beloved." Watching him as she finished speaking, she kissed him.

He picked her up in his arms and carried her to their bed. It was a moment of delicate anguish for him, and yet he felt encouraged by her elegant words. Elizabeth had a generous, loving disposition and a warmth that drew him to her, most passionately. Slipping his wife between the bed linens, he began to disrobe. "I feel the need to obtain your forgiveness, my lovely Elizabeth." His words had a mournful sound. "Sweet Fitzwilliam, you are the best of men. Shall I find the girl I was at age two and ten, or perhaps three and ten years? She would have been climbing trees in Hertfordshire. But, shall I locate her and bring her to you? If I could, you might certainly tell her all your recollections. I promise you, she would be ignorant of the things you would wish to relate to her. Instead, close your eyes my darling, please." She kissed his eyelids and whispered in his ear. "Let us not continue to speak of this, my love. I wish only to hear you say how much you love me. Delight me with your kisses once again, caress my curves and enjoy my touches. I very much desire to demonstrate my affections. Love me in a most leisurely manner, darling. Let me feel the wonder of having my own husband violently in love with me, whilst most tenderly touching me. Love me, Fitzwilliam, please." She smiled as she watched the awkwardness and anxiety leave him. How she loved seeing expressions of heart-felt relief, contentment, and complete delight— diffuse over his handsome face— as she loved him most passionately.

Pemberly had never looked so beautiful, nor so much like home to them. Fitzwilliam and Elizabeth were more than pleased to be back in Derbyshire and situated in the life and place they would raise their family. Much preparation was needed, and all could begin now that Darcy knew he was to become a father, and they had left the past, in the past. The nursery and birthing room must be prepared, baby furniture must be selected and refinished, and redecorating was required in both rooms. Clothing for the child awaited fabrication as well as the ever-important christening gown. Edith would be busier than she could imagine in helping her daughter prepare for the arrival of the heir of Pemberly. The joy she had experienced in providing their wedding, was nothing when compared with this current happiness. She was now, a devoted mama, and very soon to be a proud grandmama. Edith Hamilton was exuberant. This was her most cherished placement.

The hiring of a nanny and midwife was critical. Darcy had agreed to a midwife, rather than the physician he had wanted, on the condition that she be installed and retained on duty immediately and for two months following the birth. He would take no chances with the health and wellness, of his wonderful wife, and his expected child. Elizabeth made it plain to her husband that the use of a wet-nurse would be unthinkable. She refused to have any woman take part in the nourishment of their child. God forbid that anyone would have the ability to suggest, later in their son's life, that she had made a contribution to his strength and wellbeing. The heir of Pemberly would not need to thank a strange woman for providing his food. His own mother would provide his first food, then his papa would put food on his table. Pemberly's tenants were very proud of their mistress upon hearing this gossip. They thought Elizabeth was a strong, vibrant woman. They well understood that only a strong, healthy woman could nurse her child.

During this time, the final preparations for the Assistance Agency of London were completed. The staff eagerly anticipated the grand opening of the facility, and the date was set for August five. Elizabeth suffered great disappointment to miss the event, yet she, of all people, insisted that the celebrations, and most important, the work of the agency move forward. There were hundreds, maybe thousands, of women and girls in need, and the work must not wait solely upon her ability to attend a ceremony.

Edith wrote to her friend Lady Catherine de Bourgh and asked that she and Anne attend the London ceremony as stand-ins, to represent herself and her own daughter, Elizabeth. She secretly reveled in the fact that Catherine, ever greedy for the public eye, had agreed. The woman nearly drooled at the opportunity to shine in the spotlight, offer remarks, and then read about herself in the *London Times*.

With humour Edith looked forward to reading the regrets sent by Mr. Fitzwilliam Darcy, his wife, Elizabeth, and his mother-in-law, Lady Edith Hamilton—all major contributors—yet unable to attend the opening, due to a blessed event which was expected in Pemberly, on August ten. She smiled at the thought of the number of times Catherine would be forced to tell all their friends of Edith's daughter and son-in-law expecting their child's arrival on the tenth of August. She thought it most delicious.

The August sunrise was warm, promising a heat wave by late afternoon. The staff opened all the windows and prayed for a gentle breeze to flow through the house. Mrs. Reynolds consulted the calendar as was her early-morning habit. She sipped her coffee and thought about Lady Hamilton's warning that today was to be the arrival of baby Darcy. Thinking it unlikely that the woman could predict with accuracy, she concerned herself with the birthday celebration for Mrs. Bingley.

The day brought great excitement throughout Pemberly. Every servant had several jobs to do, and each family member was busy preparing for the festivities. By one o'clock the activities were underway, and the excitement continued to build.

Inside the home, Fitzwilliam's voice rang in the halls as he called for his wife. He had been searching in every known or even probable location and was growing panicky. He located Mrs. Reynolds and ordered her to put staff members on the search for his wife. The man was frantic.

Spotting his mama, he inquired of her, feeling that she could help. "Darcy, have you been to the nursery or the birthing chamber?" she asked matter-of-factly. With a sudden look of relief, he kissed her cheek and turned on his heels.

Elizabeth was just quitting the nursery as he prepared to enter. They met face to face and he grabbed her and kissed her in his relief. "Elizabeth, we should be at the door meeting the carriages as they arrive. Are you well?"

"Quite, husband," she responded with a twinkle in her eye. "I shall be with you in one moment. I just wish to speak with Mrs. Reynolds briefly, and then we shall meet our guests, my love." The two walked the hallways hand in hand, and when she spotted Mrs. Reynolds, Elizabeth took the woman's arm and spoke quickly into her ear. "Of course, Mrs. Darcy, thank you." Mrs. Reynolds smiled, Nodding her head, she continued down the hallway. It would have seemed mysterious to Darcy, had he paid them any attention.

Mr. and Mrs. Darcy welcomed their numerous guests on the great lawn. Jane was so pleased with the honour shown to her birthday celebration. The music was beautiful and the aromas filling the air were adding to everyone's anticipation of the delicious meal. Just as the cake was being brought outside, Spencer approached and silently inquired of Mr. Darcy. Fitzwilliam indicated he wished Edith to attend Elizabeth whilst he joined his man. This done, the men set out to the far portion of the great lawn.

Walking away from the crowd and the music to speak privately, Spencer began his report. "Mr. Darcy, you wished to be told about Madamoiselle Suzette Simoneaux." Darcy nodded. "I learned that she has lived in London for the past twenty years, sir. I acquired my information from her former lady's maid, who had been with her from that time until last year when she dismissed the maid, because of poor finances. It seems that Madamoiselle Simoneaux first learned of you by reading the *London Times*. A story of your graduation from Cambridge was printed that described your role as master of Pemberly, along with your other land holdings. The two of them set out for Paris to await you, as the story detailed that you would spend one year in Italy studying the art masters, then one in Paris. She arranged your meeting. After you departed Paris, she returned to London, angry that she had failed to secure a proposal of marriage. At that time she became mistress to a Mr. Metz, a German gentleman of some means. From him, I am sorry to tell you, she went from being a mistress, to a prostitute in Fielding Street, London."

Darcy's heart nearly froze upon hearing these words. He had been given to understand that Suzette was the daughter of a very wealthy count and countess who'd met with the guillotine during the French Revolution. She'd told him of her father's influence, and that of her own import throughout the country. Suzette lived in a mansion in Paris, and the two had visited her holdings in Nice on more than one occasion.

Darcy put up his hand, to halt the report and ask a question. Spencer stopt. "Please tell me how this is possible, when I lived with her in her mansion whilst in Paris, and joined her on more than one visit to her holdings in Nice."

"Ay, sir." Spencer looked at his boots to avoid the man's eyes. "She used these properties in return for her ah—*favours*' to a wealthy viscount who was out of country for political reasons, Mr. Darcy. As to the Nice holdings, those documents were fabricated by a talented Frenchman whose payment was remitted ah— *personally* by Madamoiselle Simoneaux."

Spencer was sorry to have caused Mr. Darcy pain. He was fully aware of his employer's sincere affection for Suzette. Nevertheless, he faithfully continued his report: "Um— ah— as I was saying, sir—Madamoiselle Simoneaux went to Fielding Street in London to ply her—ah— to establish her— *trade?*" Darcy nodded his understanding— Spencer continued.

"She spent several years at that house, and then she read of you once again in the *London Times* when you were honoured by the Crown. That was when she packed all her belongings, and with her lady's maid in tow, presented herself to you—once again, sir, claiming she had just arrived from Paris. She celebrated her four-and-thirty-year birthday on that self-same day, Mr. Darcy." Spencer waited to hear a response from his employer. "Nine years older..." Fitzwilliam muttered to himself. "Pardon, sir?" Spencer inquired, but Darcy was silent, so he concluded. "She told you she was returning to Paris, but she came back to London. She used the money you gave her to purchase passage for herself and her lady's maid to return to Paris. That money, added to the travel expense funds you provided, was combined and used to let a small house in London town. Sir, it seems she was not content to remain secluded in London. She wished to reach out, far beyond her own class. She used intelligence she had gained in her— uh— please forgive me— *relationship*— with you— Mr. Darcy...

"Guided by the *London Times*, she would seek out those of your acquaintance. As they hosted social gatherings, her lady's maid would enter those functions feigning an urgent missive for her. Some she met in theatres. Thus she began to have her name frequently heard and very often spoken in wealthy circles. After a time, she was able to attend those gatherings, as she was believed to be, a wealthy woman of influence. She was always careful to avoid gatherings where you might be in attendance, sir.

"Her most recent lover released her. Suffering from lack of funds, she was able to retain only her butler, who related her latest scheme to me. Sir, I beg your pardon— but he revealed that she planned to take you as her lover. Being self-assured of your devotion and ardent love for her, she was confident that you would take her to live with you at Darcy House. She relished the opportunity to show all of London that she was, indeed, your mistress. It was her desire to ah—um— once again— please forgive me, sir; but she said she wanted to be equal in your eyes with Mrs. Darcy. She wanted to have the same level of devotion as— uh— you show to Mrs. Darcy. She had gone so far as to consult with your personal jeweller, and Mrs. Darcy's own modiste. I am sorry to inform you that she as much as told both of them to expect her extravagant purchases in the very near future. She assured them, that you would very soon be establishing her own credit, in your name, of course. Darcy blanched at this news, yet he remained silent and Spencer concluded.

"Apparently she came to Darcy House on the Tuesday of your dinner party, entered without knocking, and told her butler she saw you and listened to you and Mrs. Darcy as you made the announcement of your child's expected birth. This dashed her designs on you, sir. Her last hope to obtain a financial benefactor, was Mr. Bottsworth, and Lady Hamilton was apparently her undoing in that regard. She has since dismissed her butler and returned to her Fielding Street occupation, sir."

Darcy, his head reeling, thanked Spencer. He was shocked to have been duped by this older woman who had lied, deceiving him about everything. Had he been blind or simply not wished to see her as a fortune seeker and an opportunist? It was only his responsibility to Georgie that had caused him to turn from Suzette. For all his mighty orations about the elevated qualities he required in a wife, he had narrowly escaped being wed to a common prostitute. It made him feel quite ill indeed. This was a secret he would take to his grave. Dreading the necessity to make an additional request of Spencer he directed the man to make haste for London. It was Darcy's desire that both the jeweller and the modiste be made aware that Mr. Darcy disavowed all claims made by Madamoiselle Simoneaux. Perhaps if possible, Spencer and Collot might also look into the possibility of property and monies awaiting the woman in France. If a suitable 'inheritance' might be located, the mid-aged courtesan just might change countries. A talented solicitor in southern France might serve well. Perhaps conditions upon taking the ownership of such a home, might include her prohibition of ever returning to England. Collot, being French, should know his way around the country well enough to be of great benefit. Darcy was angry with himself at the thought of once again putting money into Suzette's hands, but it was the only way of being free of this cursed woman. He would not risk her being able to embarrass him or his family with tales of her past attachment to Fitzwilliam Darcy. He had certainly reached the limit of his patience where women from his past were concerned. He wished to look only at the present, and into the future; his future with Mrs. Elizabeth Darcy, and their soon to arrive son. Once again he felt a burning desire to live clean with his wife. He wanted to honour Elizabeth, and this time he would seriously consider telling her the truth.

Fitzwilliam made an effort to collect himself and joined Elizabeth once again. Sitting beside her under the canopy, he knew he did not deserve her. What would she think if she knew the truth? It was a sad and embarrassing truth.

Suddenly Elizabeth took Fitzwilliam's hand and squeezed it very hard. She whispered in his ear, "We need to go inside *now*, my husband. Please take me to our birthing room and stay with me, my love. Our child wants to join the celebration!"

Just as she had dreamt, Darcy was so excited he could not speak to his guests. He tried to tell Bingley, but Charles just smiled and said, "Ay! We are having a wonderful time! Thank you so very much, Darcy." Georgie got up to follow them, and Fitzwilliam asked her to wait with her sisters and brother Charles. Elizabeth asked that someone find her mama and send her to them. Darcy understood her request and gave thanks that his wife could have a loving mother to encourage her, and himself as well.

Once in the birthing chamber, Elizabeth was met by her midwife. Darcy wondered how the woman knew to be there, but he was too excited to ask. She took charge immediately, barking orders to Fitzwilliam and speaking gently to Elizabeth. Fitzwilliam was as helpful as he could be. He sat behind his labouring wife and rubbed her back. He told her what a wonderful job she was doing and thanked her for her nine months of effort and discomfort, and for the pain she was enduring for the baby's birth.

Elizabeth did not hear him. She had entered the final stages of labour when her midwife asked her to cry out and scream as needed. This was thought to assist the muscles in pushing the baby out of the birth canal.

The midwife called to Fitzwilliam and asked him to stand next to her. She bade him to make haste, for Elizabeth had previously told the woman that she wanted him to see his child as he entered the world. Darcy felt woozy as he saw his wife's body stretched to such enormous dimensions.

"Elizabeth I can see his head, it is full of dark hair!" He stopt himself just before adding a commentary on the size of the head. In seconds the baby was out. The midwife cut his cord and put him in a blanket. She handed him to Darcy and said, "Here is your son, be sure his mama gets a good look at him." The baby was announcing his presence in loud bellows.

The proud parents took a very close look at their son. They counted fingers and toes and inspected the inside of his mouth. They looked him over carefully from top to bottom, front to back. Mrs. Reynolds took the baby from them to clean him up, and the midwife finished with delivery of the afterbirth.

At last the new family retired to their bed. They heard a light tap upon the door. Edith slowly opened it and peered inside, saying, "Did you call for me, Lizzy?"

Elizabeth propped herself up on her elbows and nodded her head, "Ay, Mama please do come in and meet our sweet boy, your grandson."

Smiling widely, Edith tiptoed in and looked at the babe. Always knowing the best course to take, she smoothed her daughter's hair and kissed her cheek. "You did such a wonderful job, my darling Lizzy. He is such a beautiful baby! Now, you and your husband and my little grandson need some sleep. I shall see all three of you later, child!"

After a four-hour nap, Elizabeth opened her eyes to find her husband staring at her. She smiled at him as she got out of bed to take their son from his nearby cradle. Getting back into bed, she opened her gown and put the baby to her breast. Darcy stretched out beside them, and watched in wonder, silently pondering how soon it would be his turn.

"Darling," he asked, " shall we not name our son?" Elizabeth suggested their father's names. Darcy offered, "Perhaps for our second son, darling. I was wondering if we might possibly name him Charles Fitzwilliam Darcy. Had it not been for Charles nagging me into coming out to Hertfordshire, I would not have been at Netherfield when you and Jane were caught in that storm. I wanted to name my son Fitzwilliam, but it would be too confusing. This way, he has my name, yet Charles's as well. What do you say, darling?"

"I think Charles Fitzwilliam Darcy is the best name we could give the next master of Pemberly! He could be C. Fitzwilliam Darcy, in his professional life, could he not? He is a fine-looking baby! Have you noticed he looks just like you, Fitzwilliam?"

"Ay," he sighed, smiling, "but he has your beautiful lavender eyes, my love."

Mrs. Reynolds entered and told them that the family was gathered in the grand salon. The birthday celebration had ended and all were waiting to hear the news. The proud grandmama would give nothing away, wishing the parents to make the announcement. Mrs. Reynolds asked what they wanted to do about the announcement to the family. Elizabeth surprised her husband by asking for a morning gown. Her lady's maid entered and helped her into the garment. She arranged her hair and Elizabeth looked as beautiful as ever. Darcy protested, but she would have none of his prohibitions. He insisted upon carrying her to the grand salon, and it was finally agreed that Elizabeth would hold

Charles Fitzwilliam, and Darcy would carry his entire family down the hall and into the grand salon. He was thankful it was on the same floor.

Mrs. Reynolds went ahead of them and asked everyone to be seated. The little family would stay only ten minutes. They entered the room, and Fitzwilliam put his wife and child onto a nearby sofa. Then he stood protectively next to them. Looking at his family and friends, he said, "Elizabeth and I would like to introduce Master Charles Fitzwilliam Darcy, the future master of Pemberly Park, Derbyshire."

Charles and Jane jumped to their feet. Charles had tears in his eyes. "I am, I am—to say I am honoured is an understatement, my brother. What an unexpected and undeserved homage! Charles Fitzwilliam Darcy. Thank you, Lizzy and Darcy. I suppose I shall need to watch my Ps and Qs now that I am an uncle with a namesake."

The MacDougals and Gardiners announced their joy at being present to welcome the first baby of the family's next generation. Lizzy stretched out her hand to Edith. She called to her, "Come hold your grandson, Grandmama!"

All of the new aunties gathered around Edith as she held the newborn. They admired his handsome face and decided he looked like a composite of both his parents. Edith looked to Lizzy, and said, "I love you, daughter."

Lizzy replied, "I love you as well, Mama. I am so pleased that you love your new grandson. I somewhat suspect you will be spending quite a bit of time with him, will you not?" Edith laughed along with everyone, and in good humour she confessed her desire to dedicate as much time as possible to the beautiful lad. She had already engaged an artist to paint the entire family. She planned to generously supply Lady Catherine and others with numerous silhouettes and miniatures of the child.

Darcy put his hand upon Edith's shoulder as she held his firstborn. "Mama, I must tell you that I also love you." He was obviously holding back tears as he looked into her eyes. "I would like to tell you how much it means to me, having you as Elizabeth's mother, and as such, my own mother as well." Looking at Georgiana, he continued. "I should like you to understand my heart, Mama. Please receive my words as a tribute to your love and devotion. I hold in my mind, many sweet scenes of you, visiting my own dear mother here at Pemberly. Oftentimes, I enter this very room, and in my mind, I can see the two of you, sitting on the sofa with the morning light streaming through the window. I hear your laughter and bless Heaven for you both. I dearly wish my parents could be here to share in this joy, as I know Elizabeth wishes the same of her own father. I would like to think they are all watching— as part of that great cloud of witness on high. But, dear Mama, in you, my own mother is here. I wish you could have the pleasure of knowing my joy, as I see you holding our son, and hearing your devotion to my precious wife. You give Elizabeth more than warm female friendship, you are in truth her very own mother. There is no other light in which to view it, you are her loving mother, and therefore, the true grandmother to our son. There are no solicitors clever enough to devise legal papers, nor judges with enough authority to pronounce you Elizabeth's mother. Only God can do so, and I am very thankful that he has so done!"

Georgiana was filled with emotion at her brother's words. "Oh, Aunt. I have no such memories of you and my mother, but I always feel such joy in being near you. You are my dearest Aunt Edith and I treasure you, too." Edith put her hand upon Georgie's hand. "My wonderful little Georgie. How dearly your precious mother loved you. Somehow I know she is well pleased that we live under the same roof. Starting tomorrow, I shall tell you one story of your mother each day, child." Georgiana responded in tears, for this promise greatly touched her tender heart.

"This shall not do!" Darcy cried to anyone, and everyone. "My son shall not be baptized with his grandmother's tears whilst everyone in the room looks on and cries. Now, Aunt Mary, kindly open up the instrument and play a lively jig. Your nephew needs merriment on the day of his birth!" Everyone laughed much at this suggestion, and Mary went to the pianoforte.

Ten minutes later the proud papa announced bedtime for the Darcy family. Elizabeth stood up but he would not allow her to walk. Picking up his wife and son, they bade their guests a good night and headed for their rooms. Georgiana followed behind, as they reached their door, the girl took Elizabeth's hand and kissed it. "Oh, Elizabeth, I thank you so much. You became my dearest sister, you have given me sisters, and now I am an aunt with a beautiful little nephew. Lizzy, we are a true family, are we not? I love my sisters, all of you and now I love my sweet little nephew! I am Aunt Georgiana! I can scarcely believe it. Before Mary, and then Kitty came to live with me, I was so lonely. But now, I am so joyful, and upon my word, my brother also has never been so happy. I dare say, Fitzwilliam was a lonely fellow before he met and fell in love with you, Lizzy. Thank you, Lizzy!" She kissed her brother on the cheek, "Oh, and thank you, too, brother! You met and married Elizabeth, and now you have a son and an heir."

"Ay! Indeed, I did have a part in this, Georgie!" He called after her, laughing as she left.

Elizabeth put the baby in his cradle next to their bed. She bent over him and stroked his head softly, "Good-night, sweet little Fitzie! Your Mama and Papa love you so much!" Fitzwilliam drew her close and embraced her asking, "Fitzie? We are going to call him Fitzie, my love?"

She leaned her head back to look at him and laughed at his wrinkled brow. "Do not worry, darling," she smiled, smoothing his wrinkled forehead with her finger," it will be what his mama calls him, if you do not like it as a family nickname."

"I have suffered being called Fitzie. It was an agony! How about Fitz? May we not call him Fitz?" he begged, hoping that she would agree.

Elizabeth smiled with a mischievous sparkle in her lavender eyes. "Very well, we shall see, my darling man. We shall see."

Sleep came quickly to the proud and happy parents. All was quiet in their room, each sleeping peacefully, when suddenly Elizabeth sat straight up in bed. This rush of movement awakened Fitzwilliam and he reached out and caught her by the shoulders before she could rise.

"Darling, please. Are you well?" He spoke in a whisper because of the nearness of their son, sleeping in his cradle. Fitzwilliam placed his lips upon her ear and murmured, "Whatever is the matter, my love? Please lie back and tell me." Elizabeth sat straight up, and threw her arms around him. Kissing his neck she said, "Oh, Fitzwilliam, I had a dream! It was the most spectacular dream I have ever experienced. My love, may I please tell you of my dream? It all seemed quite real to me. Oh darling, please do believe me, the first part of my dream was exceedingly wonderful…"

2439106R00144

Made in the USA
San Bernardino, CA
22 April 2013